IMAGE
COMICS

PRESENTS

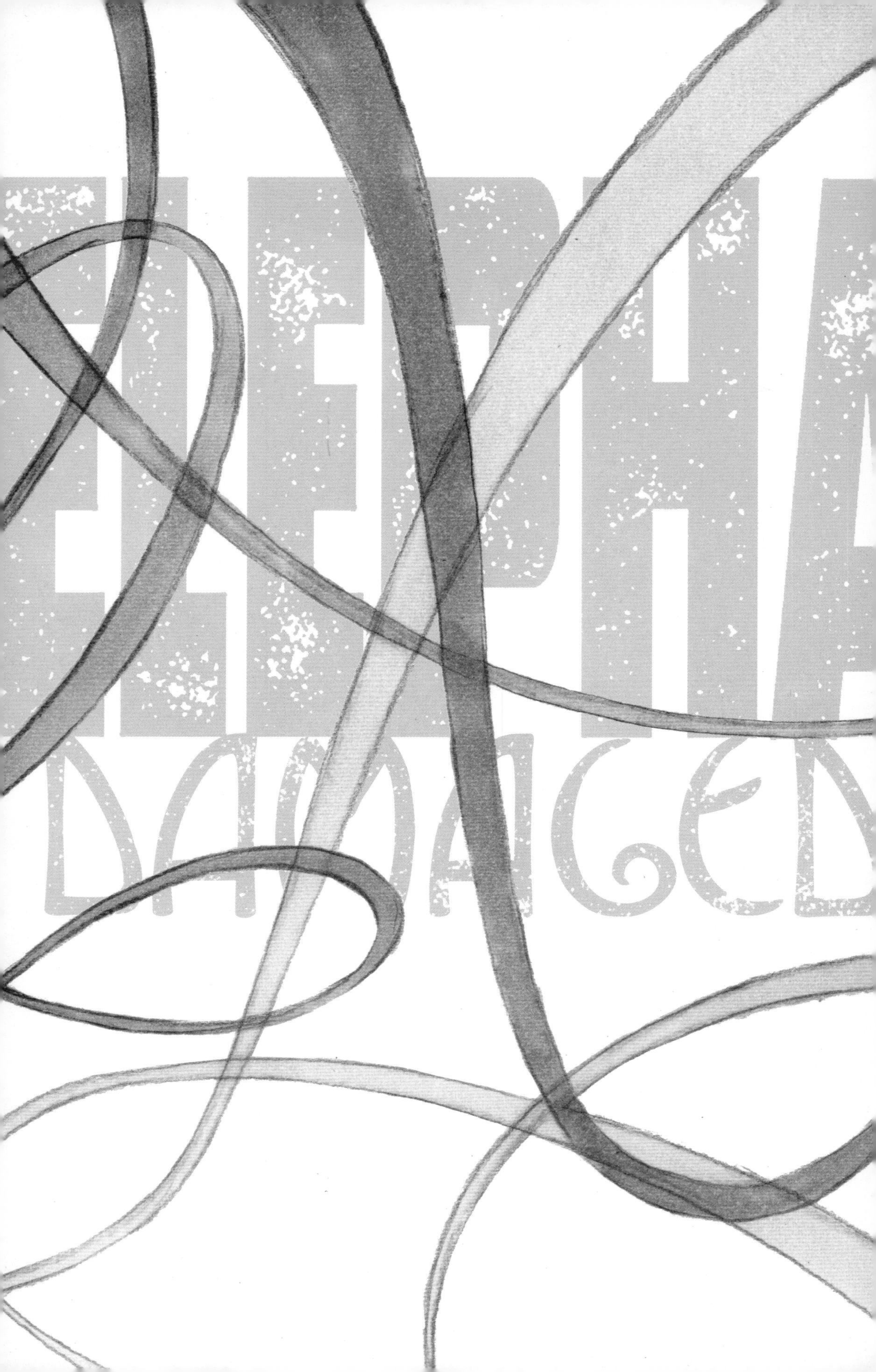

NTMEN GOODS

by
RICHARD
STARKINGS
& MARIAN
CHURCHLAND

ACTIVE IMAGES

COMICRAFT SINCE 1992

RICHARD STARKINGS
PRESIDENT & FIRST TIGER

JOHN 'JG' ROSHELL
SECRET WEAPON

SANTIAGO PEREZ
WRANGLER

Made possible by the following Comicraft
Fonts (available at ComicBookFonts.com):

MARIANCHURCHLAND
GRANDE GUIGNOL
Paranoid Android
DESIGNER GENES
DUTCH COURAGE
WICCAN
CheekyMonkey
Matinee Idol
SLAPHAPPY
PhatBoi

image

ELEPHANTMEN: DAMAGED GOODS.
Published by Image Comics, Inc.,
Office of publication: 2134 Allston
Way, Second Floor, Berkeley, California
94704. Originally published in magazine
form as ELEPHANTMEN #18-20. Copyright ©
2009 Active Images. All rights reserved. HIP
FLASK®, MYSTERY CITY™ and ELEPHANTMEN™
(including all prominent characters featured in
this issue), its logo and all character likenesses
are trademarks of Active Images, unless
otherwise noted. Image Comics® is a trademark
of Image Comics, Inc. All rights reserved. No
part of this publication may be reproduced or
transmitted, in any form or by any means
(except for short excerpts for review
purposes) without the express written
permission of Image Comics, Inc. All
names, characters, events and locales
in this publication are entirely
fictional. Any resemblance to
actual persons (living or
dead), events or places,
without satiric intent, is
coincidental.
PRINTED IN CHINA

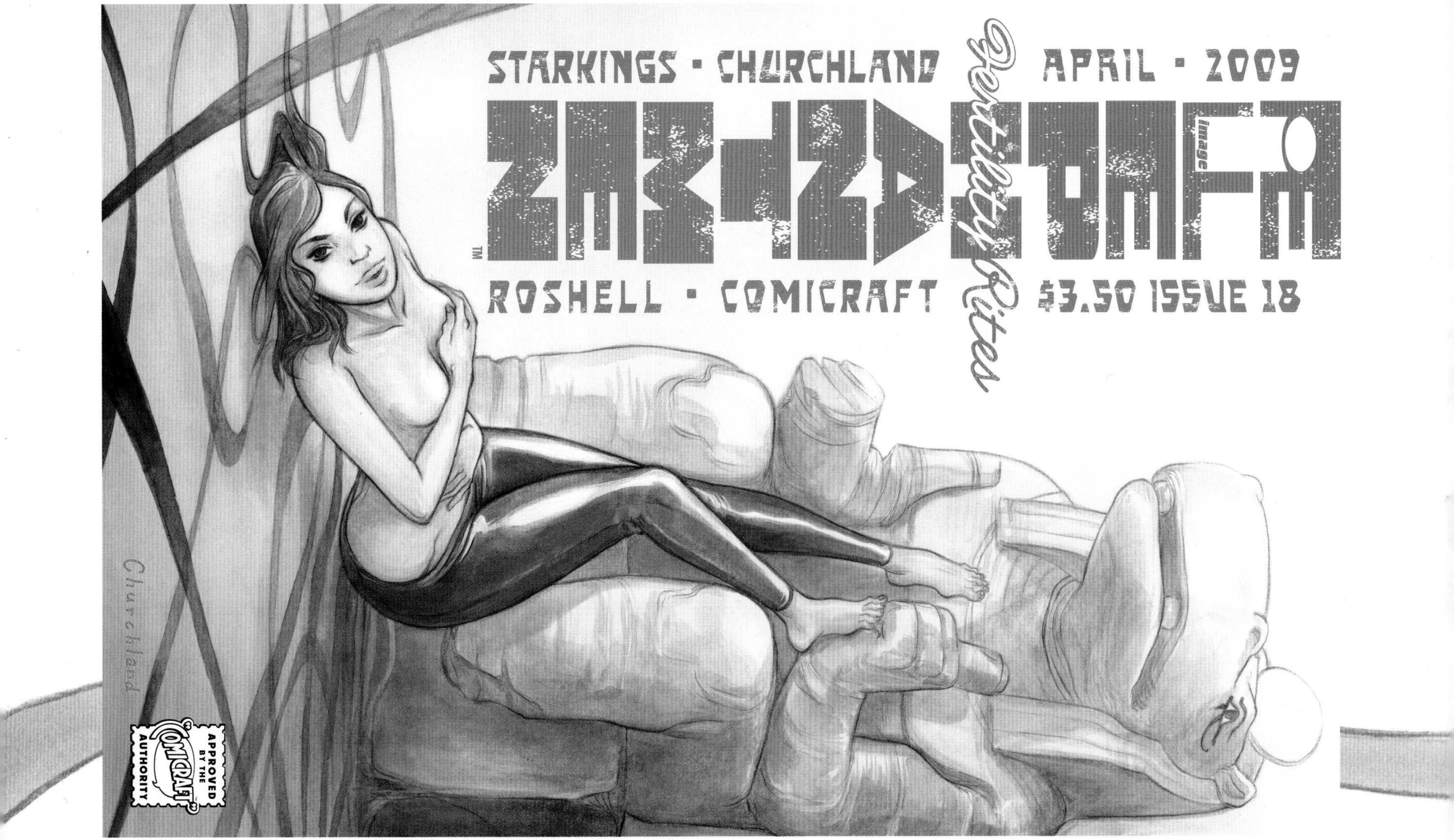
STARKINGS · CHURCHLAND
APRIL · 2009
ELEPHANTMEN™
image
Fertility Rites
ROSHELL · COMICRAFT
$3.50 ISSUE 18
Churchland
APPROVED BY THE "COMICRAFT" AUTHORITY

MIKI

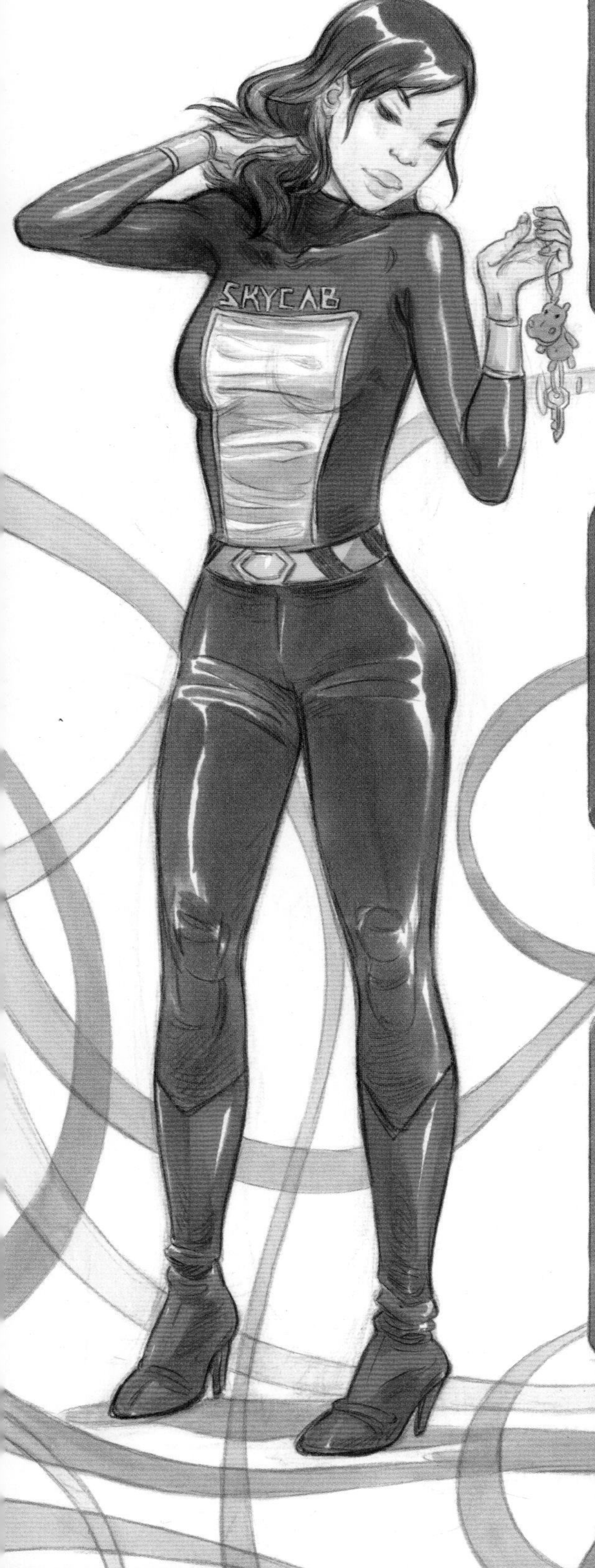
SKYCAB

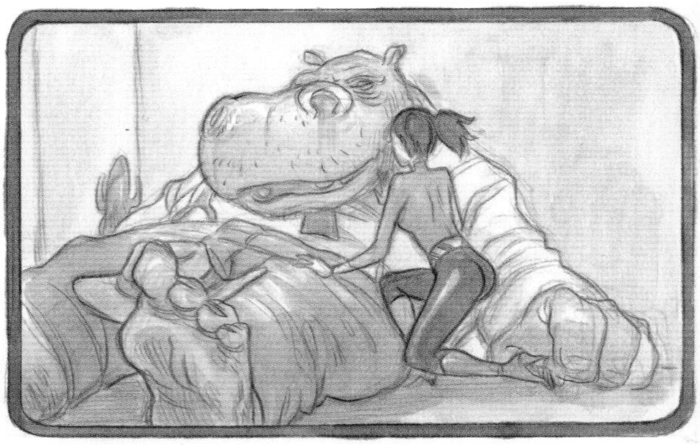

Cab Driver Hiromi Kiyoko, Miki to her friends, stumbled upon the wounded Elephantman known as Hip Flask by the Los Angeles river.

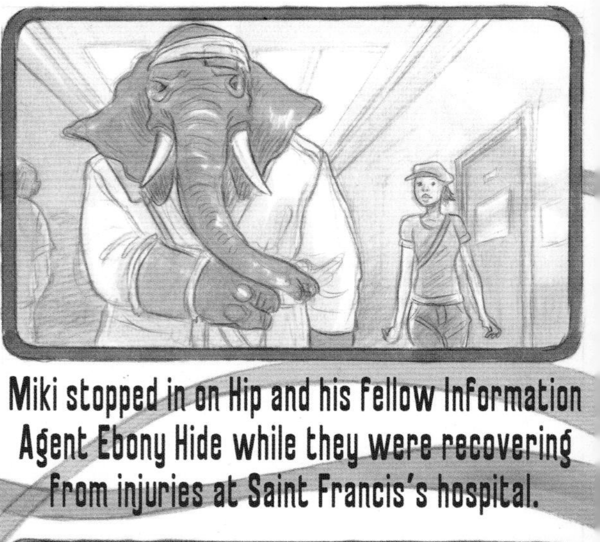

Miki stopped in on Hip and his fellow Information Agent Ebony Hide while they were recovering from injuries at Saint Francis's hospital.

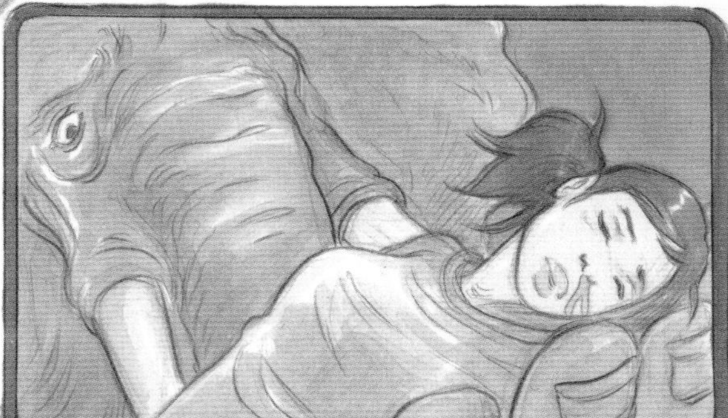

Now her life has become increasingly involved in, and endangered by, the world of the Elephantmen...

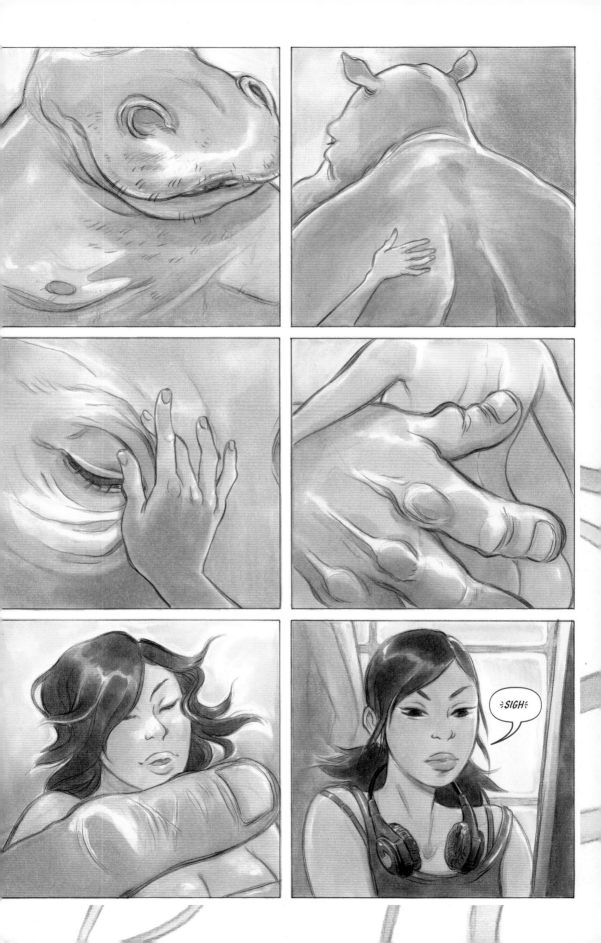

SIGH

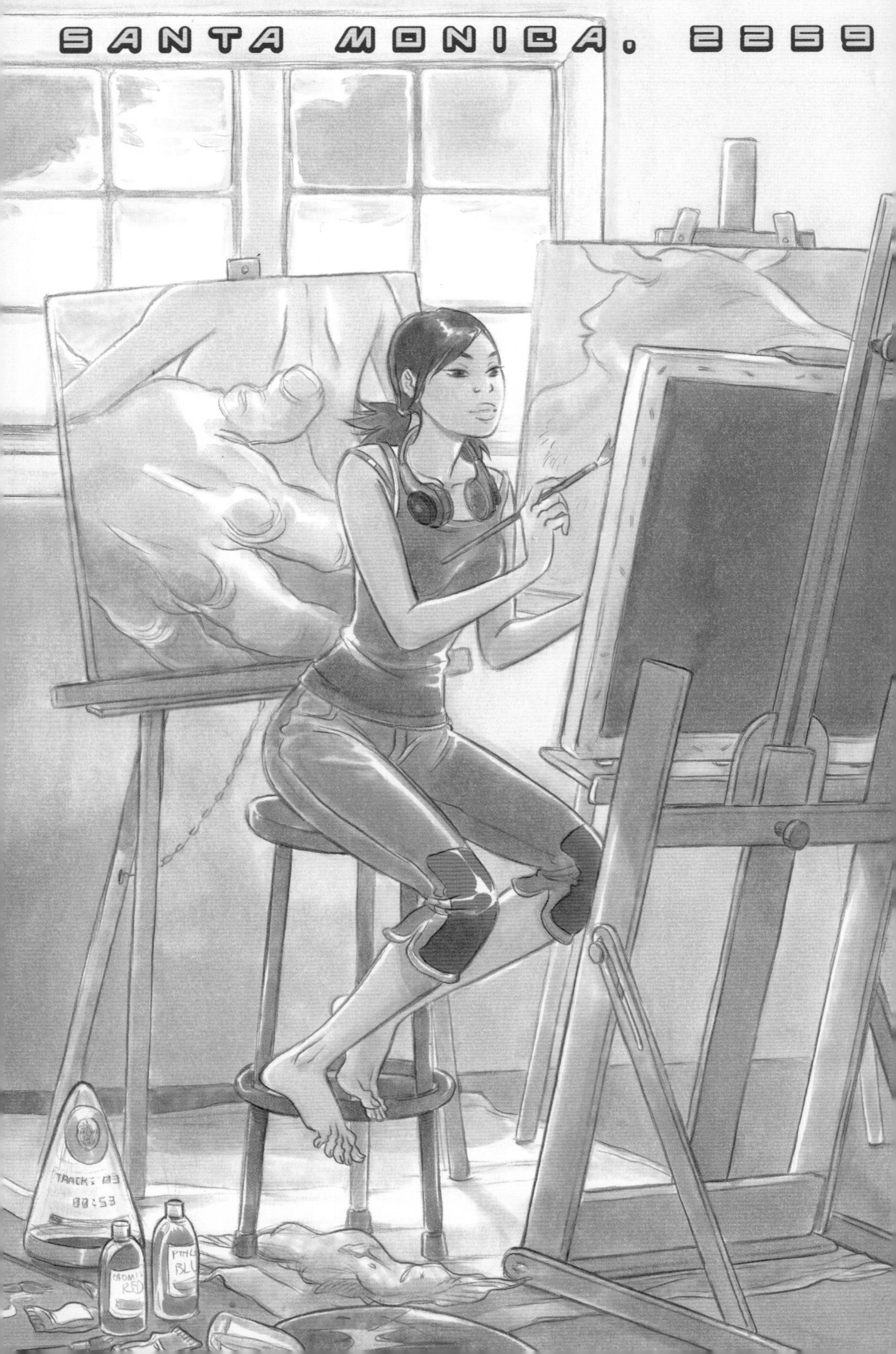
SANTA MONICA, 2259
TRACK: 03
00:53

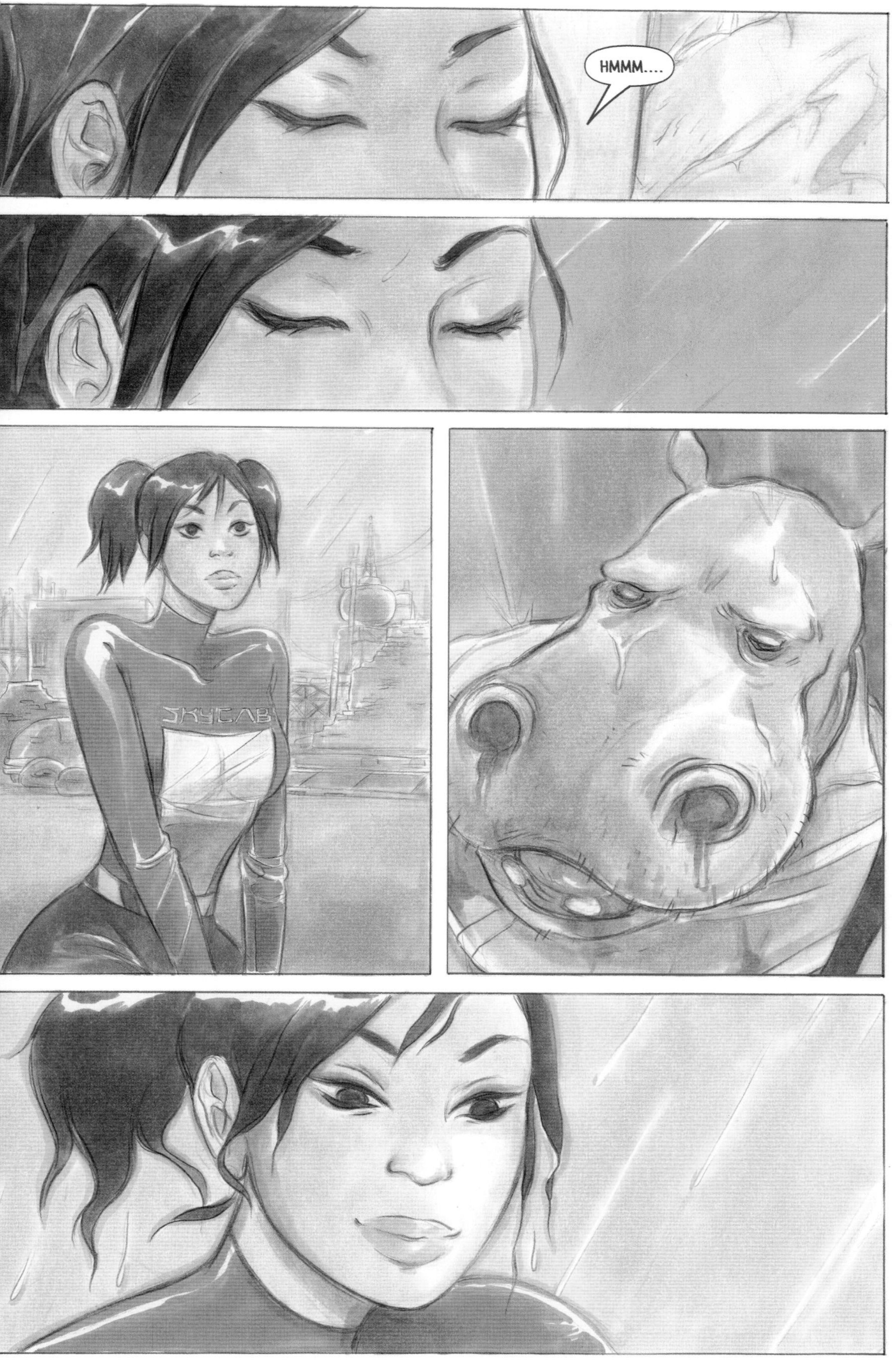
HMMM....
SKYCAB

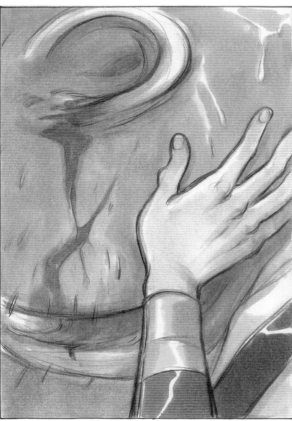

HIROMI!

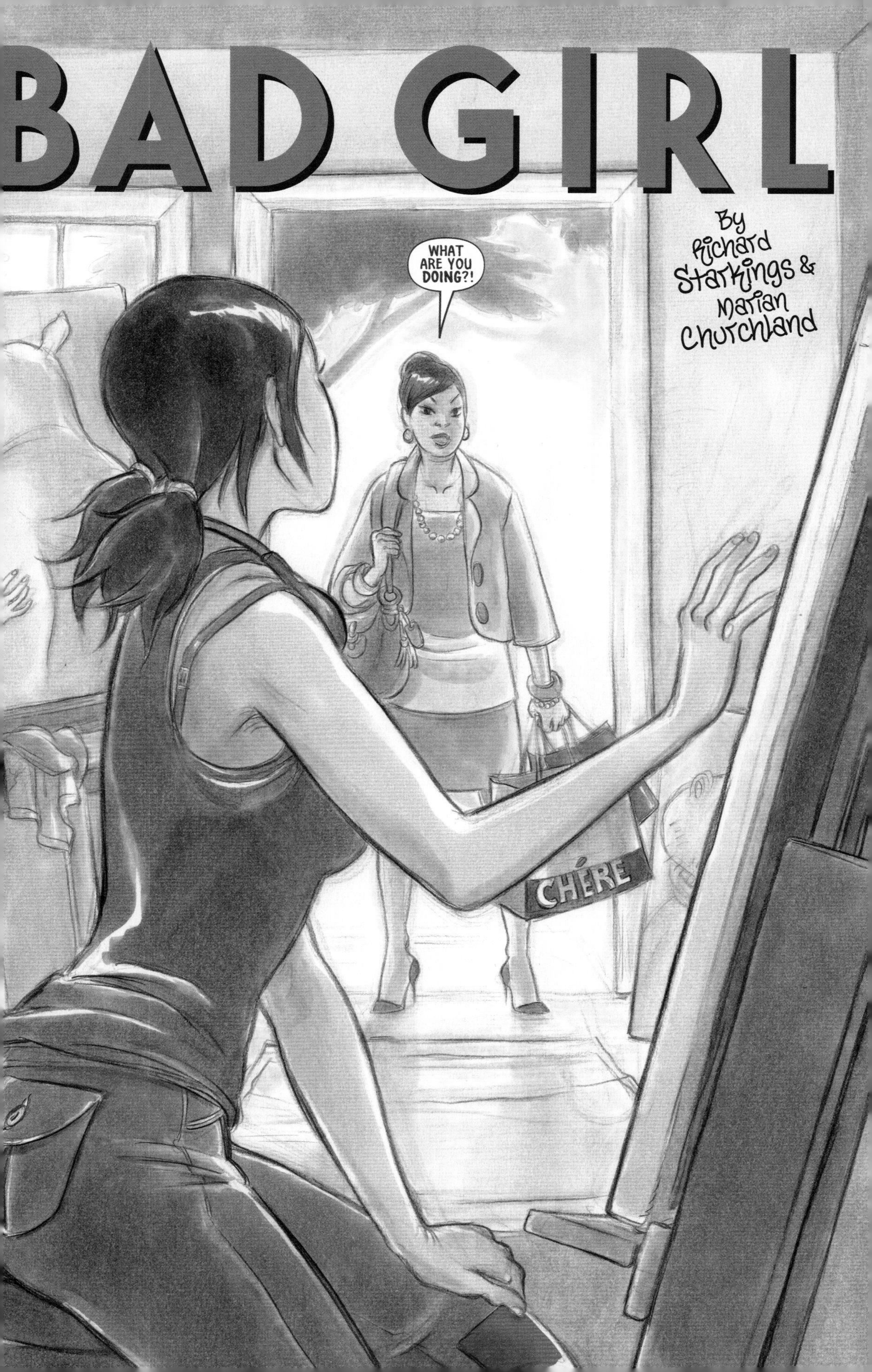
BAD GIRL
By Richard Starkings & Marian Churchland
WHAT ARE YOU DOING?!
CHÉRE

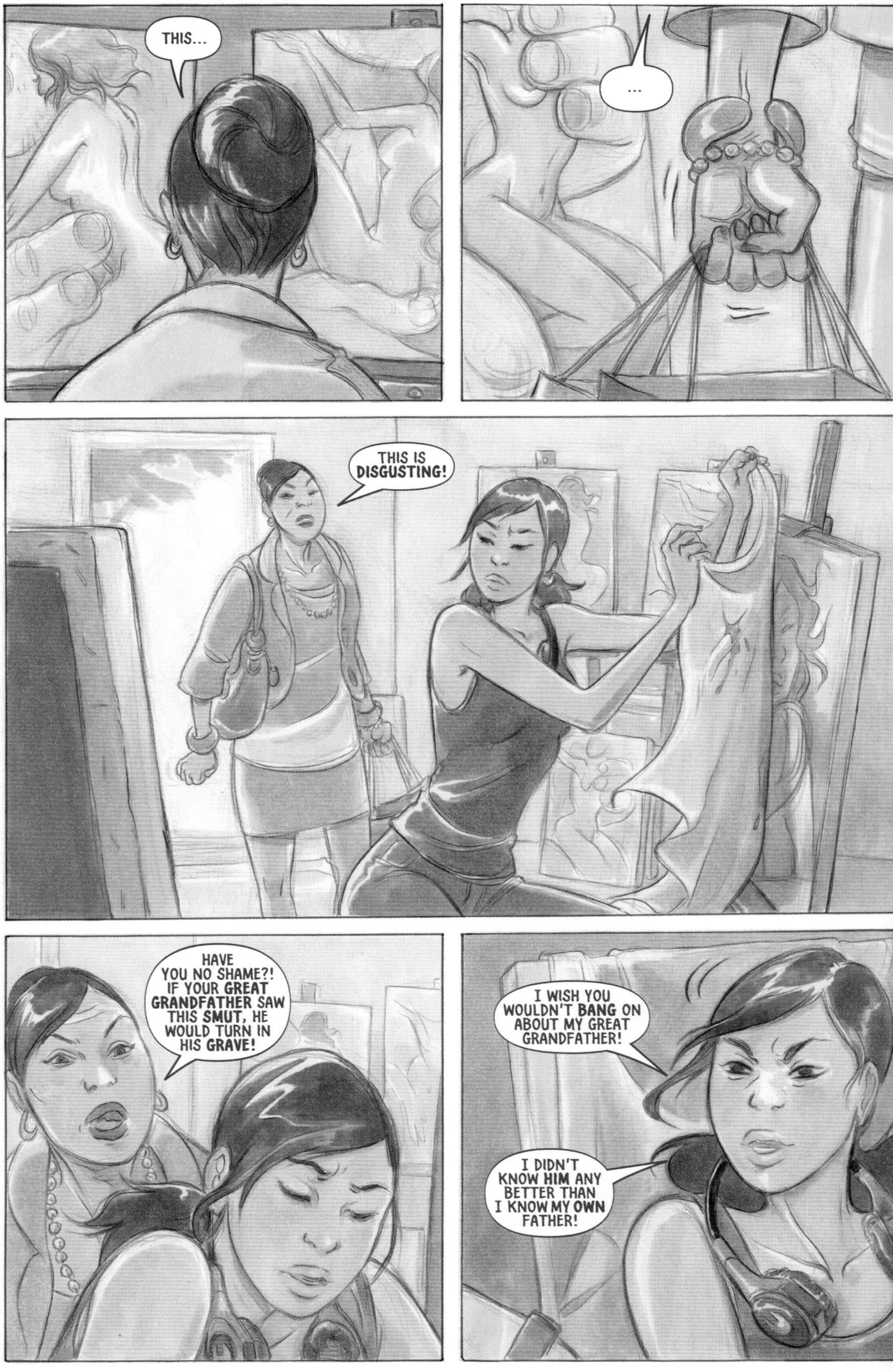

THIS...
...
THIS IS DISGUSTING!
HAVE YOU NO SHAME?! IF YOUR GREAT GRANDFATHER SAW THIS SMUT, HE WOULD TURN IN HIS GRAVE!
I WISH YOU WOULDN'T BANG ON ABOUT MY GREAT GRANDFATHER!
I DIDN'T KNOW HIM ANY BETTER THAN I KNOW MY OWN FATHER!

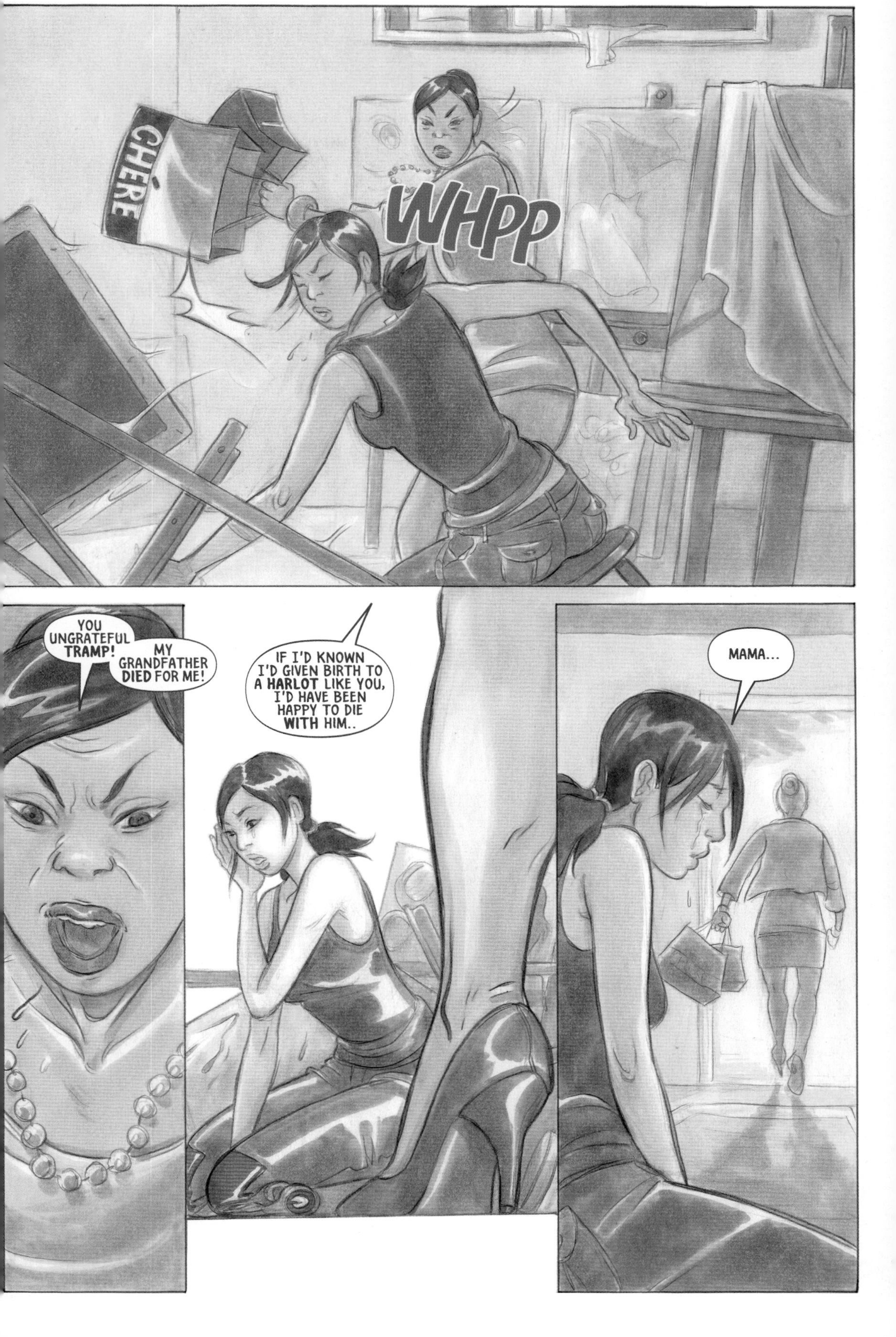

CHÈRE
WHPP
YOU UNGRATEFUL TRAMP!
MY GRANDFATHER DIED FOR ME!
IF I'D KNOWN I'D GIVEN BIRTH TO A HARLOT LIKE YOU, I'D HAVE BEEN HAPPY TO DIE WITH HIM..
MAMA...

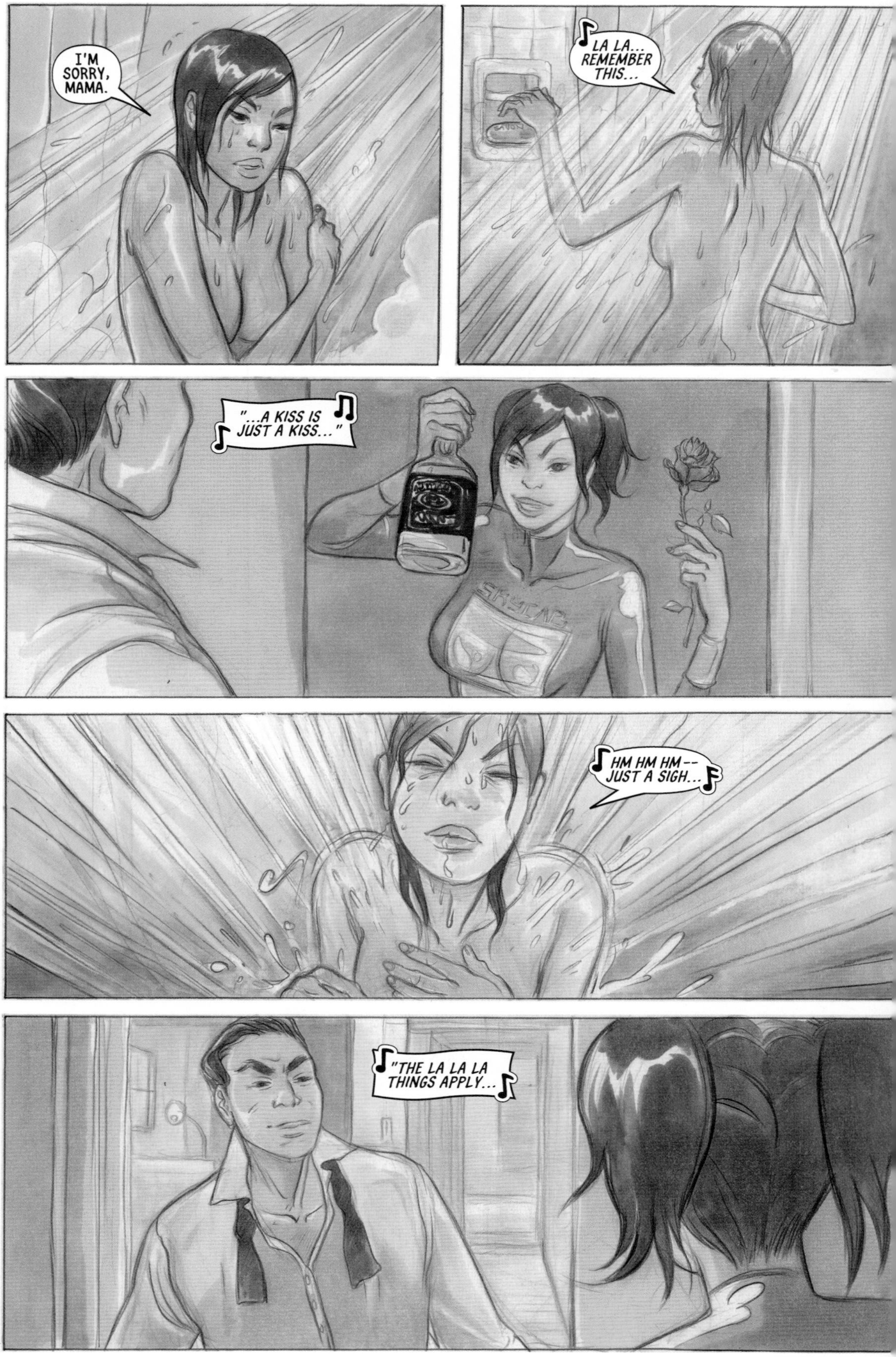
I'M SORRY, MAMA.
LA LA... REMEMBER THIS...
"...A KISS IS JUST A KISS..."
HM HM HM-- JUST A SIGH...
"THE LA LA LA THINGS APPLY...

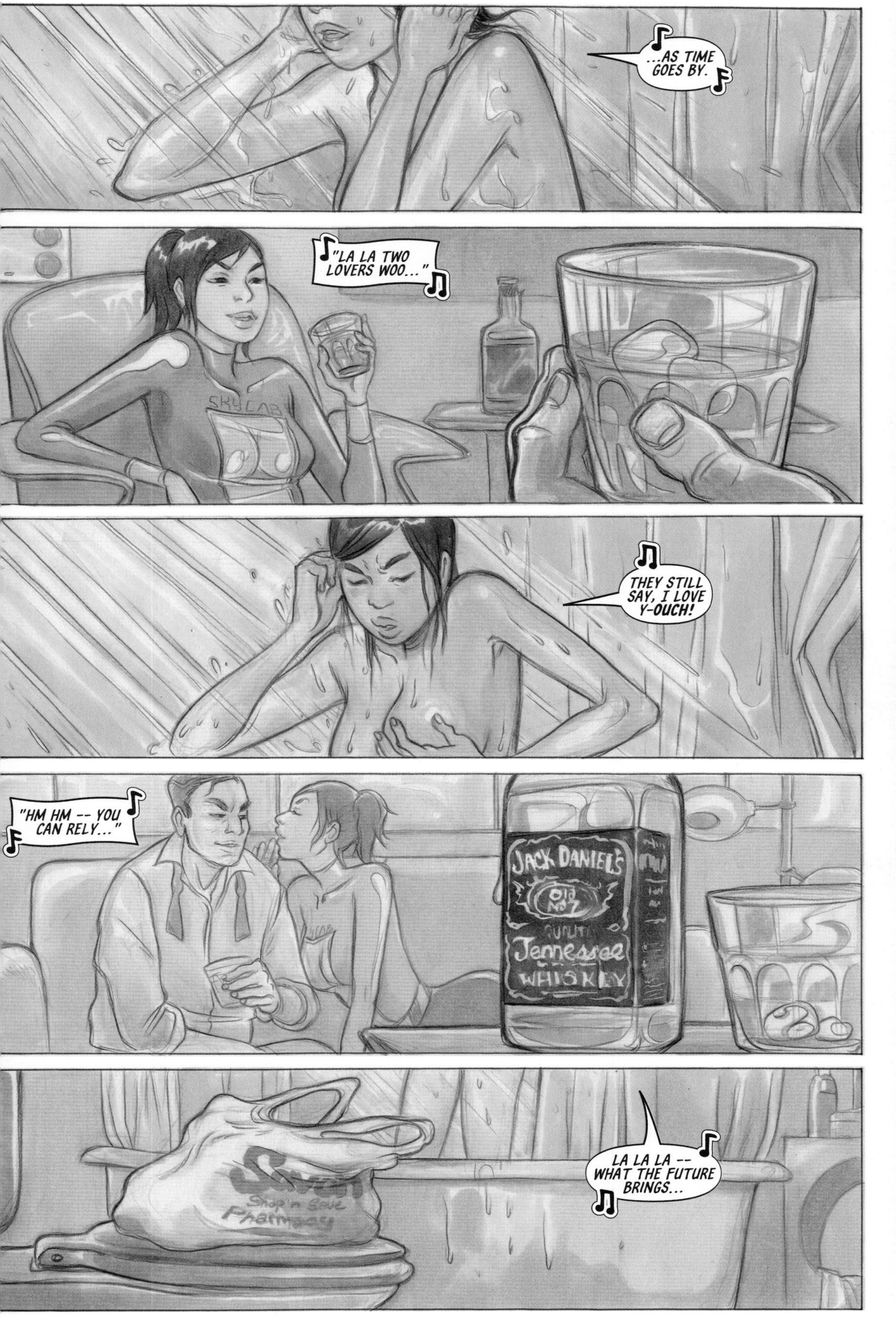
...AS TIME GOES BY.
"LA LA TWO LOVERS WOO..."
THEY STILL SAY, I LOVE Y-OUCH!
"HM HM -- YOU CAN RELY..."
JACK DANIEL'S
WHISKEY
LA LA LA -- WHAT THE FUTURE BRINGS...

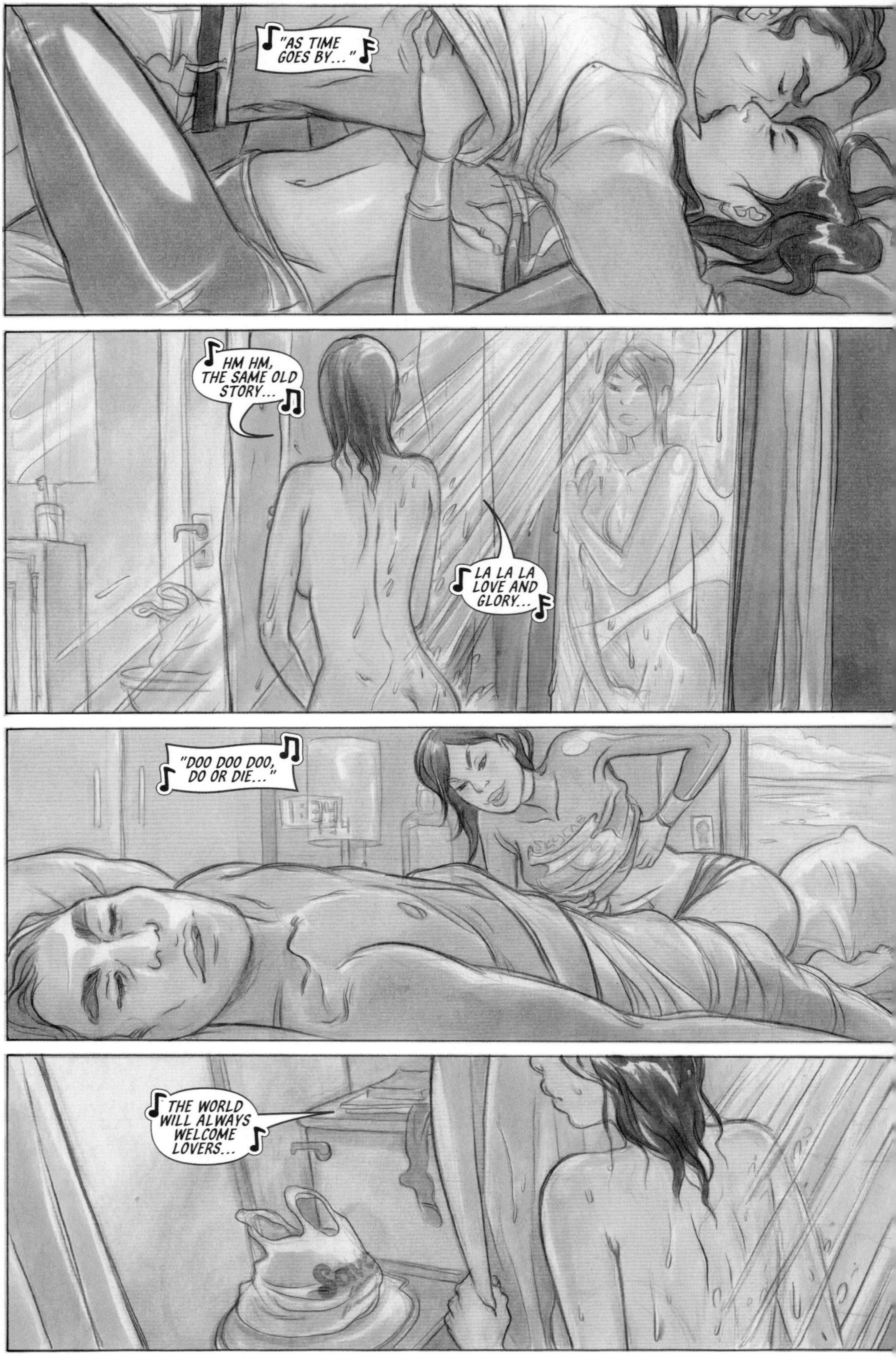
"AS TIME GOES BY..."
HM HM, THE SAME OLD STORY...
LA LA LA LOVE AND GLORY...
"DOO DOO DOO, DO OR DIE..."
THE WORLD WILL ALWAYS WELCOME LOVERS...

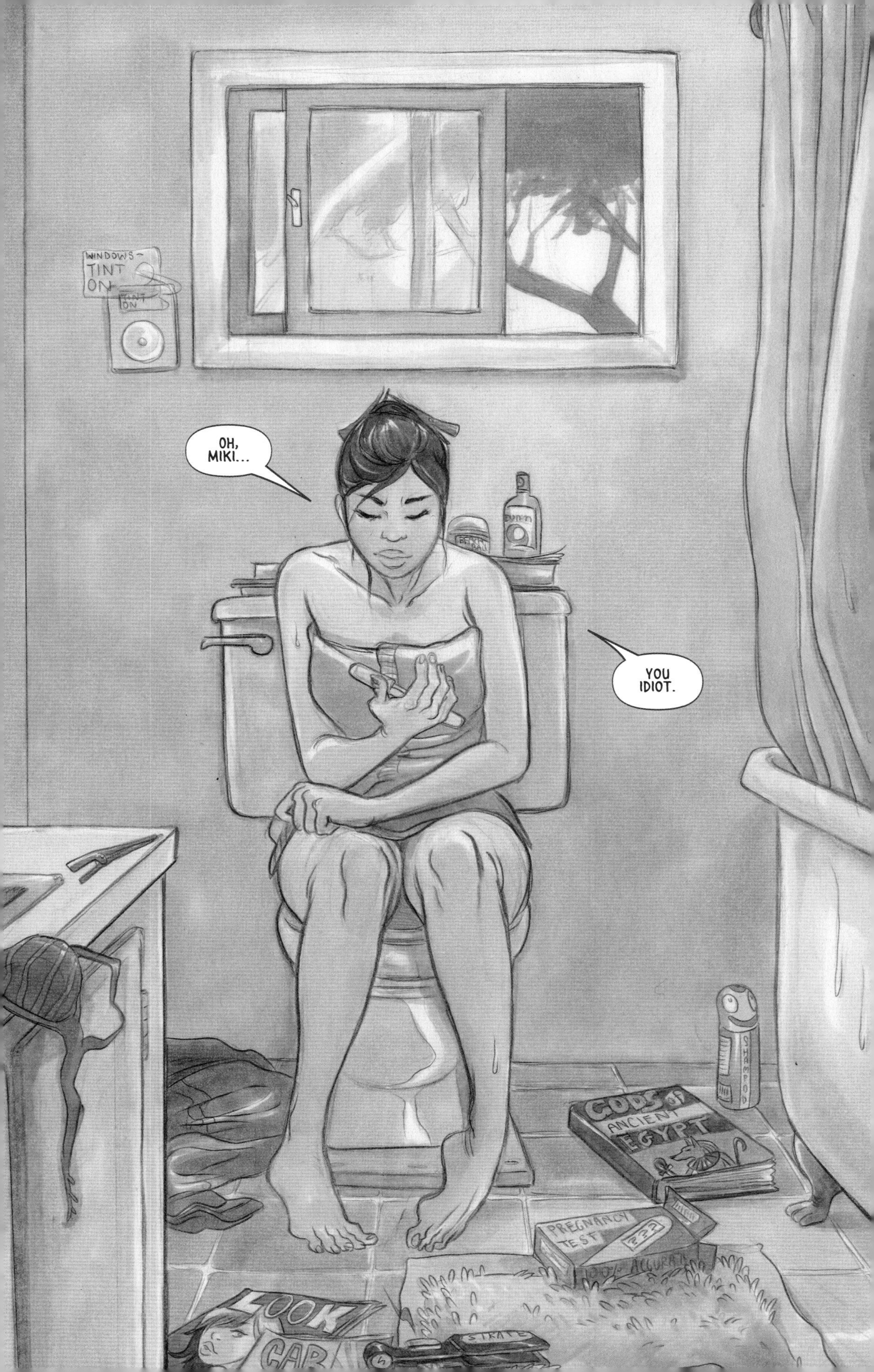
OH, MIKI...
YOU IDIOT.
WINDOWS- TINT ON
TINT ON
GODS OF ANCIENT EGYPT
PREGNANCY TEST
SHAMPOO
LOOK

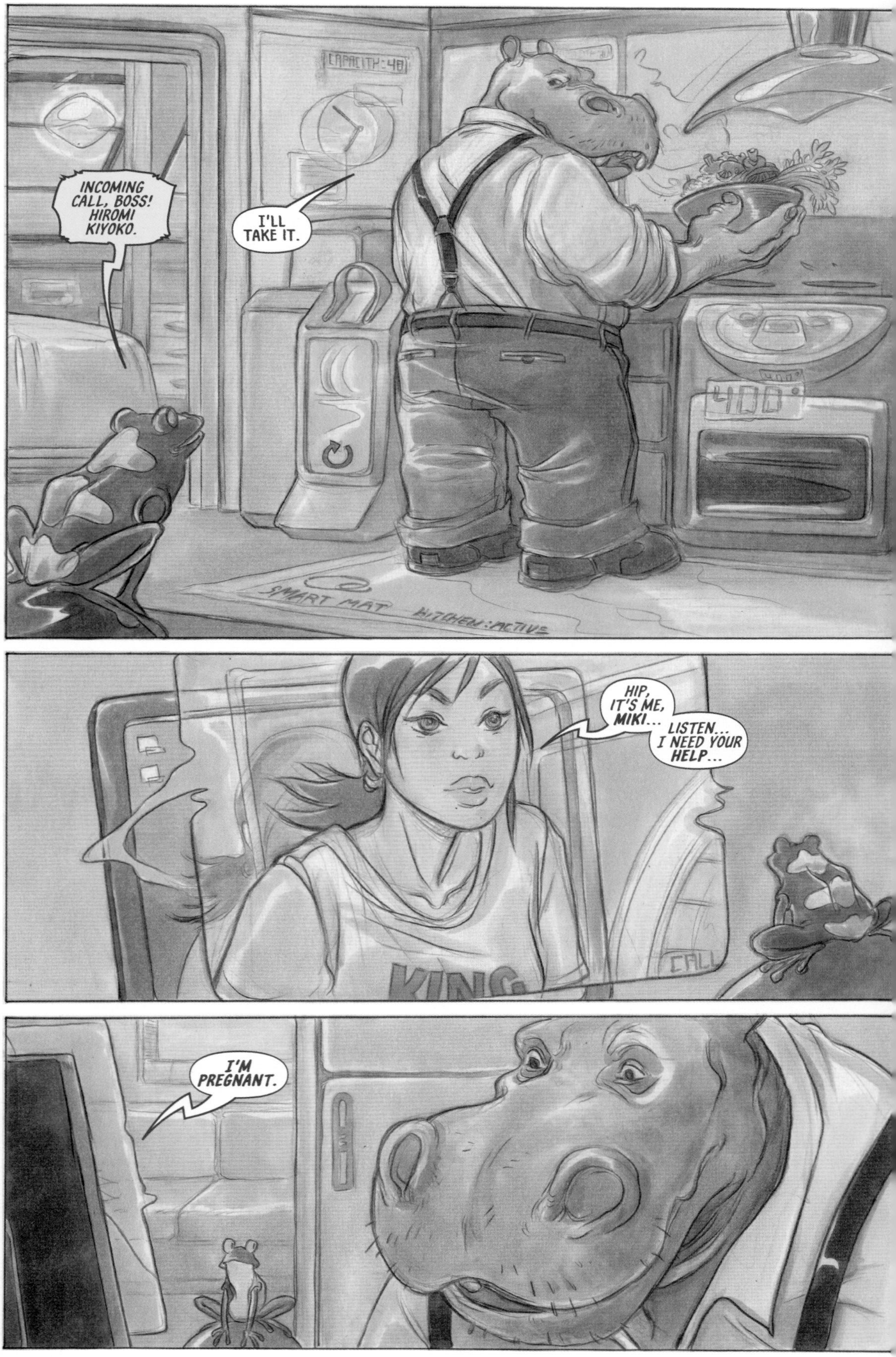
CAPACITY:40
INCOMING CALL, BOSS! HIROMI KIYOKO.
I'LL TAKE IT.
400
SMART MAT
HIP, IT'S ME, MIKI...
LISTEN... I NEED YOUR HELP...
CALL
KING
I'M PREGNANT.

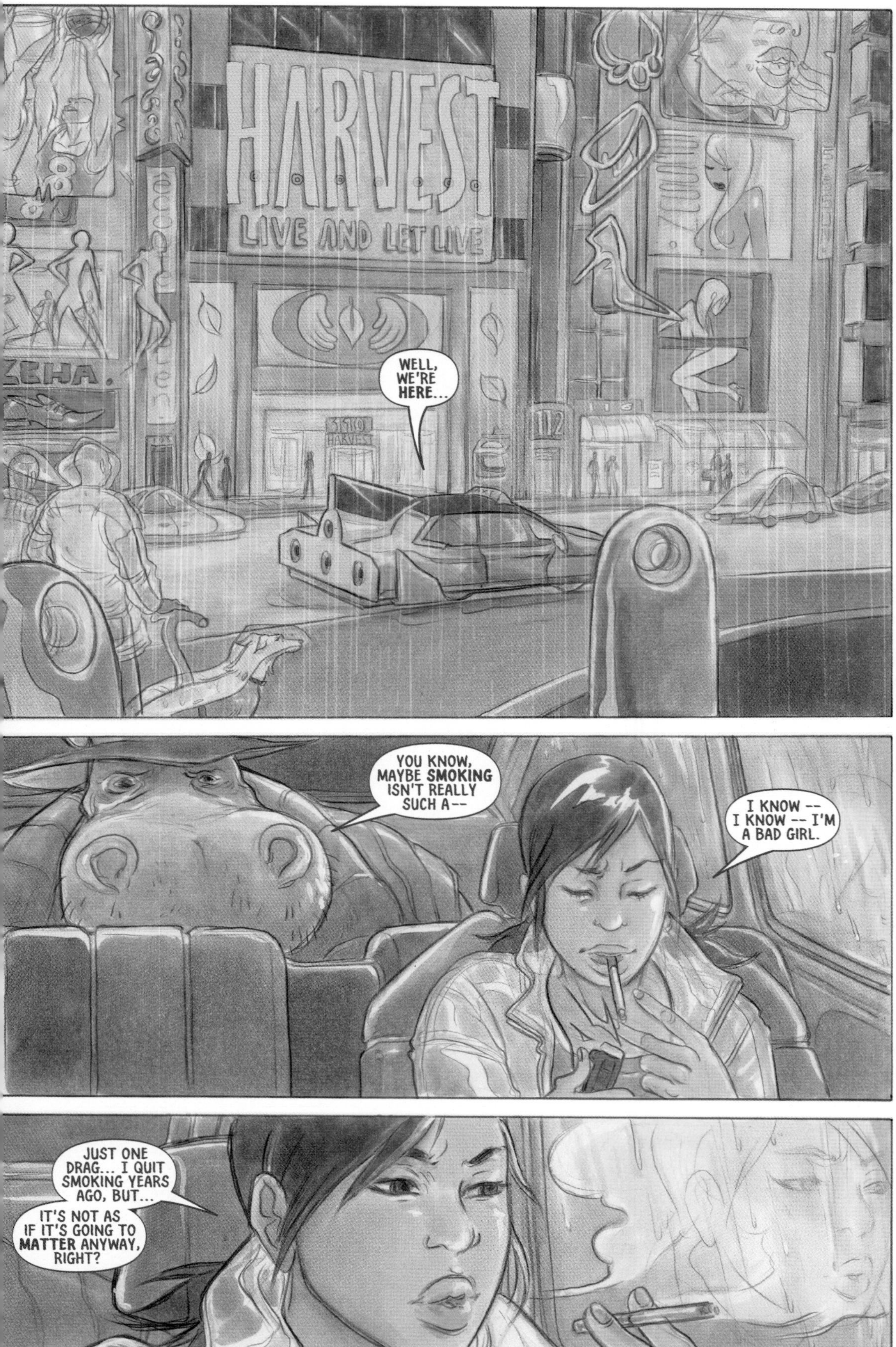
HARVEST
LIVE AND LET LIVE
112
WELL, WE'RE **HERE**...
YOU KNOW, MAYBE **SMOKING** ISN'T REALLY SUCH A--
I KNOW -- I KNOW -- I'M A BAD GIRL.
JUST ONE DRAG... I QUIT SMOKING YEARS AGO, BUT...
IT'S NOT AS IF IT'S GOING TO **MATTER** ANYWAY, RIGHT?

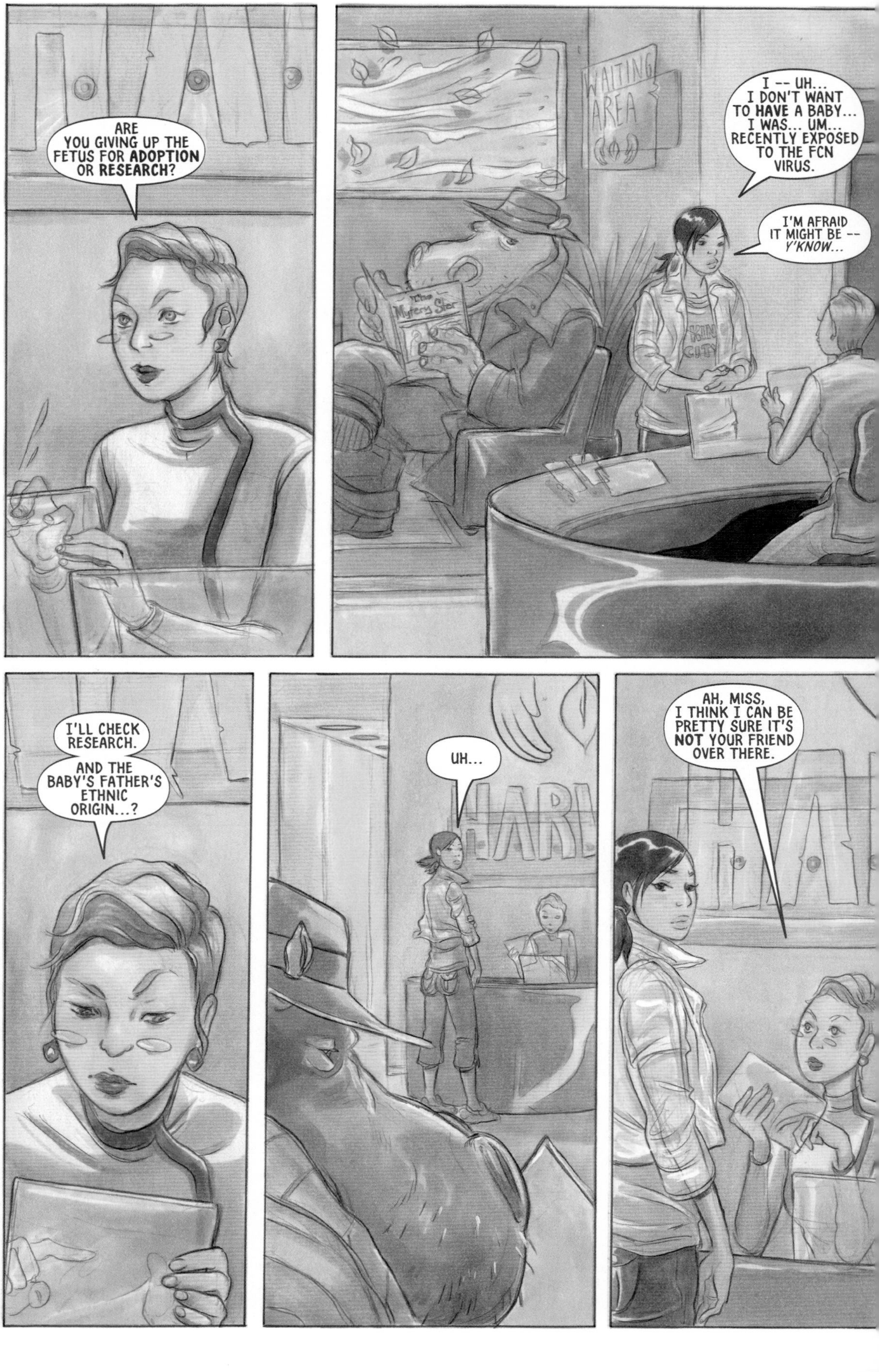
ARE YOU GIVING UP THE FETUS FOR ADOPTION OR RESEARCH?
WAITING AREA
The Mystery Star
KING CITY
I -- UH... I DON'T WANT TO HAVE A BABY... I WAS... UM... RECENTLY EXPOSED TO THE FCN VIRUS.
I'M AFRAID IT MIGHT BE -- Y'KNOW...
I'LL CHECK RESEARCH.
AND THE BABY'S FATHER'S ETHNIC ORIGIN...?
UH...
AH, MISS, I THINK I CAN BE PRETTY SURE IT'S NOT YOUR FRIEND OVER THERE.

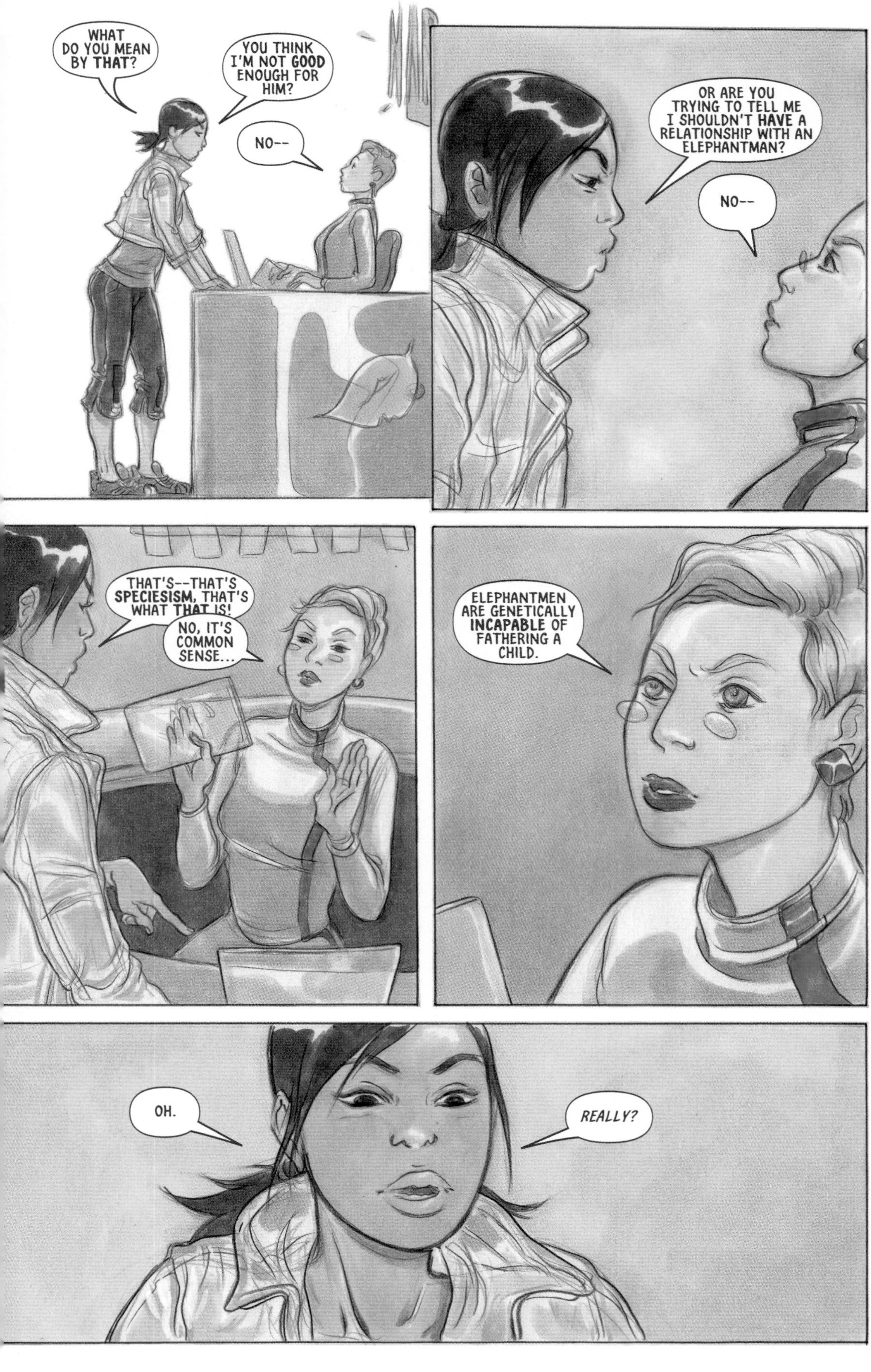
WHAT DO YOU MEAN BY THAT?
YOU THINK I'M NOT GOOD ENOUGH FOR HIM?
NO--
OR ARE YOU TRYING TO TELL ME I SHOULDN'T HAVE A RELATIONSHIP WITH AN ELEPHANTMAN?
NO--
THAT'S--THAT'S SPECIESISM, THAT'S WHAT THAT IS!
NO, IT'S COMMON SENSE...
ELEPHANTMEN ARE GENETICALLY INCAPABLE OF FATHERING A CHILD.
OH.
REALLY?

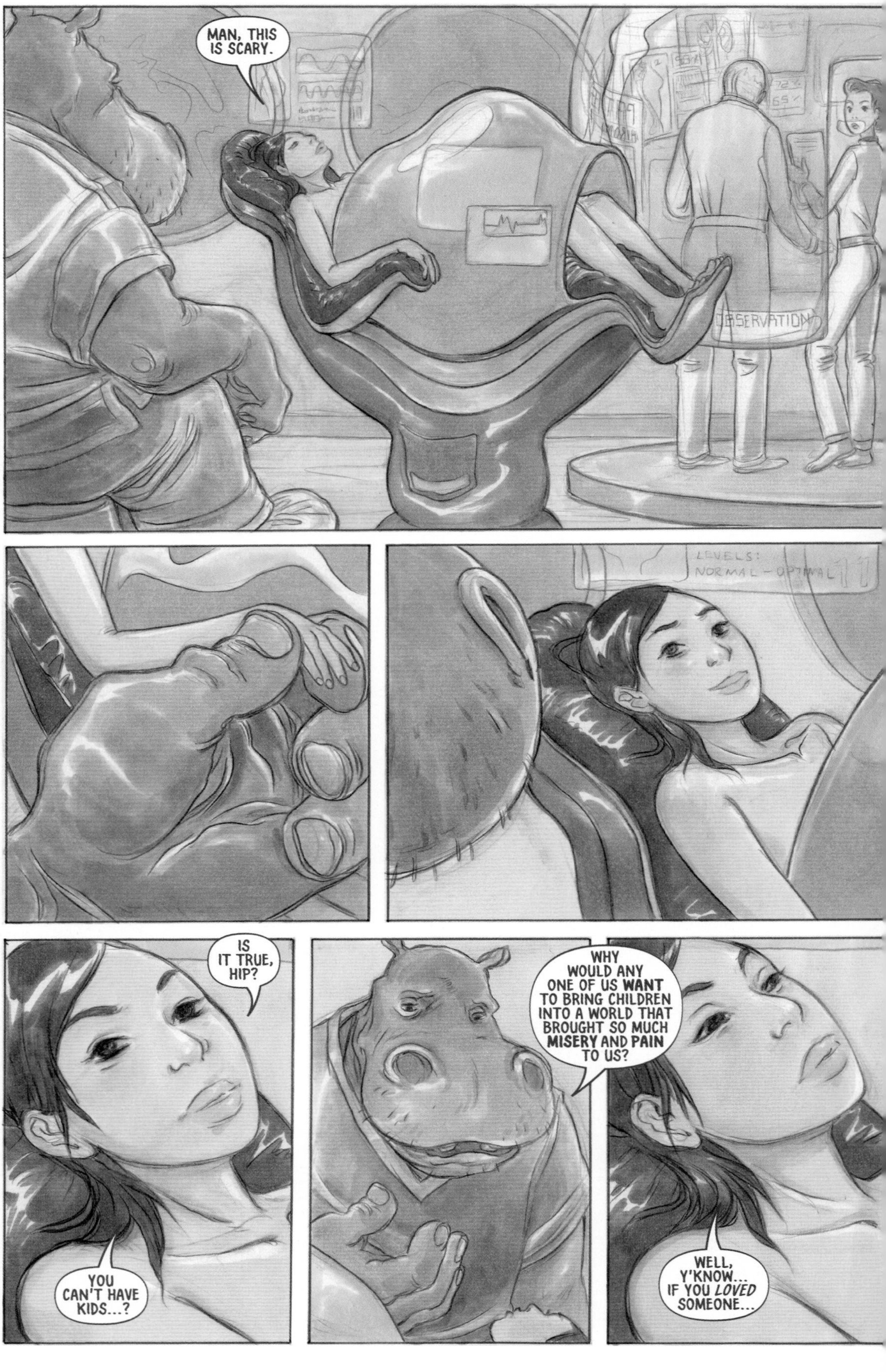
MAN, THIS IS SCARY.
OBSERVATION
LEVELS: NORMAL - OPTIMAL
IS IT TRUE, HIP?
YOU CAN'T HAVE KIDS...?
WHY WOULD ANY ONE OF US **WANT** TO BRING CHILDREN INTO A WORLD THAT BROUGHT SO MUCH **MISERY** AND **PAIN** TO US?
WELL, Y'KNOW... IF YOU *LOVED* SOMEONE...

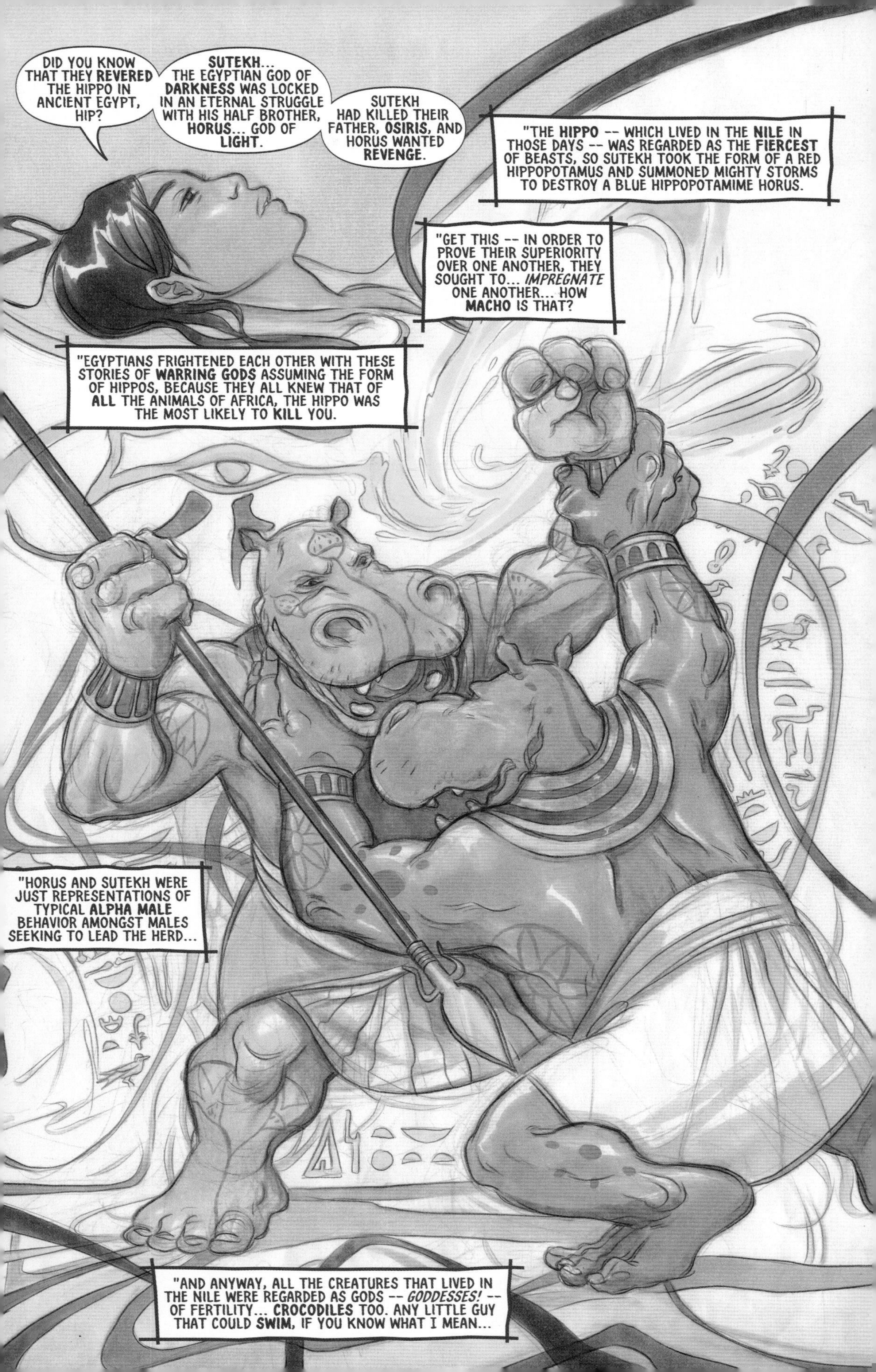

DID YOU KNOW THAT THEY **REVERED** THE HIPPO IN ANCIENT EGYPT, HIP?
SUTEKH... THE EGYPTIAN GOD OF **DARKNESS** WAS LOCKED IN AN ETERNAL STRUGGLE WITH HIS HALF BROTHER, **HORUS**... GOD OF **LIGHT**.
SUTEKH HAD KILLED THEIR FATHER, **OSIRIS**, AND HORUS WANTED **REVENGE**.
"THE **HIPPO** -- WHICH LIVED IN THE **NILE** IN THOSE DAYS -- WAS REGARDED AS THE **FIERCEST** OF BEASTS, SO SUTEKH TOOK THE FORM OF A RED HIPPOPOTAMUS AND SUMMONED MIGHTY STORMS TO DESTROY A BLUE HIPPOPOTAMIME HORUS.
"GET THIS -- IN ORDER TO PROVE THEIR SUPERIORITY OVER ONE ANOTHER, THEY SOUGHT TO... *IMPREGNATE* ONE ANOTHER... HOW **MACHO** IS THAT?
"EGYPTIANS FRIGHTENED EACH OTHER WITH THESE STORIES OF **WARRING GODS** ASSUMING THE FORM OF HIPPOS, BECAUSE THEY ALL KNEW THAT OF **ALL** THE ANIMALS OF AFRICA, THE HIPPO WAS THE MOST LIKELY TO **KILL** YOU.
"HORUS AND SUTEKH WERE JUST REPRESENTATIONS OF TYPICAL **ALPHA MALE** BEHAVIOR AMONGST MALES SEEKING TO LEAD THE HERD...
"AND ANYWAY, ALL THE CREATURES THAT LIVED IN THE NILE WERE REGARDED AS GODS -- *GODDESSES!* -- OF FERTILITY... **CROCODILES** TOO. ANY LITTLE GUY THAT COULD **SWIM**, IF YOU KNOW WHAT I MEAN...

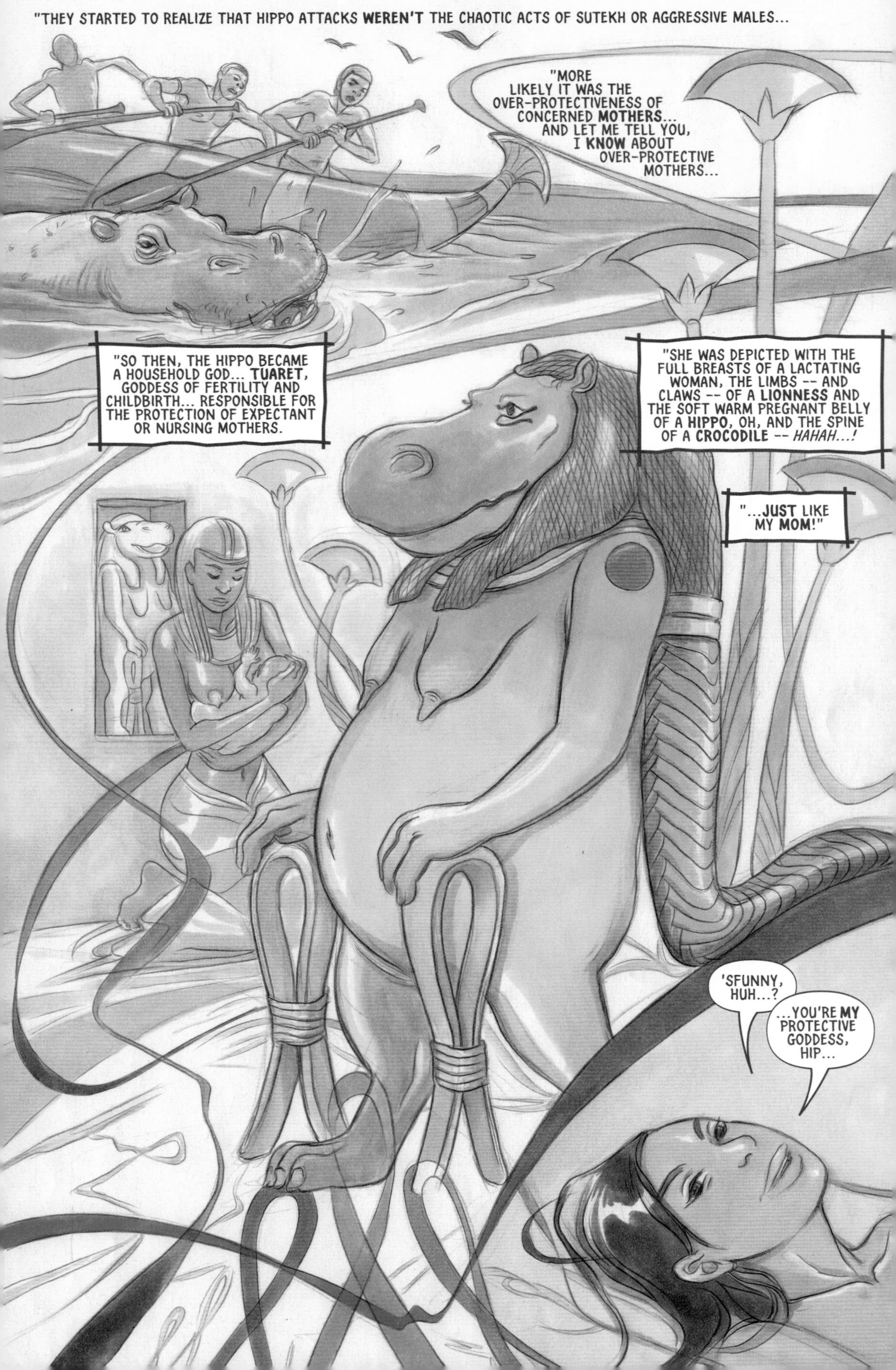
"THEY STARTED TO REALIZE THAT HIPPO ATTACKS **WEREN'T** THE CHAOTIC ACTS OF SUTEKH OR AGGRESSIVE MALES...
"MORE LIKELY IT WAS THE OVER-PROTECTIVENESS OF CONCERNED **MOTHERS**... AND LET ME TELL YOU, I **KNOW** ABOUT OVER-PROTECTIVE MOTHERS...
"SO THEN, THE HIPPO BECAME A HOUSEHOLD GOD... **TUARET**, GODDESS OF FERTILITY AND CHILDBIRTH... RESPONSIBLE FOR THE PROTECTION OF EXPECTANT OR NURSING MOTHERS.
"SHE WAS DEPICTED WITH THE FULL BREASTS OF A LACTATING WOMAN, THE LIMBS -- AND CLAWS -- OF A **LIONNESS** AND THE SOFT WARM PREGNANT BELLY OF A **HIPPO**, OH, AND THE SPINE OF A **CROCODILE** -- *HAHAH...!*
"...**JUST** LIKE MY **MOM**!"
'SFUNNY, HUH...?
...YOU'RE **MY** PROTECTIVE GODDESS, HIP...

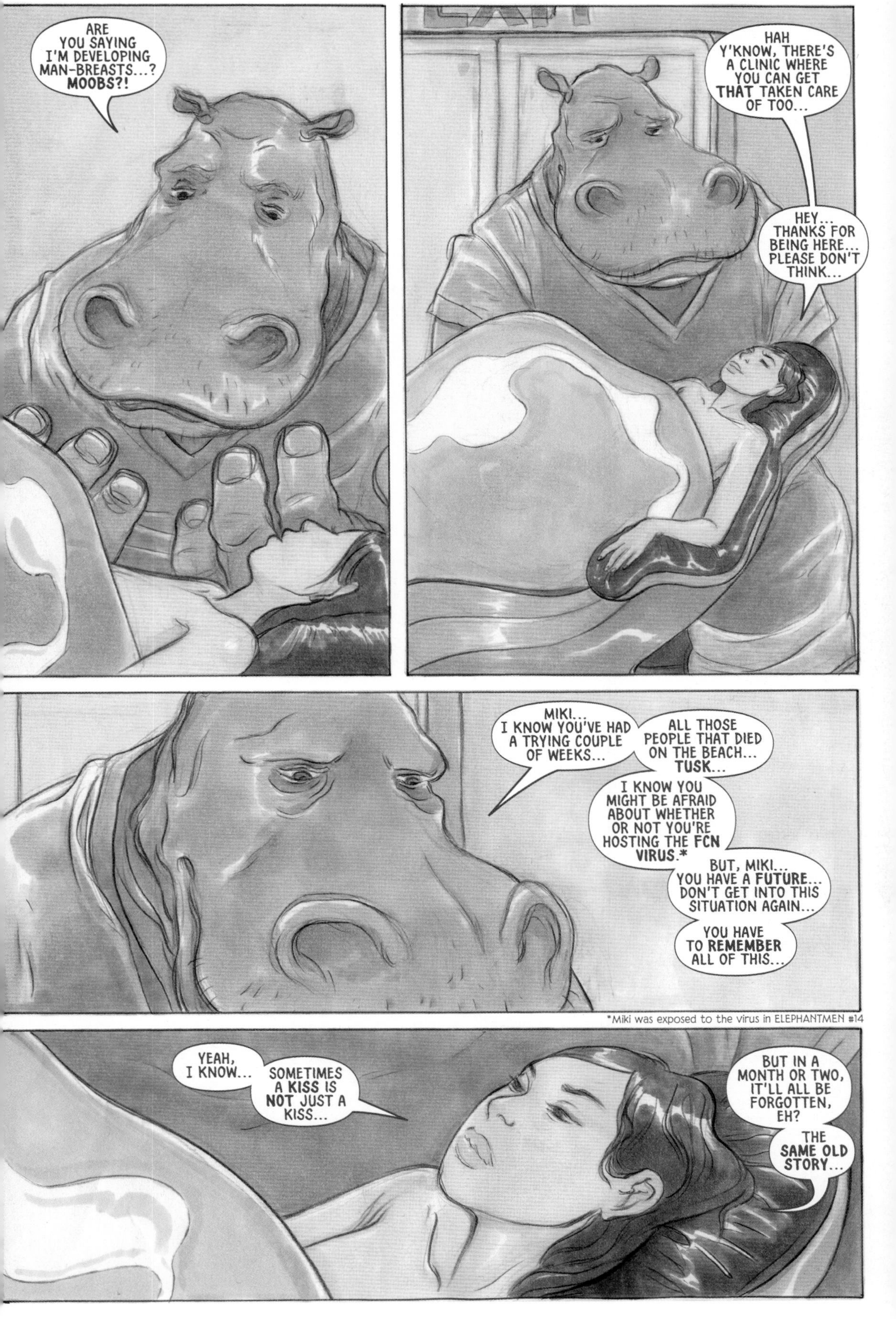
ARE YOU SAYING I'M DEVELOPING MAN-BREASTS...? MOOBS?!
HAH Y'KNOW, THERE'S A CLINIC WHERE YOU CAN GET THAT TAKEN CARE OF TOO...
HEY... THANKS FOR BEING HERE... PLEASE DON'T THINK...
MIKI... I KNOW YOU'VE HAD A TRYING COUPLE OF WEEKS...
ALL THOSE PEOPLE THAT DIED ON THE BEACH... TUSK...
I KNOW YOU MIGHT BE AFRAID ABOUT WHETHER OR NOT YOU'RE HOSTING THE FCN VIRUS.*
BUT, MIKI... YOU HAVE A FUTURE... DON'T GET INTO THIS SITUATION AGAIN...
YOU HAVE TO REMEMBER ALL OF THIS...
*Miki was exposed to the virus in ELEPHANTMEN #14
YEAH, I KNOW...
SOMETIMES A KISS IS NOT JUST A KISS...
BUT IN A MONTH OR TWO, IT'LL ALL BE FORGOTTEN, EH?
THE SAME OLD STORY...

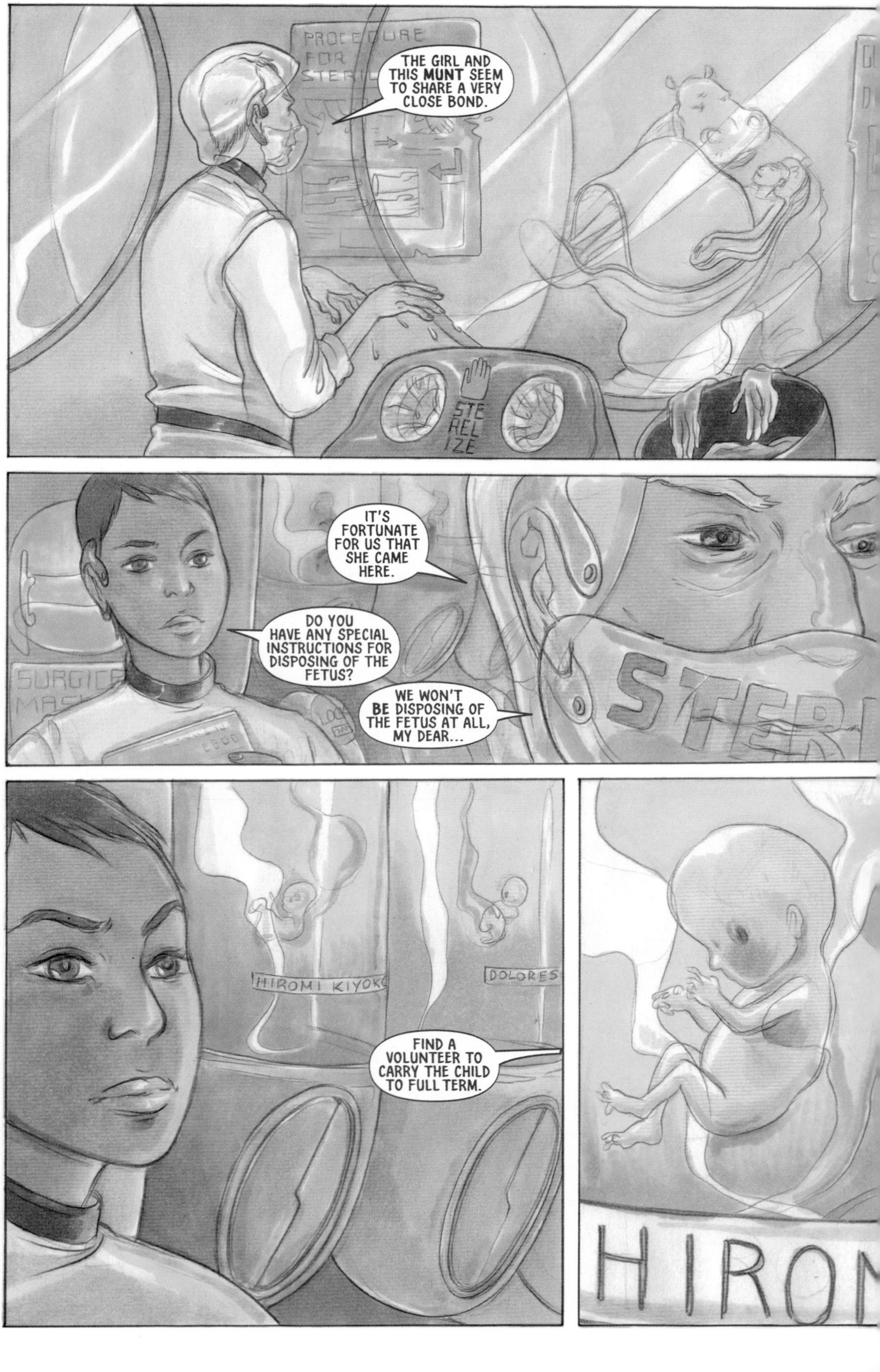
THE GIRL AND THIS **MUNT** SEEM TO SHARE A VERY CLOSE BOND.
IT'S FORTUNATE FOR US THAT SHE CAME HERE.
DO YOU HAVE ANY SPECIAL INSTRUCTIONS FOR DISPOSING OF THE FETUS?
WE WON'T **BE** DISPOSING OF THE FETUS AT ALL, MY DEAR...
HIROMI KIYOKO
DOLORES
FIND A VOLUNTEER TO CARRY THE CHILD TO FULL TERM.

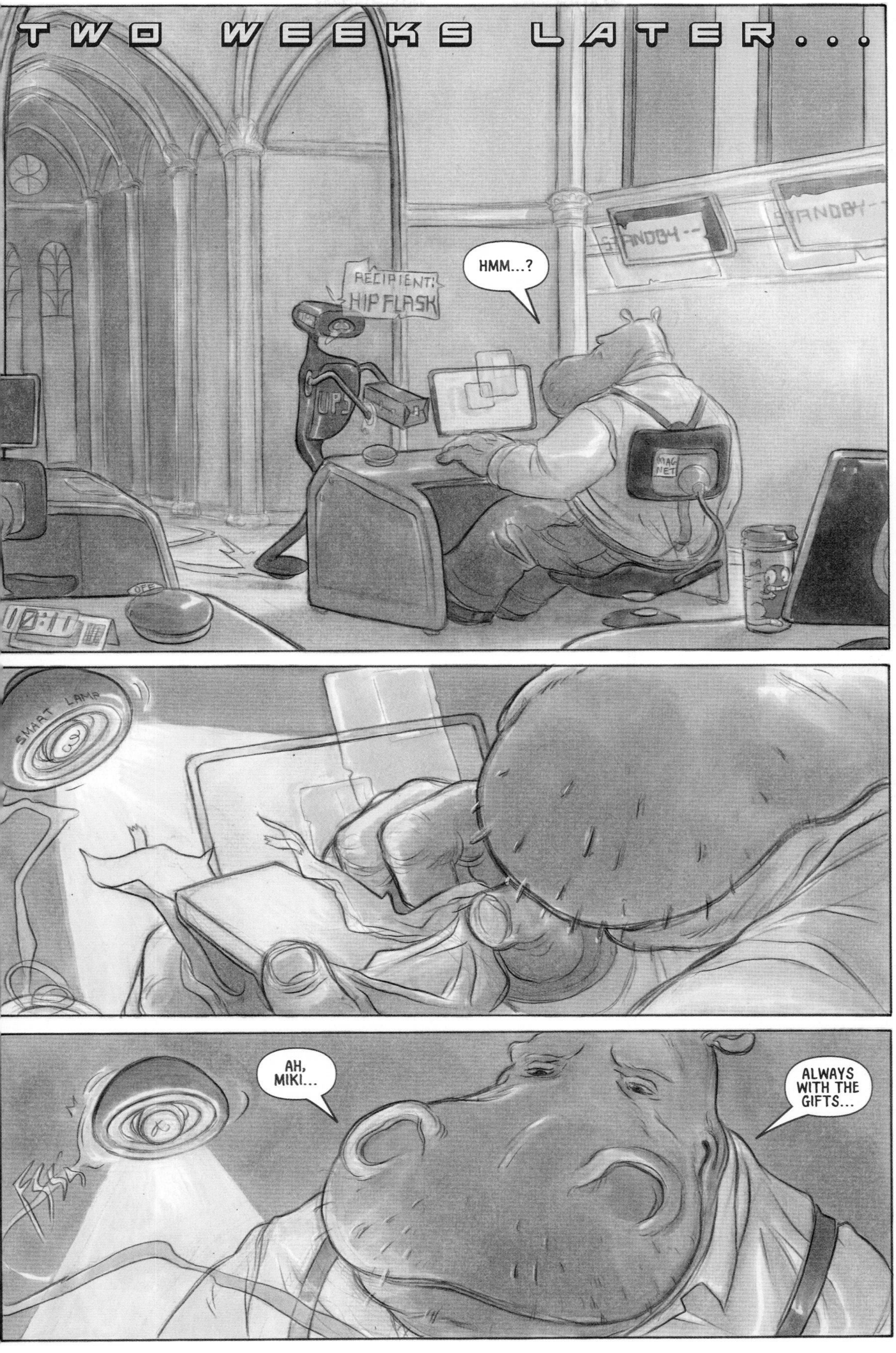
TWO WEEKS LATER...
STANDBY --
STANDBY --
RECIPIENT: HIP FLASK
HMM...?
UPS
MAG NET
OFF
SMART LAMP
AH, MIKI...
ALWAYS WITH THE GIFTS...

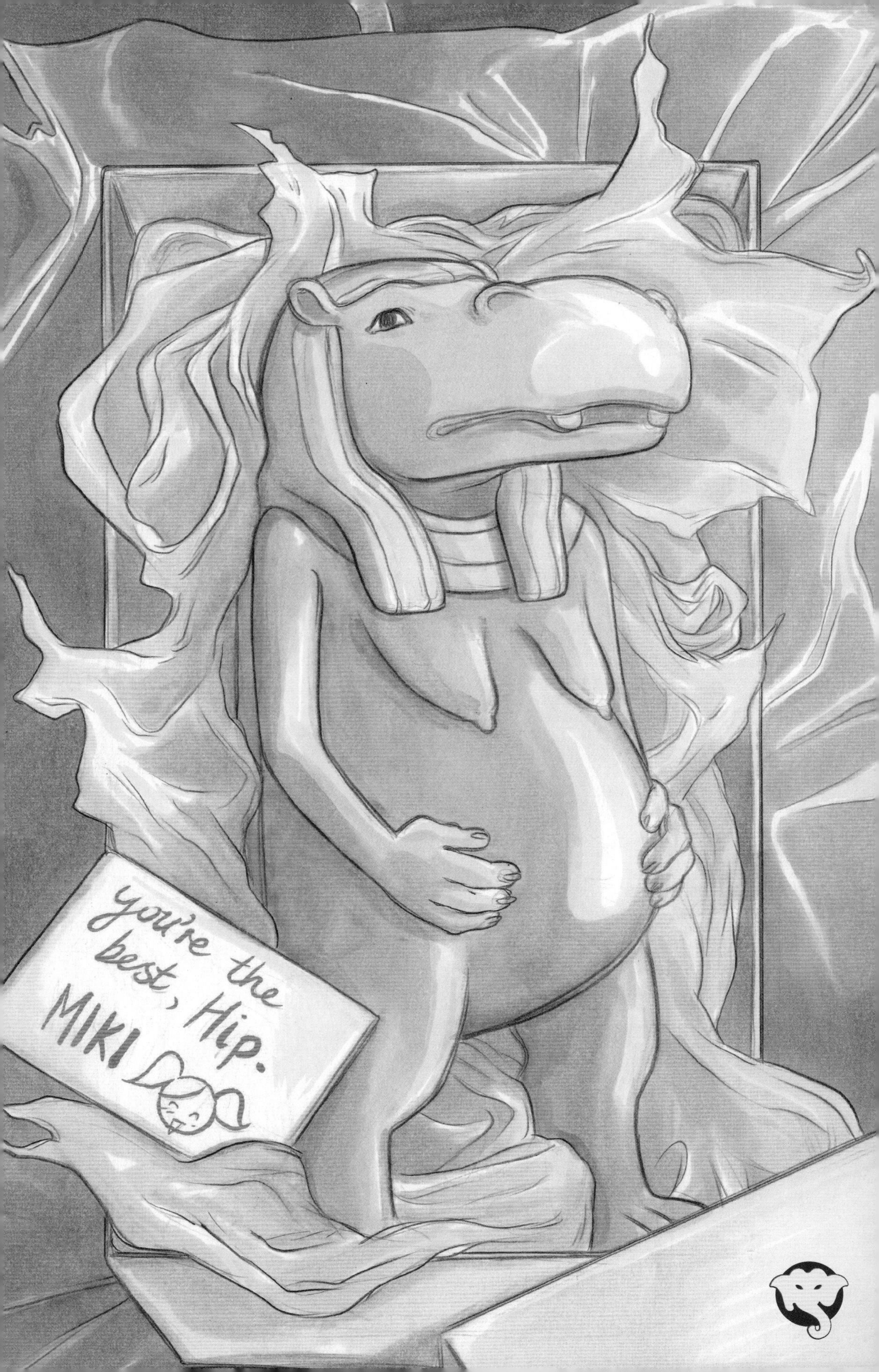
you're the
best, Hip.
MIKI

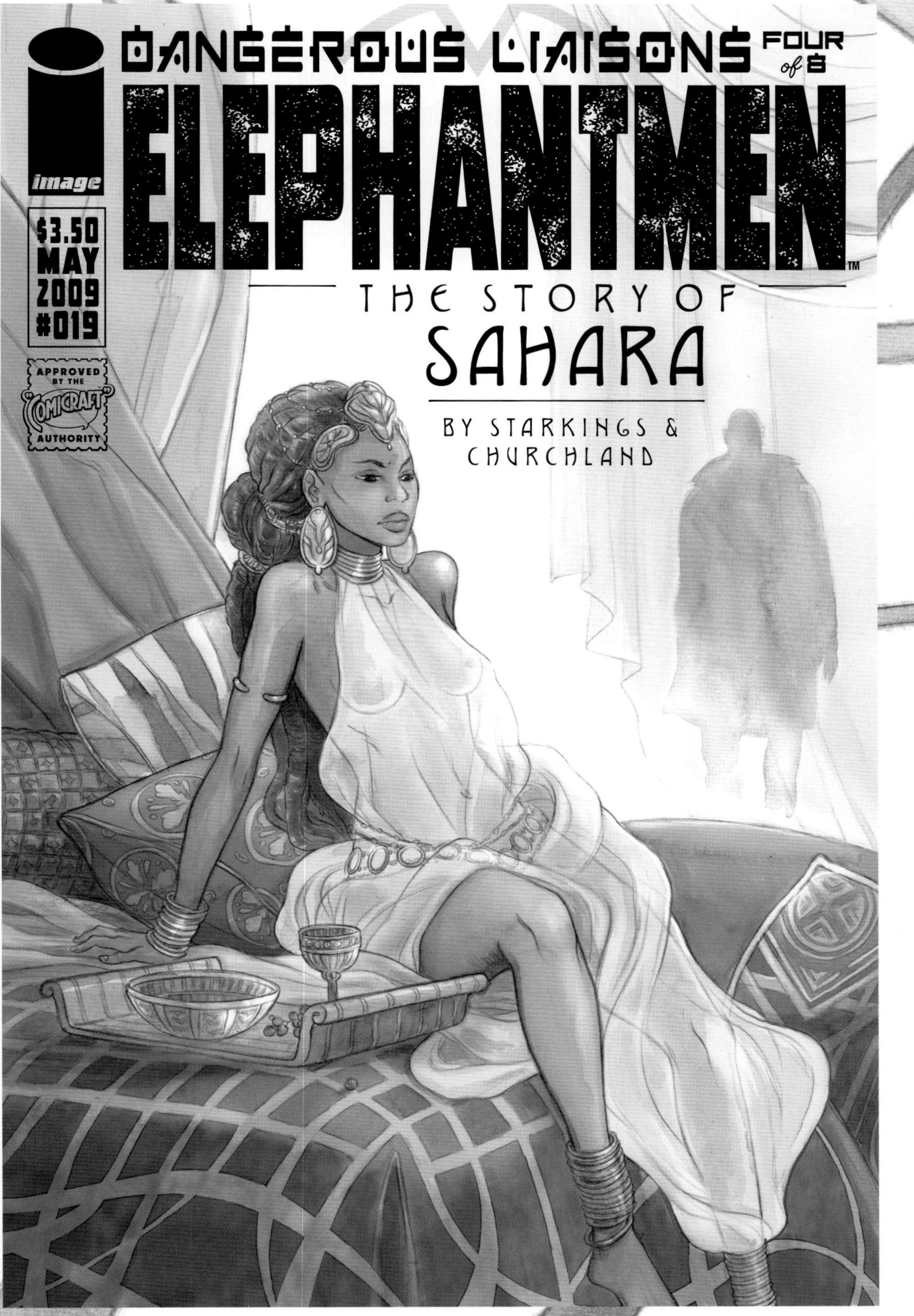

DANGEROUS LIAISONS FOUR of 8
ELEPHANTMEN™
image
$3.50
MAY
2009
#019
APPROVED BY THE COMICRAFT AUTHORITY
THE STORY OF
SAHARA
BY STARKINGS &
CHURCHLAND

SAHARA

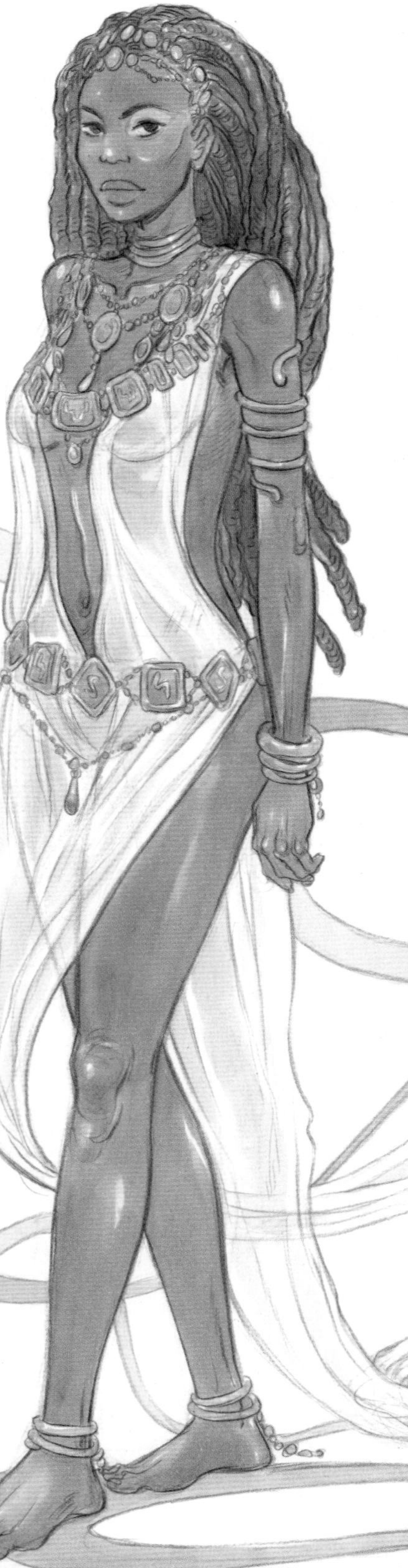

She is the unwanted daughter of African crimelord Joshua Serengheti and his mistress, Kala. Many years after Serengheti sold her mother to MAPPO as breeding stock for production of Elephantmen...

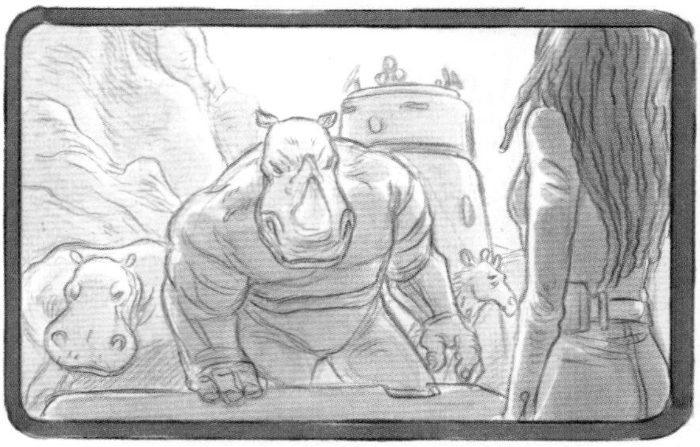

...Sahara became involved in the UN's Elephantmen rehabilitation program, where she met and fell in love with Obadiah Horn, now the most celebrated Elephantman of all.

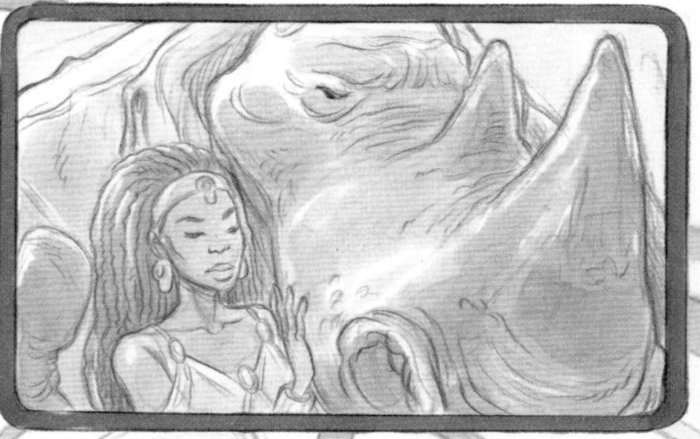

Injured in a car crash, Horn and Sahara were taken to the transgenics hospital for treatment. When Serengheti, now based in Los Angeles, heard of their location, he led an armed gang to the hospital to kill Horn and take Sahara back...

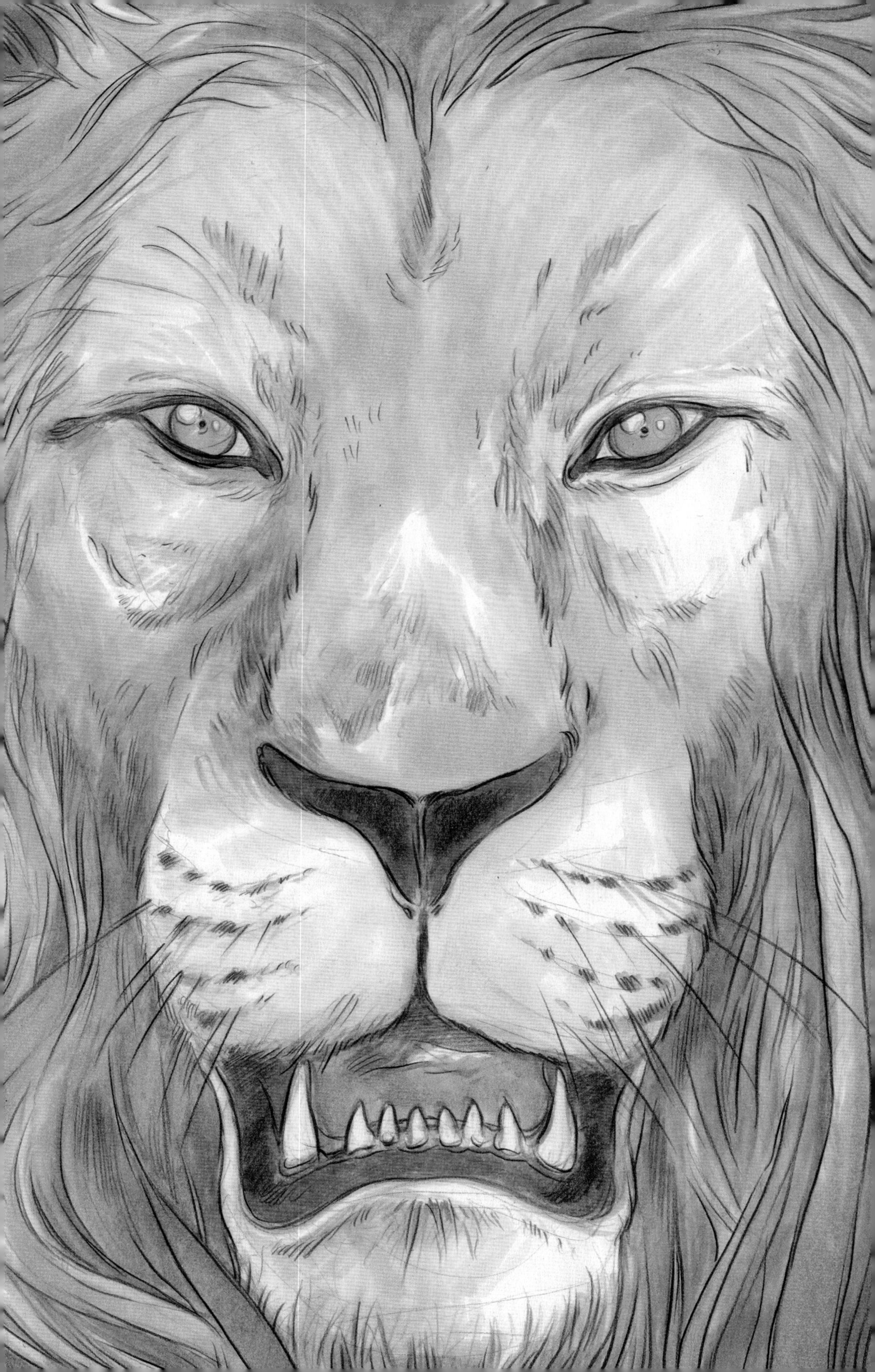

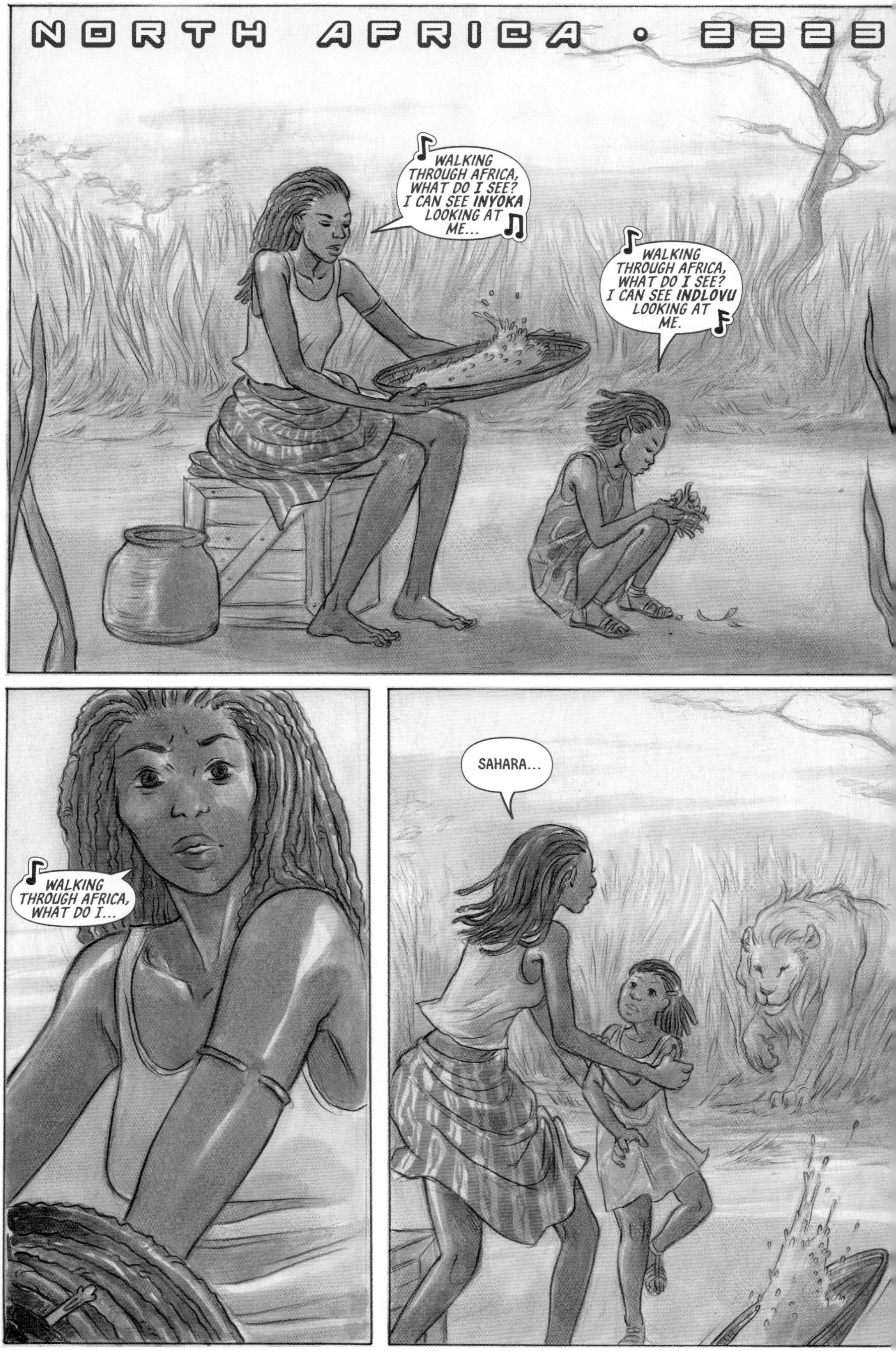
NORTH AFRICA • 2223
WALKING THROUGH AFRICA, WHAT DO I SEE? I CAN SEE INYOKA LOOKING AT ME...
WALKING THROUGH AFRICA, WHAT DO I SEE? I CAN SEE INDLOVU LOOKING AT ME.
WALKING THROUGH AFRICA, WHAT DO I...
SAHARA...

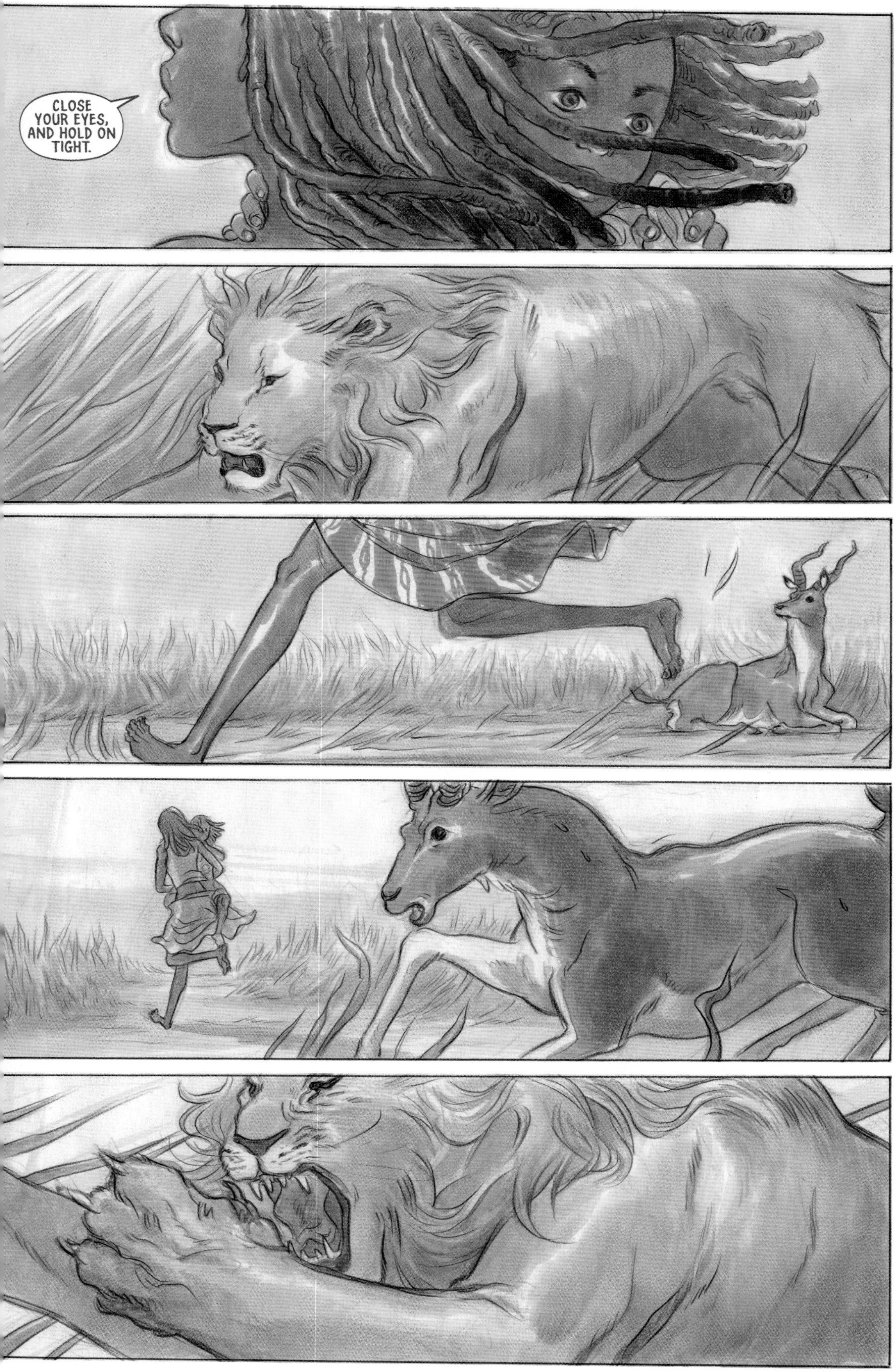
CLOSE YOUR EYES, AND HOLD ON TIGHT.

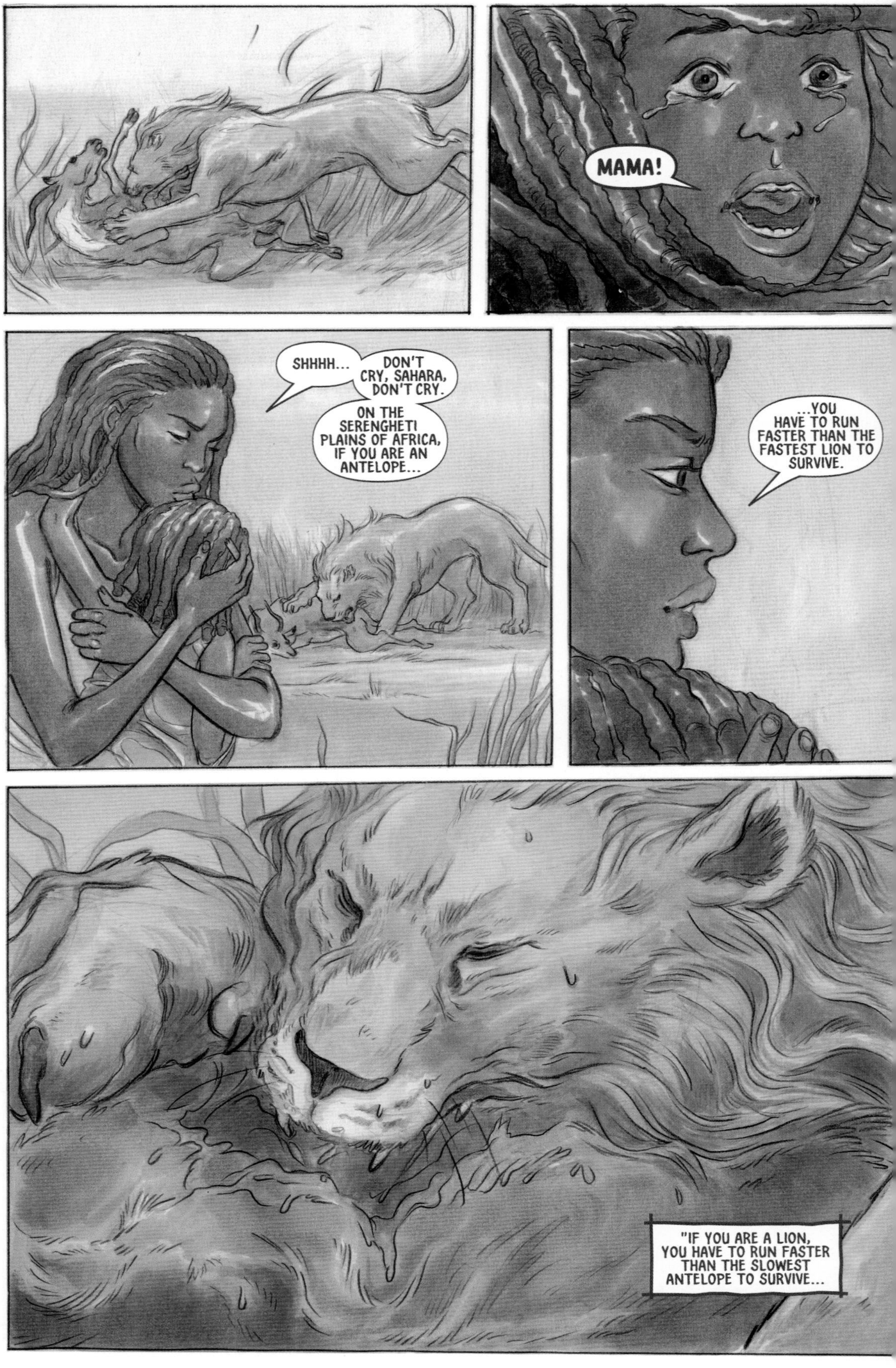
MAMA!
SHHHH...
DON'T CRY, SAHARA, DON'T CRY.
ON THE SERENGHETI PLAINS OF AFRICA, IF YOU ARE AN ANTELOPE...
...YOU HAVE TO RUN FASTER THAN THE FASTEST LION TO SURVIVE.
"IF YOU ARE A LION, YOU HAVE TO RUN FASTER THAN THE SLOWEST ANTELOPE TO SURVIVE...

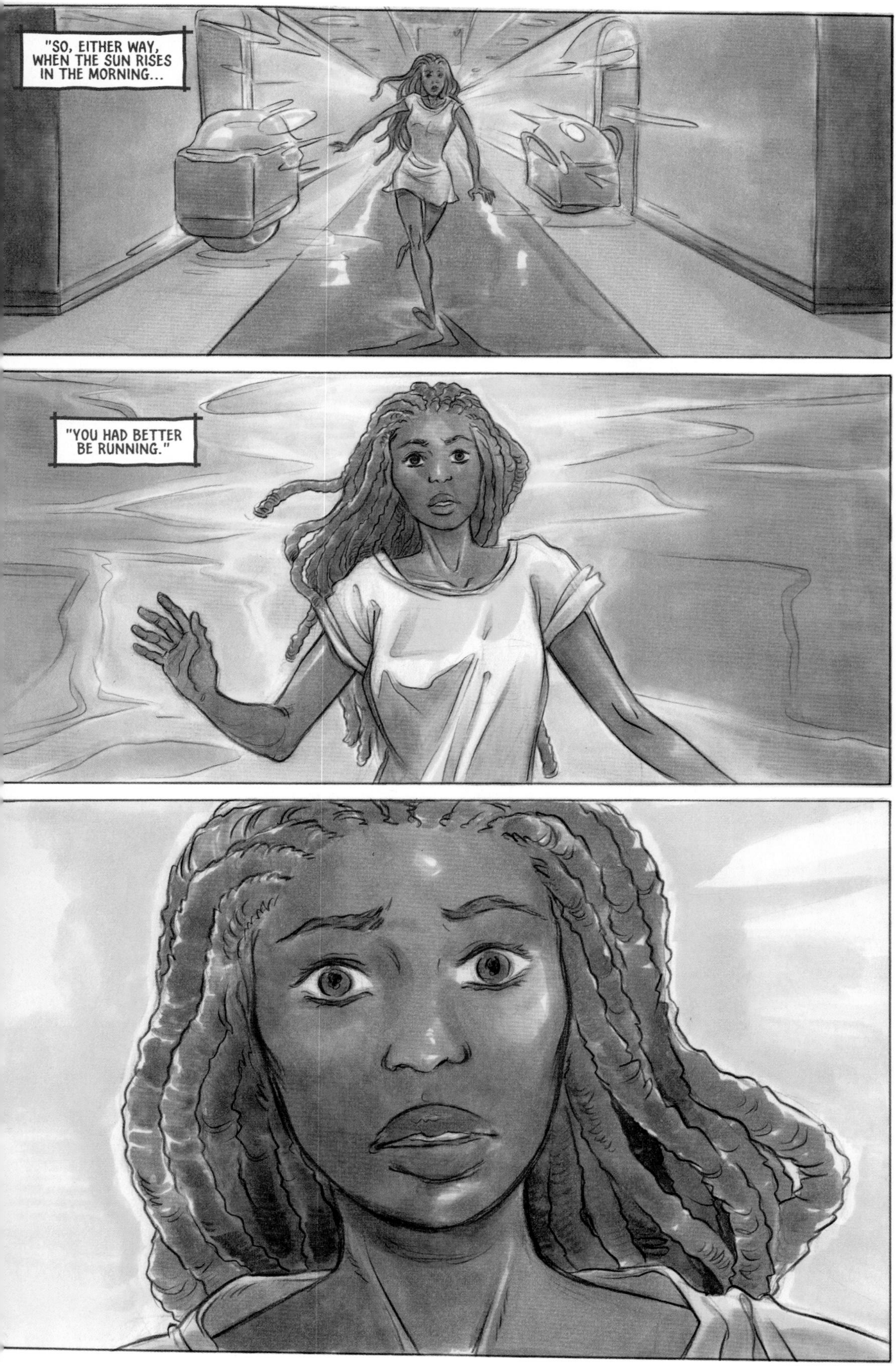
"SO, EITHER WAY, WHEN THE SUN RISES IN THE MORNING...
"YOU HAD BETTER BE RUNNING."

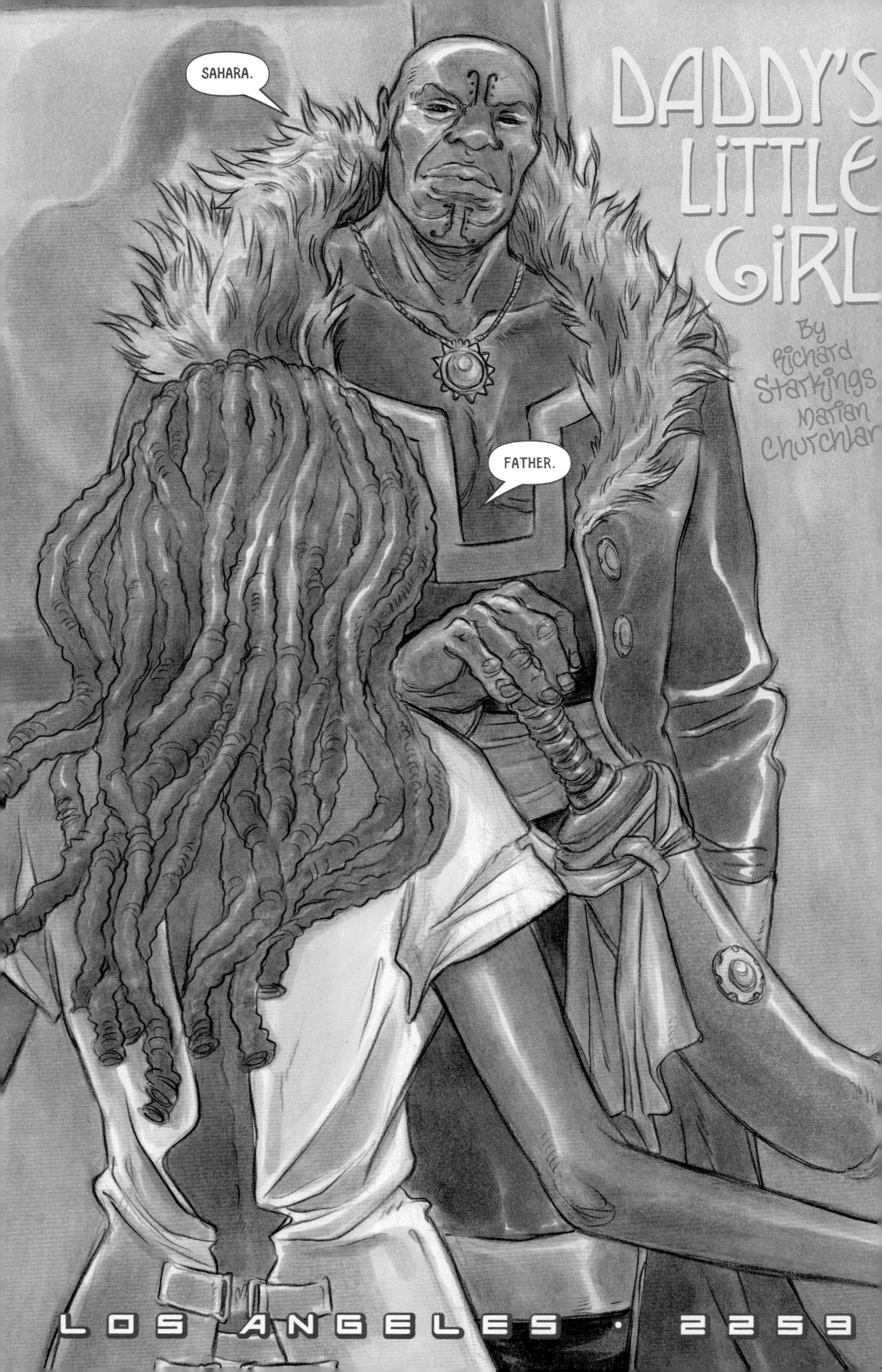
SAHARA.
DADDY'S LITTLE GIRL
By Richard Starkings Marian Churchland
FATHER.
LOS ANGELES · 2259

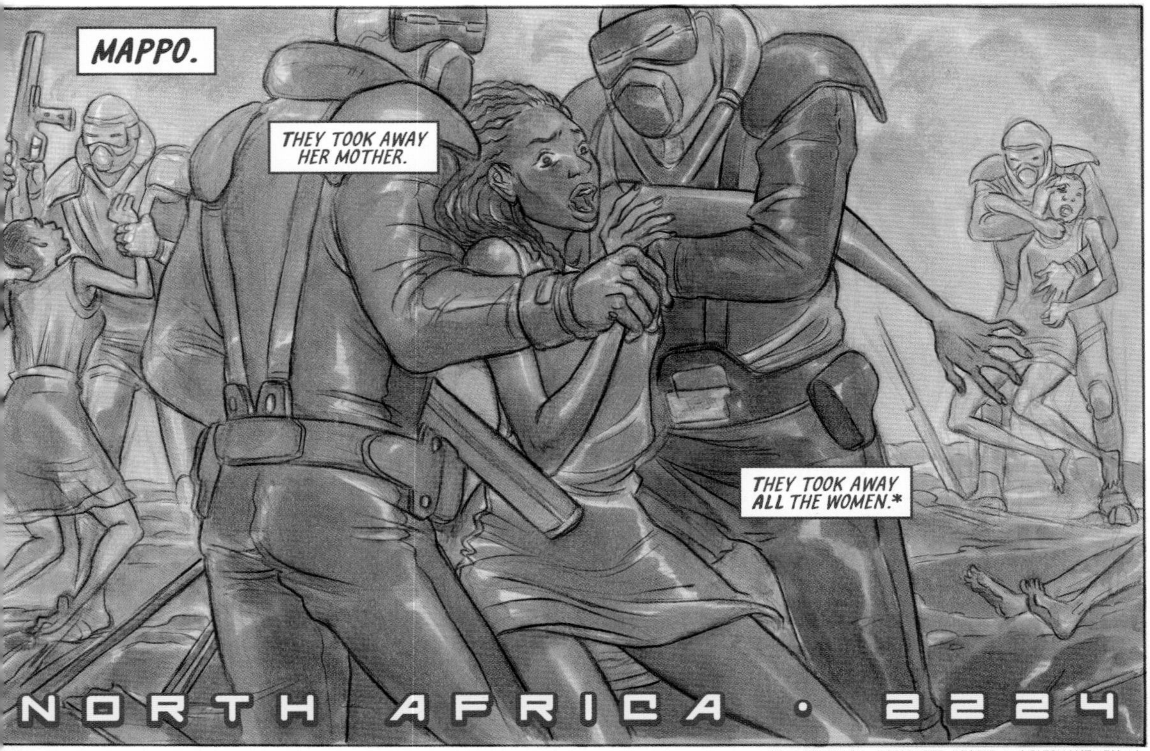
MAPPO.
THEY TOOK AWAY HER MOTHER.
THEY TOOK AWAY ALL THE WOMEN.*
NORTH AFRICA • 2224

*See HIP FLASK: CONCRETE JUNGLE and ELEPHANTMEN #6

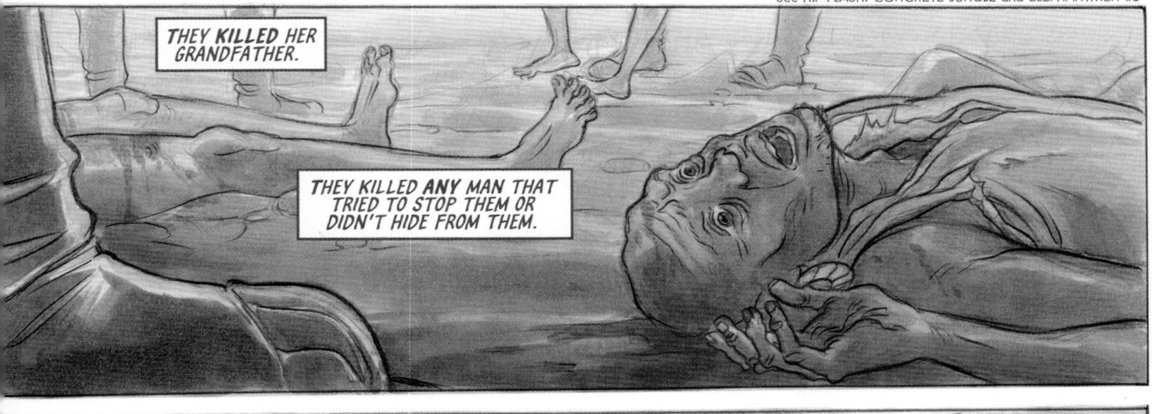
THEY KILLED HER GRANDFATHER.
THEY KILLED ANY MAN THAT TRIED TO STOP THEM OR DIDN'T HIDE FROM THEM.

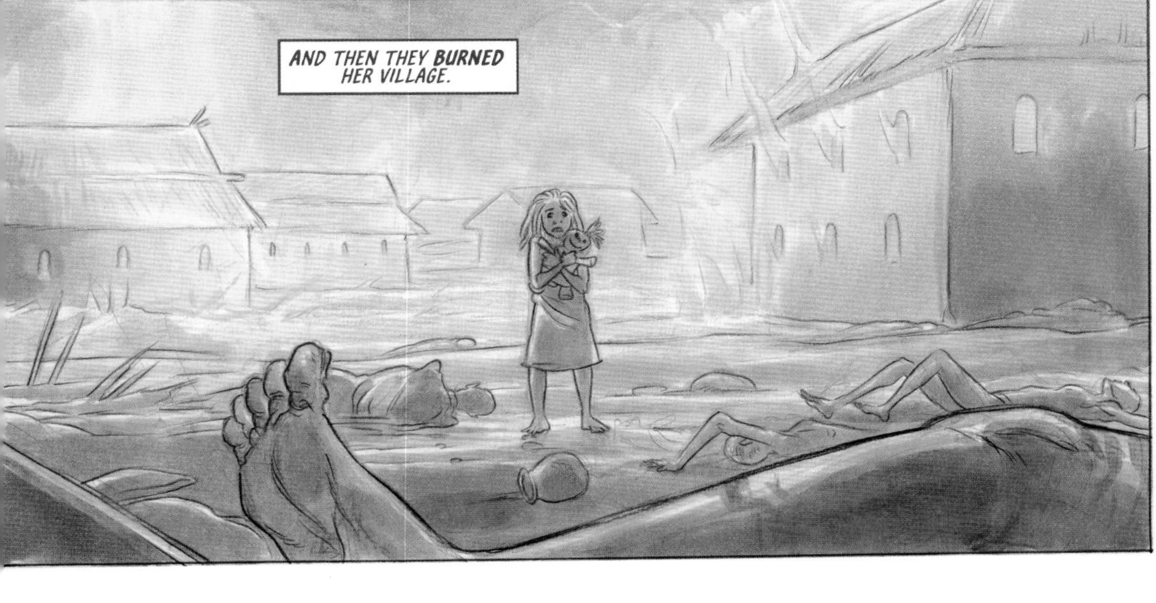
AND THEN THEY BURNED HER VILLAGE.

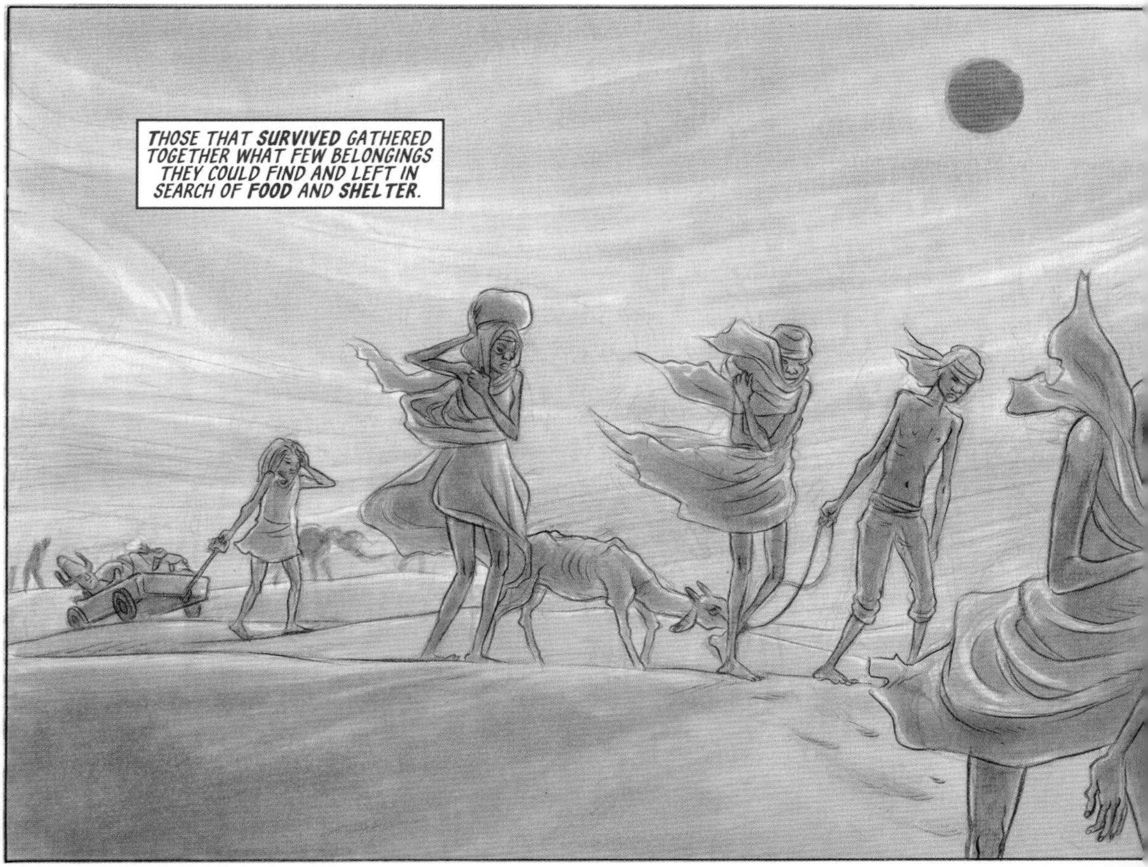
THOSE THAT SURVIVED GATHERED TOGETHER WHAT FEW BELONGINGS THEY COULD FIND AND LEFT IN SEARCH OF FOOD AND SHELTER.

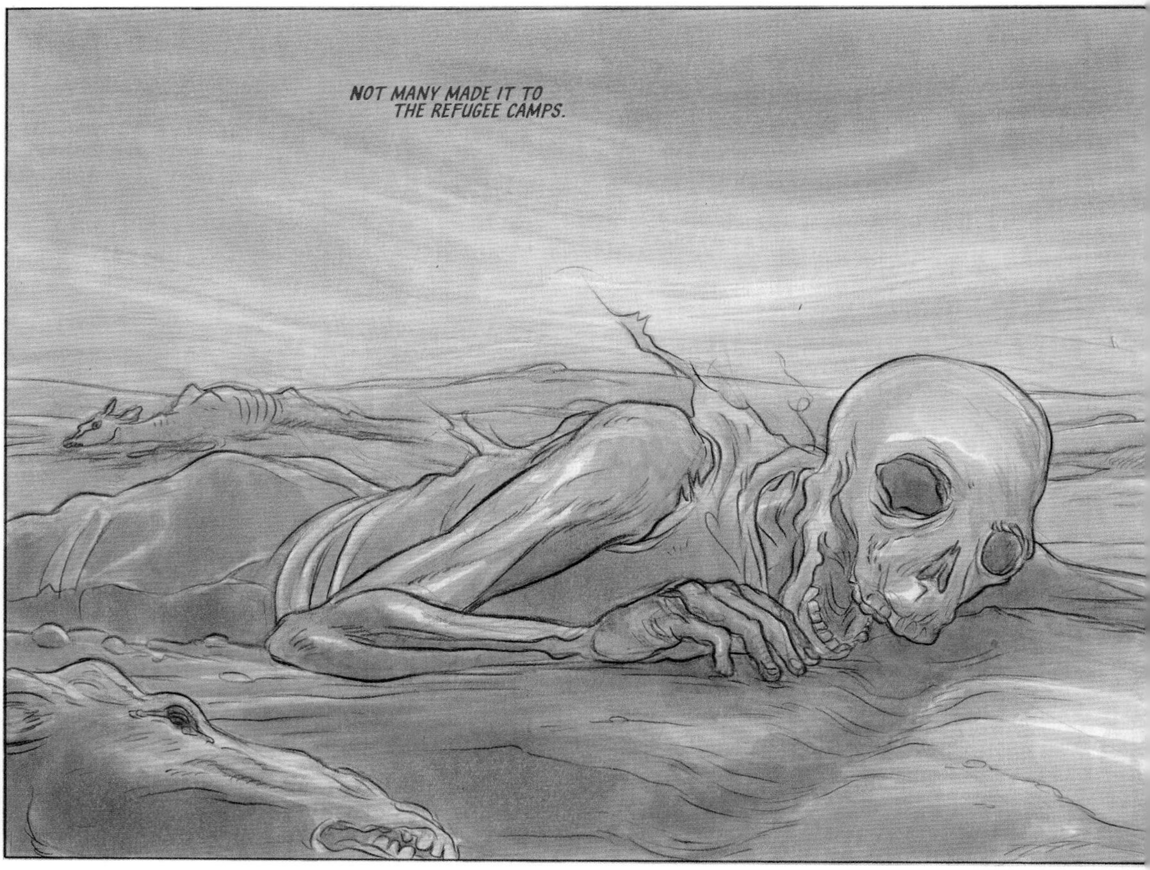
NOT MANY MADE IT TO THE REFUGEE CAMPS.

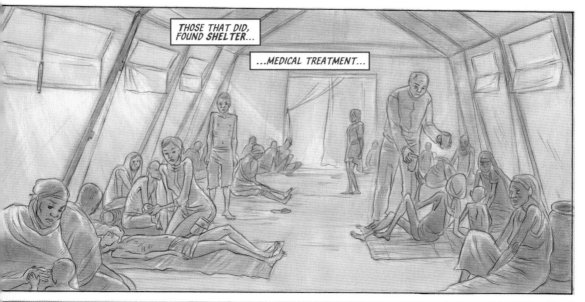

THOSE THAT DID, FOUND **SHELTER**...

...MEDICAL TREATMENT...

AND SOME...

...SOME WERE **REUNITED** WITH RELATIVES.

SAHARA?

DADDY...?

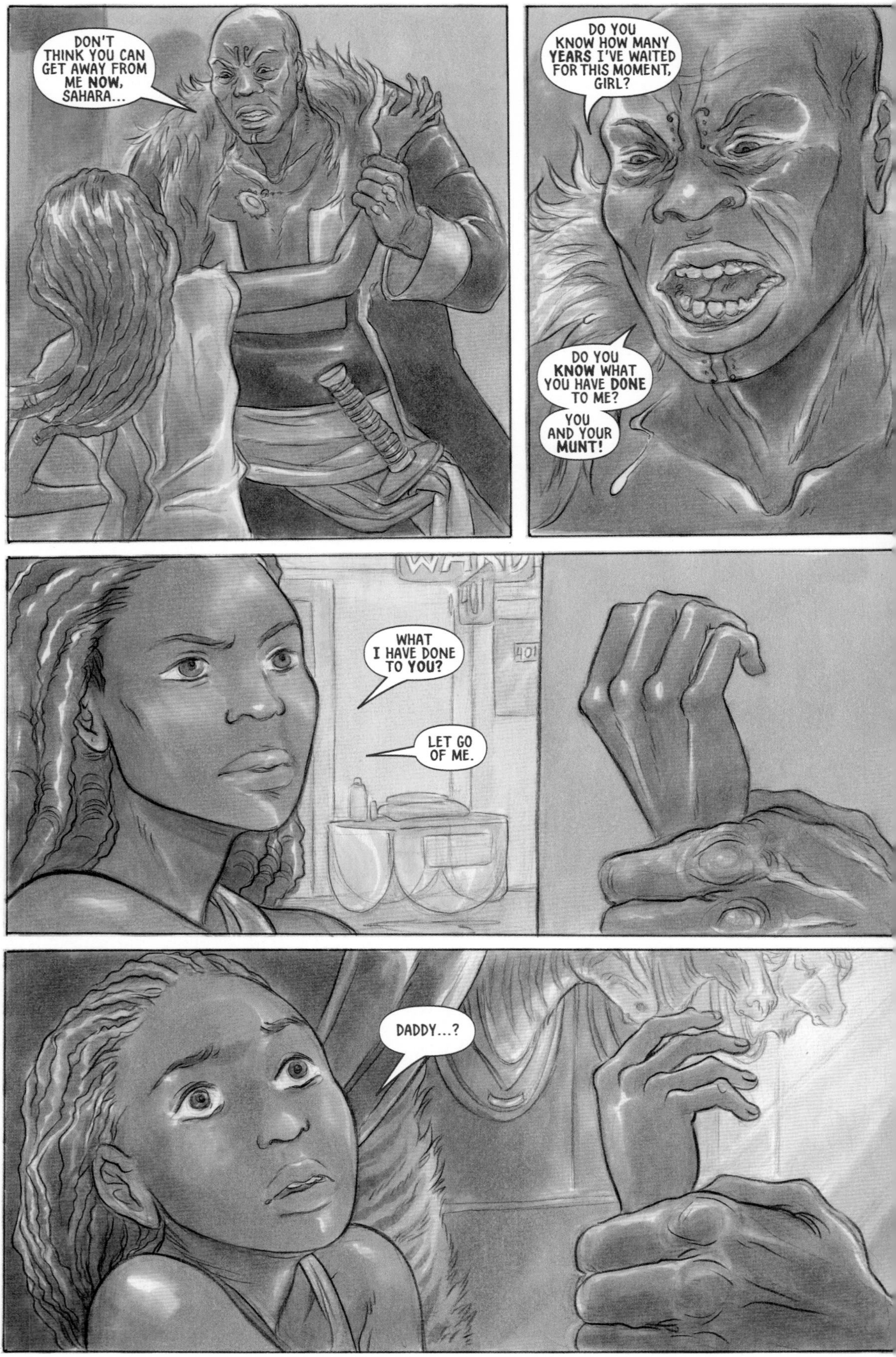

DON'T THINK YOU CAN GET AWAY FROM ME NOW, SAHARA...
DO YOU KNOW HOW MANY YEARS I'VE WAITED FOR THIS MOMENT, GIRL?
DO YOU KNOW WHAT YOU HAVE DONE TO ME?
YOU AND YOUR MUNT!
WHAT I HAVE DONE TO YOU?
LET GO OF ME.
DADDY...?

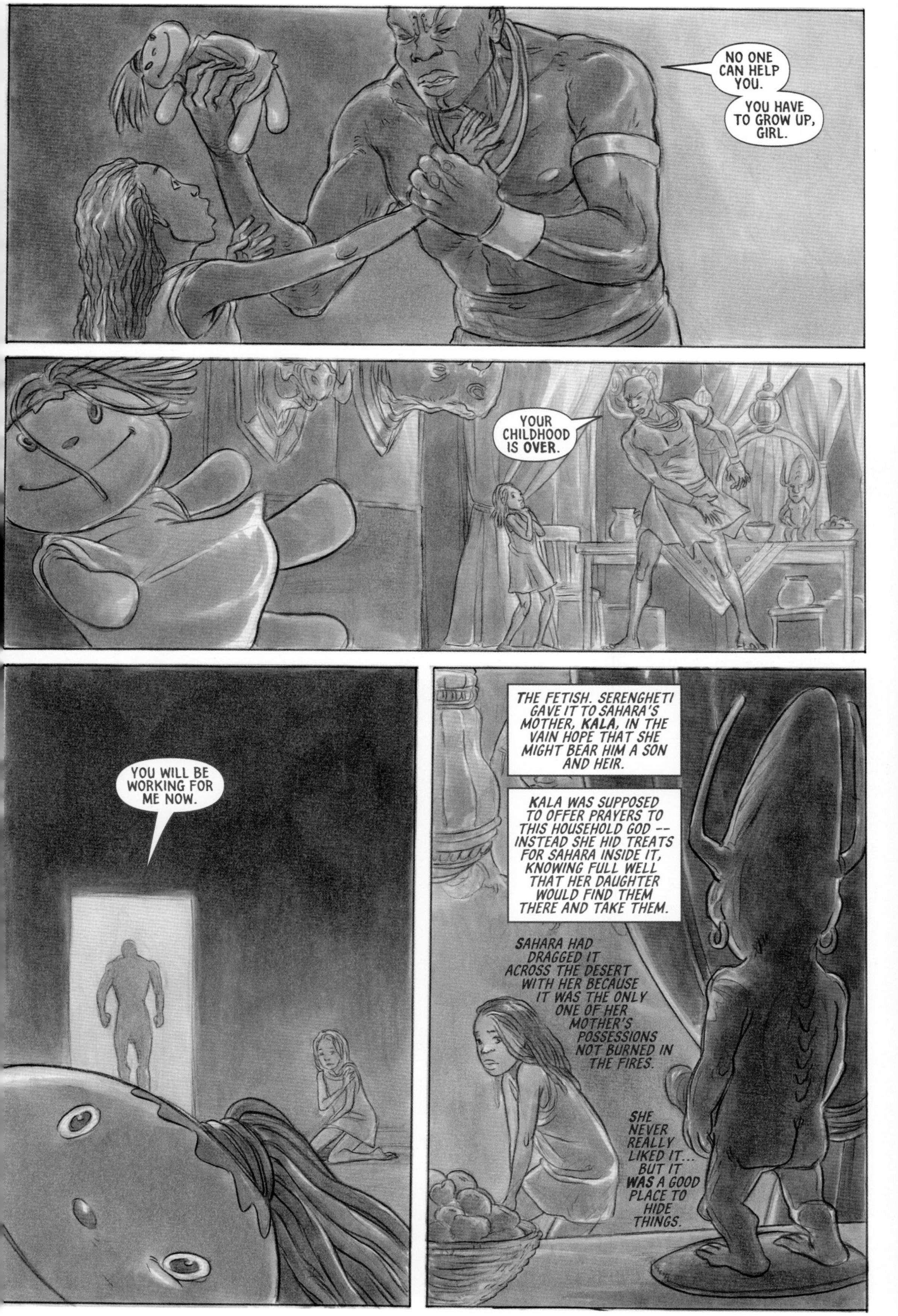
NO ONE CAN HELP YOU.
YOU HAVE TO GROW UP, GIRL.
YOUR CHILDHOOD IS OVER.
YOU WILL BE WORKING FOR ME NOW.
THE FETISH. SERENGHETI GAVE IT TO SAHARA'S MOTHER, KALA, IN THE VAIN HOPE THAT SHE MIGHT BEAR HIM A SON AND HEIR.
KALA WAS SUPPOSED TO OFFER PRAYERS TO THIS HOUSEHOLD GOD -- INSTEAD SHE HID TREATS FOR SAHARA INSIDE IT, KNOWING FULL WELL THAT HER DAUGHTER WOULD FIND THEM THERE AND TAKE THEM.
SAHARA HAD DRAGGED IT ACROSS THE DESERT WITH HER BECAUSE IT WAS THE ONLY ONE OF HER MOTHER'S POSSESSIONS NOT BURNED IN THE FIRES.
SHE NEVER REALLY LIKED IT... BUT IT WAS A GOOD PLACE TO HIDE THINGS.

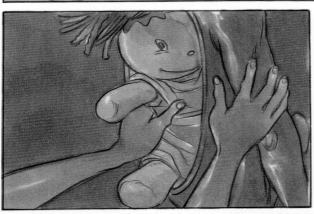

WHAT ARE YOU DOING?

OH! NUH-- NOTHING...

WHO-- WHO ARE YOU?

YOUR HUSBAND.
YOUR FIRST HUSBAND.
WH-WHAT DO YOU MEAN...
DON'T WORRY GIRLY...
YOU'LL LEARN TO LIKE IT... EVENTUALLY.
NO... NO... MAMA... MAMA!
CALL FOR HER, GIRLY...

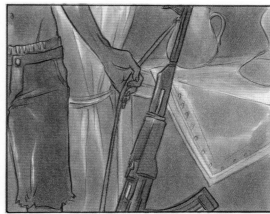

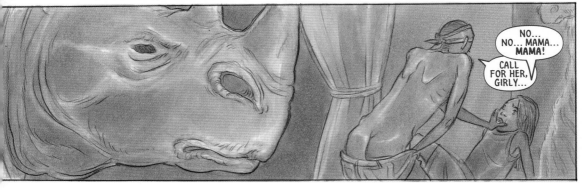

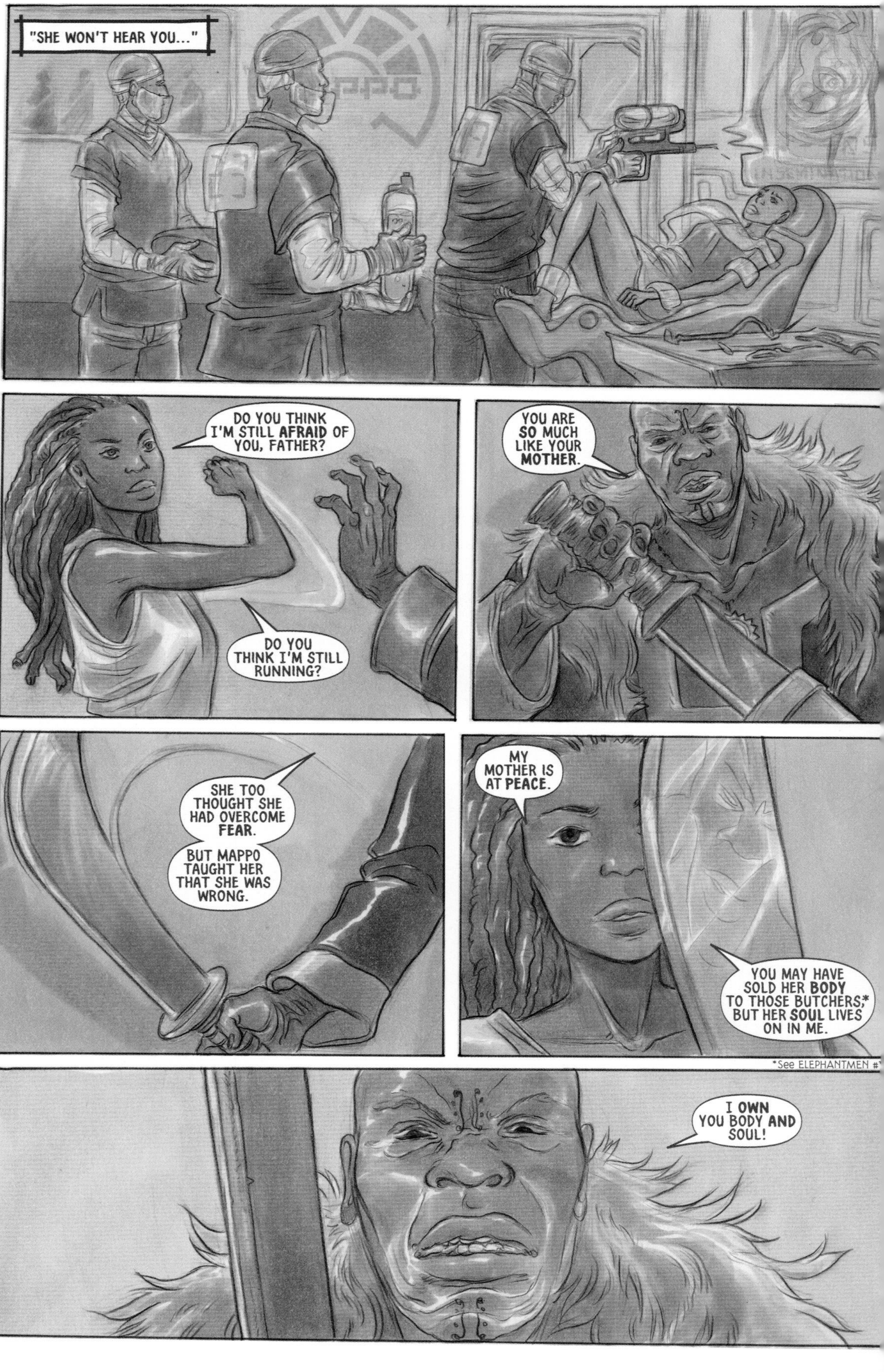
"SHE WON'T HEAR YOU..."
DO YOU THINK I'M STILL AFRAID OF YOU, FATHER?
DO YOU THINK I'M STILL RUNNING?
YOU ARE SO MUCH LIKE YOUR MOTHER.
SHE TOO THOUGHT SHE HAD OVERCOME FEAR.
BUT MAPPO TAUGHT HER THAT SHE WAS WRONG.
MY MOTHER IS AT PEACE.
YOU MAY HAVE SOLD HER BODY TO THOSE BUTCHERS,* BUT HER SOUL LIVES ON IN ME.
*See ELEPHANTMEN #
I OWN YOU BODY AND SOUL!

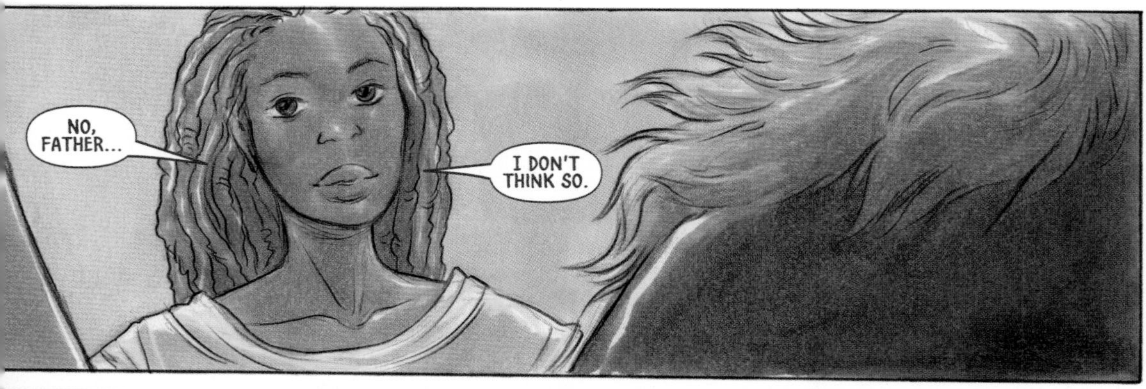
NO, FATHER...
I DON'T THINK SO.

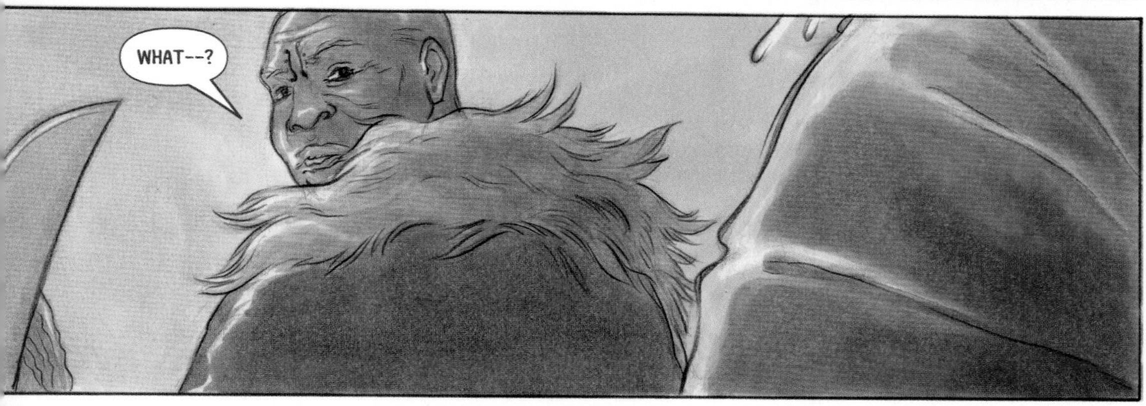
WHAT--?

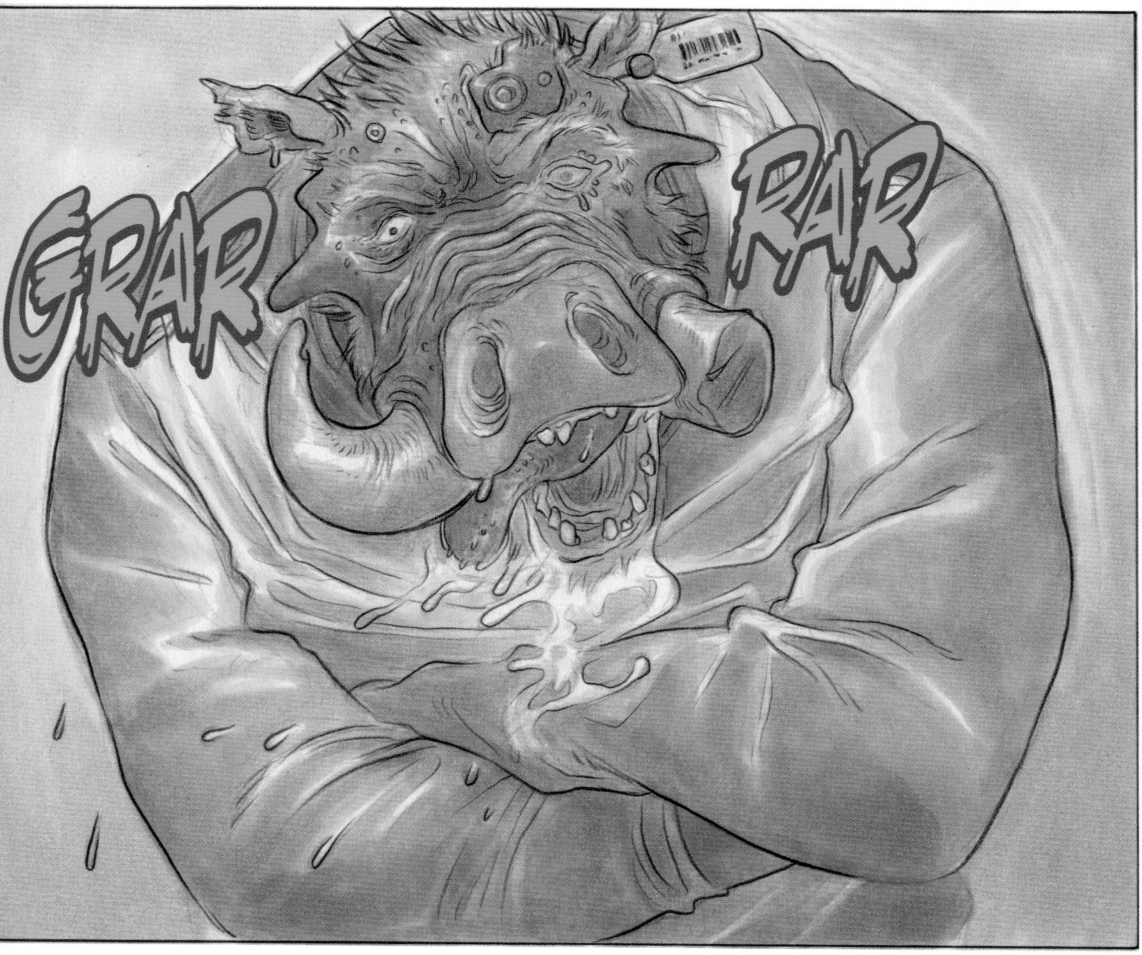
GRAR
RAR

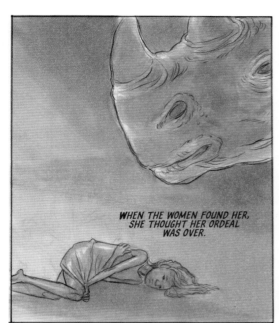

WHEN THE WOMEN FOUND HER,
SHE THOUGHT HER ORDEAL
WAS OVER.

THEIR FACES SEEMED KIND,
AS IF THEY UNDERSTOOD.
AS IF THEY COULD
SAVE HER.

THEY SPOKE TO HER WITH
GENTLE REASSURING WORDS.
THEIR TOUCH SOOTHED HER.

THEY BATHED HER
AND SANG SONGS
THAT CALMED HER.

WHEN THEY DRESSED
HER IN LINEN AND
PREPARED FRUIT FOR
HER, SHE STARTED TO WONDER IF
HER EXPERIENCES WERE ALL JUST
SOME KIND OF **BAD DREAM**...

SHE WONDERED IF
PERHAPS THEY WERE
PREPARING HER
FOR THE RETURN OF
HER MOTHER.

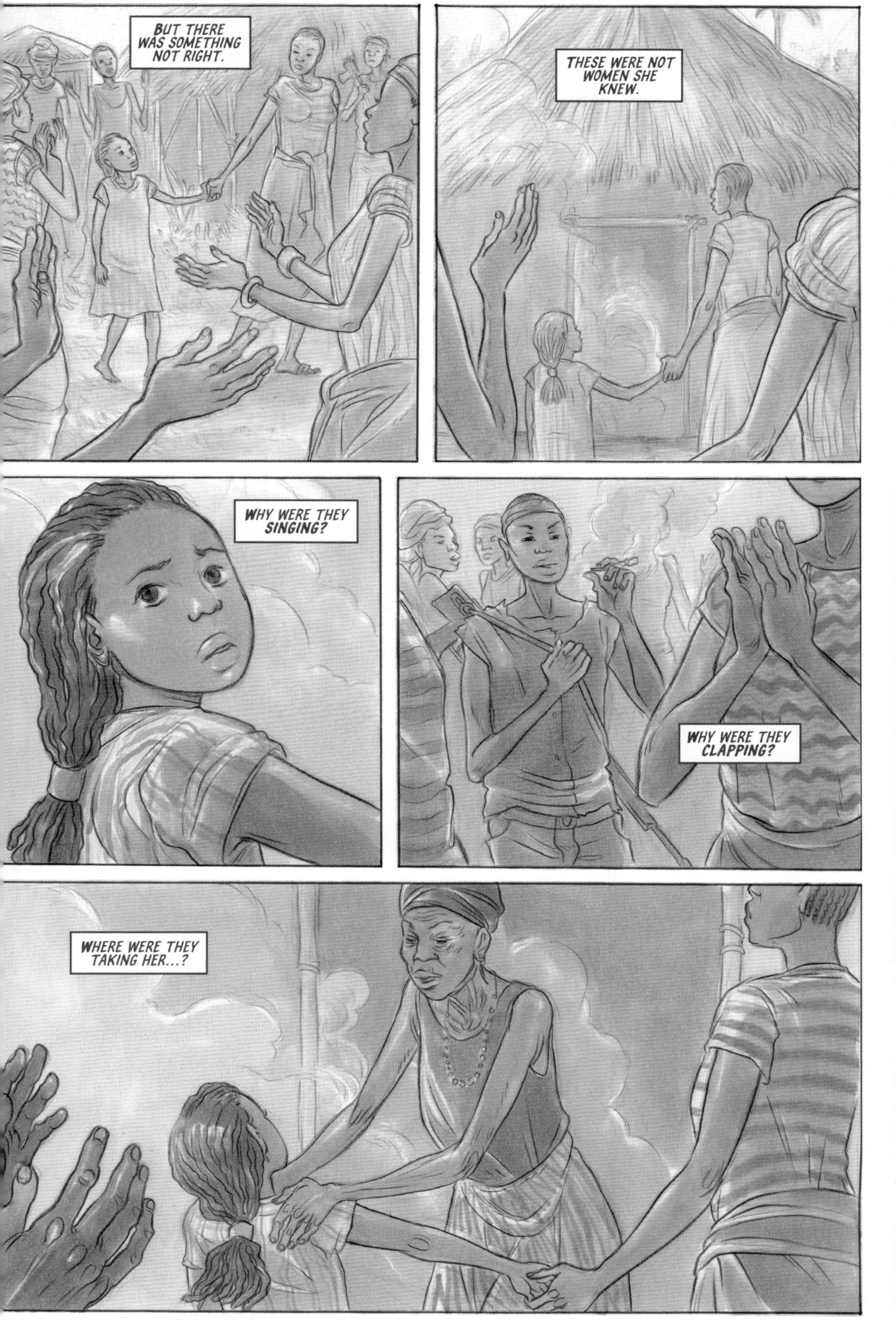
BUT THERE WAS SOMETHING NOT RIGHT.
THESE WERE NOT WOMEN SHE KNEW.
WHY WERE THEY SINGING?
WHY WERE THEY CLAPPING?
WHERE WERE THEY TAKING HER...?

THIS WAS NO DREAM.

THIS WAS A NIGHTMARE THAT WAS **NEVER** GOING TO END.

THEY CUT HER.

THEY CIRCUMCIZED HER.

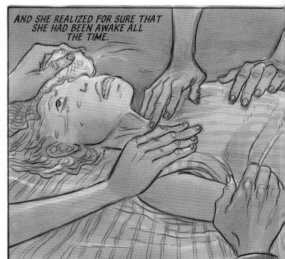

AND SHE REALIZED FOR SURE THAT SHE HAD BEEN AWAKE ALL THE TIME.

MAMAAAAAAA!

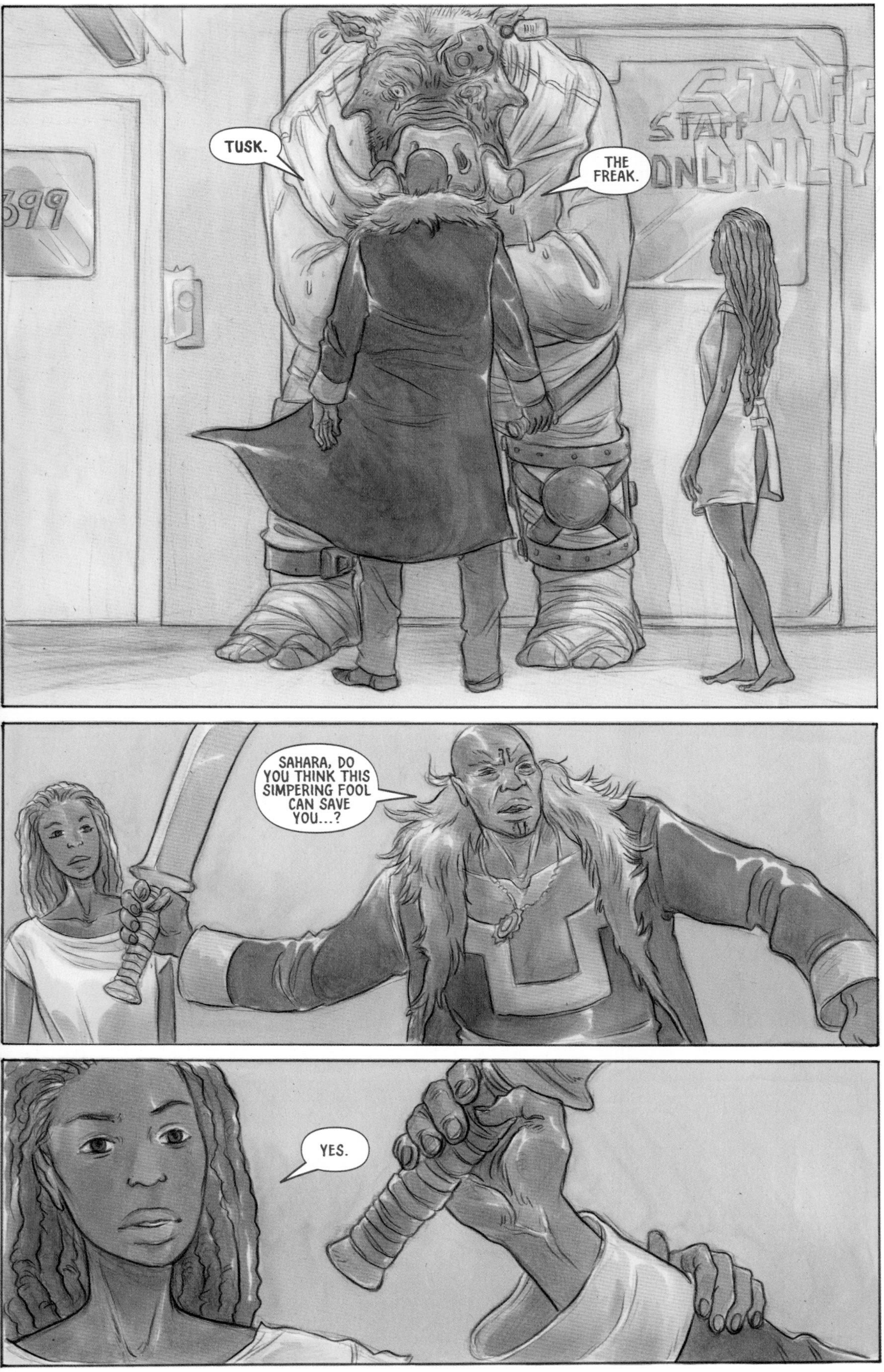
TUSK.
THE FREAK.
STAFF ONLY
STAFF ONLY
SAHARA, DO YOU THINK THIS SIMPERING FOOL CAN SAVE YOU...?
YES.

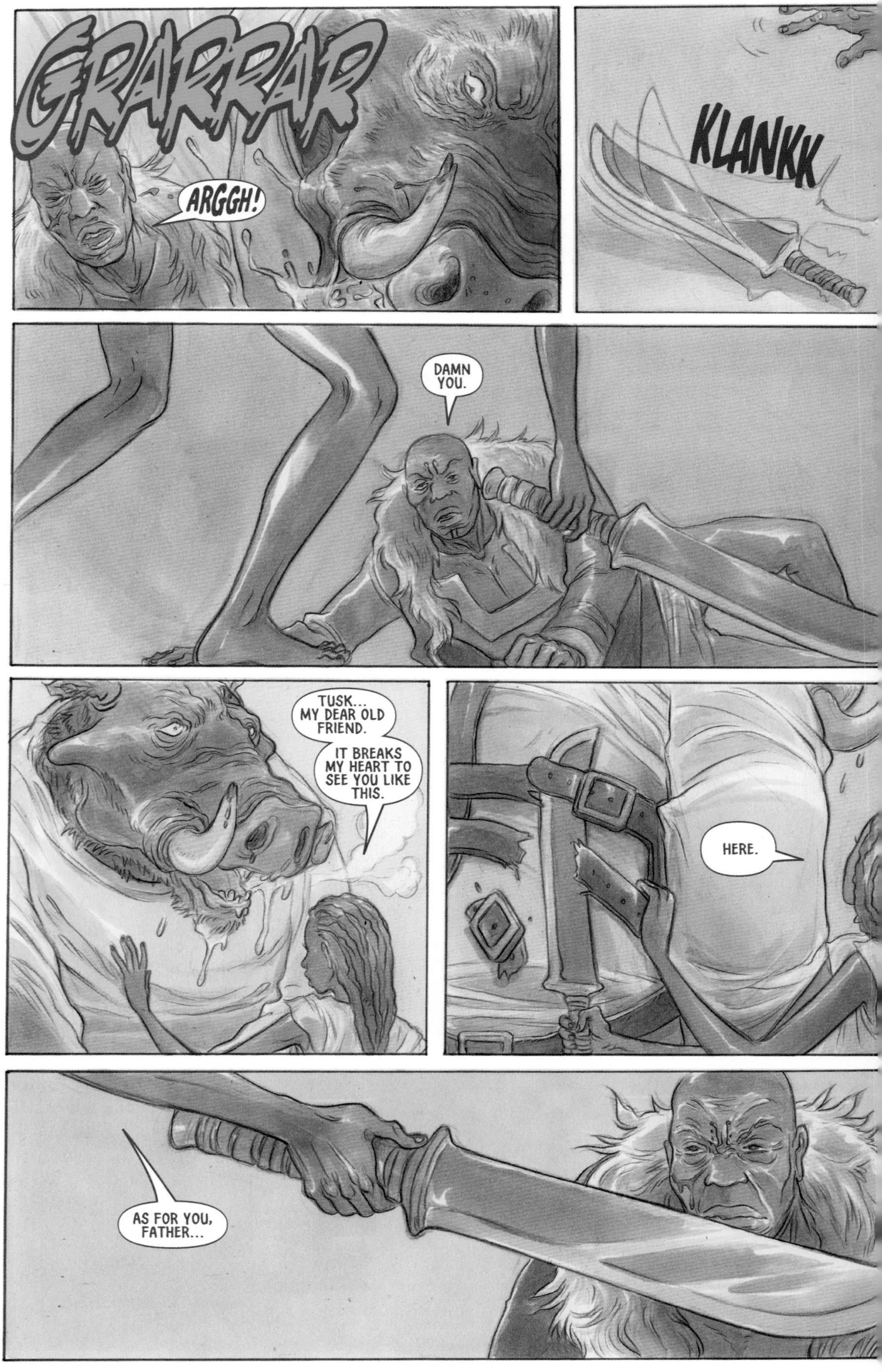
GRARRAR
ARGGH!
KLANKK
DAMN YOU.
TUSK... MY DEAR OLD FRIEND.
IT BREAKS MY HEART TO SEE YOU LIKE THIS.
HERE.
AS FOR YOU, FATHER...

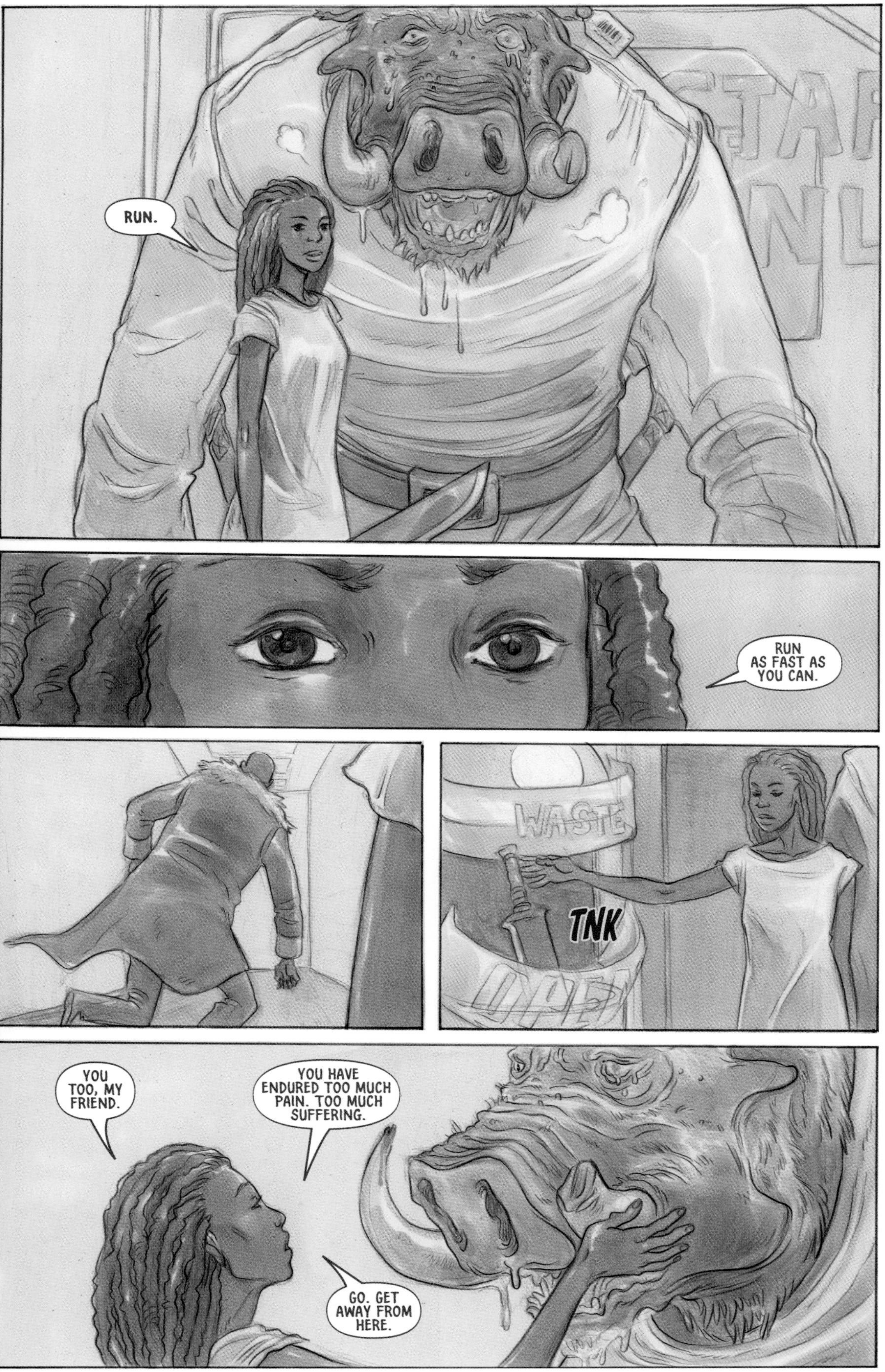
RUN.
RUN AS FAST AS YOU CAN.
WASTE
TNK
YOU TOO, MY FRIEND.
YOU HAVE ENDURED TOO MUCH PAIN. TOO MUCH SUFFERING.
GO. GET AWAY FROM HERE.

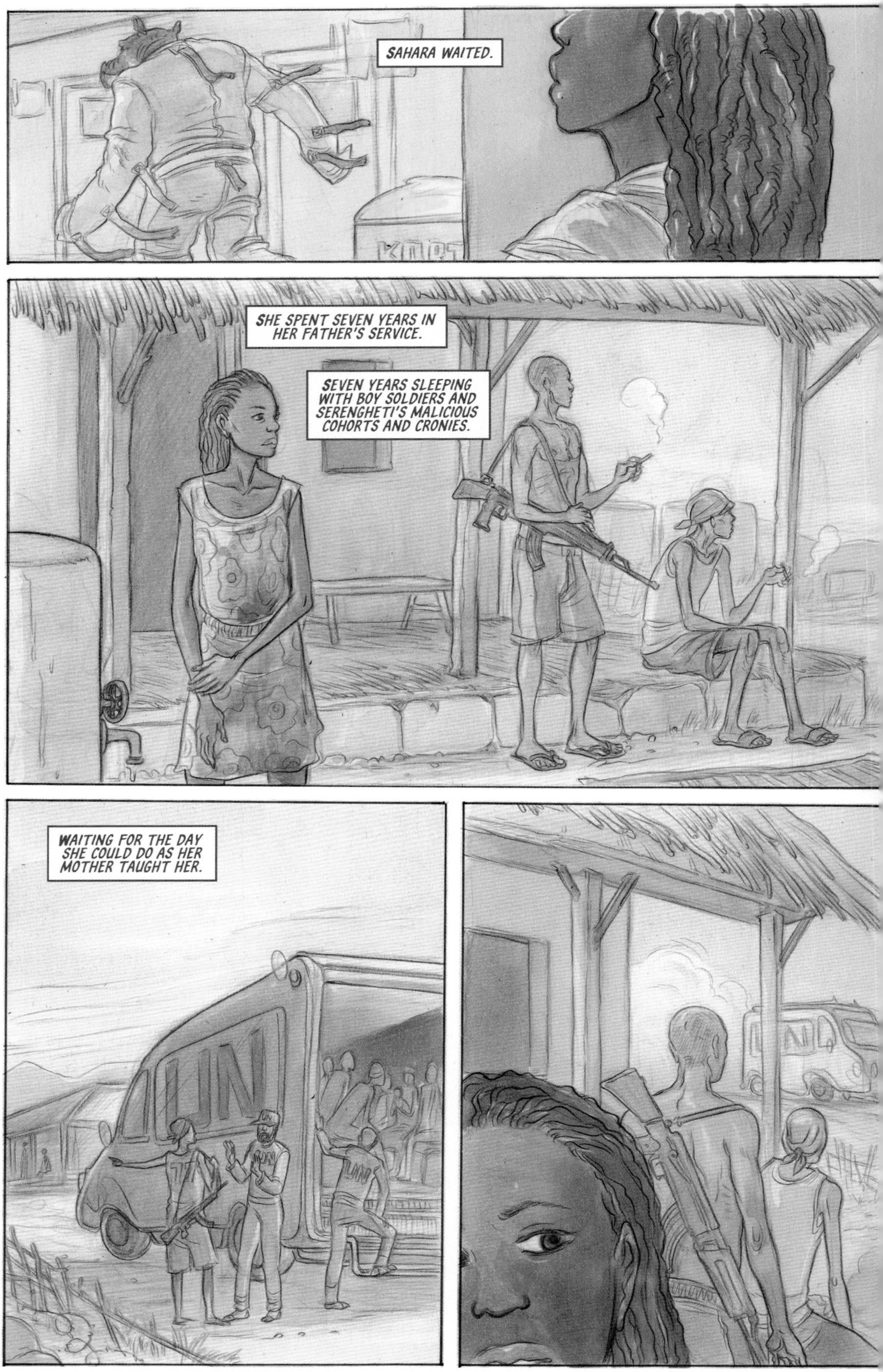
SAHARA WAITED.
SHE SPENT SEVEN YEARS IN HER FATHER'S SERVICE.
SEVEN YEARS SLEEPING WITH BOY SOLDIERS AND SERENGHETI'S MALICIOUS COHORTS AND CRONIES.
WAITING FOR THE DAY SHE COULD DO AS HER MOTHER TAUGHT HER.
UN

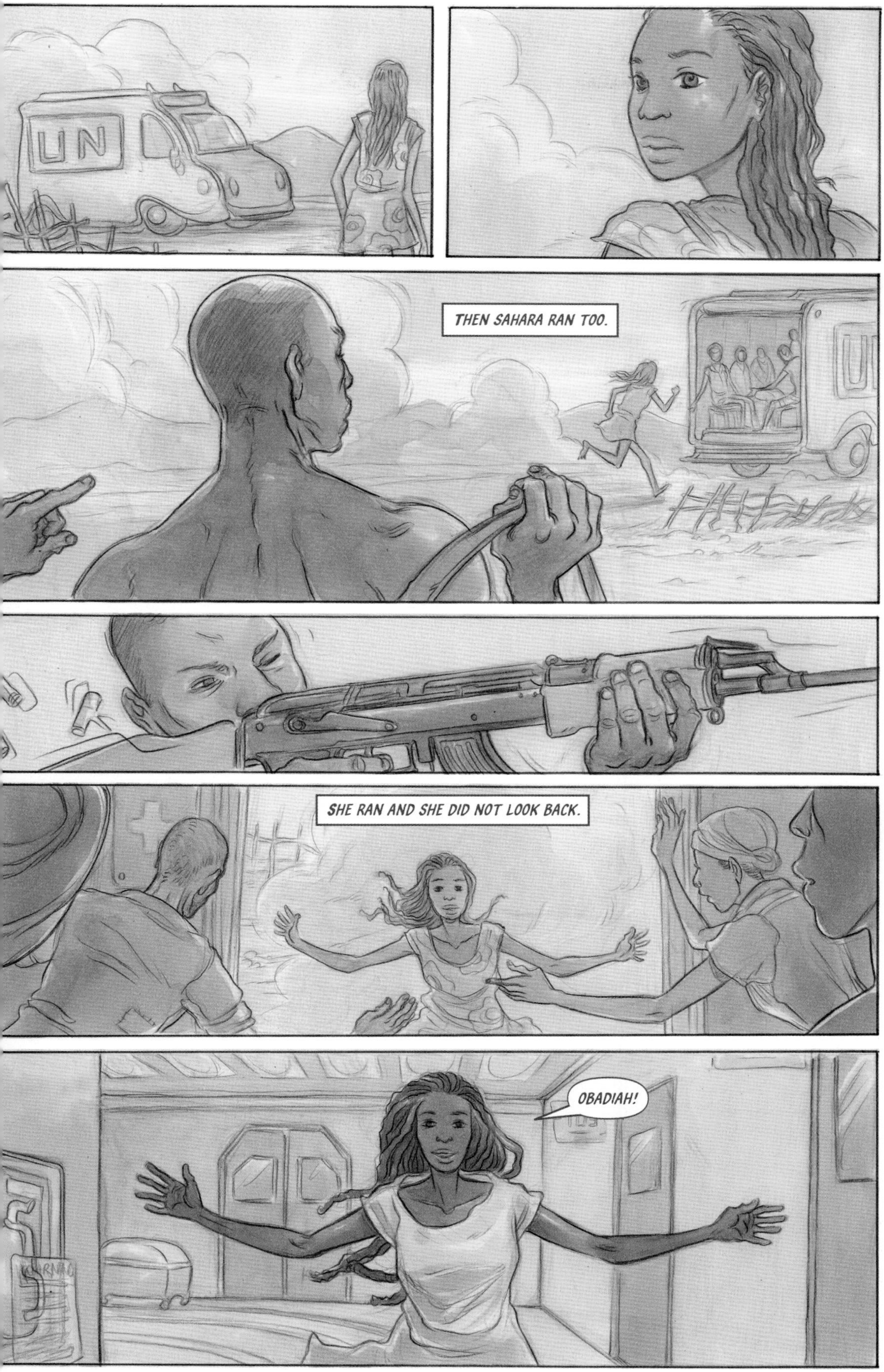
UN
THEN SAHARA RAN TOO.
SHE RAN AND SHE DID NOT LOOK BACK.
OBADIAH!

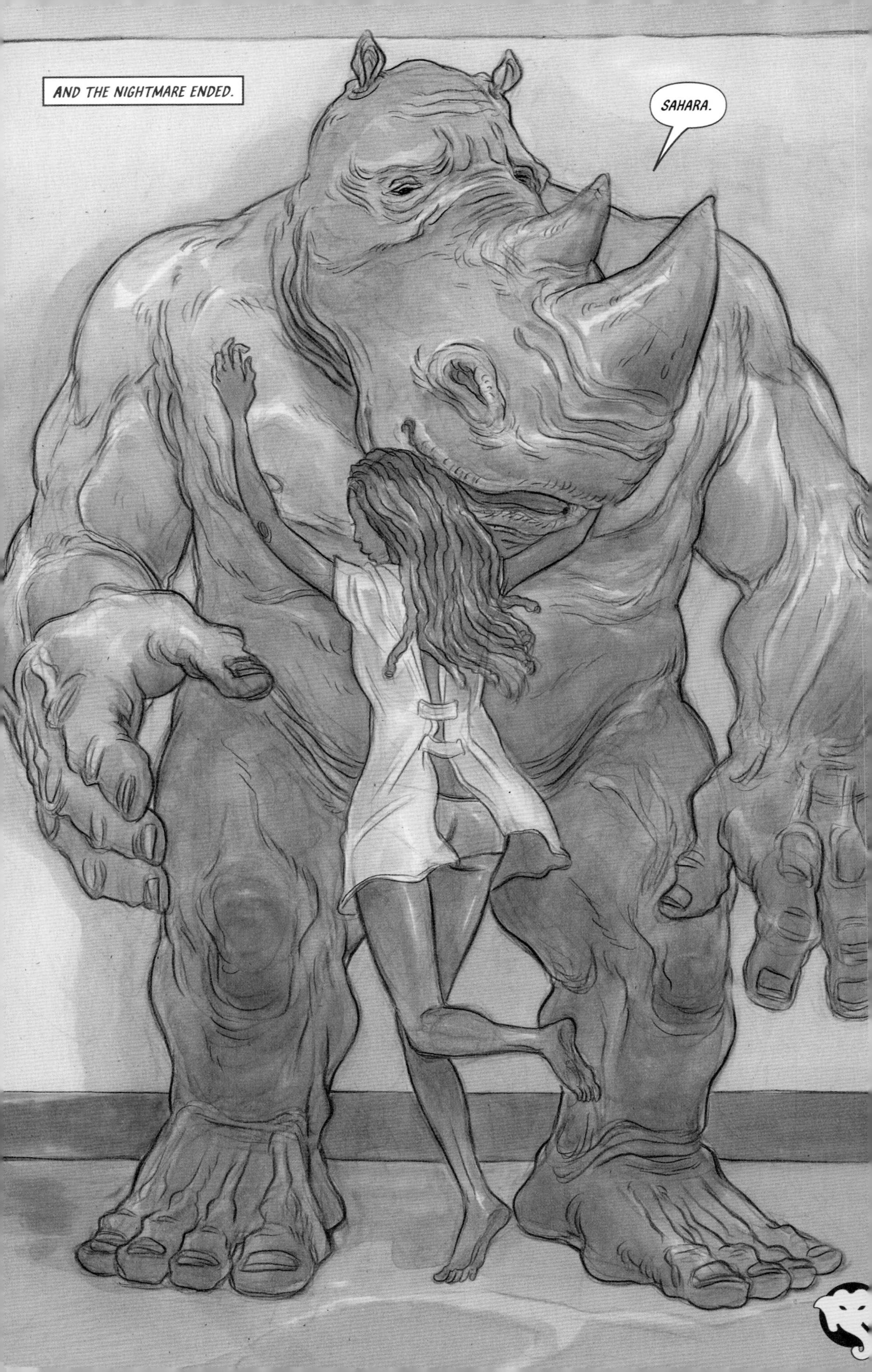
AND THE NIGHTMARE ENDED.
SAHARA.

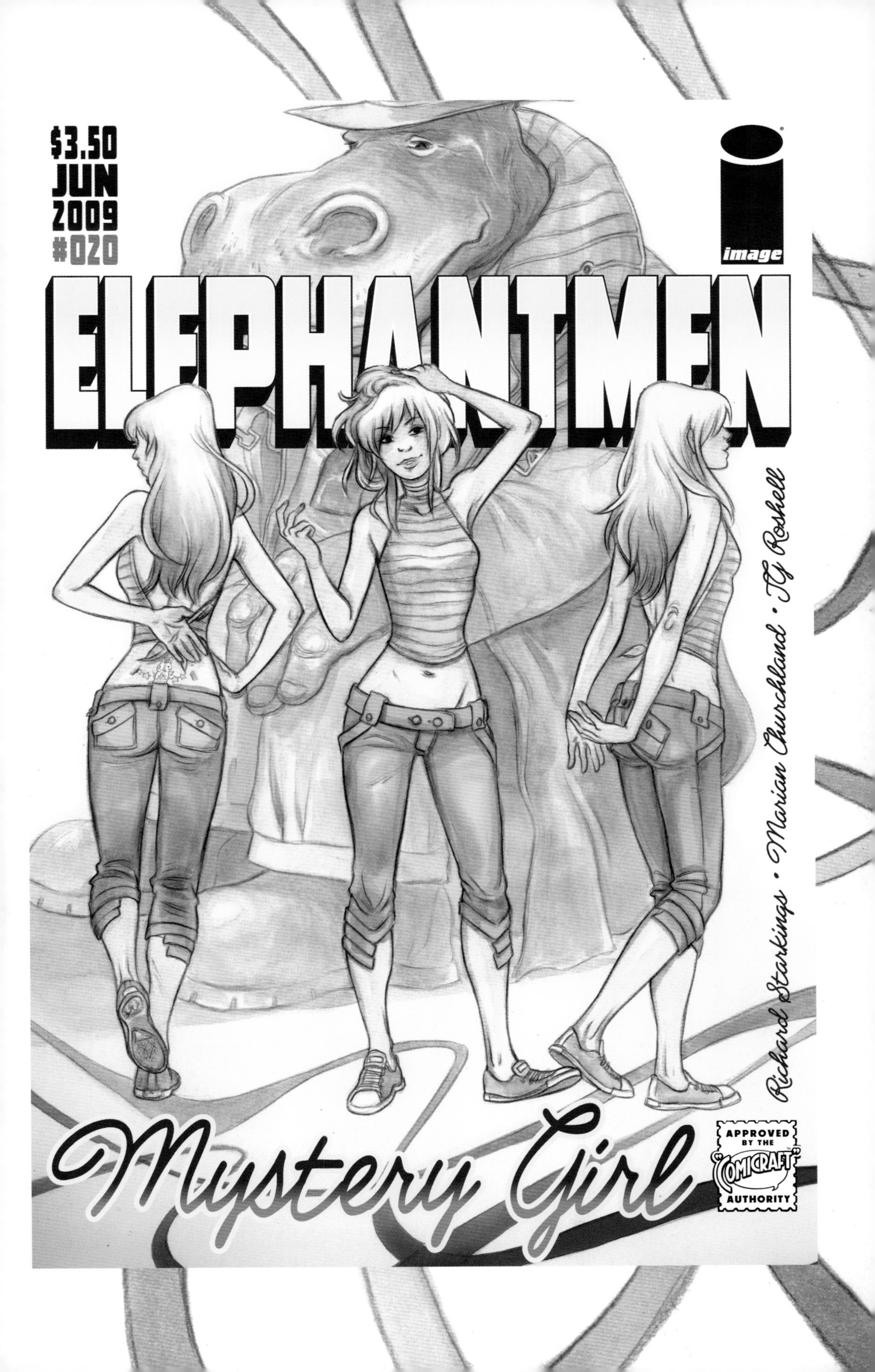

$3.50
JUN
2009
#020
image
ELEPHANTMEN
Richard Starkings • Marian Churchland • JG Roshell
Mystery Girl
APPROVED BY THE "COMICRAFT" AUTHORITY

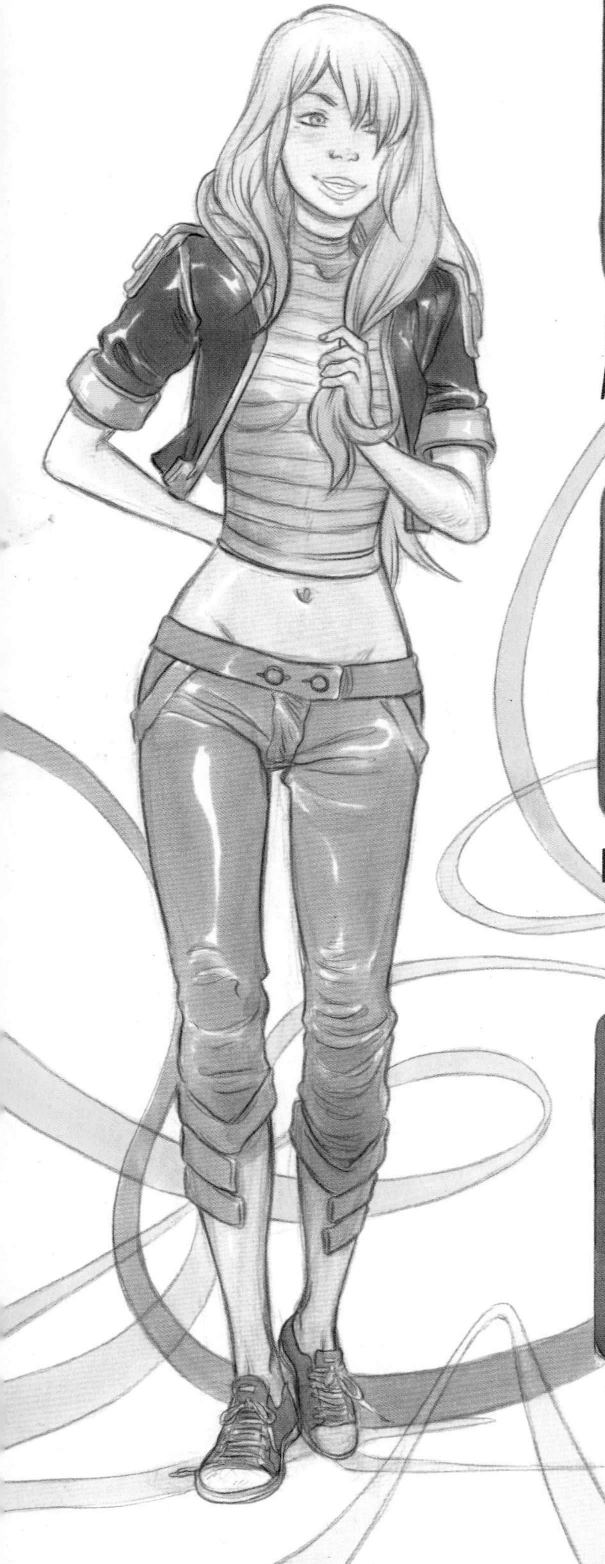

VANITY

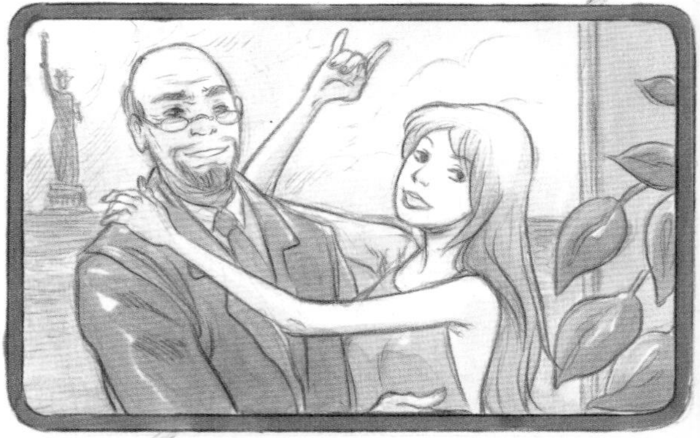

Bianca Espinosa was the daughter of Professor Alan Scott, a Forensics expert who disappeared during the course of a murder trial.

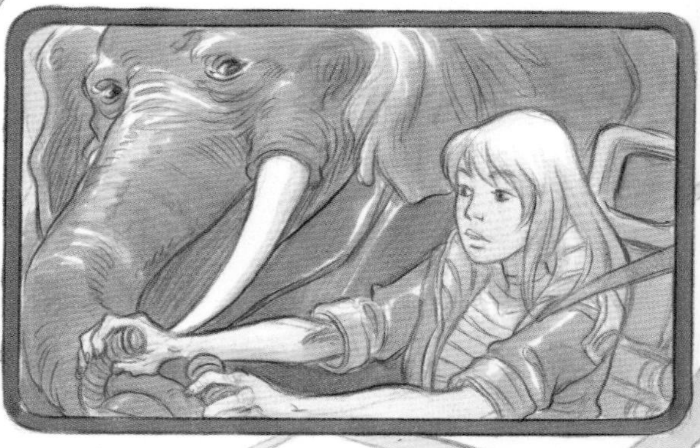

Placed in a witness protection program, Bianca was renamed Vanity Case, and given a job at the Information Agency in Venice Beach.

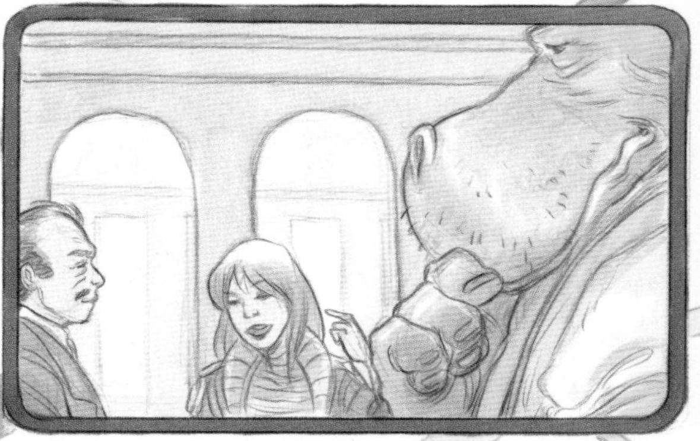

There, she was assigned to assist field agent Hieronymous "Hip" Flask...

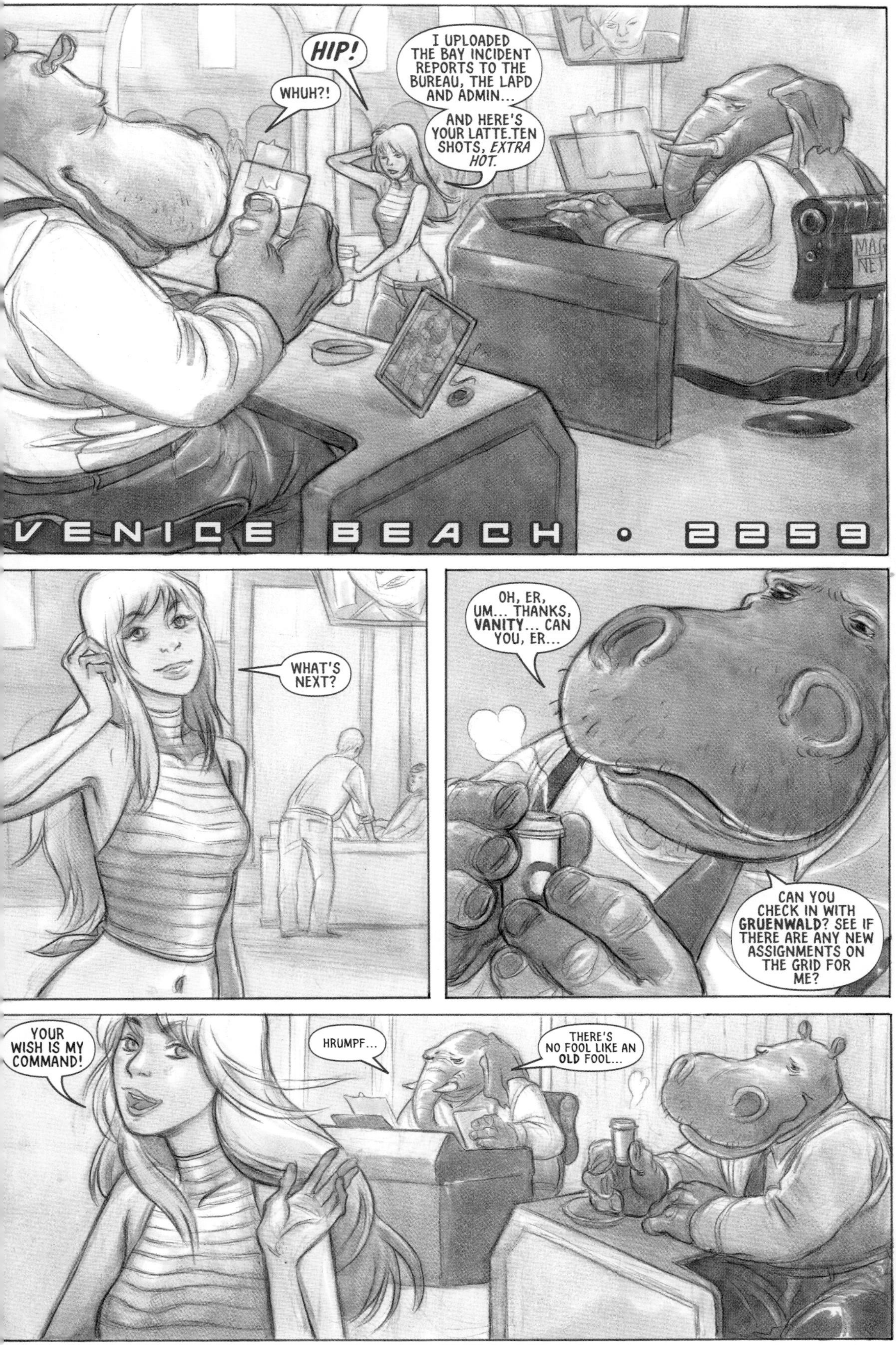
WHUH?!
HIP!
I UPLOADED THE BAY INCIDENT REPORTS TO THE BUREAU, THE LAPD AND ADMIN...
AND HERE'S YOUR LATTE.TEN SHOTS, *EXTRA HOT.*
MAG NET
VENICE BEACH • 2259
WHAT'S NEXT?
OH, ER, UM... THANKS, **VANITY**... CAN YOU, ER...
CAN YOU CHECK IN WITH **GRUENWALD**? SEE IF THERE ARE ANY NEW ASSIGNMENTS ON THE GRID FOR ME?
YOUR WISH IS MY COMMAND!
HRUMPF...
THERE'S NO FOOL LIKE AN **OLD** FOOL...

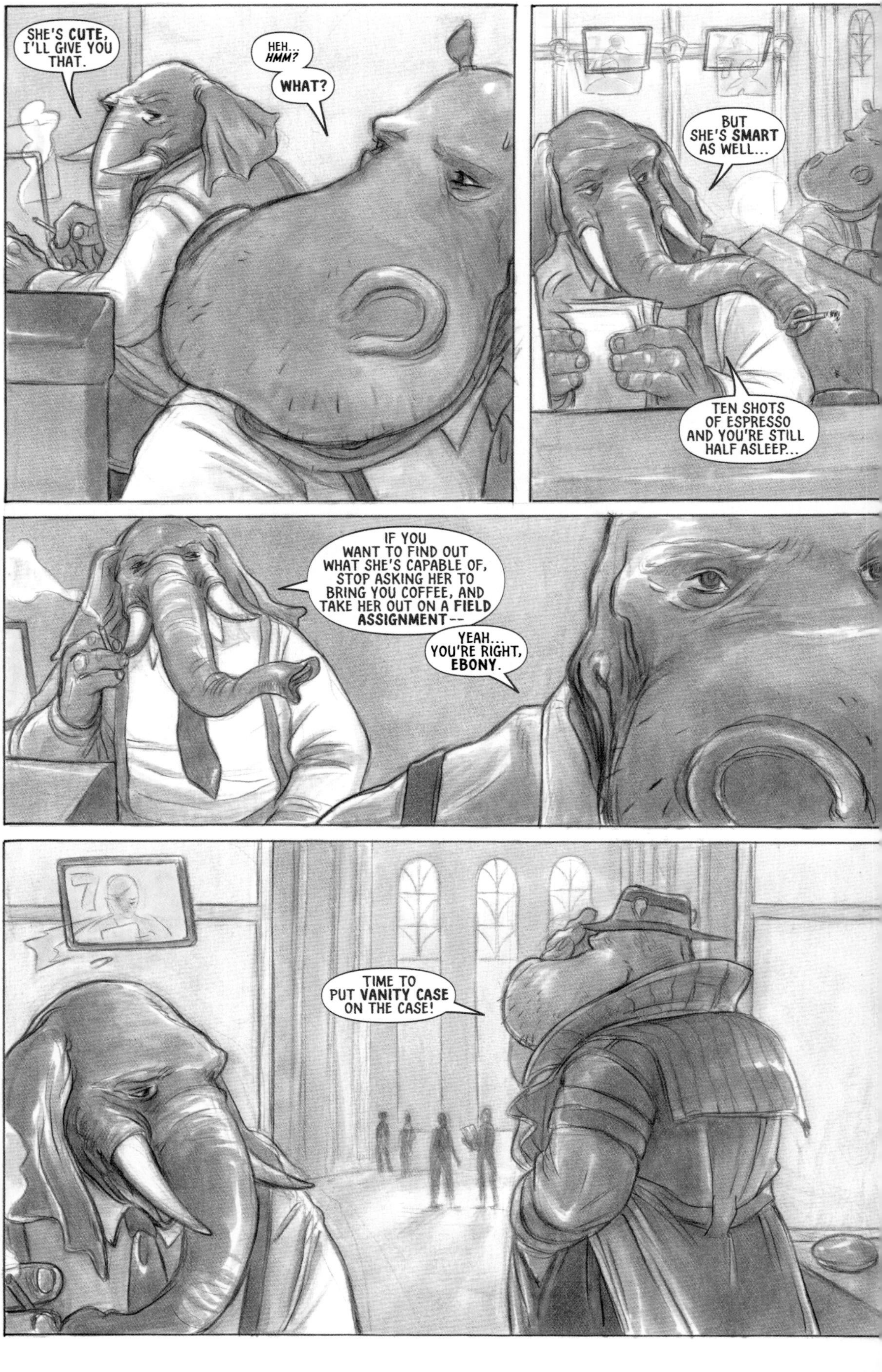
SHE'S CUTE, I'LL GIVE YOU THAT.
HEH... HMM?
WHAT?
BUT SHE'S SMART AS WELL...
TEN SHOTS OF ESPRESSO AND YOU'RE STILL HALF ASLEEP...
IF YOU WANT TO FIND OUT WHAT SHE'S CAPABLE OF, STOP ASKING HER TO BRING YOU COFFEE, AND TAKE HER OUT ON A FIELD ASSIGNMENT--
YEAH... YOU'RE RIGHT, EBONY.
TIME TO PUT VANITY CASE ON THE CASE!

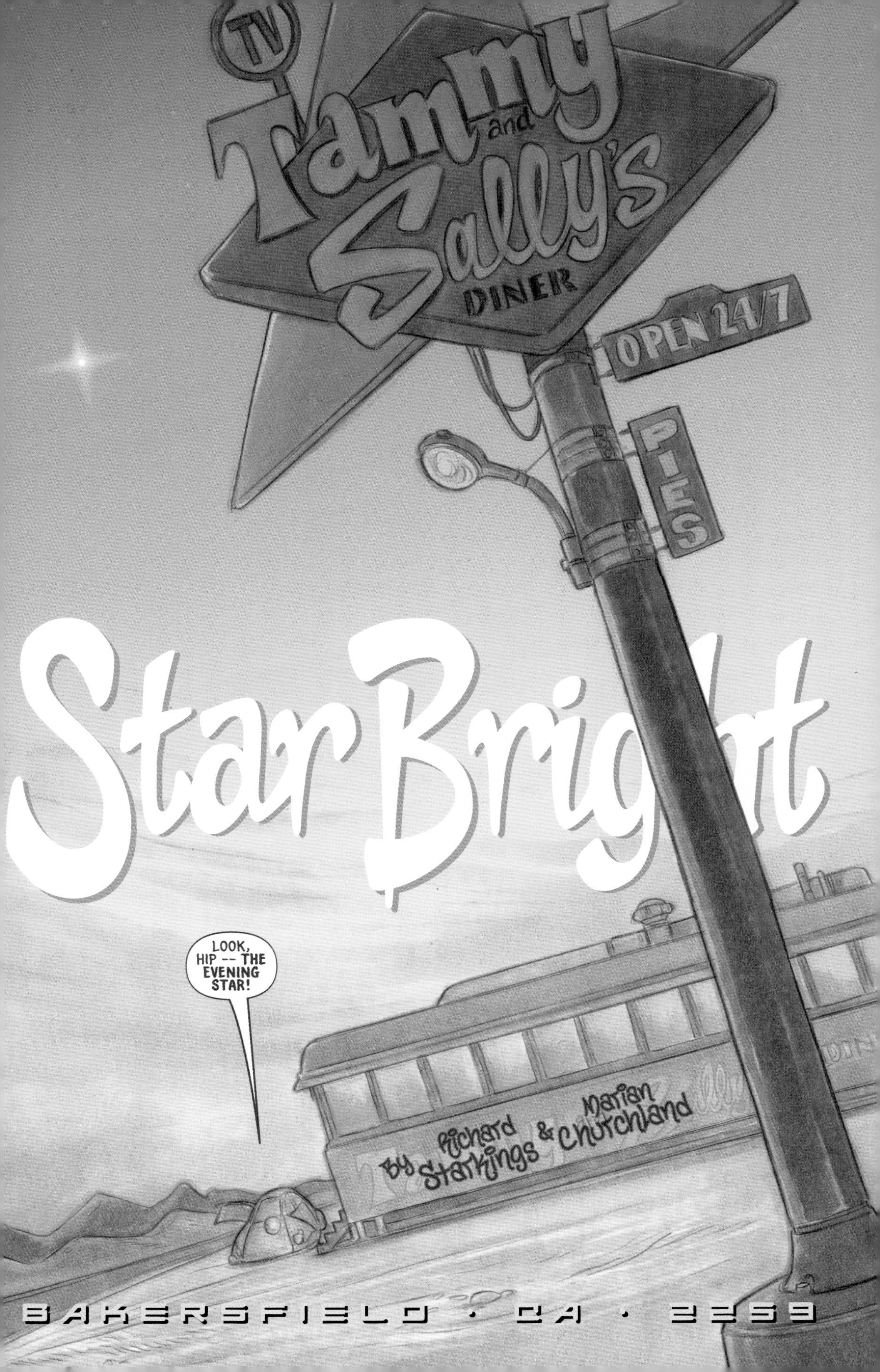
TV
Tammy and Sally's DINER
OPEN 24/7
PIES
StarBright
LOOK, HIP -- THE EVENING STAR!
By Richard Starkings & Marian Churchland
BAKERSFIELD · CA · 2259

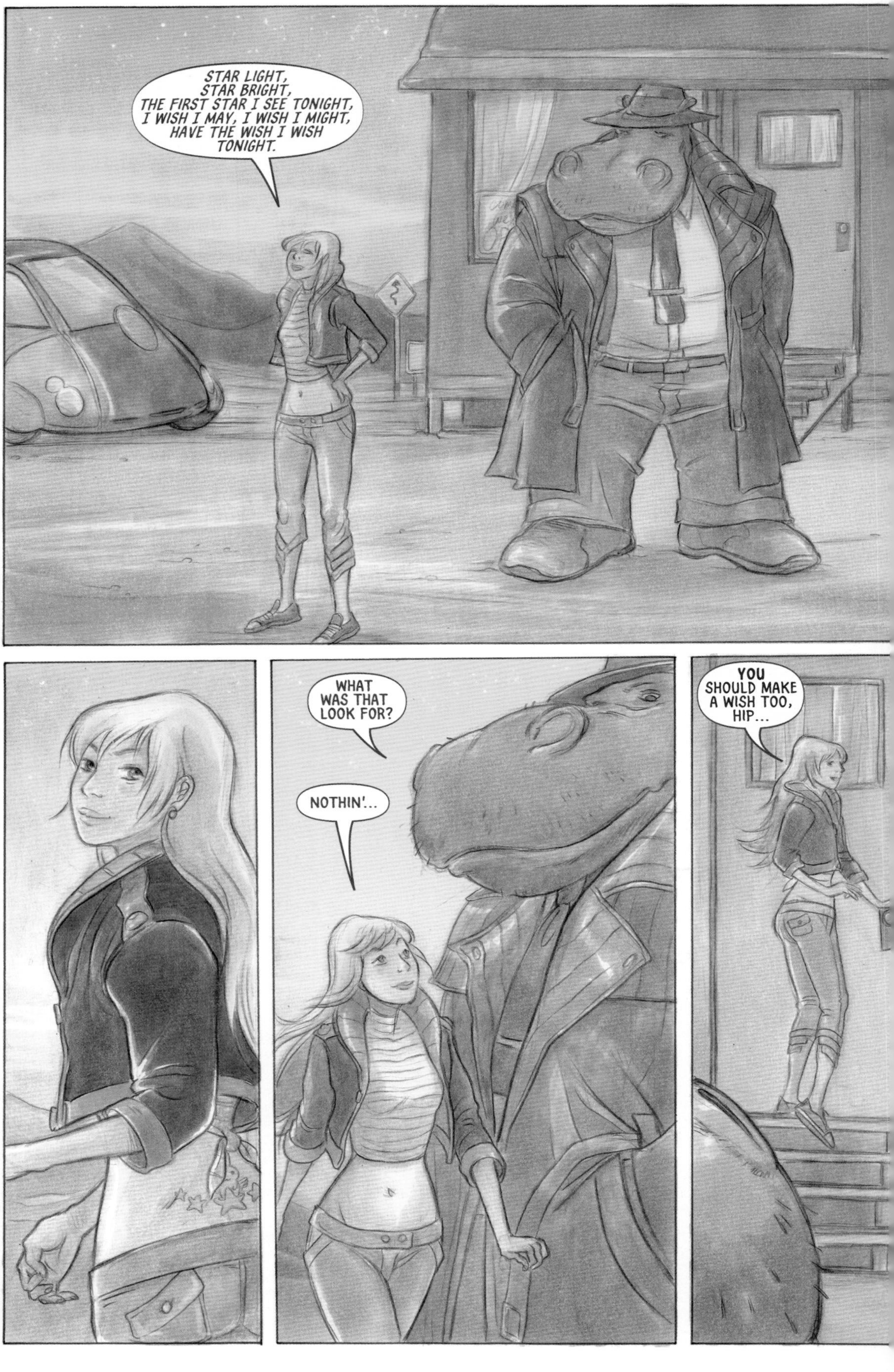
STAR LIGHT, STAR BRIGHT, THE FIRST STAR I SEE TONIGHT, I WISH I MAY, I WISH I MIGHT, HAVE THE WISH I WISH TONIGHT.
WHAT WAS THAT LOOK FOR?
NOTHIN'...
YOU SHOULD MAKE A WISH TOO, HIP...

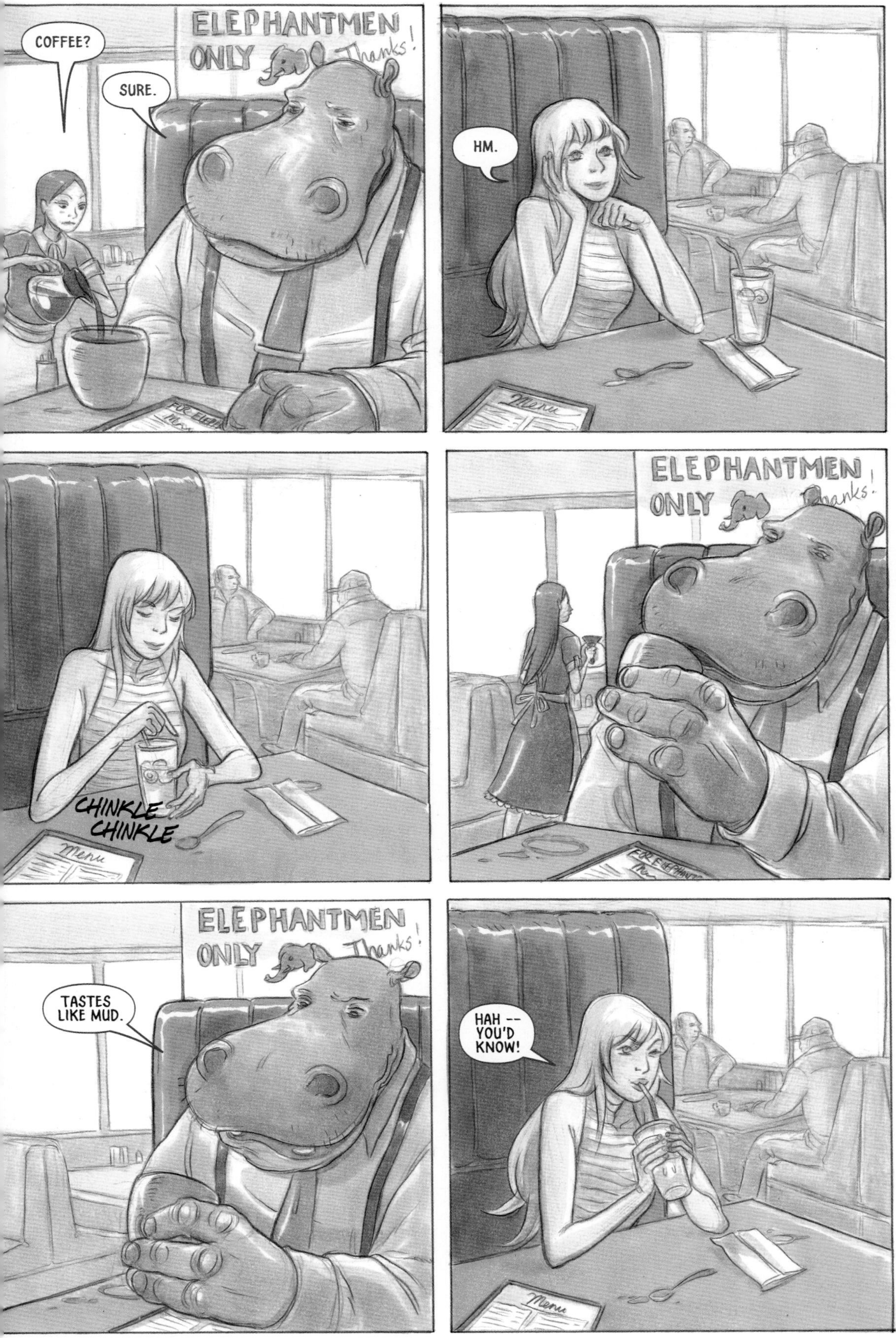
ELEPHANTMEN ONLY Thanks!
COFFEE?
SURE.
HM.
CHINKLE CHINKLE
ELEPHANTMEN ONLY Thanks!
ELEPHANTMEN ONLY Thanks!
TASTES LIKE MUD.
HAH -- YOU'D KNOW!

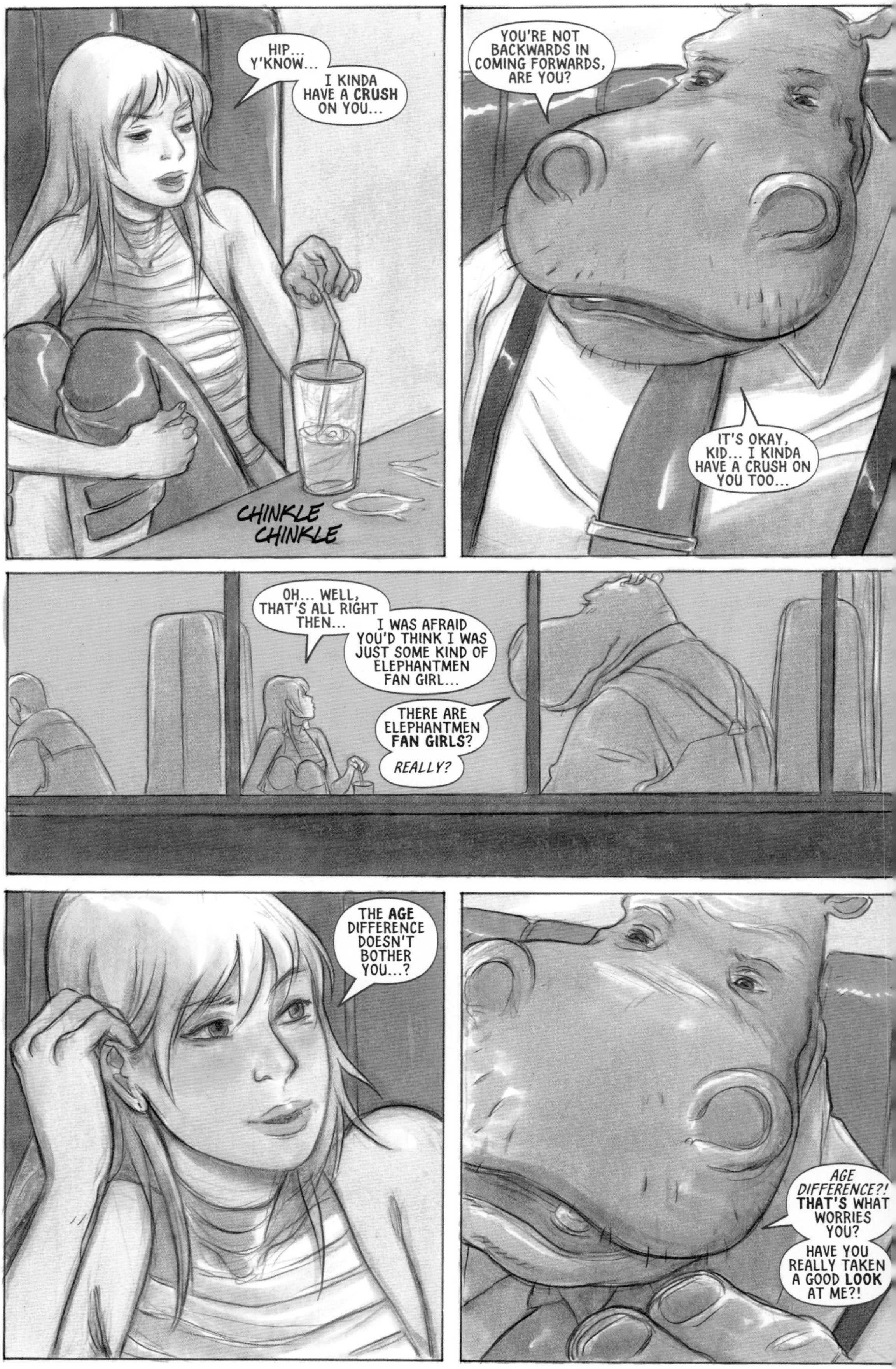
HIP... Y'KNOW... I KINDA HAVE A CRUSH ON YOU...
CHINKLE CHINKLE
YOU'RE NOT BACKWARDS IN COMING FORWARDS, ARE YOU?
IT'S OKAY, KID... I KINDA HAVE A CRUSH ON YOU TOO...
OH... WELL, THAT'S ALL RIGHT THEN...
I WAS AFRAID YOU'D THINK I WAS JUST SOME KIND OF ELEPHANTMEN FAN GIRL...
THERE ARE ELEPHANTMEN FAN GIRLS?
REALLY?
THE AGE DIFFERENCE DOESN'T BOTHER YOU...?
AGE DIFFERENCE?! THAT'S WHAT WORRIES YOU?
HAVE YOU REALLY TAKEN A GOOD LOOK AT ME?!

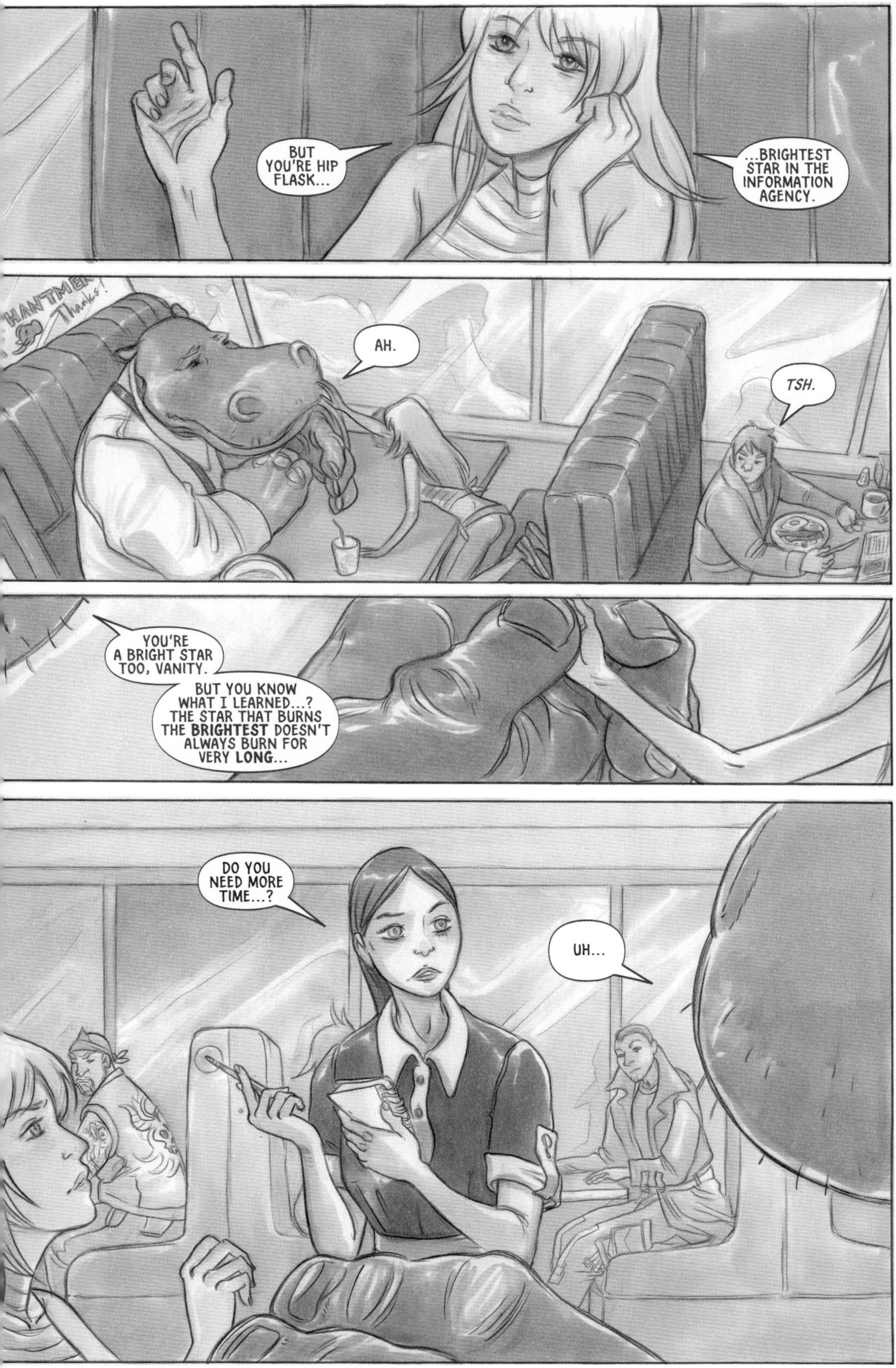
BUT YOU'RE HIP FLASK...
...BRIGHTEST STAR IN THE INFORMATION AGENCY.
AH.
TSH.
YOU'RE A BRIGHT STAR TOO, VANITY.
BUT YOU KNOW WHAT I LEARNED...? THE STAR THAT BURNS THE **BRIGHTEST** DOESN'T ALWAYS BURN FOR VERY **LONG**...
DO YOU NEED MORE TIME...?
UH...

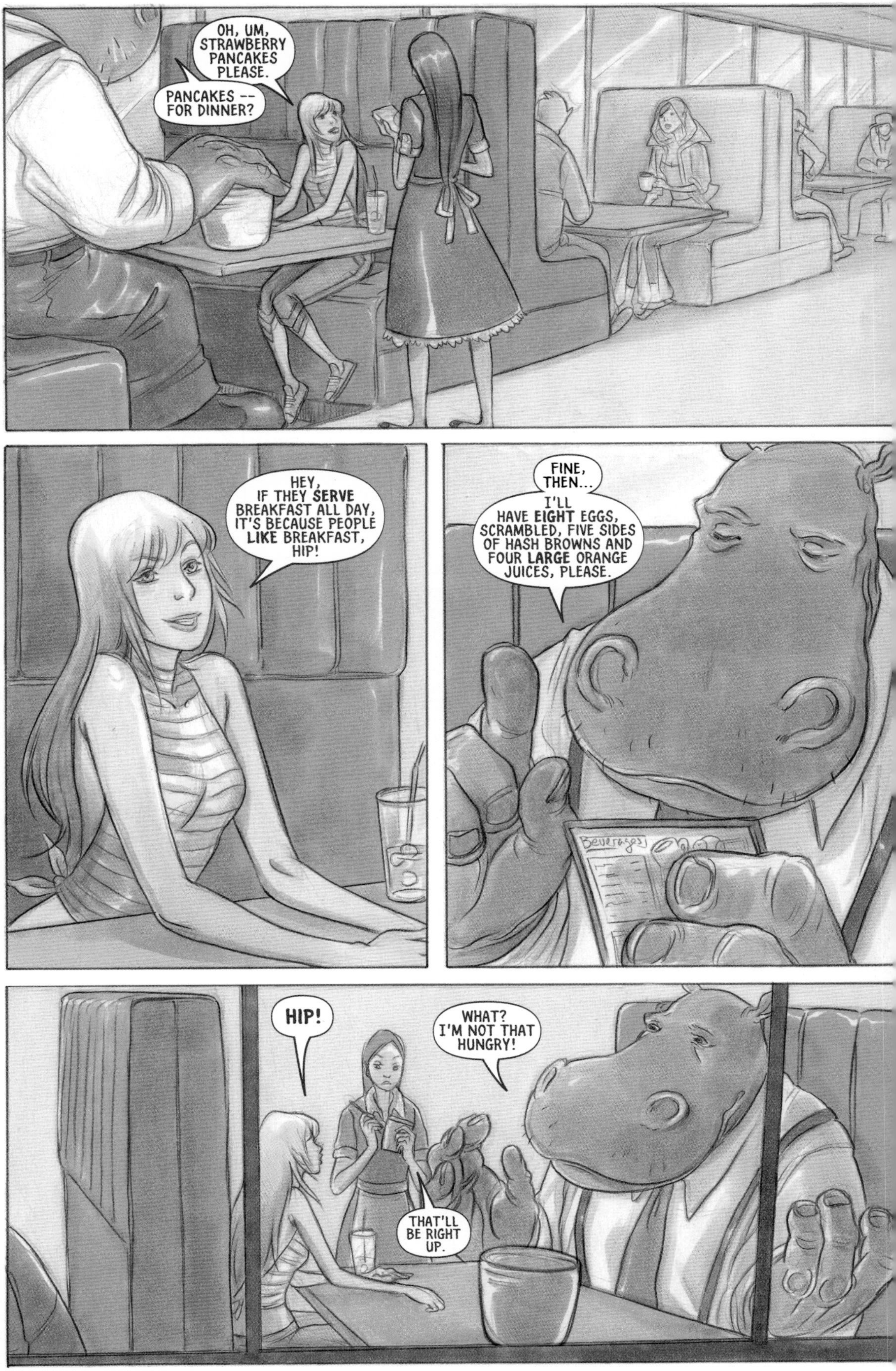
OH, UM, STRAWBERRY PANCAKES PLEASE.
PANCAKES -- FOR DINNER?
HEY, IF THEY **SERVE** BREAKFAST ALL DAY, IT'S BECAUSE PEOPLE **LIKE** BREAKFAST, HIP!
FINE, THEN...
I'LL HAVE **EIGHT** EGGS, SCRAMBLED, FIVE SIDES OF HASH BROWNS AND FOUR **LARGE** ORANGE JUICES, PLEASE.
Beverages
HIP!
WHAT? I'M NOT THAT HUNGRY!
THAT'LL BE RIGHT UP.

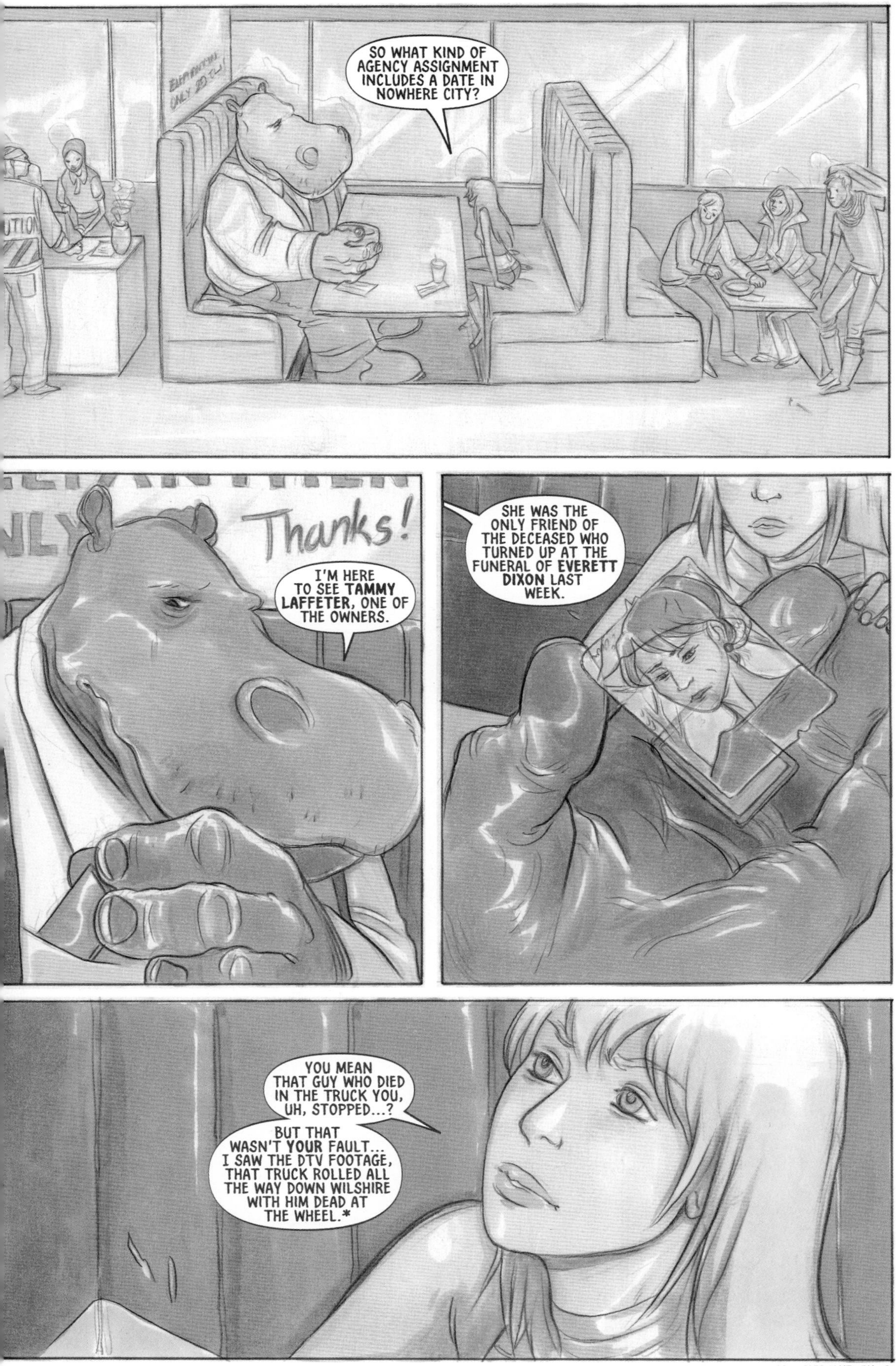

SO WHAT KIND OF AGENCY ASSIGNMENT INCLUDES A DATE IN NOWHERE CITY?
Thanks!
I'M HERE TO SEE **TAMMY LAFFETER**, ONE OF THE OWNERS.
SHE WAS THE ONLY FRIEND OF THE DECEASED WHO TURNED UP AT THE FUNERAL OF **EVERETT DIXON** LAST WEEK.
YOU MEAN THAT GUY WHO DIED IN THE TRUCK YOU, UH, STOPPED...?
BUT THAT WASN'T **YOUR** FAULT... I SAW THE DTV FOOTAGE, THAT TRUCK ROLLED ALL THE WAY DOWN WILSHIRE WITH HIM DEAD AT THE WHEEL.*

*See ELEPHANTMEN #9

ELEPHANTMEN ONLY Thanks!

SHH...
I'M NOT HERE TO *APOLOGIZE,* VANITY.

APART FROM THE FACT THAT IT'S AGENCY *POLICY* TO OFFER PERSONAL CONDOLENCES FOR ANY DEATHS THAT OCCUR IN THE LINE OF DUTY...

IT'S *ALSO* PART OF MY ONGOING *REHABILITATION* PROCESS.

AND I WAS AT ANOTHER FUNERAL WHEN THE POOR GUY WAS BURIED.*

*Tusk's. See ELEPHANTMEN

REHABILITATION PROCESS?

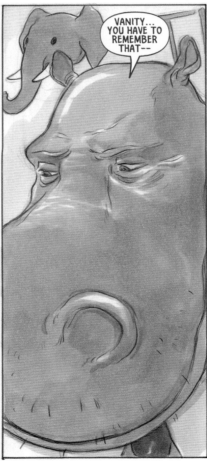

VANITY... YOU HAVE TO REMEMBER THAT--

HEY, WHAT HAPPENED TO MY *EARRING?*

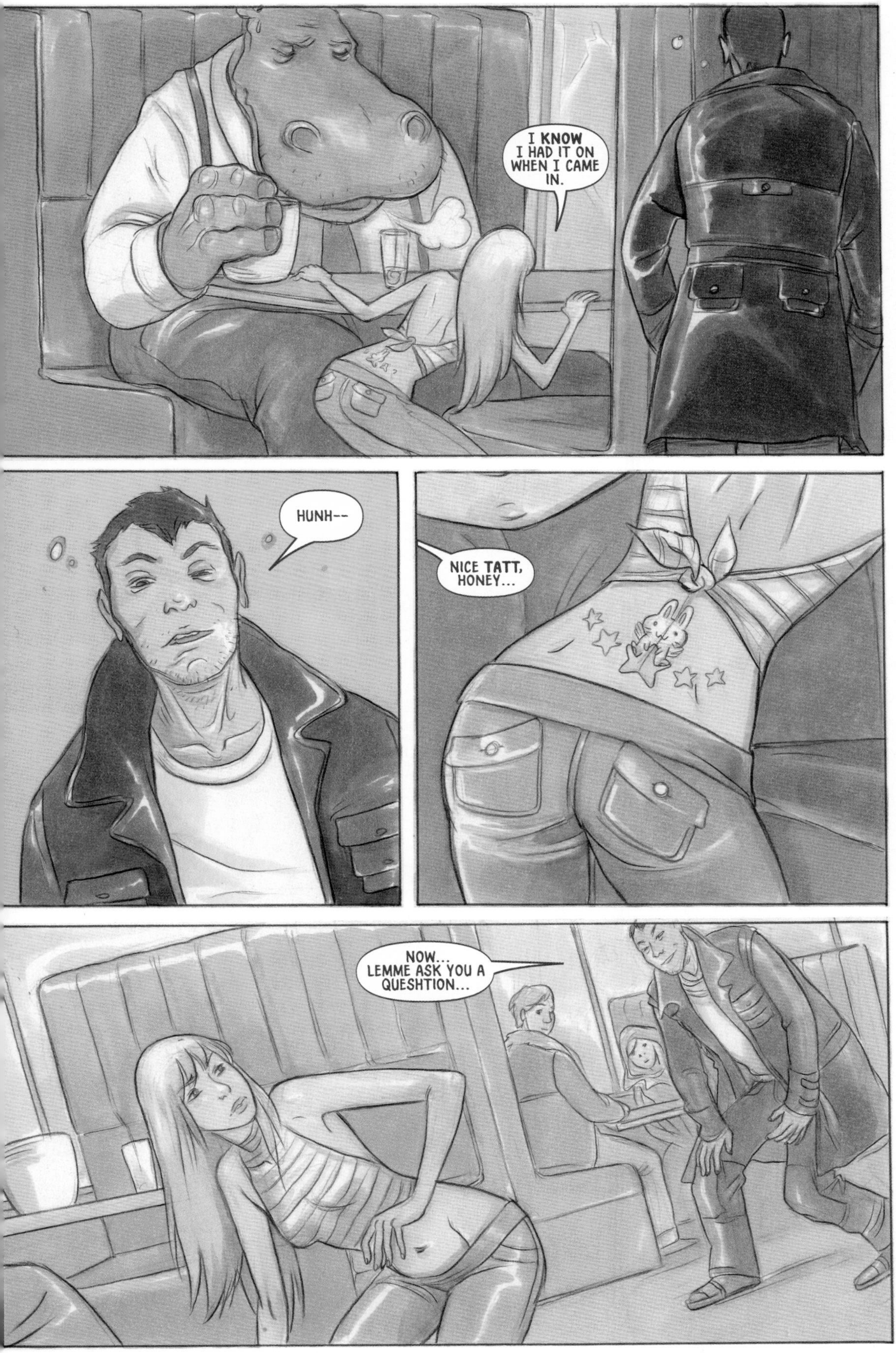
I KNOW I HAD IT ON WHEN I CAME IN.
HUNH--
NICE TATT, HONEY...
NOW... LEMME ASK YOU A QUESHTION...

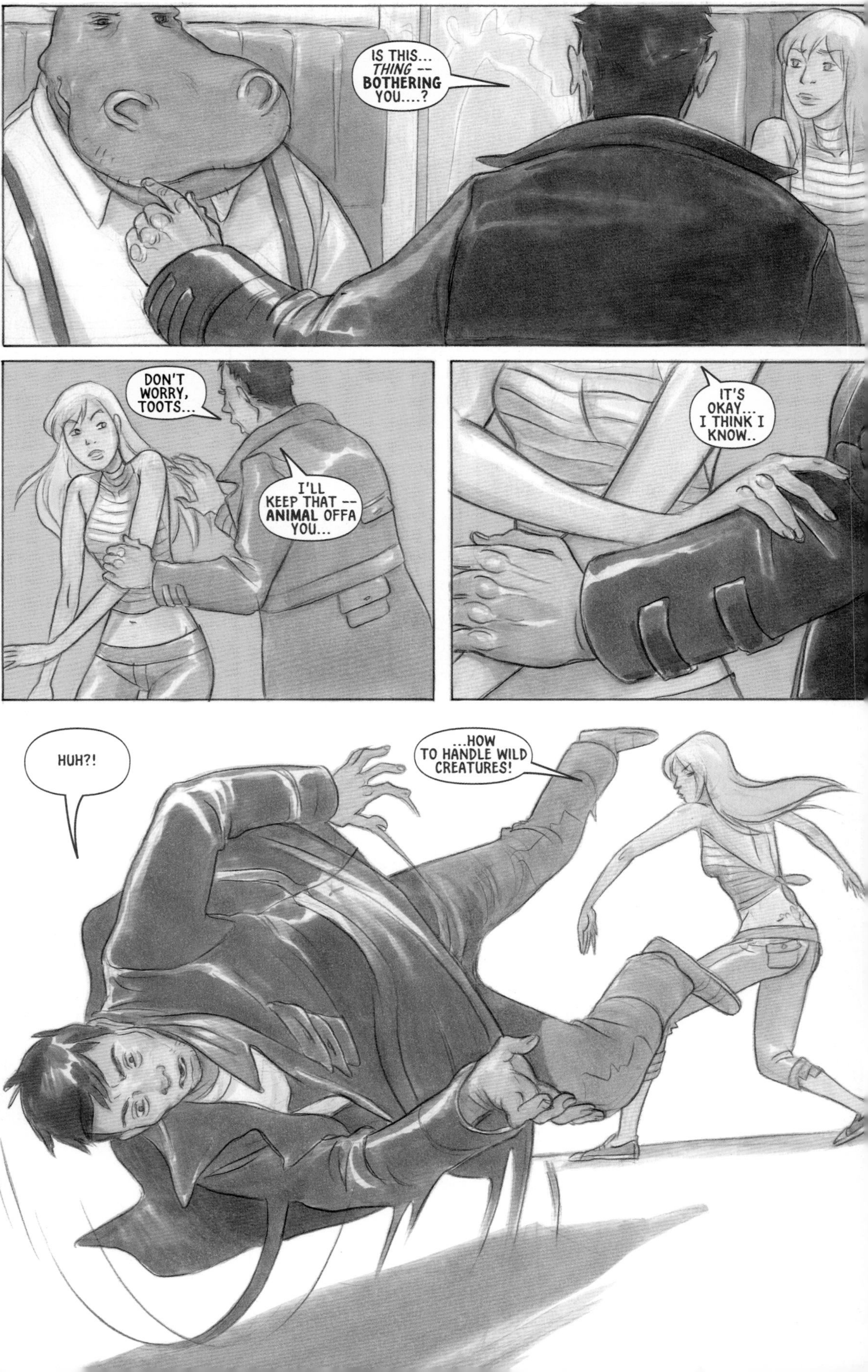
IS THIS... *THING* -- **BOTHERING** YOU....?
DON'T WORRY, TOOTS...
I'LL KEEP THAT -- **ANIMAL** OFFA YOU...
IT'S OKAY... I THINK I KNOW..
HUH?!
...HOW TO HANDLE WILD CREATURES!

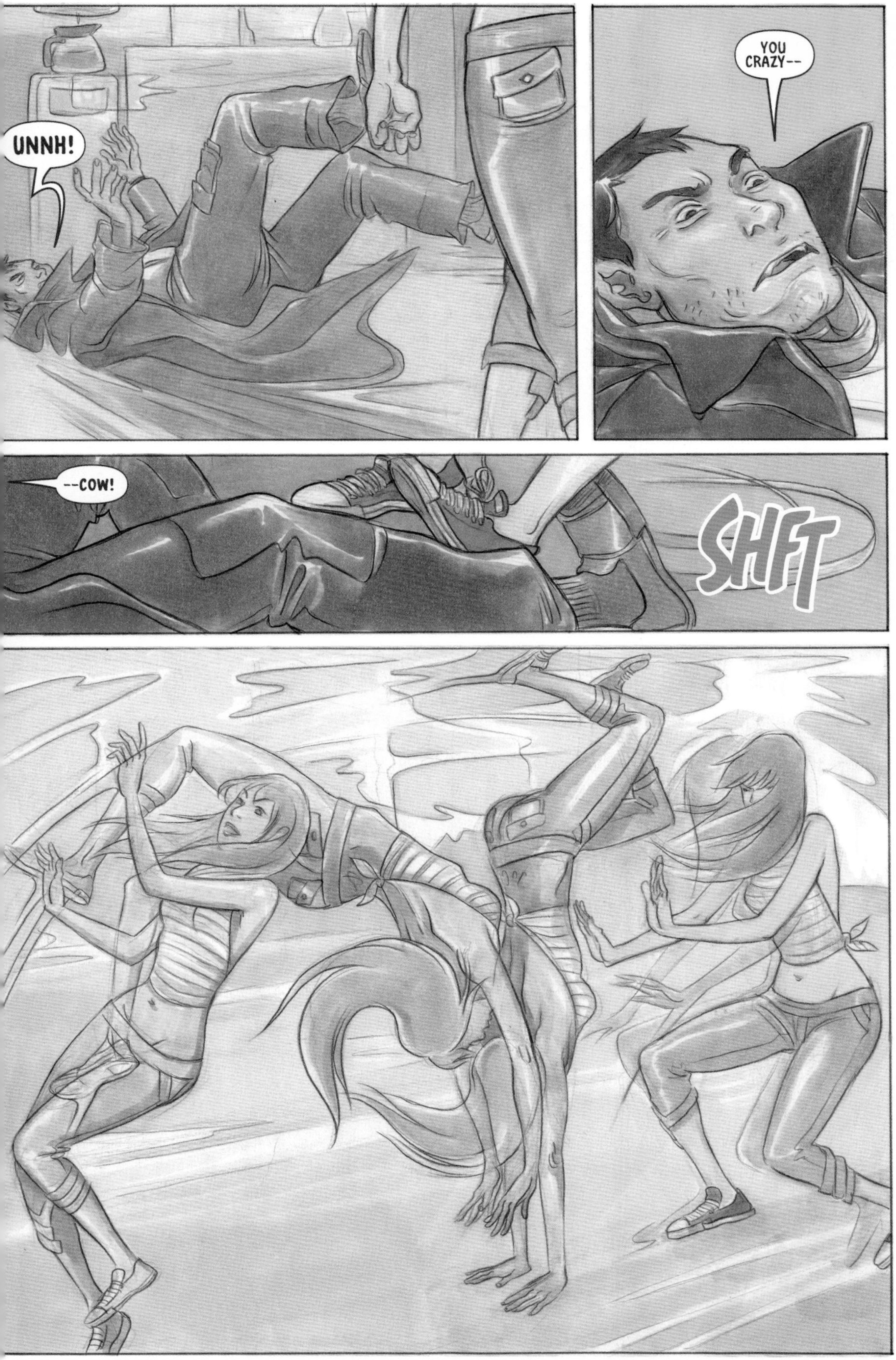
UNNH!
YOU CRAZY--
--COW!
SHFT

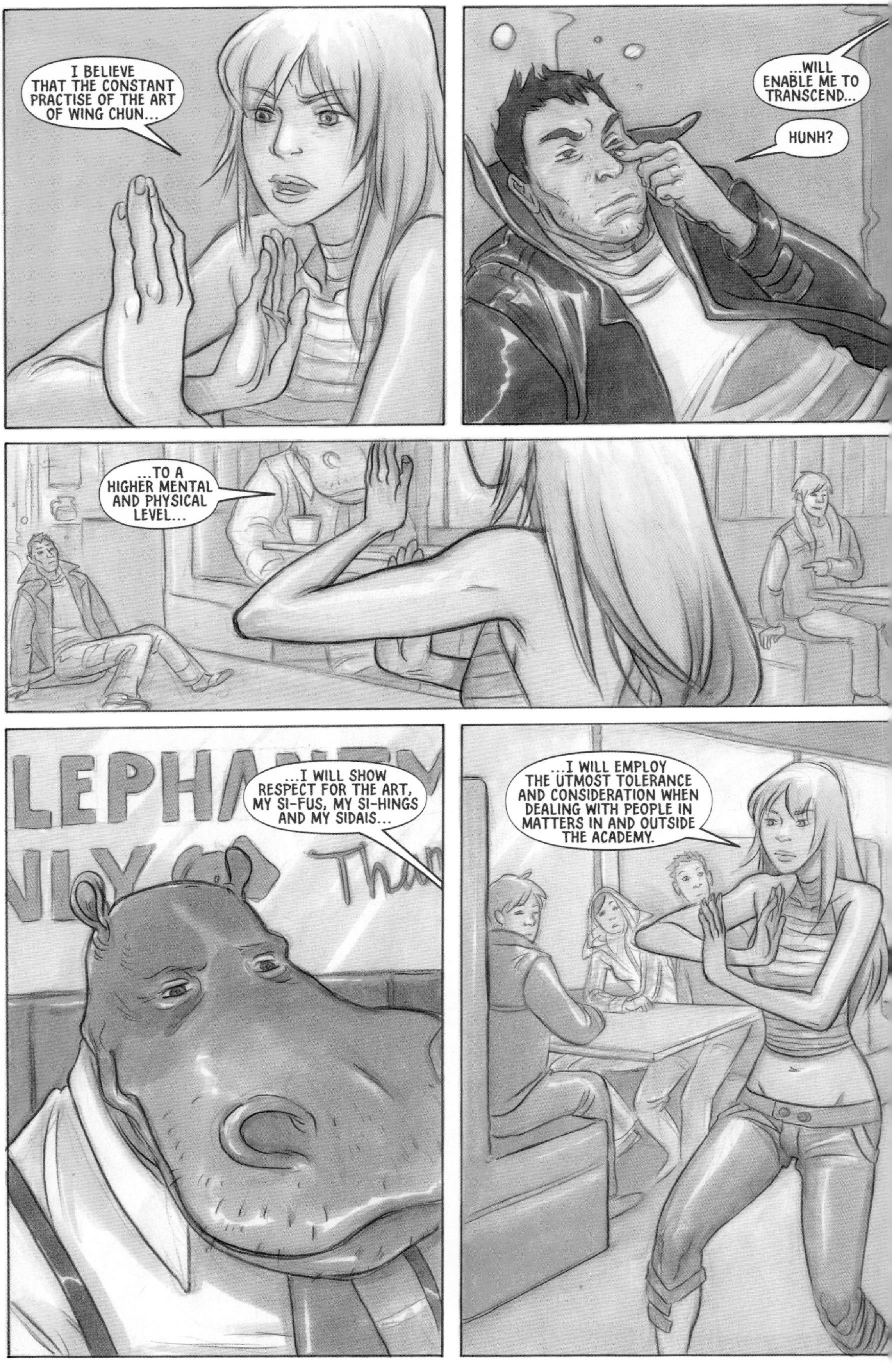
I BELIEVE THAT THE CONSTANT PRACTISE OF THE ART OF WING CHUN...
...WILL ENABLE ME TO TRANSCEND...
HUNH?
...TO A HIGHER MENTAL AND PHYSICAL LEVEL...
...I WILL SHOW RESPECT FOR THE ART, MY SI-FUS, MY SI-HINGS AND MY SIDAIS...
...I WILL EMPLOY THE UTMOST TOLERANCE AND CONSIDERATION WHEN DEALING WITH PEOPLE IN MATTERS IN AND OUTSIDE THE ACADEMY.

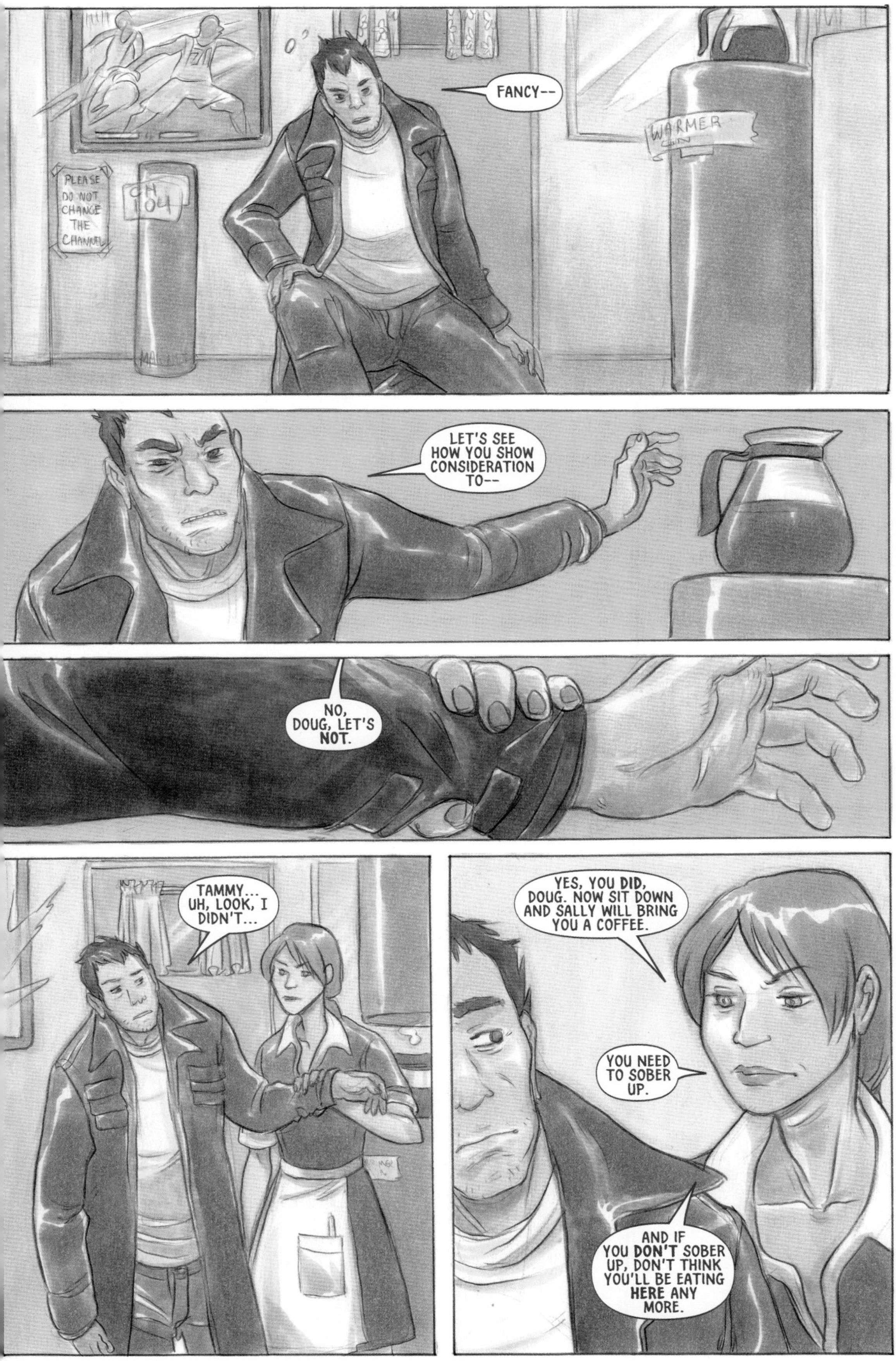
PLEASE DO NOT CHANGE THE CHANNEL
CH 104
FANCY--
WARMER
LET'S SEE HOW YOU SHOW CONSIDERATION TO--
NO, DOUG, LET'S **NOT**.
TAMMY... UH, LOOK, I DIDN'T...
YES, YOU **DID**, DOUG. NOW SIT DOWN AND SALLY WILL BRING YOU A COFFEE.
YOU NEED TO SOBER UP.
AND IF YOU **DON'T** SOBER UP, DON'T THINK YOU'LL BE EATING **HERE** ANY MORE.

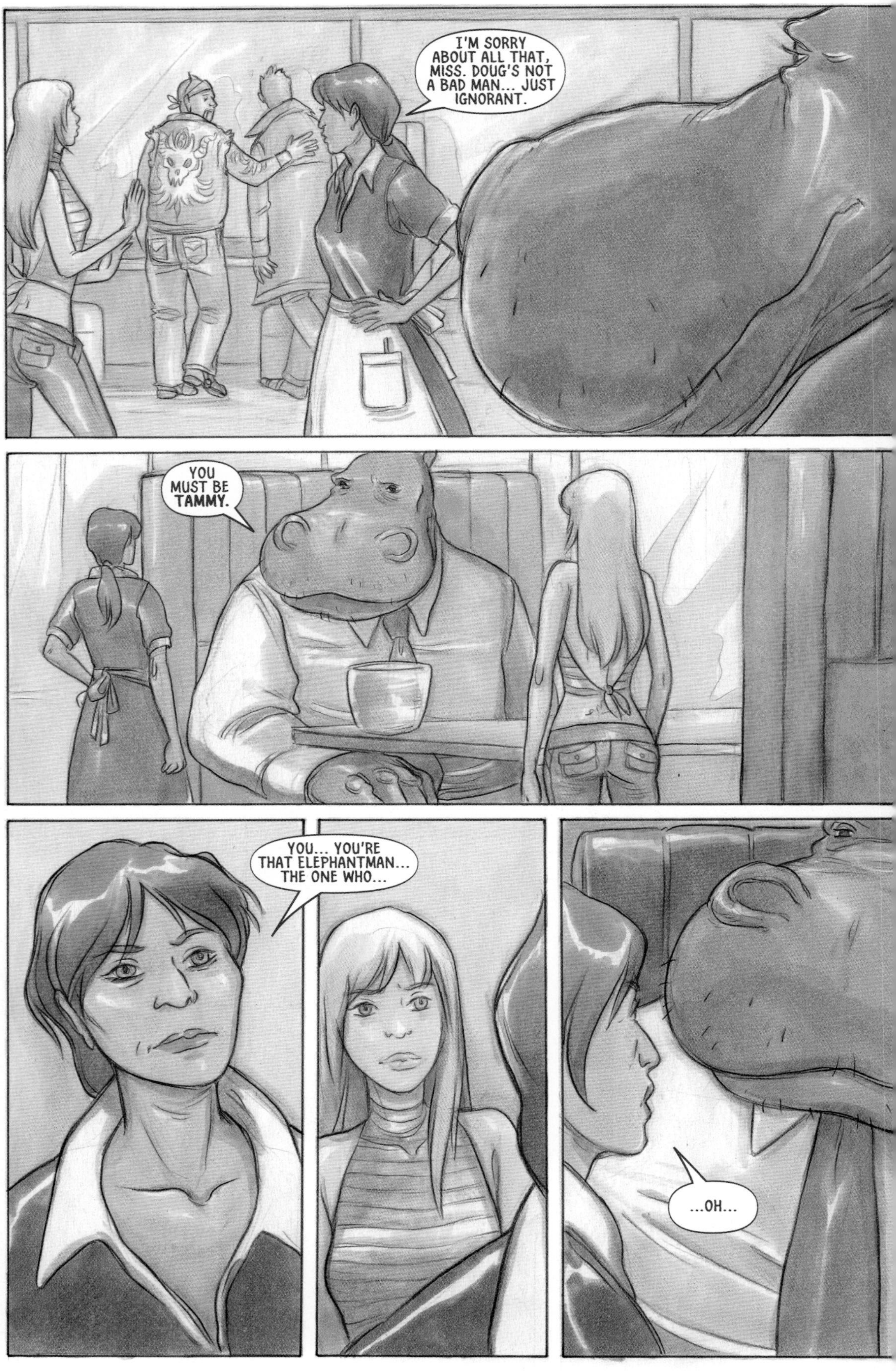
I'M SORRY ABOUT ALL THAT, MISS. DOUG'S NOT A BAD MAN... JUST IGNORANT.
YOU MUST BE **TAMMY.**
YOU... YOU'RE THAT ELEPHANTMAN... THE ONE WHO...
...OH...

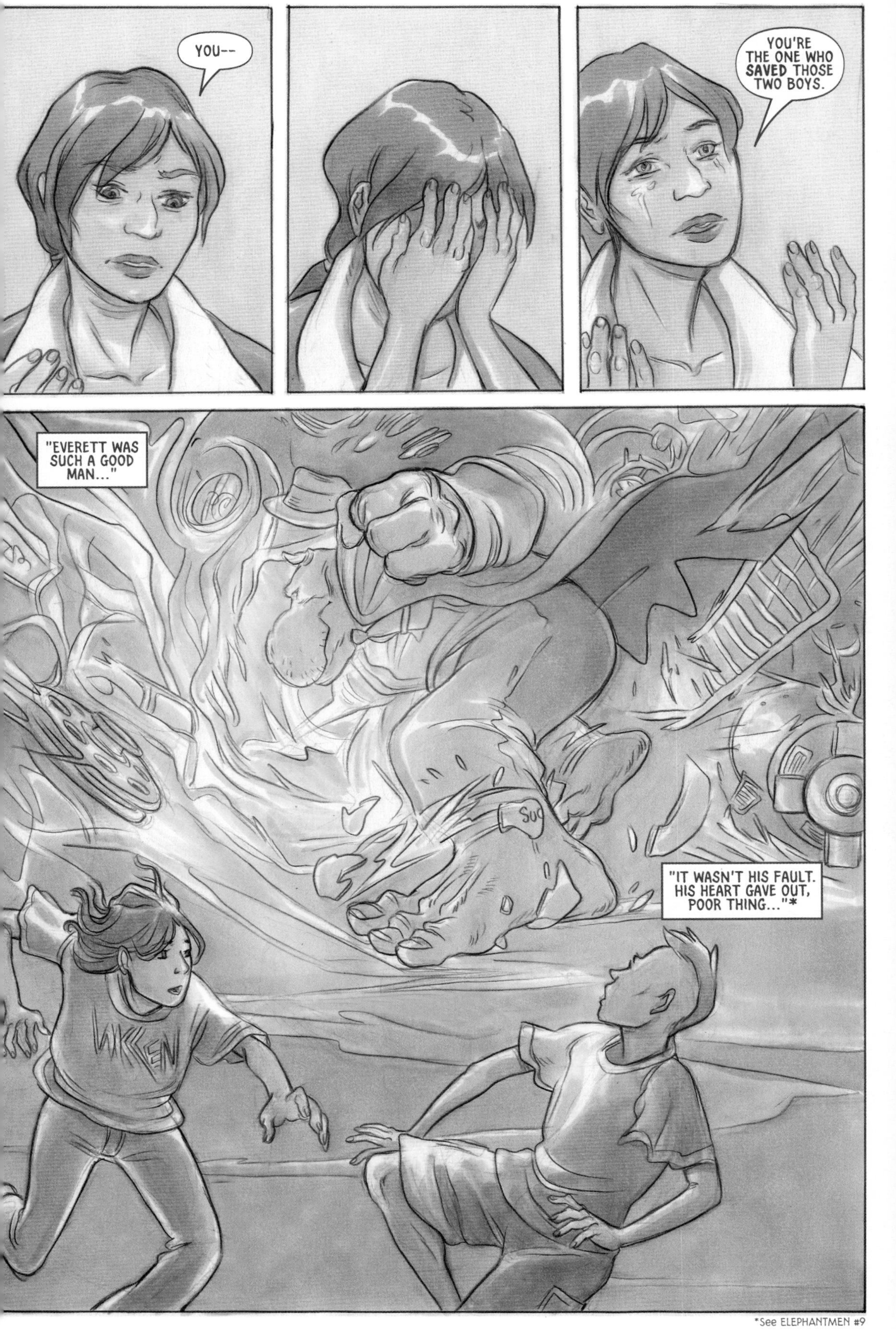
YOU--
YOU'RE THE ONE WHO SAVED THOSE TWO BOYS.
"EVERETT WAS SUCH A GOOD MAN..."
"IT WASN'T HIS FAULT. HIS HEART GAVE OUT, POOR THING..."*

*See ELEPHANTMEN #9

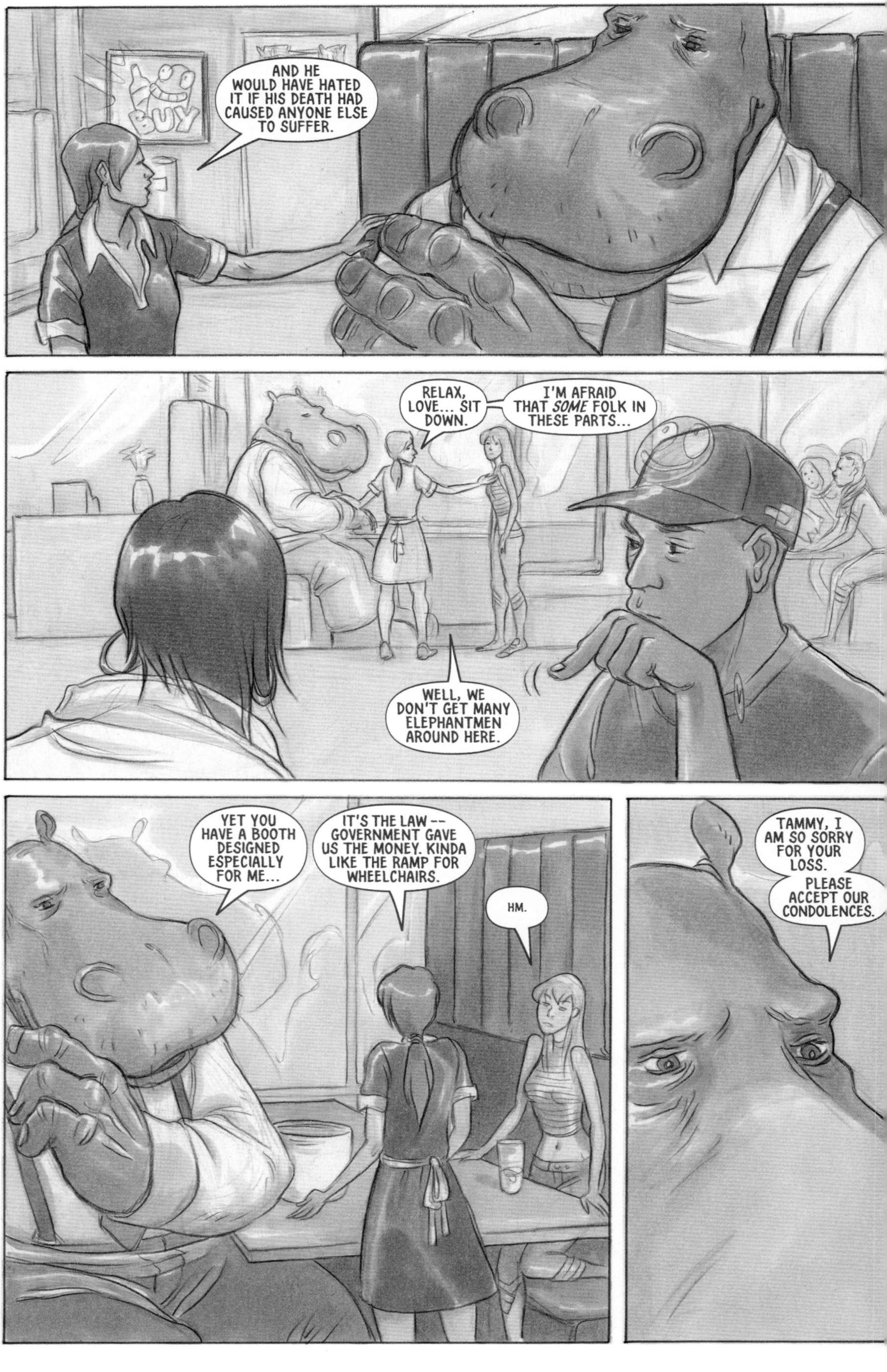

AND HE WOULD HAVE HATED IT IF HIS DEATH HAD CAUSED ANYONE ELSE TO SUFFER.
BUY
RELAX, LOVE... SIT DOWN.
I'M AFRAID THAT *SOME* FOLK IN THESE PARTS...
WELL, WE DON'T GET MANY ELEPHANTMEN AROUND HERE.
YET YOU HAVE A BOOTH DESIGNED ESPECIALLY FOR ME...
IT'S THE LAW -- GOVERNMENT GAVE US THE MONEY. KINDA LIKE THE RAMP FOR WHEELCHAIRS.
HM.
TAMMY, I AM SO SORRY FOR YOUR LOSS.
PLEASE ACCEPT OUR CONDOLENCES.

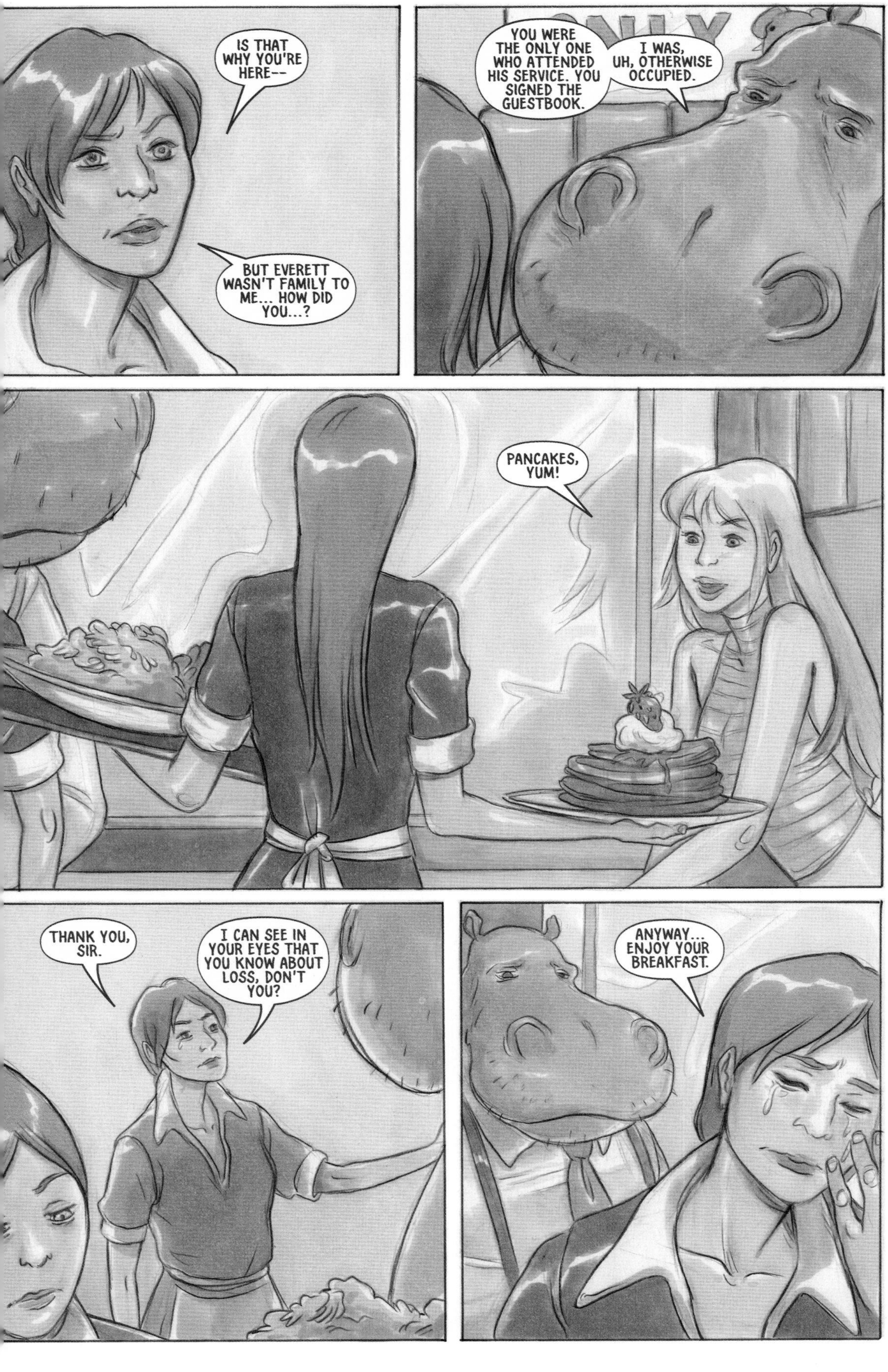
IS THAT WHY YOU'RE HERE--
BUT EVERETT WASN'T FAMILY TO ME... HOW DID YOU...?
YOU WERE THE ONLY ONE WHO ATTENDED HIS SERVICE. YOU SIGNED THE GUESTBOOK.
I WAS, UH, OTHERWISE OCCUPIED.
PANCAKES, YUM!
THANK YOU, SIR.
I CAN SEE IN YOUR EYES THAT YOU KNOW ABOUT LOSS, DON'T YOU?
ANYWAY... ENJOY YOUR BREAKFAST.

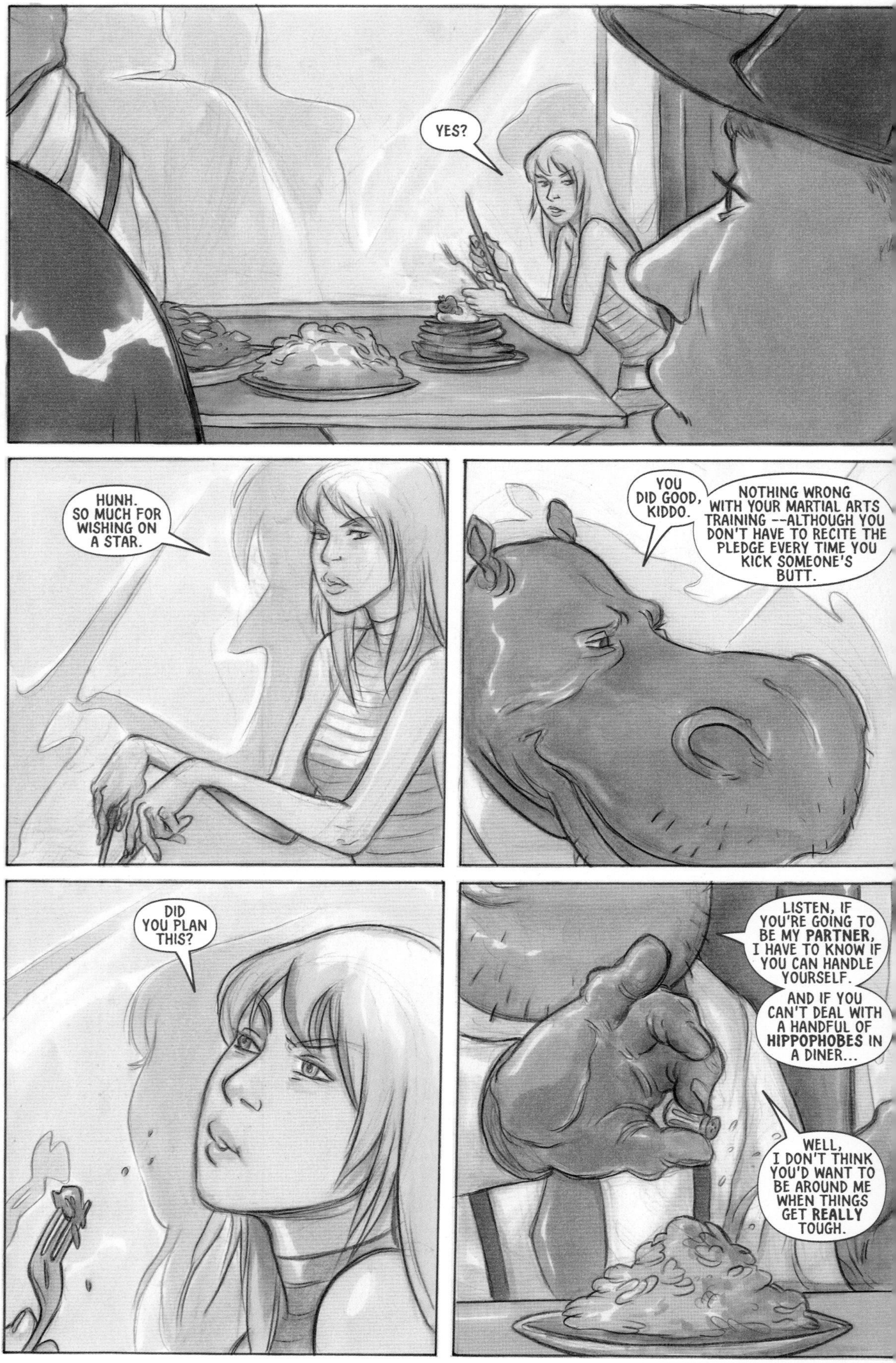
YES?
HUNH. SO MUCH FOR WISHING ON A STAR.
YOU DID GOOD, KIDDO.
NOTHING WRONG WITH YOUR MARTIAL ARTS TRAINING --ALTHOUGH YOU DON'T HAVE TO RECITE THE PLEDGE EVERY TIME YOU KICK SOMEONE'S BUTT.
DID YOU PLAN THIS?
LISTEN, IF YOU'RE GOING TO BE MY **PARTNER**, I HAVE TO KNOW IF YOU CAN HANDLE YOURSELF.
AND IF YOU CAN'T DEAL WITH A HANDFUL OF **HIPPOPHOBES** IN A DINER...
WELL, I DON'T THINK YOU'D WANT TO BE AROUND ME WHEN THINGS GET **REALLY** TOUGH.

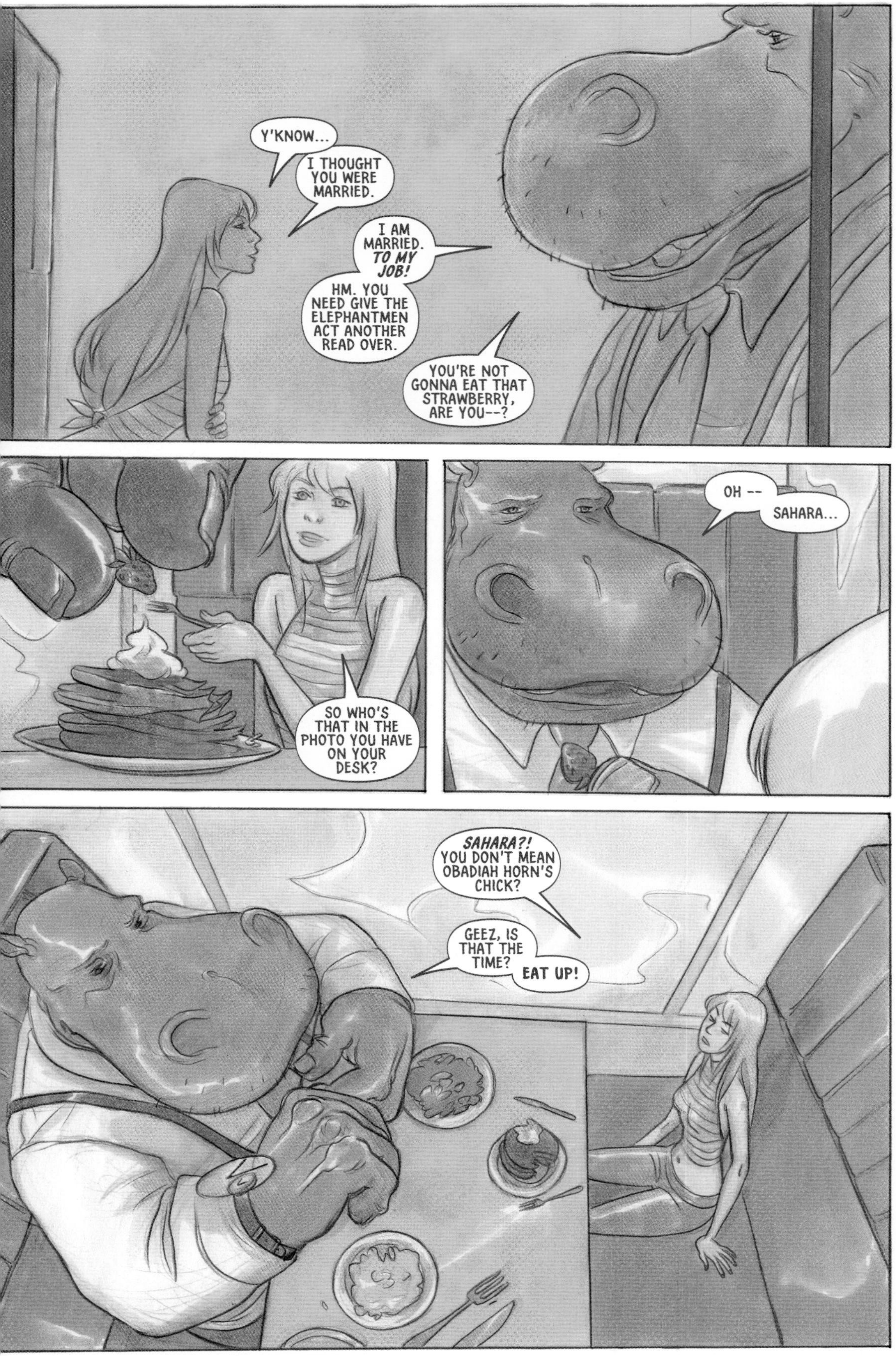

Y'KNOW...
I THOUGHT YOU WERE MARRIED.
I AM MARRIED. *TO MY JOB!*
HM. YOU NEED GIVE THE ELEPHANTMEN ACT ANOTHER READ OVER.
YOU'RE NOT GONNA EAT THAT STRAWBERRY, ARE YOU--?
SO WHO'S THAT IN THE PHOTO YOU HAVE ON YOUR DESK?
OH --
SAHARA...
SAHARA?! YOU DON'T MEAN OBADIAH HORN'S CHICK?
GEEZ, IS THAT THE TIME?
EAT UP!

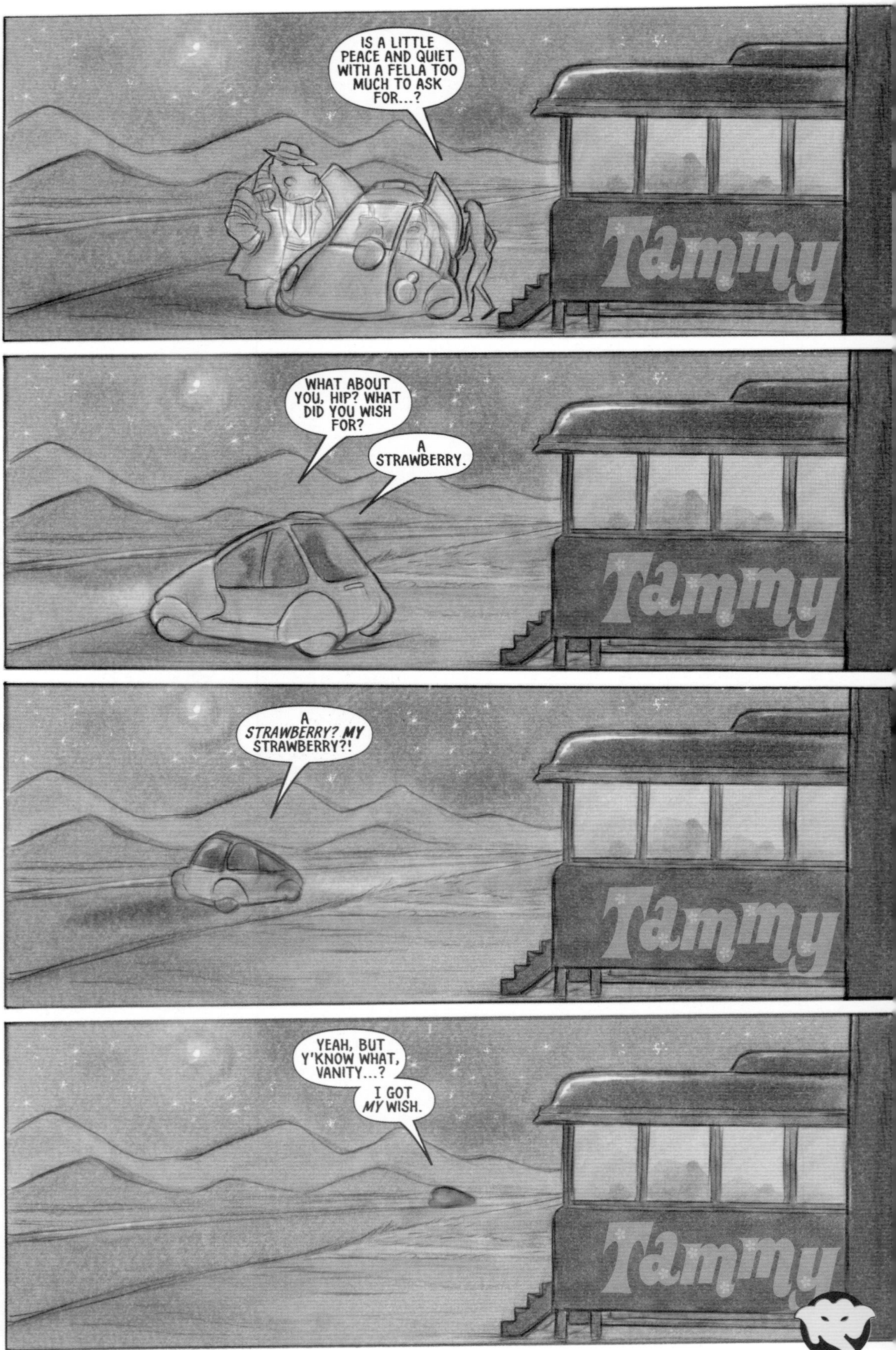
IS A LITTLE PEACE AND QUIET WITH A FELLA TOO MUCH TO ASK FOR...?
Tammy
WHAT ABOUT YOU, HIP? WHAT DID YOU WISH FOR?
A STRAWBERRY.
Tammy
A *STRAWBERRY? MY* STRAWBERRY?!
Tammy
YEAH, BUT Y'KNOW WHAT, VANITY...?
I GOT *MY* WISH.
Tammy

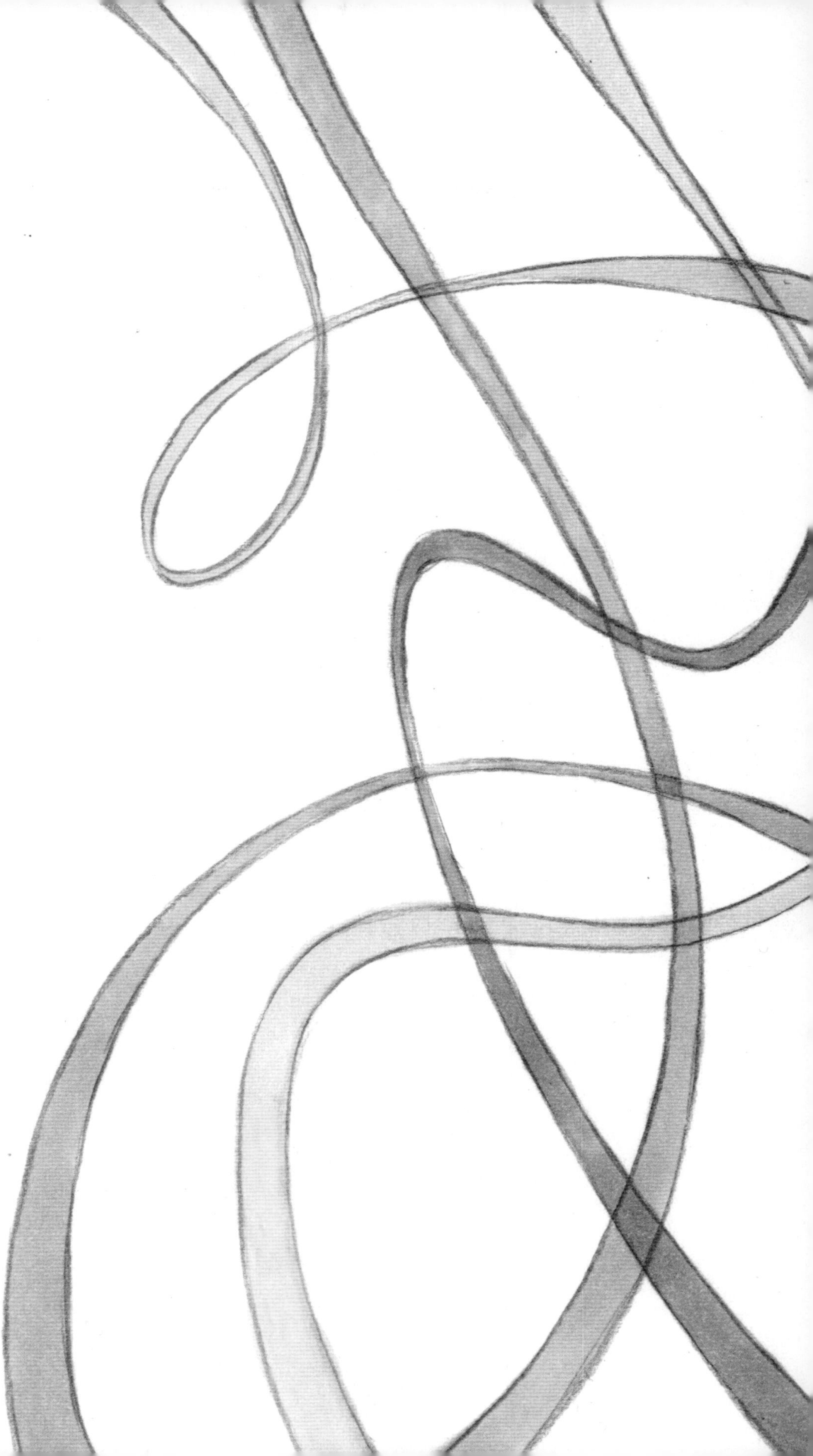

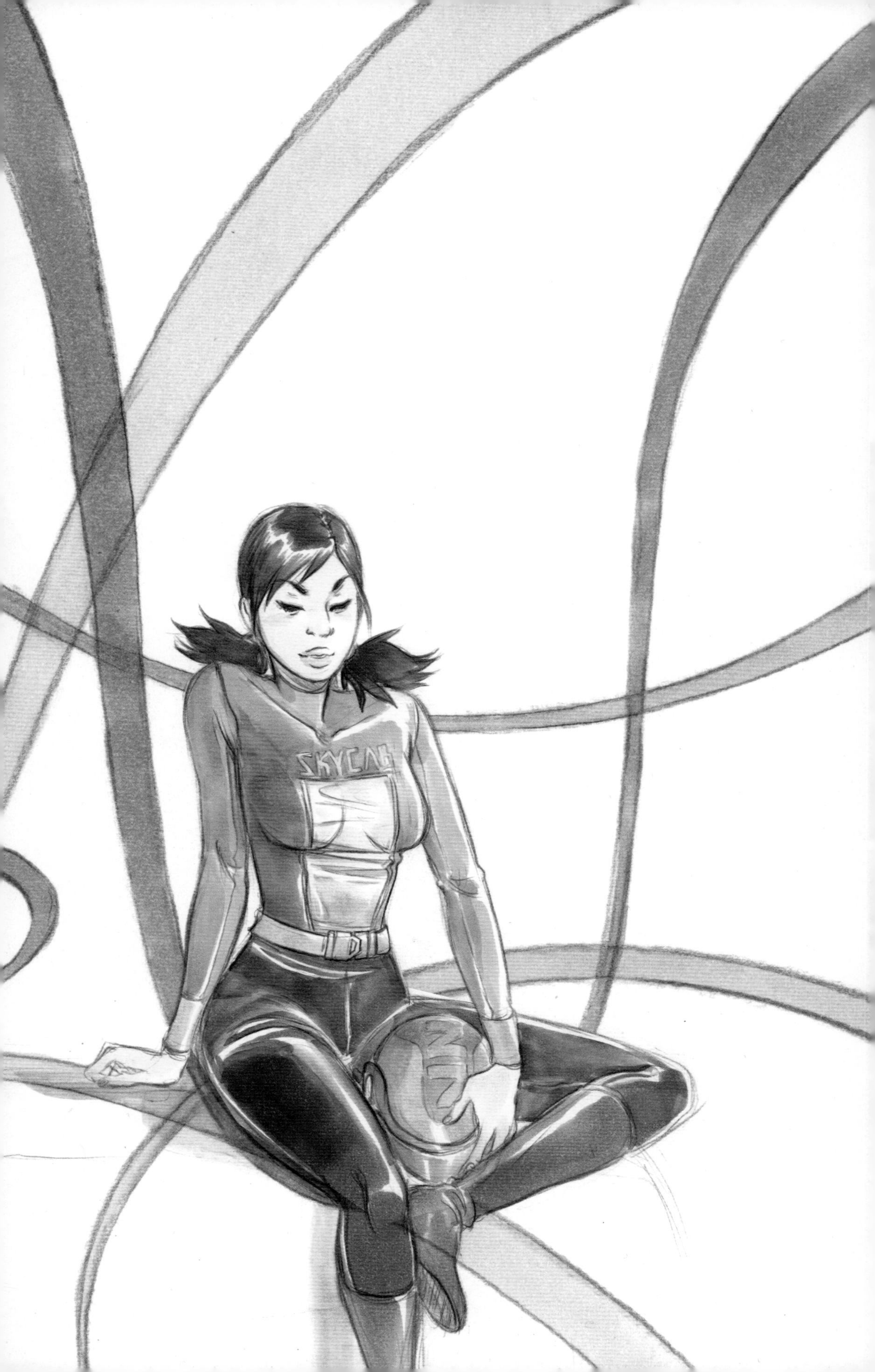
SKYCAB

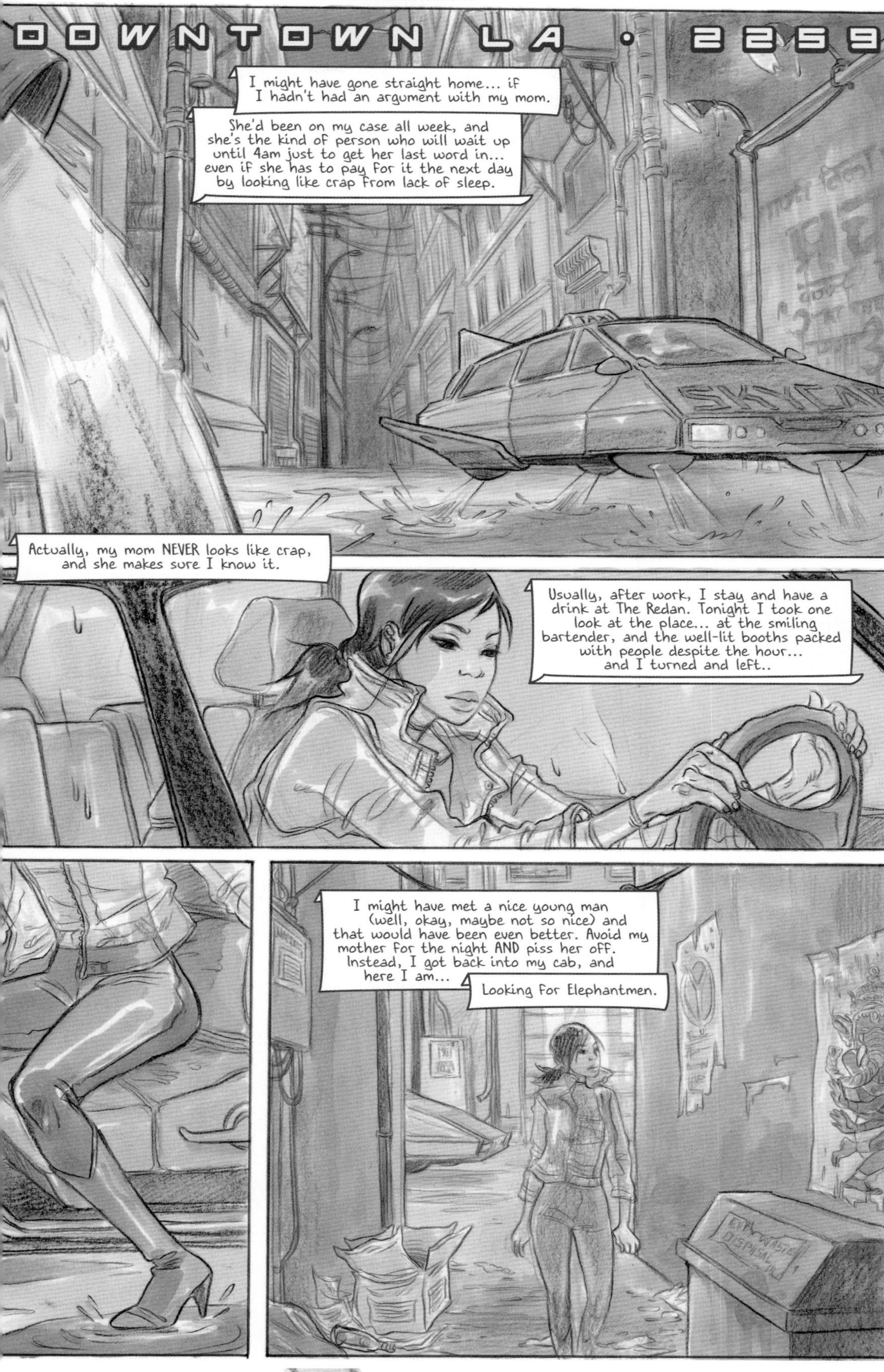
DOWNTOWN LA • 2259
I might have gone straight home... if I hadn't had an argument with my mom.
She'd been on my case all week, and she's the kind of person who will wait up until 4am just to get her last word in... even if she has to pay for it the next day by looking like crap from lack of sleep.
Actually, my mom NEVER looks like crap, and she makes sure I know it.
Usually, after work, I stay and have a drink at The Redan. Tonight I took one look at the place... at the smiling bartender, and the well-lit booths packed with people despite the hour... and I turned and left..
I might have met a nice young man (well, okay, maybe not so nice) and that would have been even better. Avoid my mother for the night AND piss her off. Instead, I got back into my cab, and here I am...
Looking for Elephantmen.

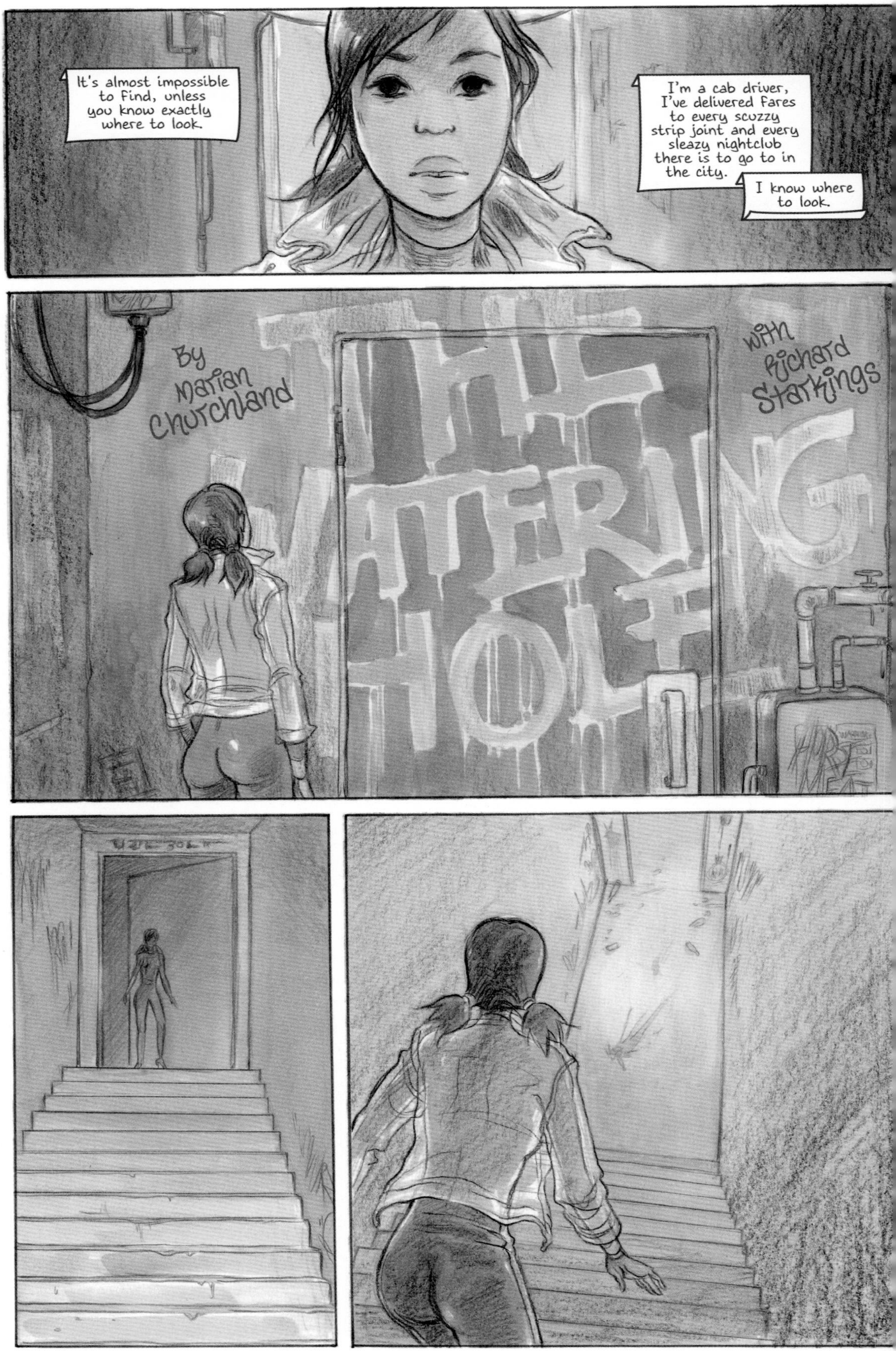
It's almost impossible to find, unless you know exactly where to look.
I'm a cab driver, I've delivered fares to every scuzzy strip joint and every sleazy nightclub there is to go to in the city.
I know where to look.
The Watering Hole
By Marian Churchland
with Richard Starkings

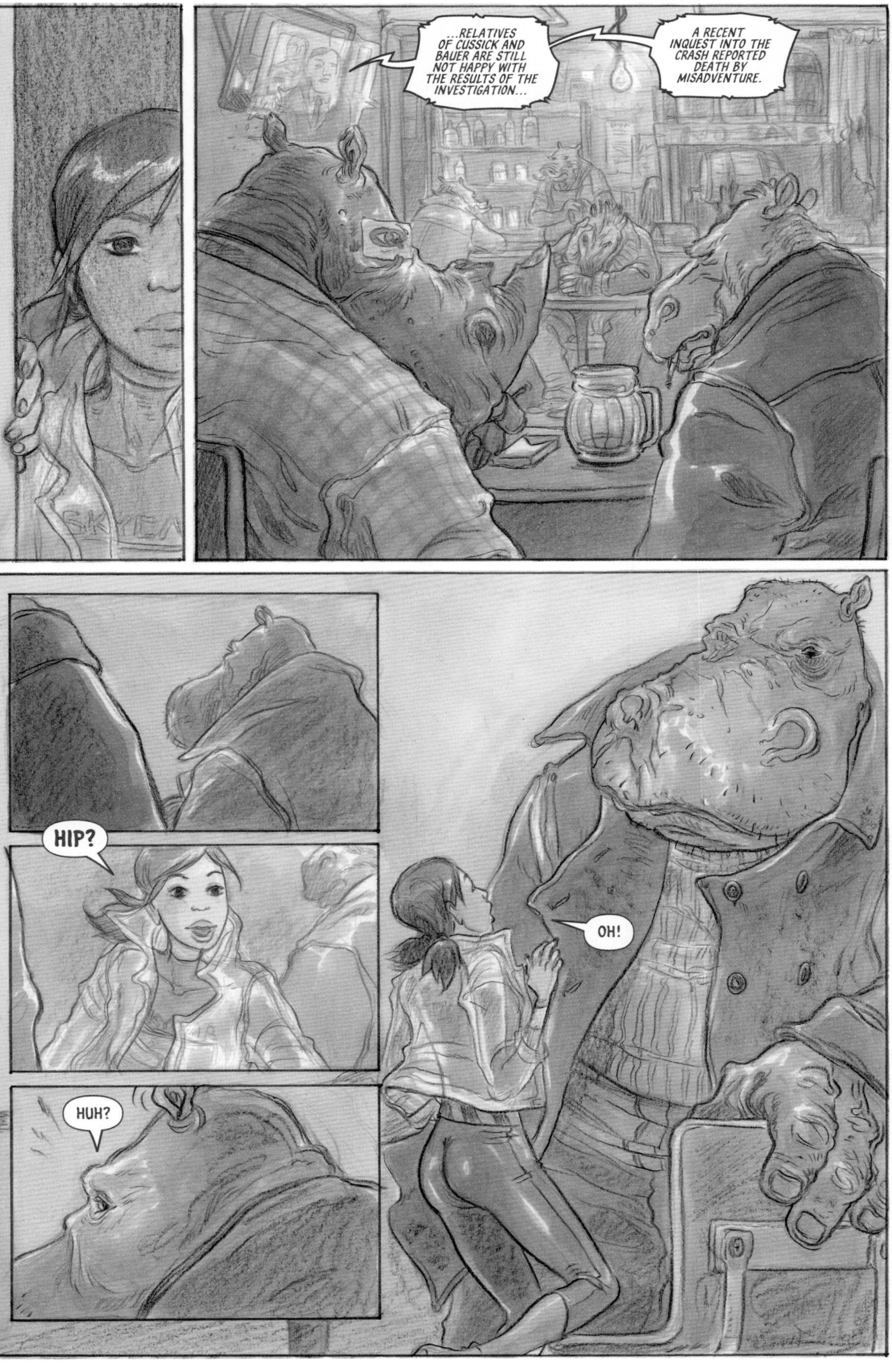
...RELATIVES OF CUSSICK AND BAUER ARE STILL NOT HAPPY WITH THE RESULTS OF THE INVESTIGATION...
A RECENT INQUEST INTO THE CRASH REPORTED DEATH BY MISADVENTURE.
HIP?
HUH?
OH!

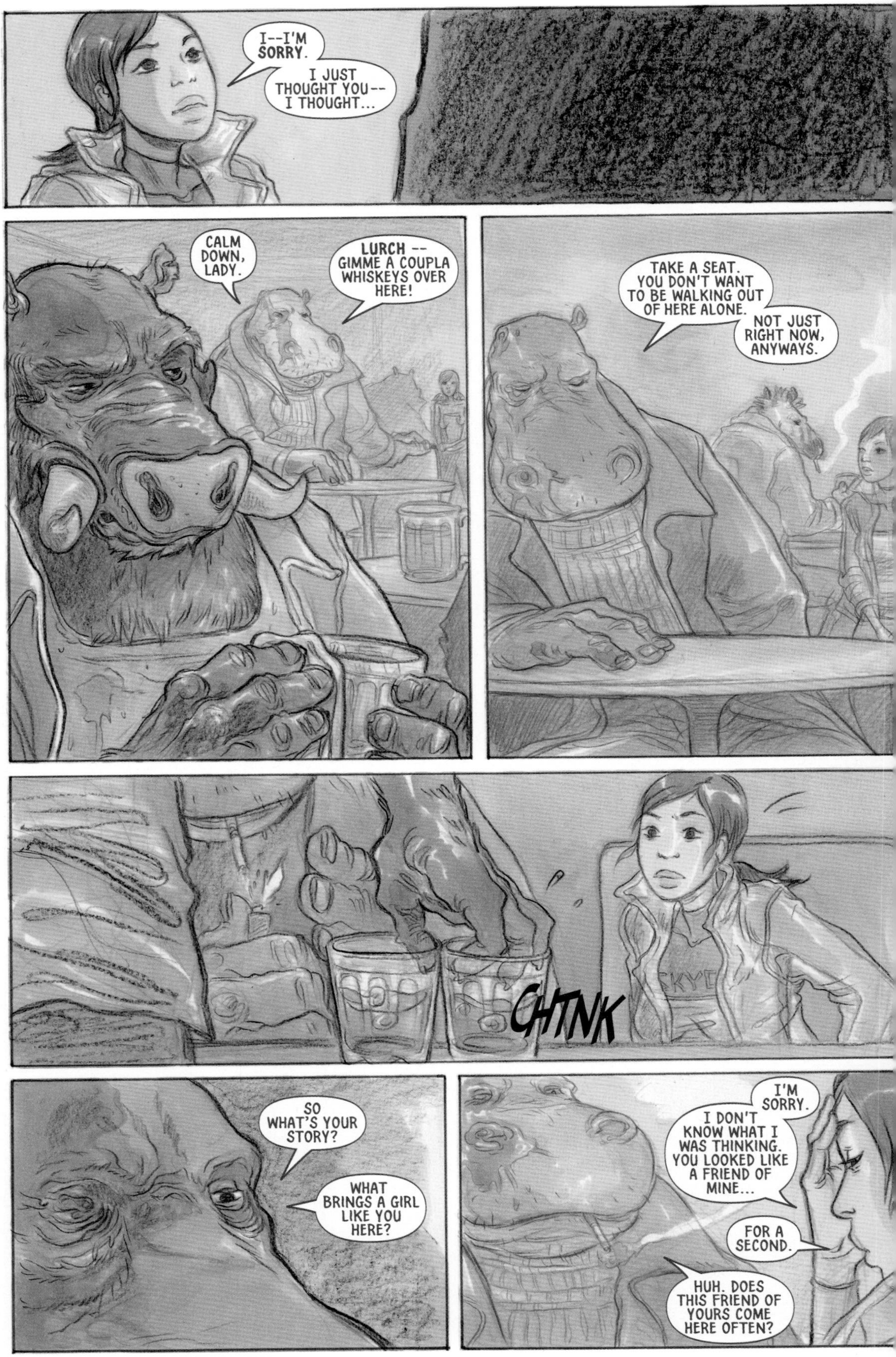
I--I'M SORRY.
I JUST THOUGHT YOU-- I THOUGHT...
CALM DOWN, LADY.
LURCH -- GIMME A COUPLA WHISKEYS OVER HERE!
TAKE A SEAT. YOU DON'T WANT TO BE WALKING OUT OF HERE ALONE.
NOT JUST RIGHT NOW, ANYWAYS.
CHTNK
SO WHAT'S YOUR STORY?
WHAT BRINGS A GIRL LIKE YOU HERE?
I'M SORRY.
I DON'T KNOW WHAT I WAS THINKING. YOU LOOKED LIKE A FRIEND OF MINE...
FOR A SECOND.
HUH. DOES THIS FRIEND OF YOURS COME HERE OFTEN?

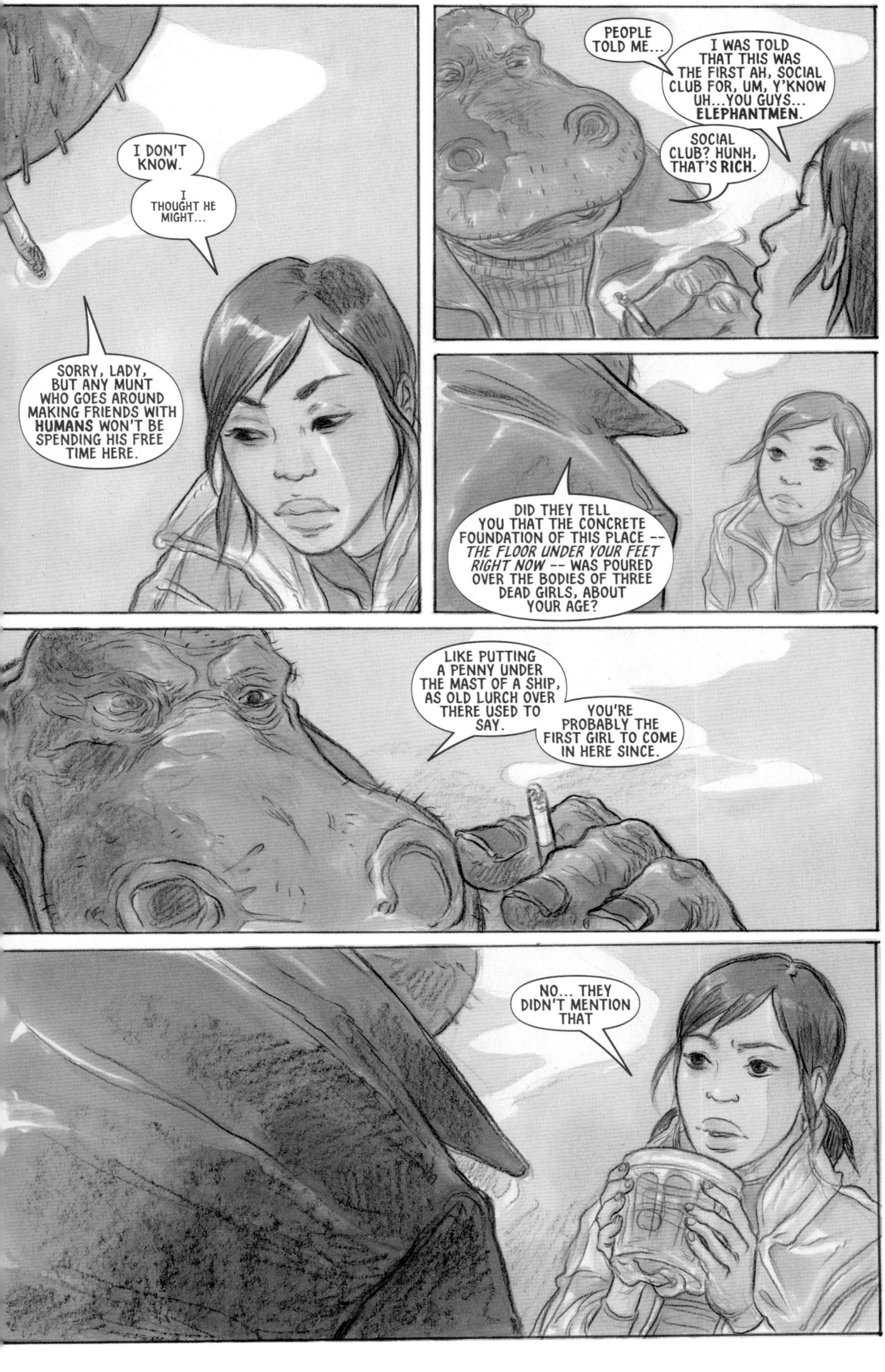
I DON'T KNOW.
I THOUGHT HE MIGHT...
SORRY, LADY, BUT ANY MUNT WHO GOES AROUND MAKING FRIENDS WITH HUMANS WON'T BE SPENDING HIS FREE TIME HERE.
PEOPLE TOLD ME...
I WAS TOLD THAT THIS WAS THE FIRST AH, SOCIAL CLUB FOR, UM, Y'KNOW UH...YOU GUYS... ELEPHANTMEN.
SOCIAL CLUB? HUNH, THAT'S RICH.
DID THEY TELL YOU THAT THE CONCRETE FOUNDATION OF THIS PLACE -- THE FLOOR UNDER YOUR FEET RIGHT NOW -- WAS POURED OVER THE BODIES OF THREE DEAD GIRLS, ABOUT YOUR AGE?
LIKE PUTTING A PENNY UNDER THE MAST OF A SHIP, AS OLD LURCH OVER THERE USED TO SAY.
YOU'RE PROBABLY THE FIRST GIRL TO COME IN HERE SINCE.
NO... THEY DIDN'T MENTION THAT

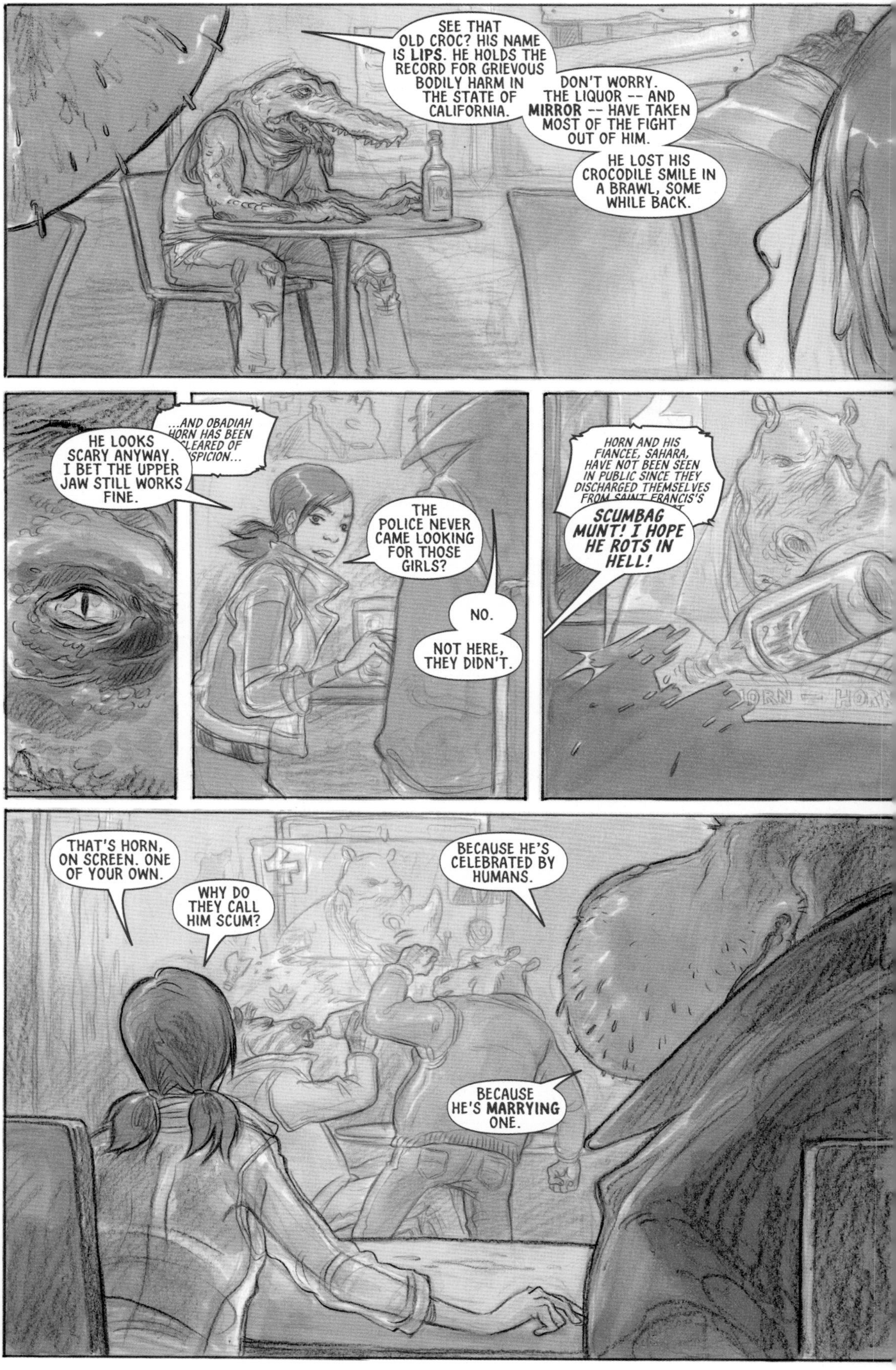
SEE THAT OLD CROC? HIS NAME IS **LIPS**. HE HOLDS THE RECORD FOR GRIEVOUS BODILY HARM IN THE STATE OF CALIFORNIA.
DON'T WORRY. THE LIQUOR -- AND **MIRROR** -- HAVE TAKEN MOST OF THE FIGHT OUT OF HIM.
HE LOST HIS CROCODILE SMILE IN A BRAWL, SOME WHILE BACK.
HE LOOKS SCARY ANYWAY. I BET THE UPPER JAW STILL WORKS FINE.
...AND OBADIAH HORN HAS BEEN
THE POLICE NEVER CAME LOOKING FOR THOSE GIRLS?
NO.
NOT HERE, THEY DIDN'T.
HORN AND HIS FIANCEE, SAHARA, HAVE NOT BEEN SEEN IN PUBLIC SINCE THEY DISCHARGED THEMSELVES
SCUMBAG MUNT! I HOPE HE ROTS IN HELL!
THAT'S HORN, ON SCREEN. ONE OF YOUR OWN.
WHY DO THEY CALL HIM SCUM?
BECAUSE HE'S CELEBRATED BY HUMANS.
BECAUSE HE'S **MARRYING** ONE.

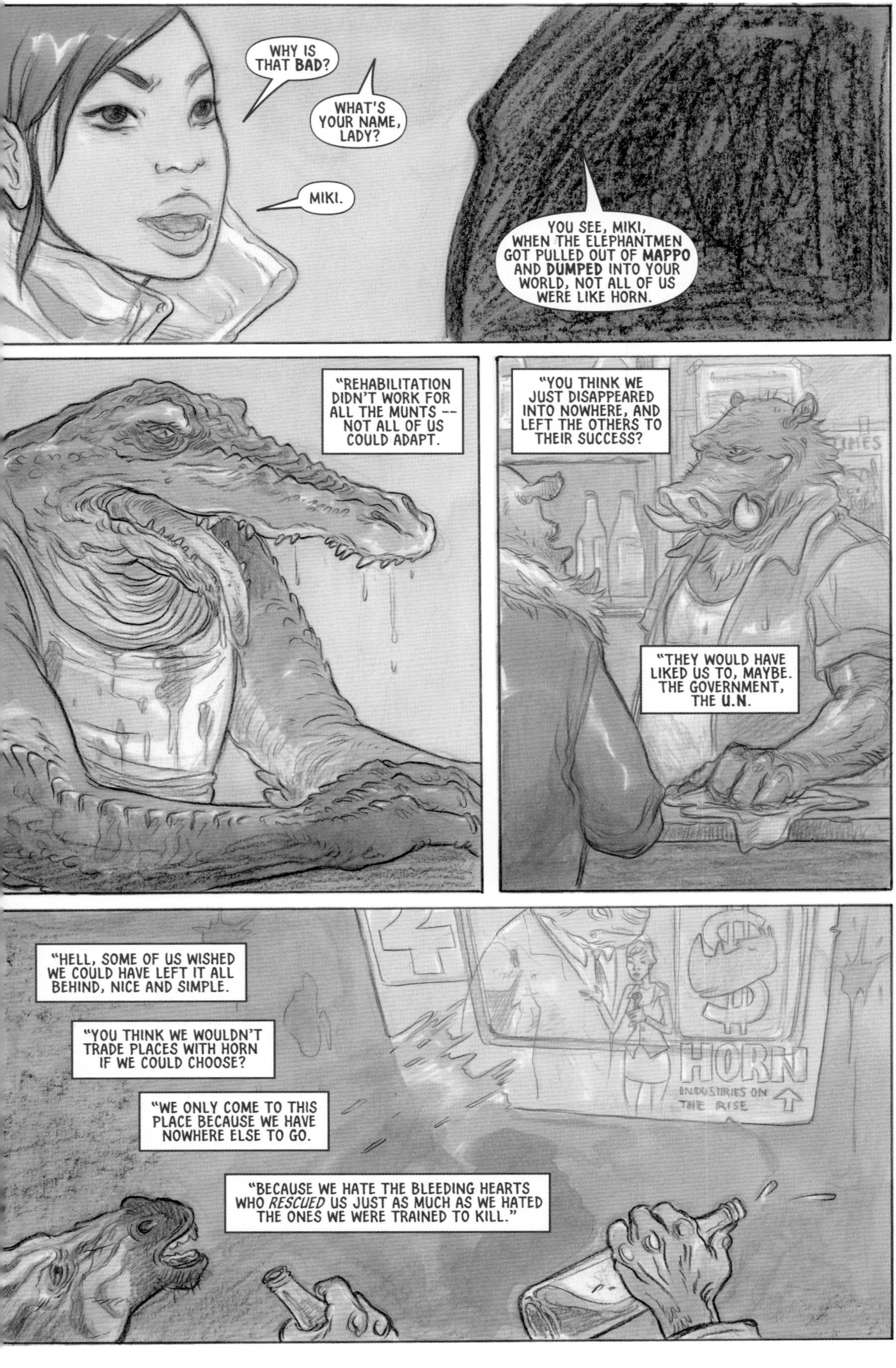
WHY IS THAT BAD?
WHAT'S YOUR NAME, LADY?
MIKI.
YOU SEE, MIKI, WHEN THE ELEPHANTMEN GOT PULLED OUT OF MAPPO AND DUMPED INTO YOUR WORLD, NOT ALL OF US WERE LIKE HORN.
"REHABILITATION DIDN'T WORK FOR ALL THE MUNTS -- NOT ALL OF US COULD ADAPT.
"YOU THINK WE JUST DISAPPEARED INTO NOWHERE, AND LEFT THE OTHERS TO THEIR SUCCESS?
"THEY WOULD HAVE LIKED US TO, MAYBE. THE GOVERNMENT, THE U.N.
"HELL, SOME OF US WISHED WE COULD HAVE LEFT IT ALL BEHIND, NICE AND SIMPLE.
"YOU THINK WE WOULDN'T TRADE PLACES WITH HORN IF WE COULD CHOOSE?
"WE ONLY COME TO THIS PLACE BECAUSE WE HAVE NOWHERE ELSE TO GO.
"BECAUSE WE HATE THE BLEEDING HEARTS WHO *RESCUED* US JUST AS MUCH AS WE HATED THE ONES WE WERE TRAINED TO KILL."
HORN
INDUSTRIES ON THE RISE

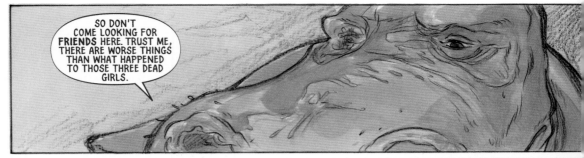

SO DON'T COME LOOKING FOR **FRIENDS** HERE. TRUST ME, THERE ARE WORSE THINGS THAN WHAT HAPPENED TO THOSE THREE DEAD GIRLS.

THERE STILL ARE.

THEY'RE DISTRACTED, NOW. I'LL SEE YOU OUT...

YOU NEVER SAID HOW THOSE GIRLS DIED. DID THAT CROC... DID HE **KILL** THEM?

HEY, CHOKER, WHERE DO YOU THINK YOU'RE GOING? WE NEED YOUR HELP IN HERE.

CHOKER...?

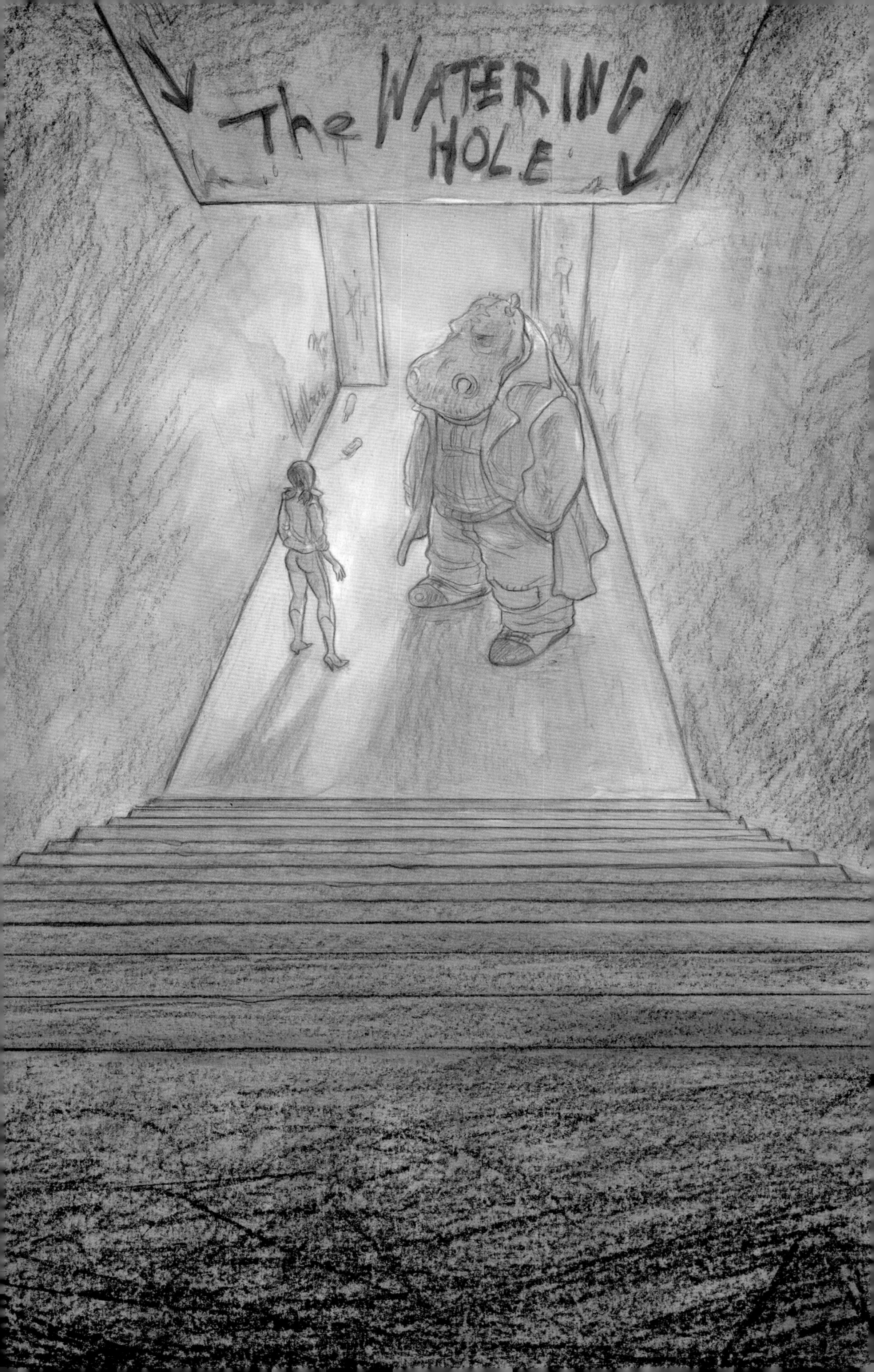
The WATERING HOLE

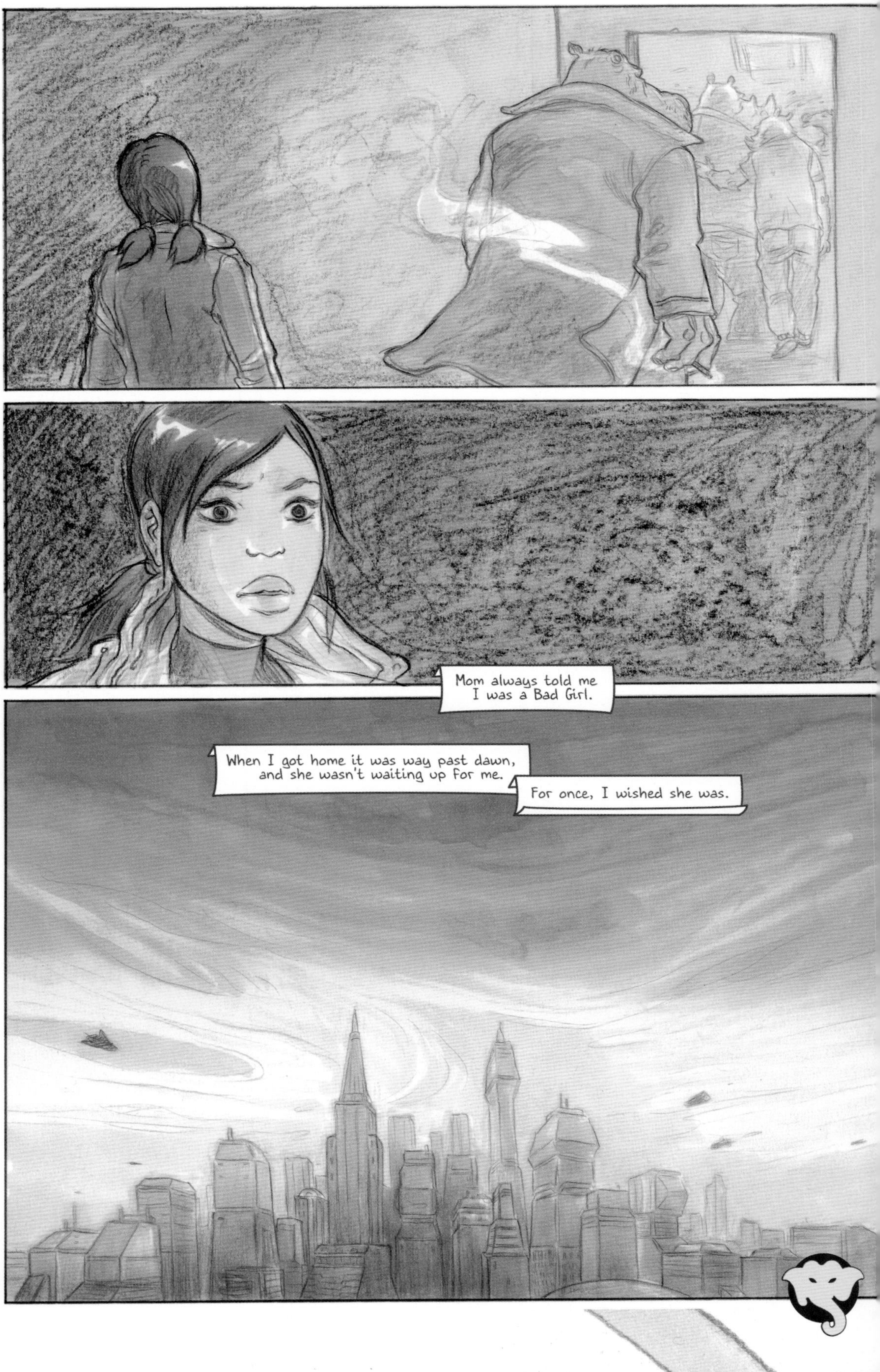

Mom always told me I was a Bad Girl.
When I got home it was way past dawn, and she wasn't waiting up for me.
For once, I wished she was.

RICHARD STARKINGS

is the creator of **HIP FLASK, ELEPHANTMEN** and his semi-autobiographical comic strip, **HEDGE BACKWARDS.** Born and raised in England, Starkings worked for five years at Marvel UK's London offices as editor, designer and occasional writer of **ZOIDS, GHOSTBUSTERS, TRANSFORMERS** and the **DOCTOR WHO** comic strip. He is perhaps best known for his work with the award-winning Comicraft design and lettering studio, which he founded in 1992 with John 'JG' Roshell. Starkings & Roshell also co-authored the best-selling books **COMIC BOOK LETTERING THE COMICRAFT WAY** and **TIM SALE: BLACK AND WHITE.**

MARIAN CHURCHLAND

was born in Canada in 1982, and was raised on a strict diet of fine literature and epic fantasy video games. She has a BA in Interdisciplinary Studies [English Literature and Visual Arts] from the University of British Columbia, and has been doing professional illustration work, including book covers and magazine articles, since she was 17. Last year, she became the first woman to solo-illustrate a **CONAN** story. She lives in Vancouver, BC with her gentleman caller [and fellow comic artist] Brandon Graham.

JG ROSHELL

grew up just an iPhone's throw from Apple headquarters in Northern California. True to his title as Comicraft's Secret Weapon, JG is currently working on a top-secret project in an undisclosed location, far from civilization.

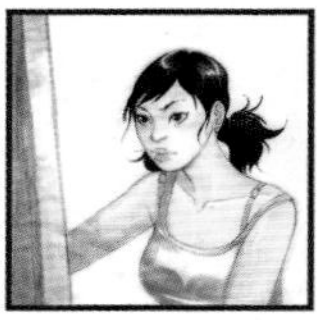

MARIAN CHURCHLAND SKETCHBOOK

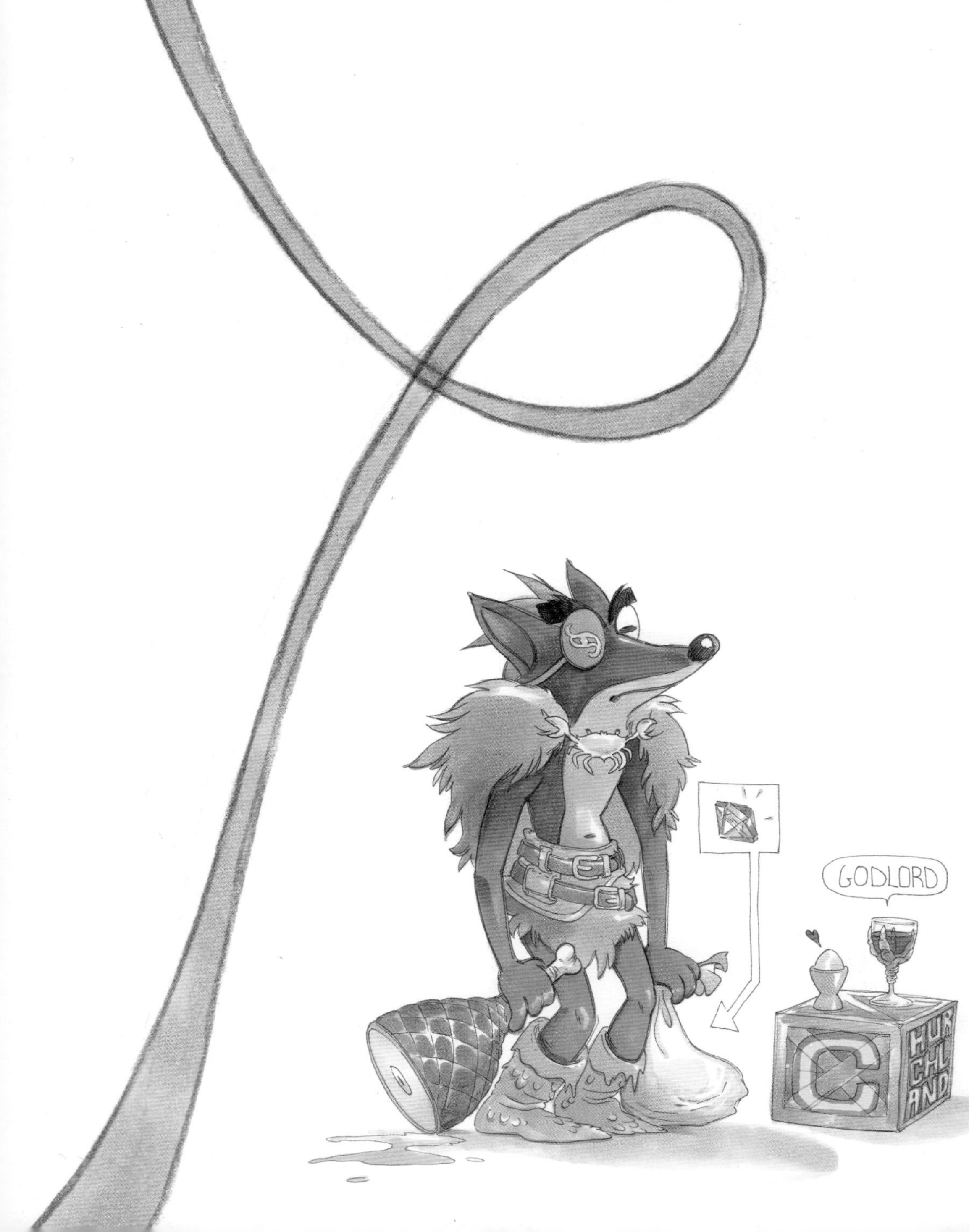

GODLORD
C
HUR
CHL
AND

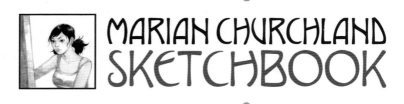

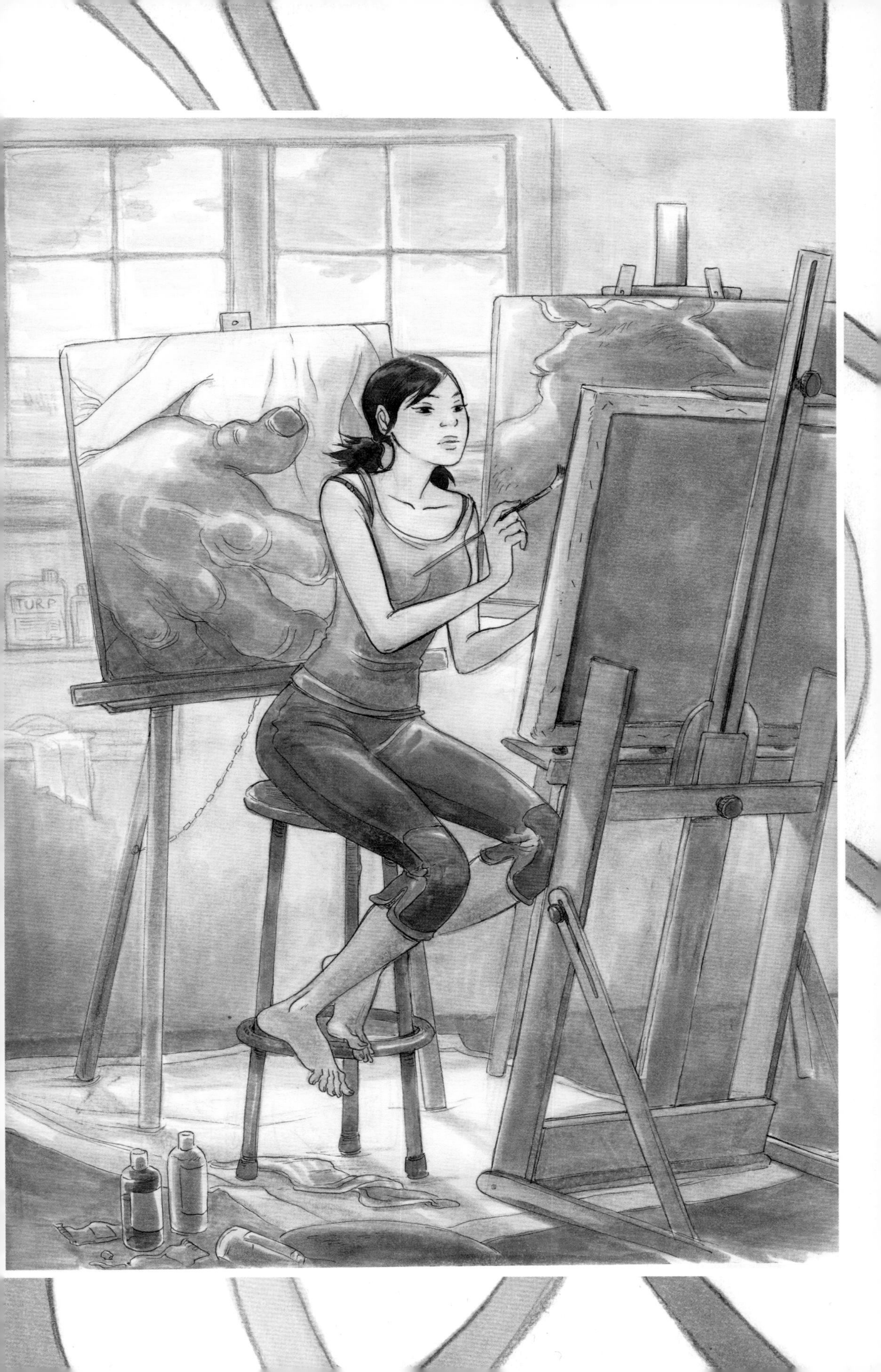
TURP

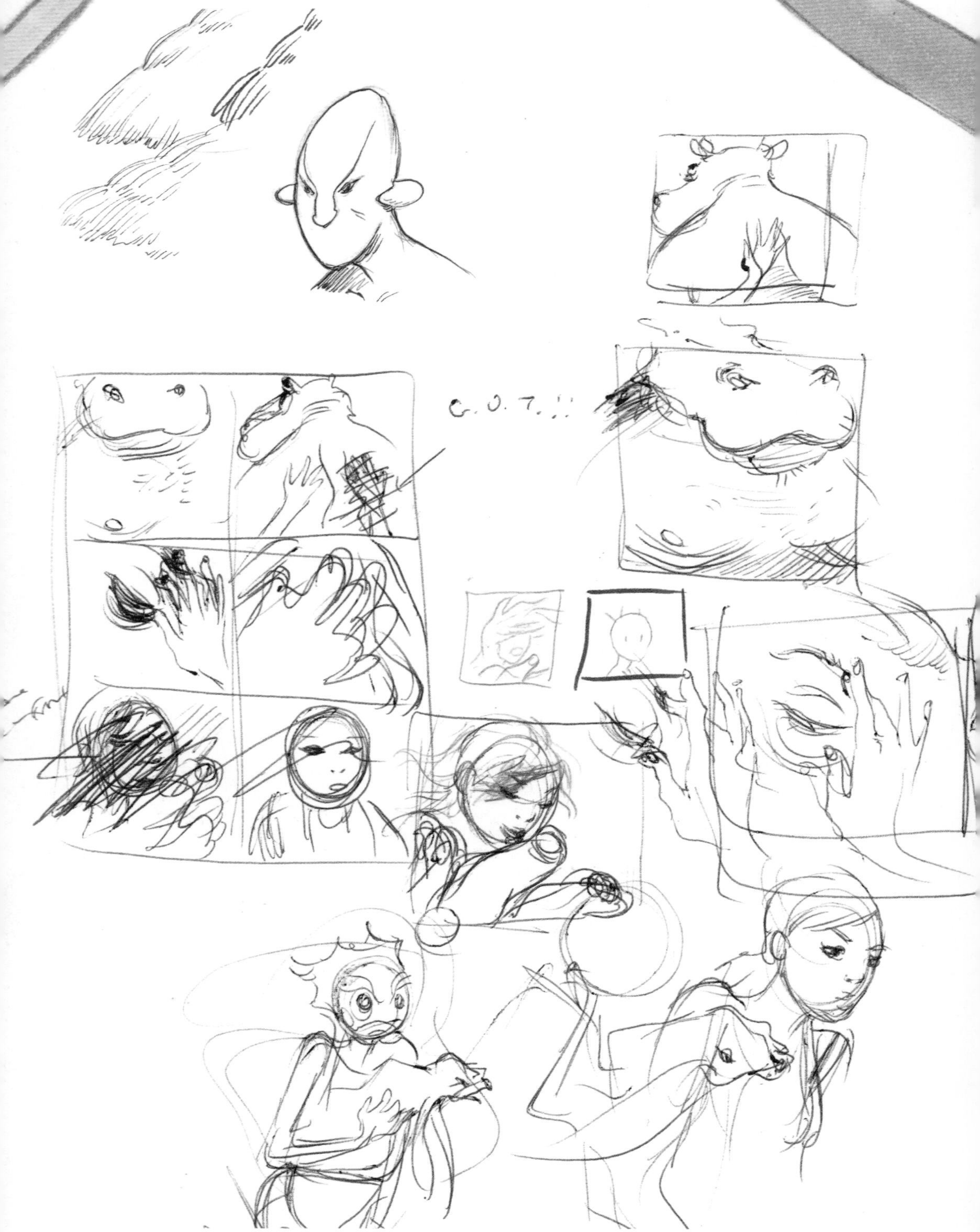
G.O.T.!!

Previous page and facing page opposite: Marian had originally intended to paint the first story in this collection in watercolours and then decided to switch to markers. She had already finished the first two pages before making her decision and recreated them with markers for the sake of consistency.

Above: Marian's thumbnails for the first page of **BAD GIRL**.
It's fun to see the mix of her character doodles with Miki and Hip.

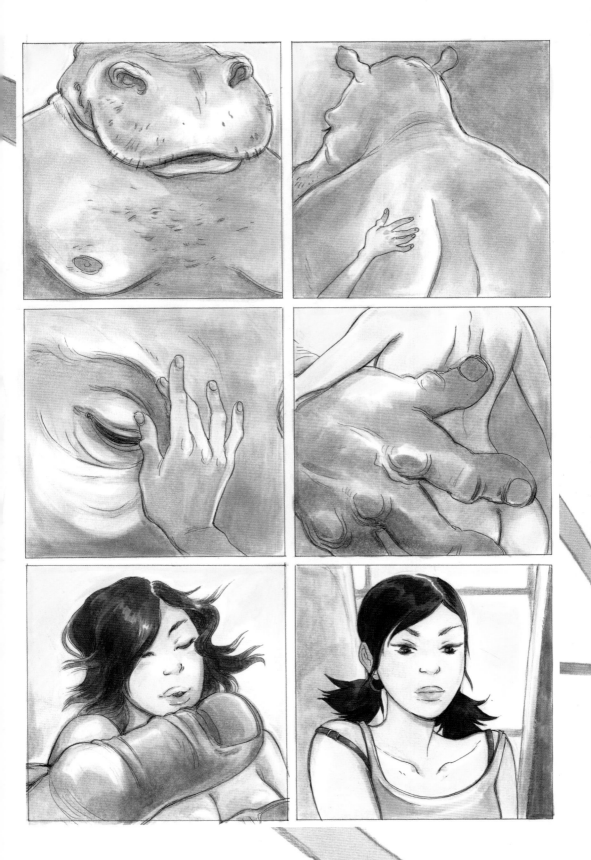

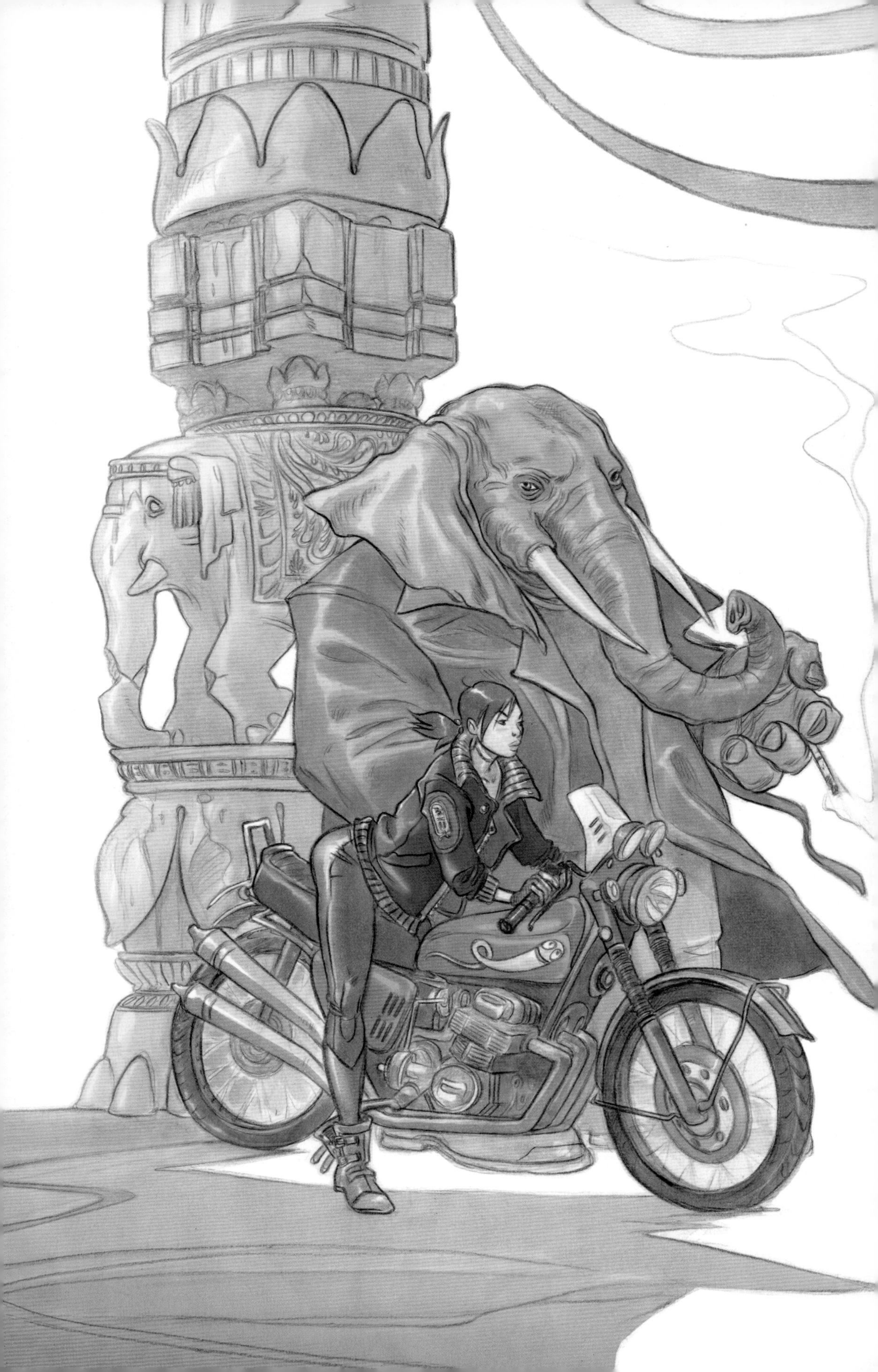

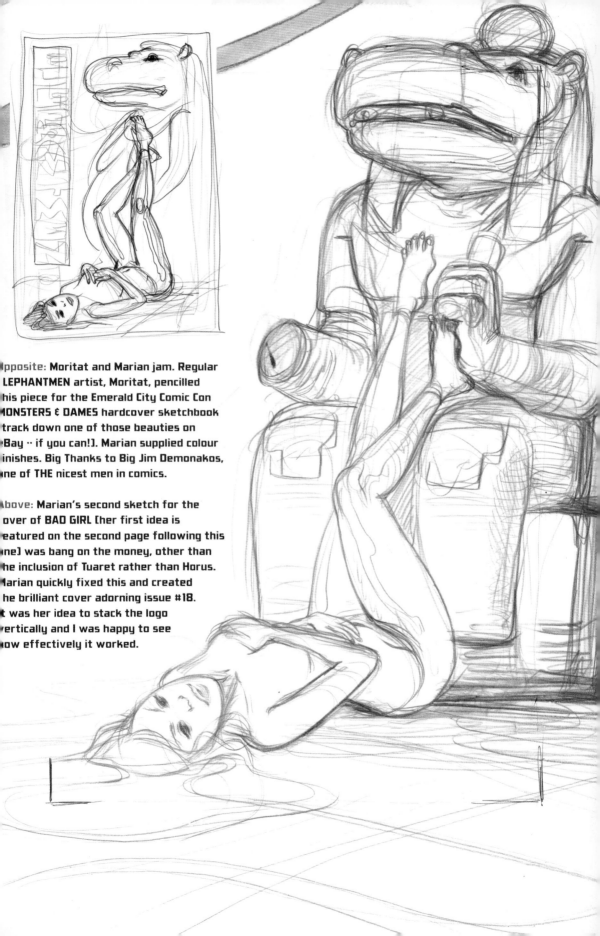

Opposite: Moritat and Marian jam. Regular ELEPHANTMEN artist, Moritat, pencilled this piece for the Emerald City Comic Con MONSTERS & DAMES hardcover sketchbook (track down one of those beauties on eBay ·· if you can!). Marian supplied colour finishes. Big Thanks to Big Jim Demonakos, one of THE nicest men in comics.

Above: Marian's second sketch for the cover of BAD GIRL (her first idea is featured on the second page following this one) was bang on the money, other than the inclusion of Tuaret rather than Horus. Marian quickly fixed this and created the brilliant cover adorning issue #18. It was her idea to stack the logo vertically and I was happy to see how effectively it worked.

Below: Marian's pencils for page 1 of THE WATERING HOLE

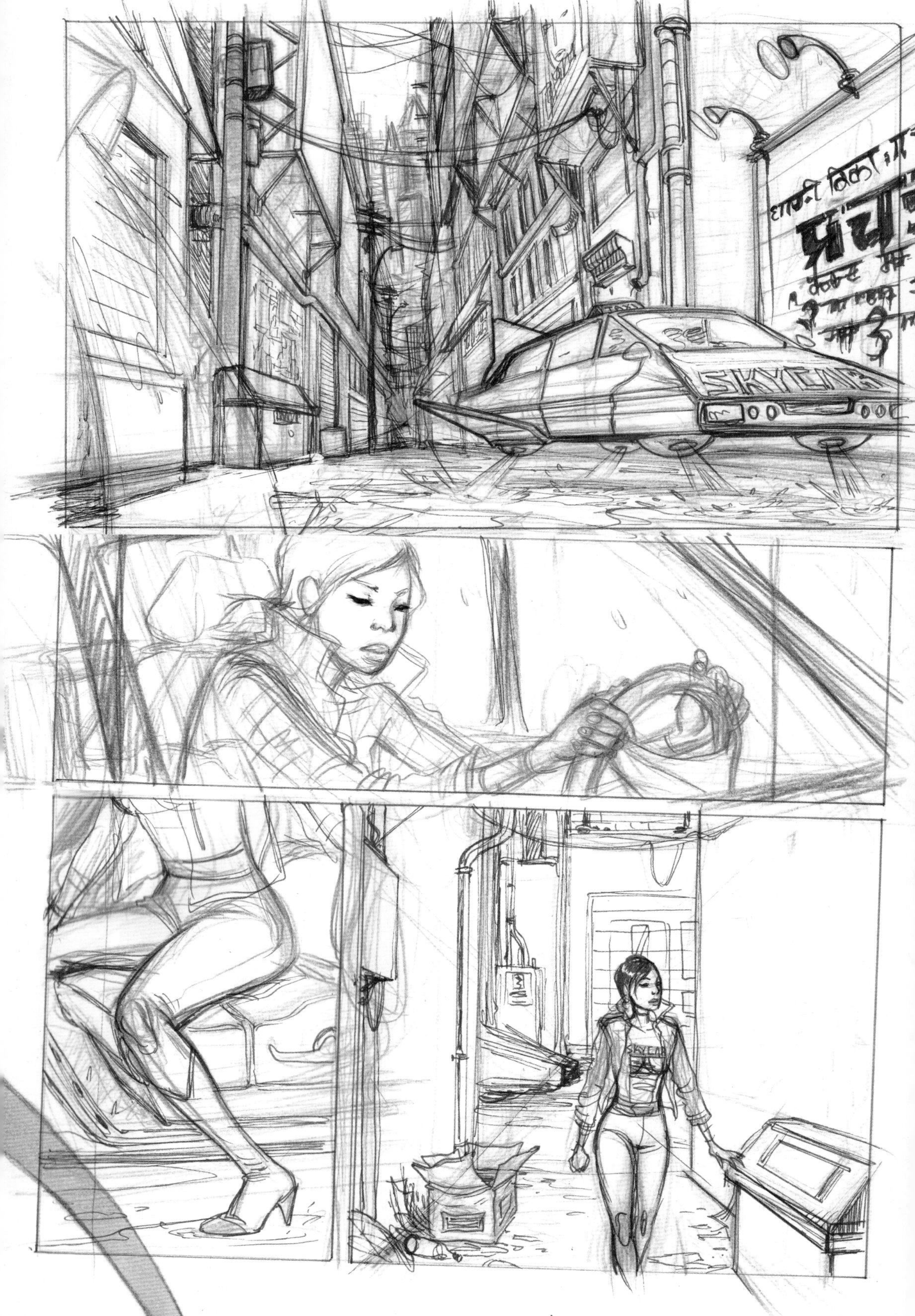
TAXI
SKYCAB

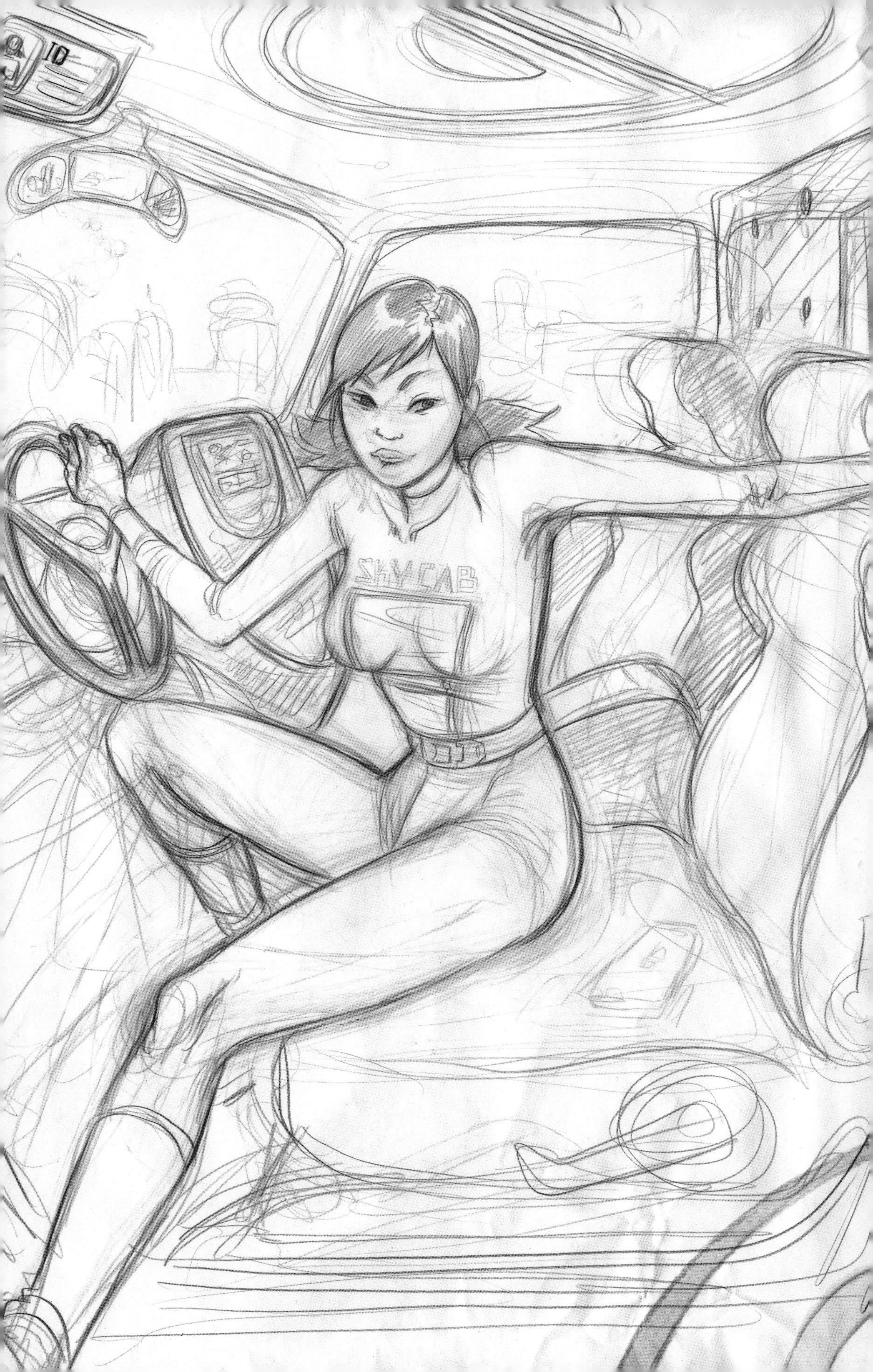
ID
SKY CAB

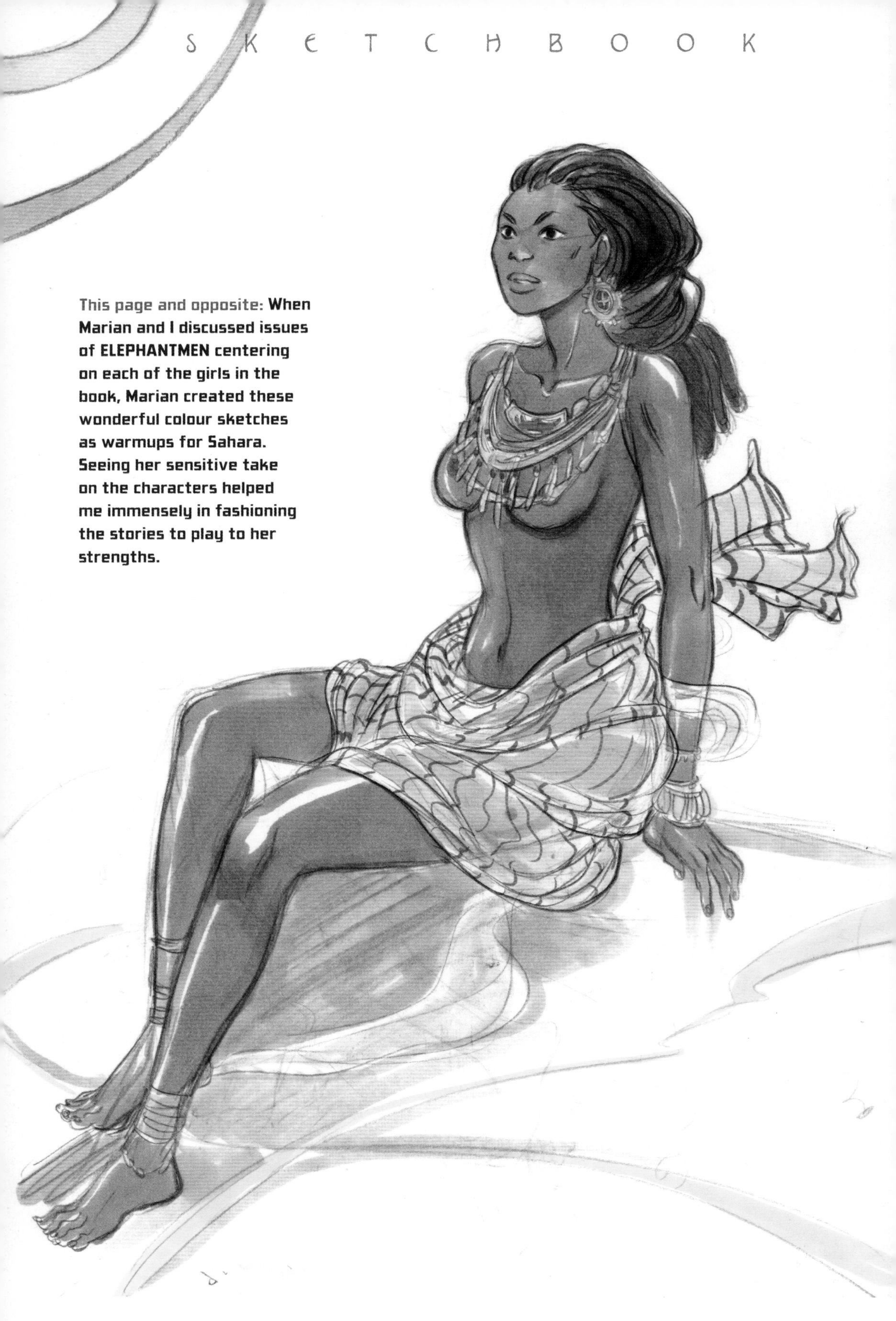

This page and opposite: **When Marian and I discussed issues of ELEPHANTMEN centering on each of the girls in the book, Marian created these wonderful colour sketches as warmups for Sahara. Seeing her sensitive take on the characters helped me immensely in fashioning the stories to play to her strengths.**

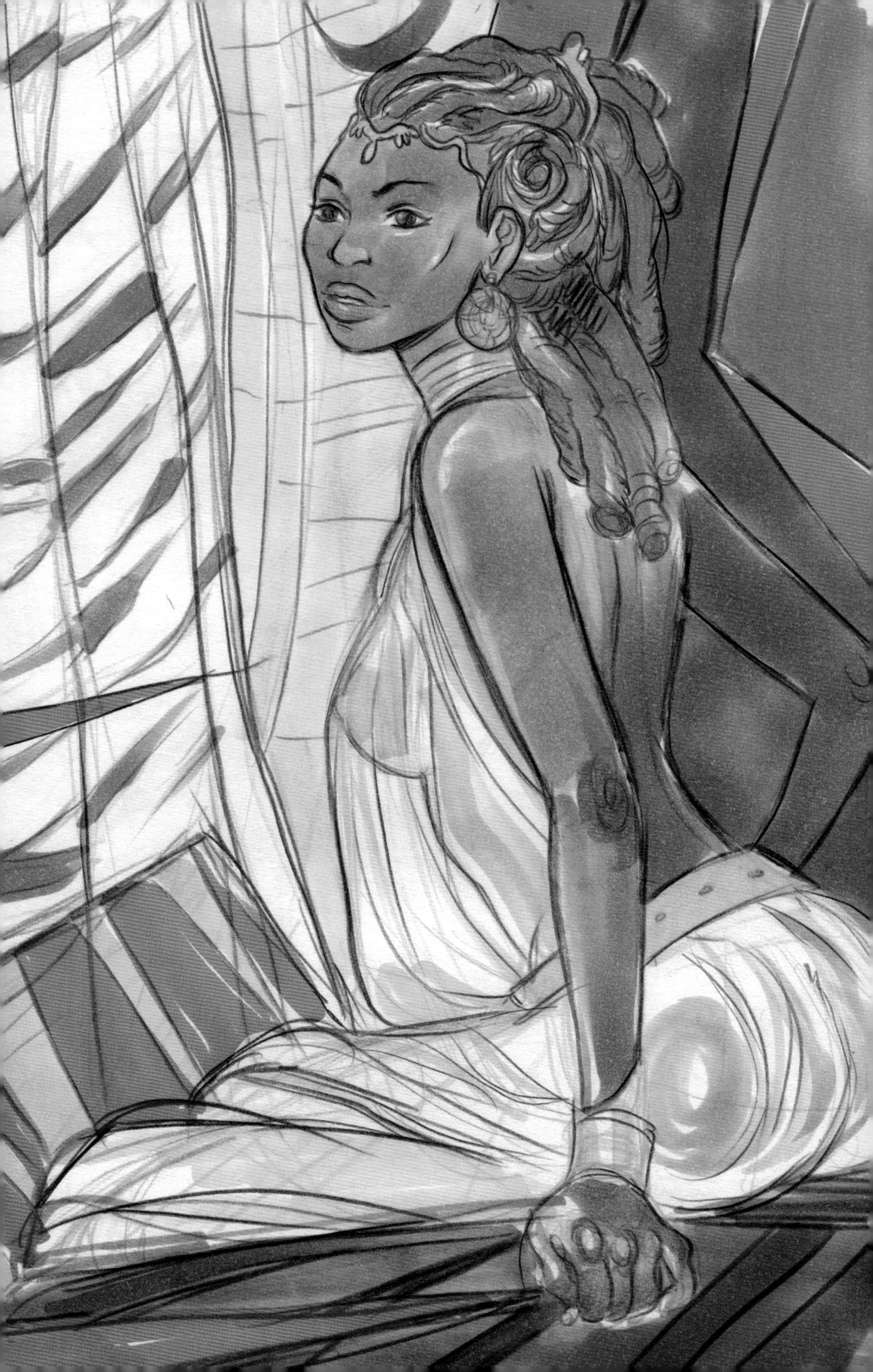

DADDY'S LITTLE GIRL was difficult to write an
Marian admitted to me that it was equall
difficult to draw. The cover was a challeng
too; you can see that Marian originall
wanted Horn's outline behind the drape i
the background. We eventually agreed tha
it was more ominous and appropriate t
suggest Serengheti's silhouette. I like tha
we can only see one of his hands – give
that he menaces Sahara with a swor
during the course of the story

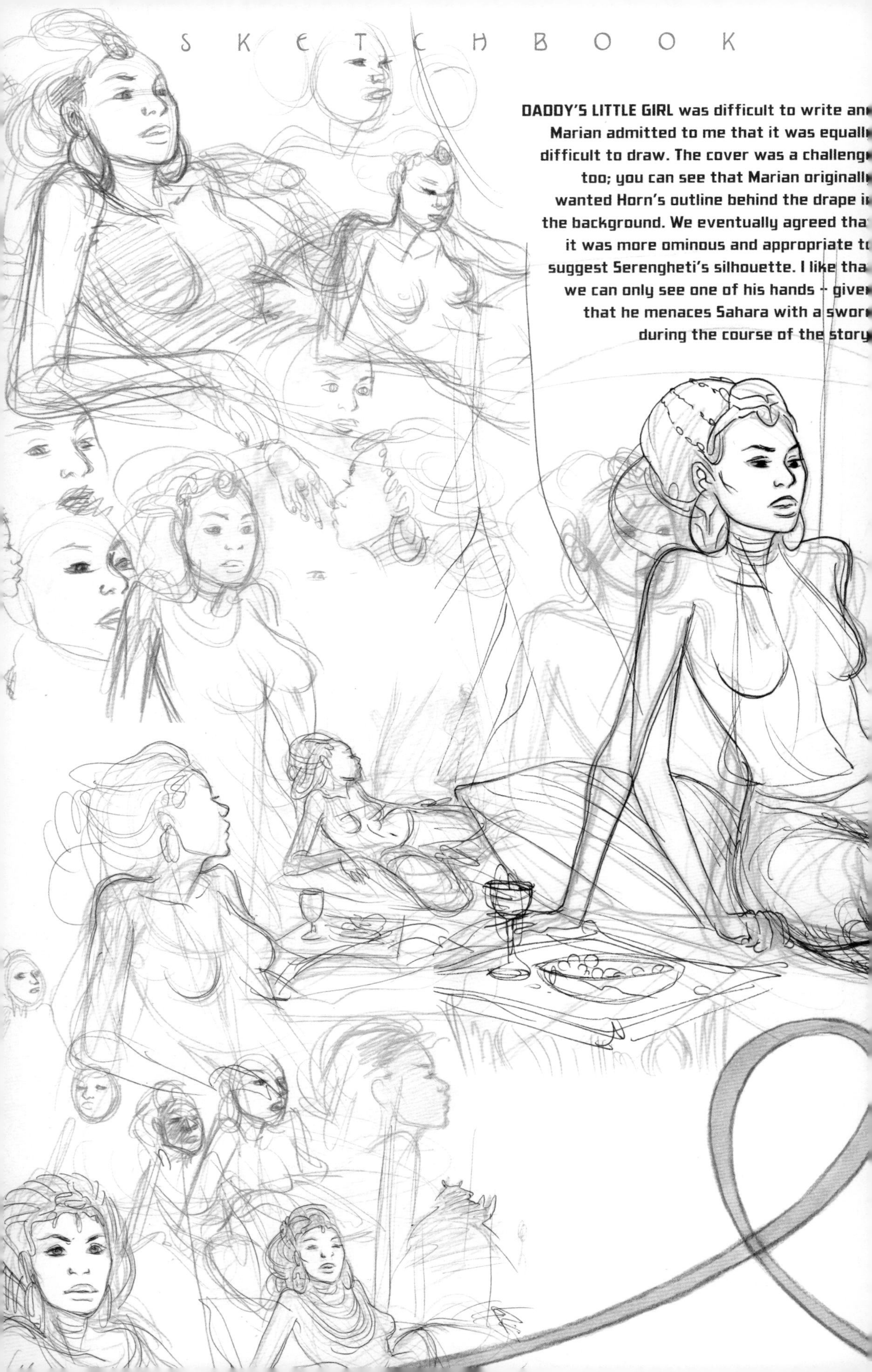

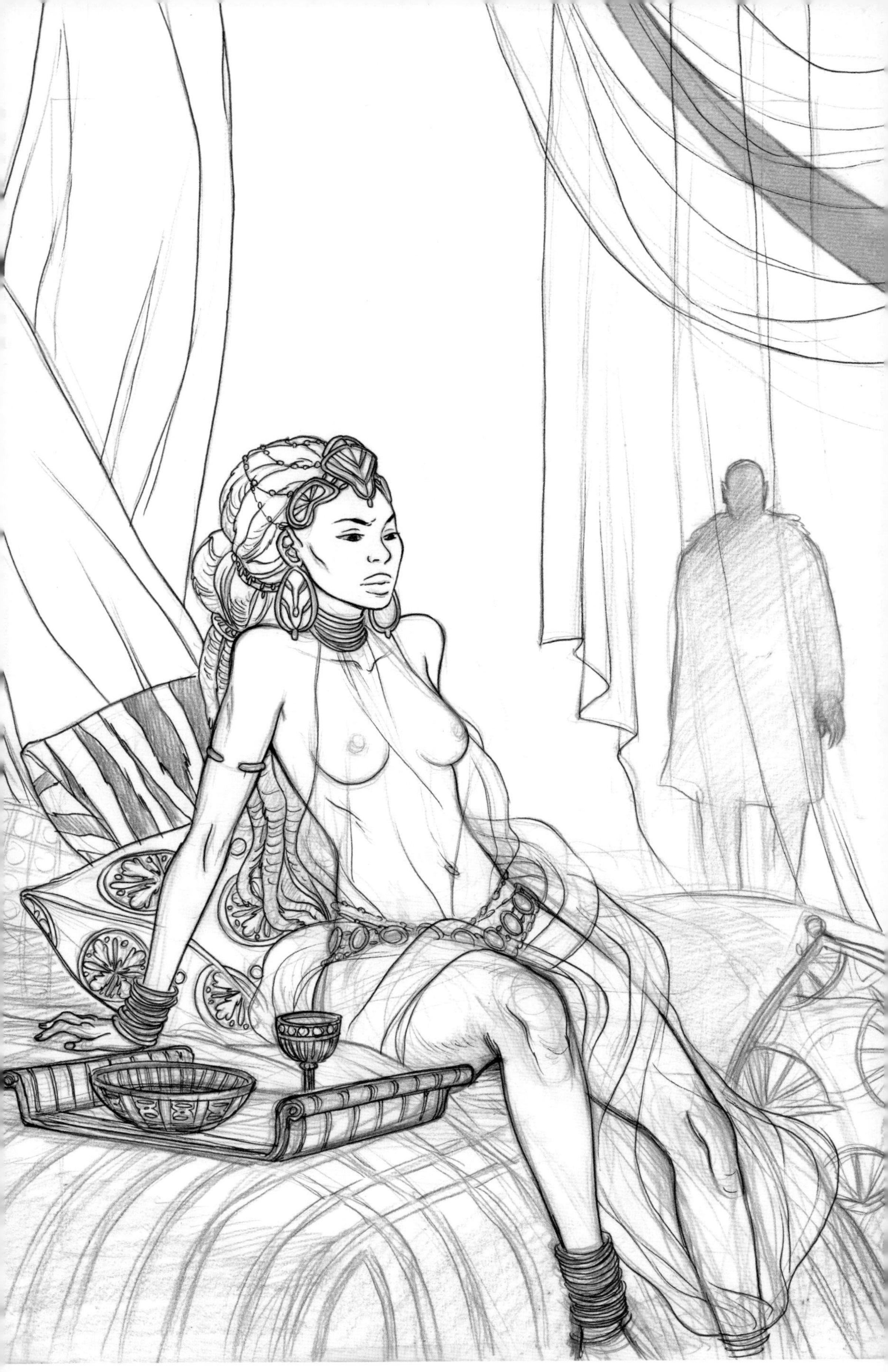

Vanity's story was actually drawn right after Miki's story. I had a very clear idea how the cover should look, but Marian made it her own nevertheless. I love the green canvas shoes Vanity is wearing. And check out the label on Vanity's jacket in the colour sketch!

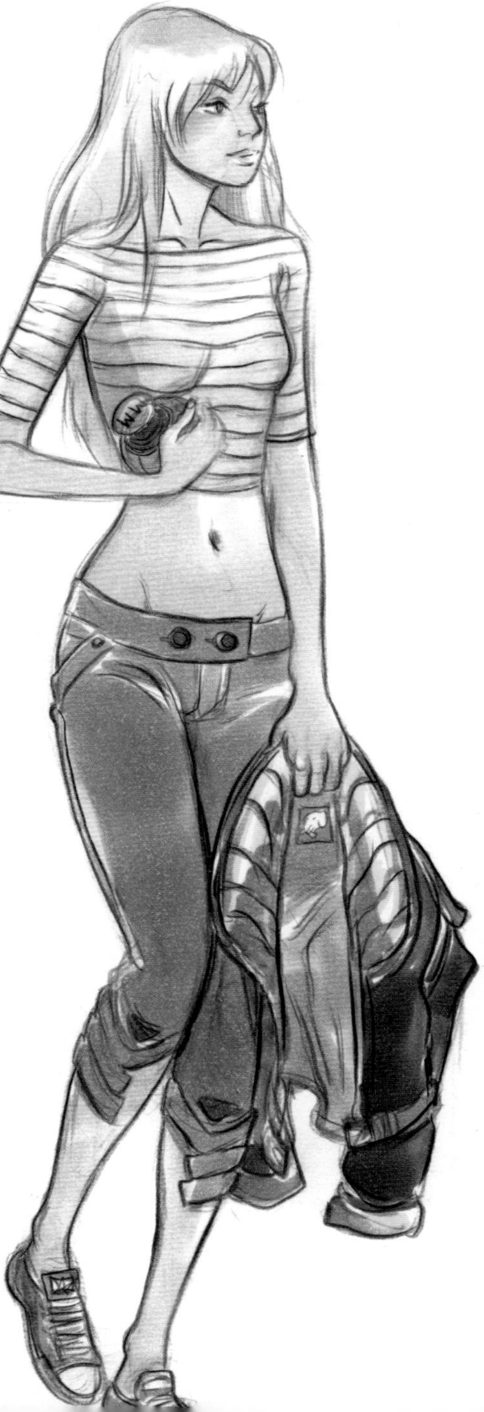

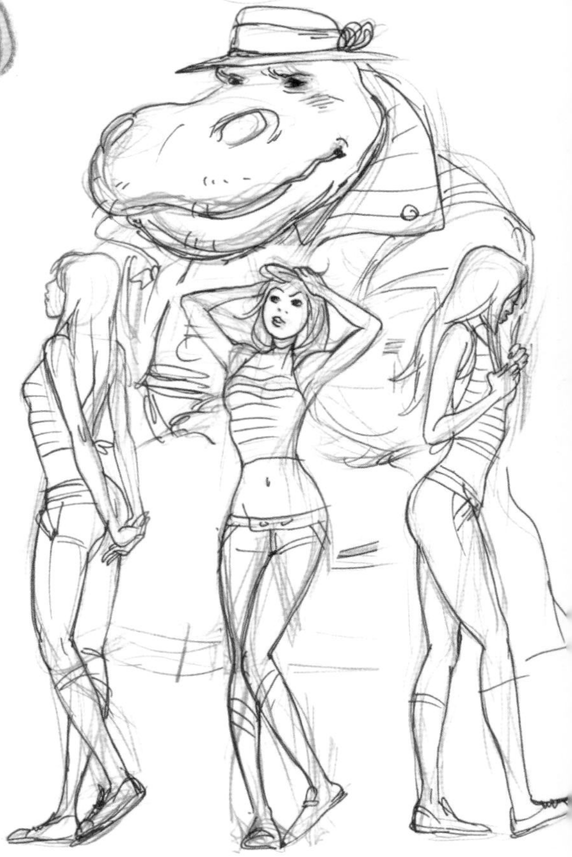

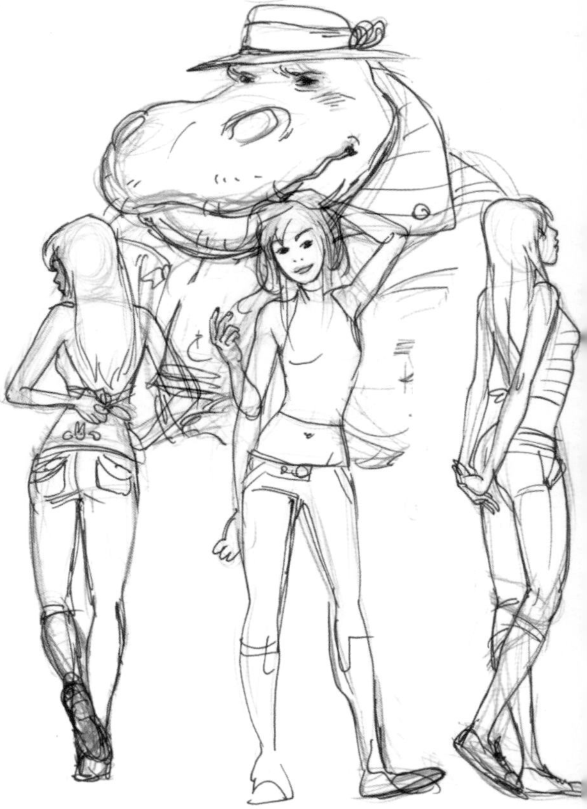

MARIAN CHURCHLAND

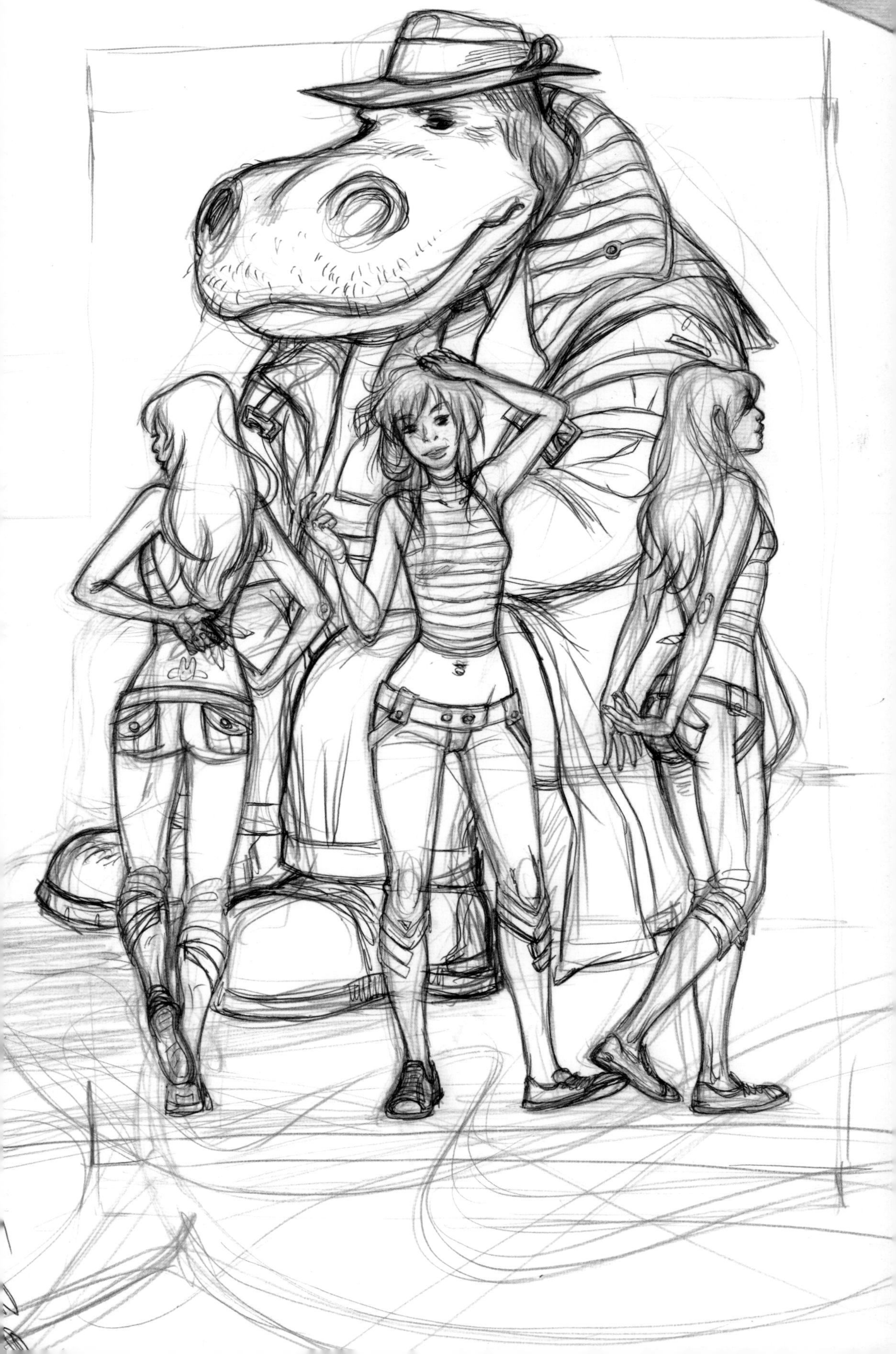

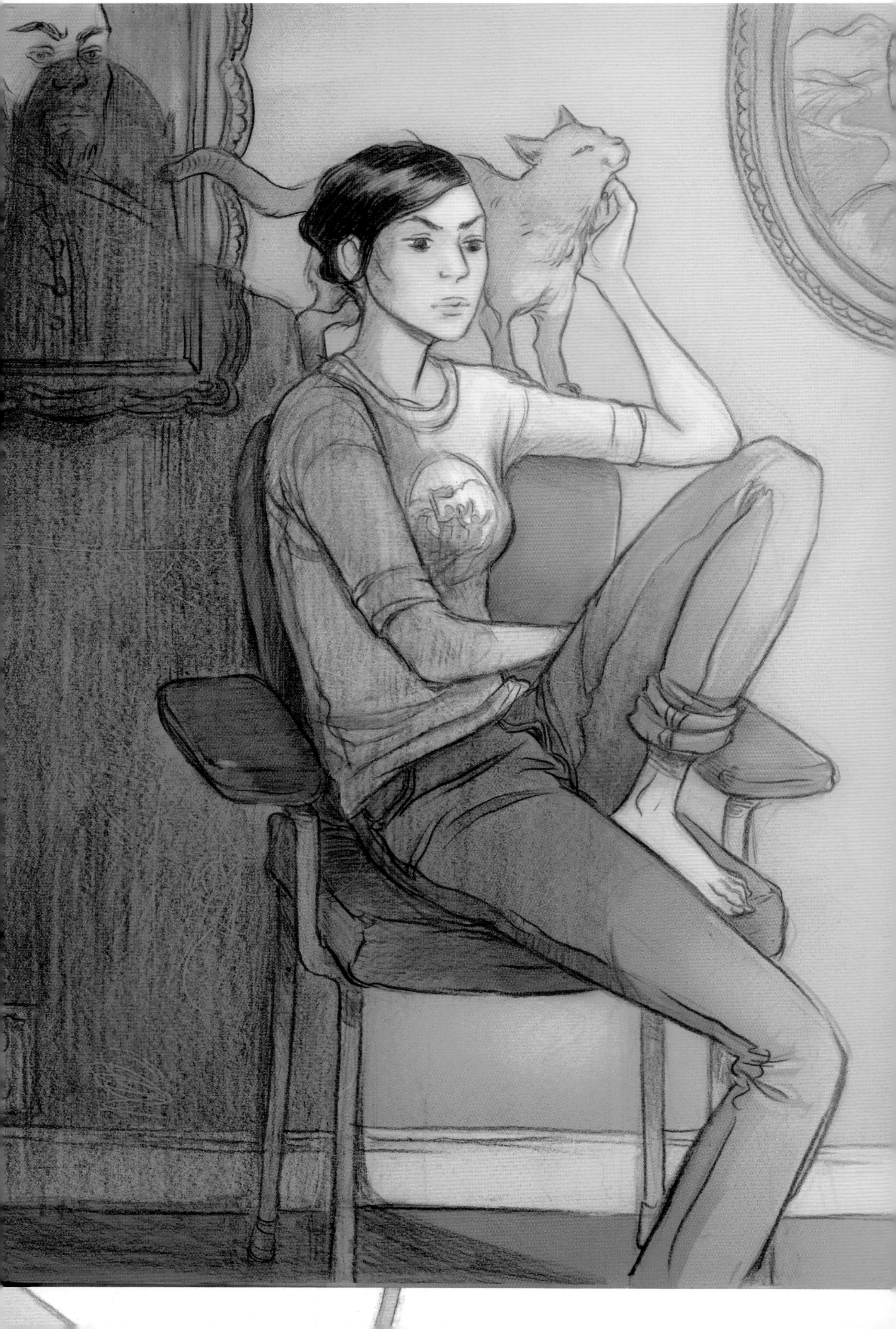

M A R I A N   C H U R C H L A N D

In the pages that follow, you'll see Marian's own imagination at work, unhampered by my clumsy attempts to have her tell MY story! Most of the drawings need no explanation, although I do want to draw your attention to the illustration of Colette opposite. Marian is still putting the finishing touches to her 150 page graphic novel, BEAST. Colette is one of the characters from the graphic novel; fingers crossed, we'll be seeing it in all good comic book stores later this year. Keep a close eye on the editorial pages of ELEPHANTMEN -- we'll let you know as soon as we know.

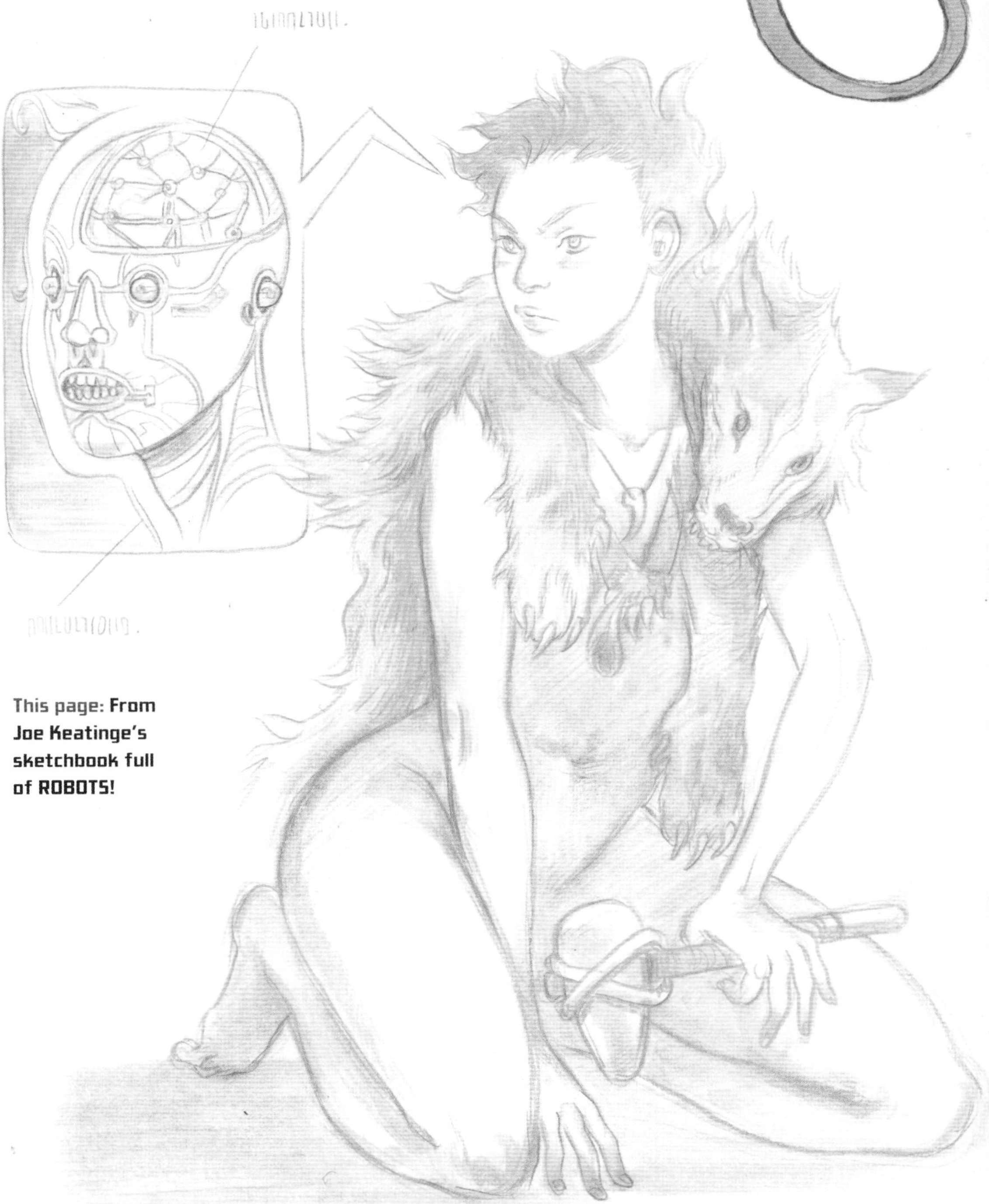

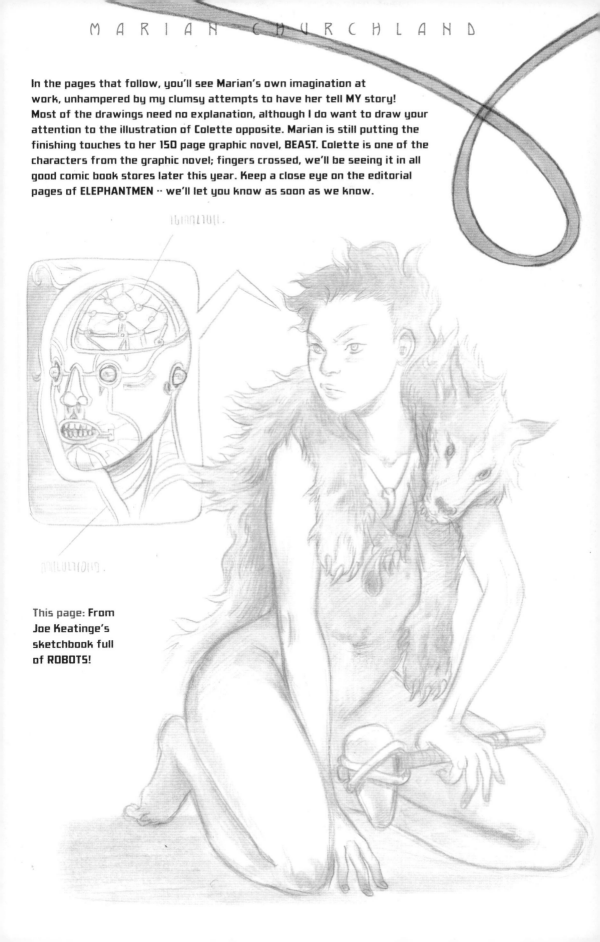

This page: **From Joe Keatinge's sketchbook full of ROBOTS!**

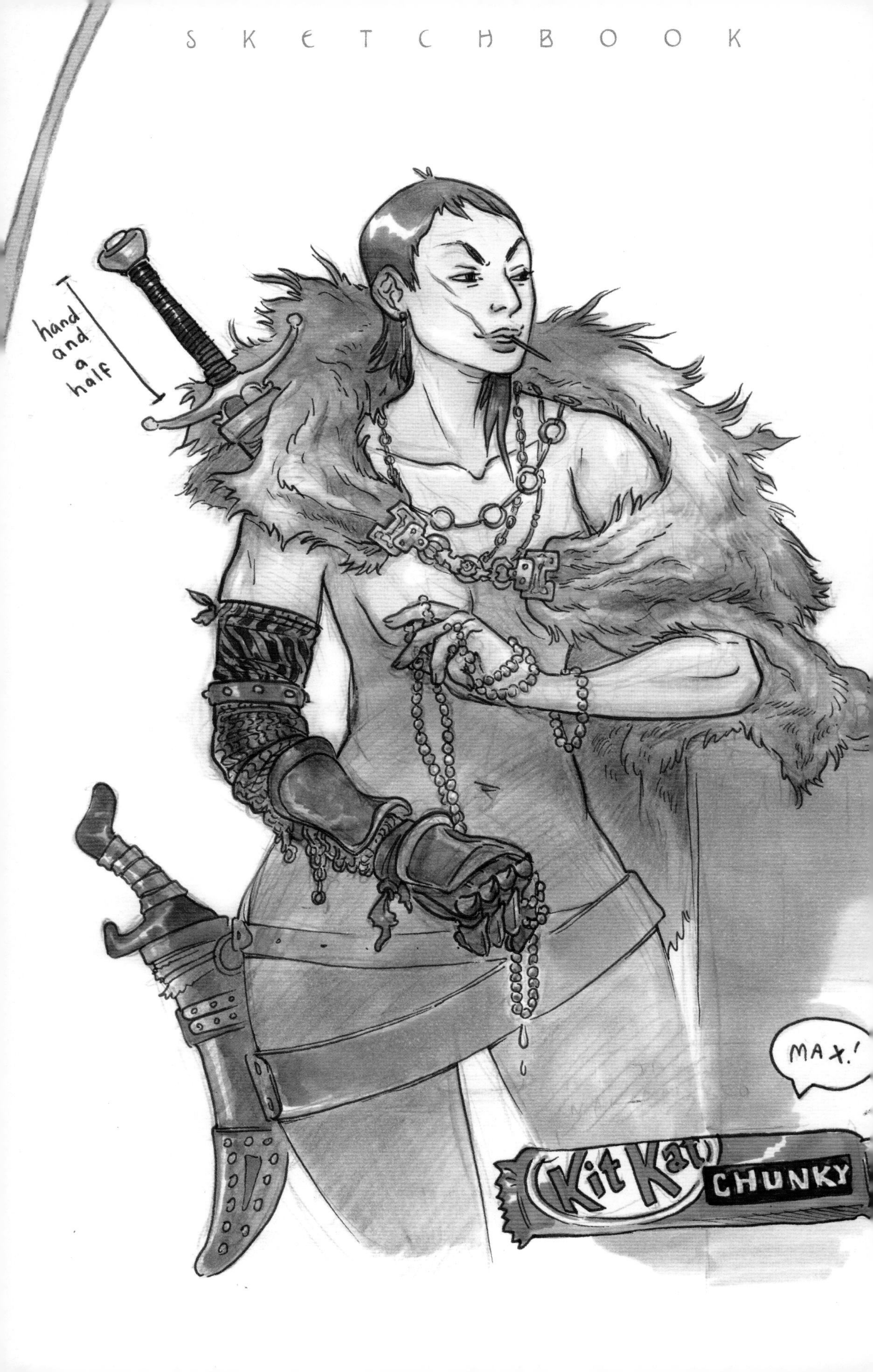
hand and a half
MAX!
KitKat
CHUNKY

M A R I A N   C H U R C H L A N D

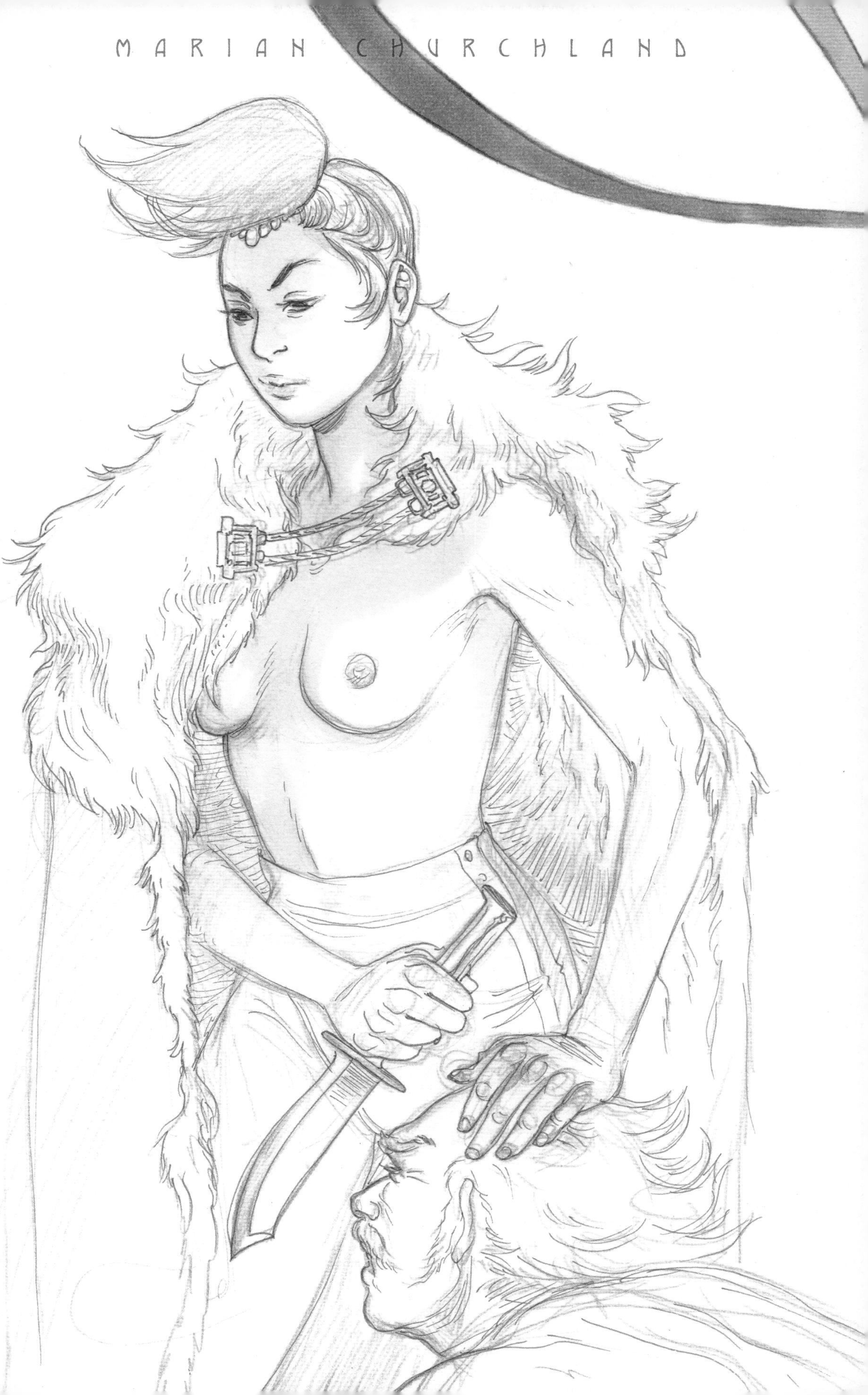

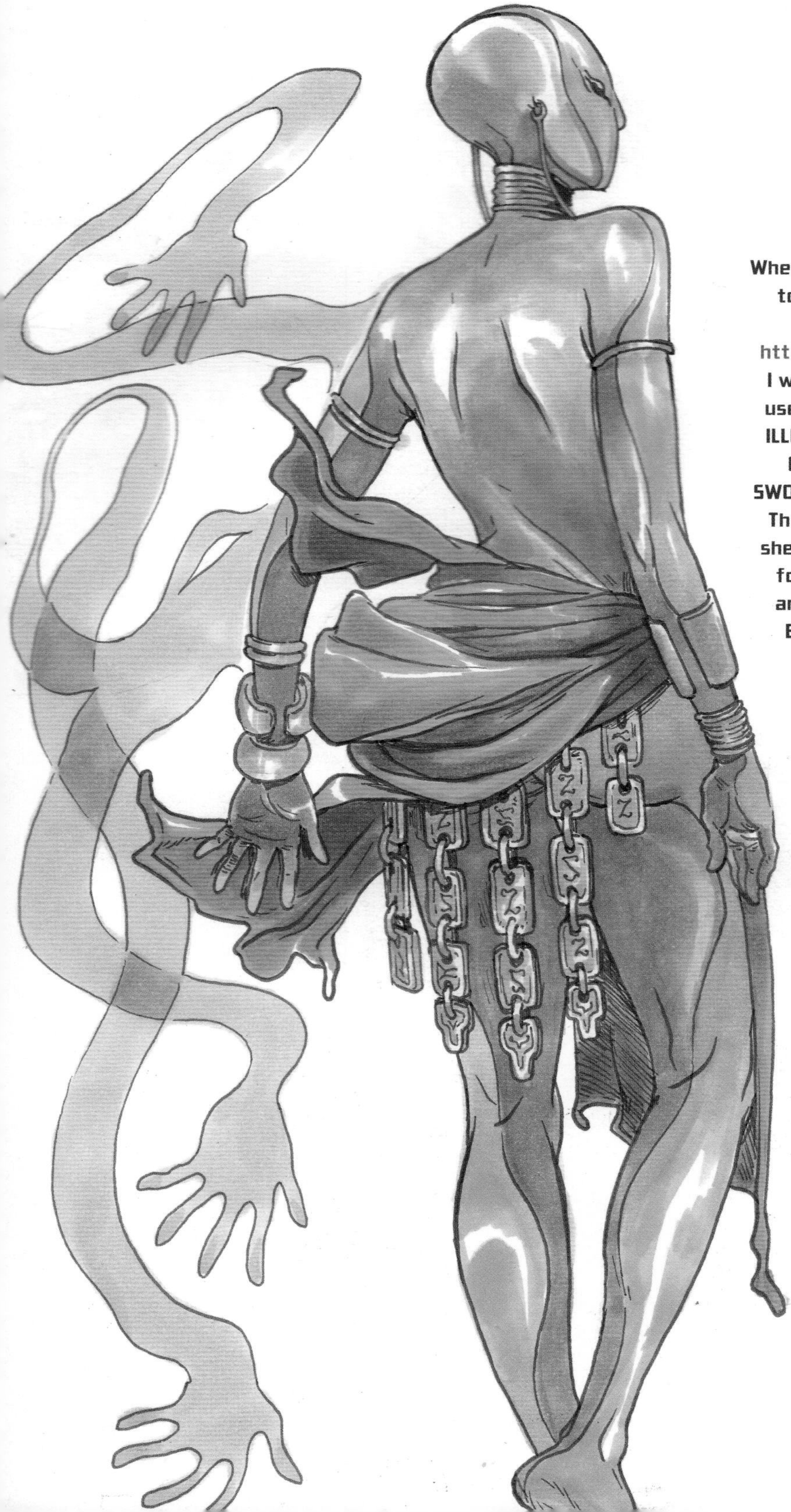

THE FIGHT

When Moritat drew my attention to the strip that follows on Marian's DeviantArt site http://nernie.deviantart.com/ I was reminded of the strips I used to love in books like EPIC ILLUSTRATED, edited by Archie Goodwin and THE SAVAGE SWORD OF CONAN, edited by Roy Thomas. and I instantly knew she'd be able to handle a story for ELEPHANTMEN... Moritat arranged an introduction at ECCC in 2008 and here we are three issues later!

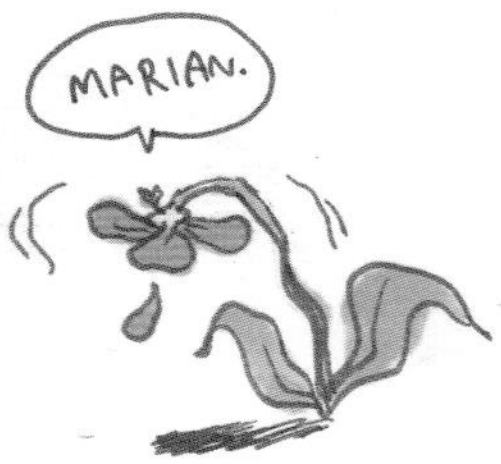
MARIAN.

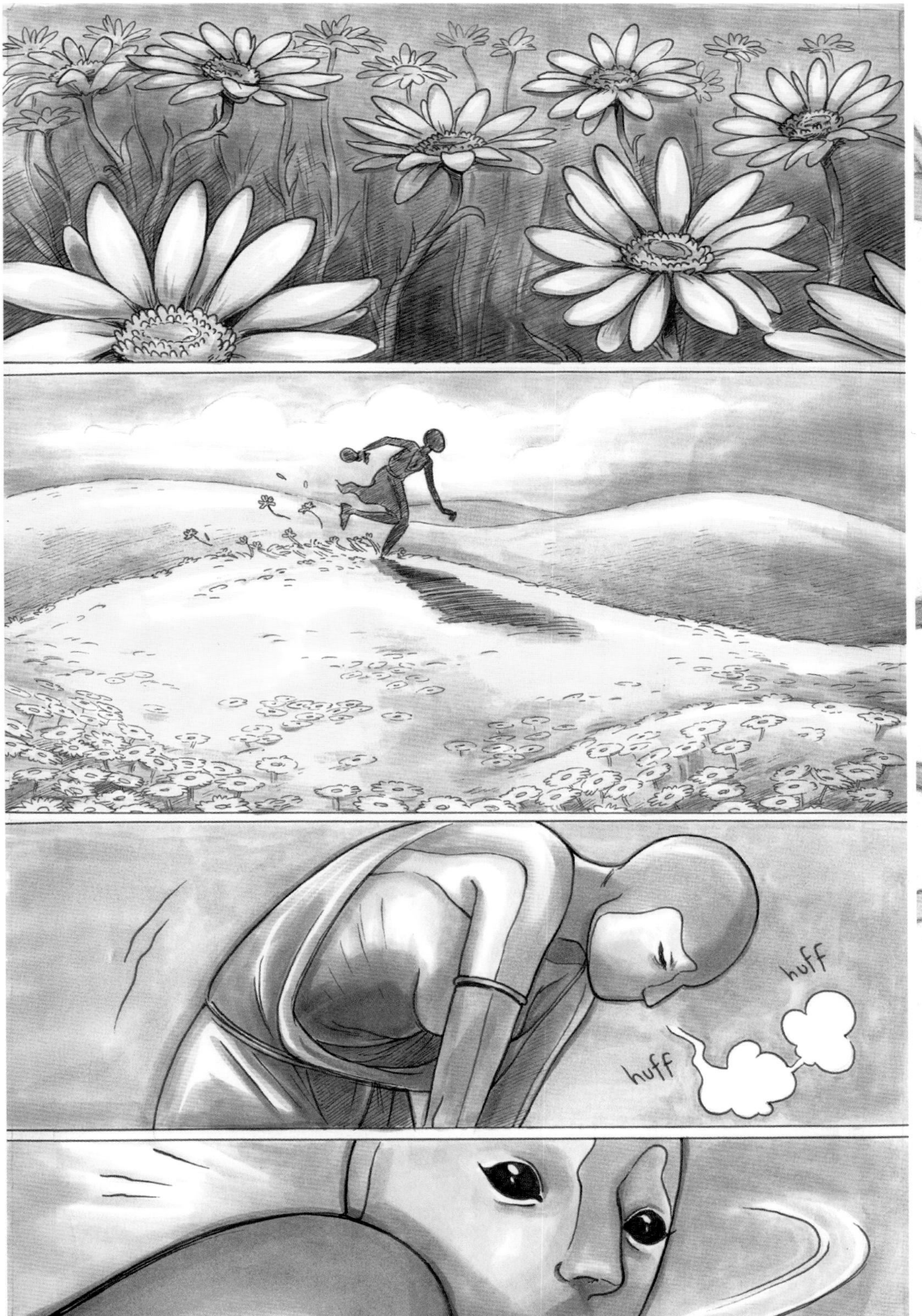
huff
huff

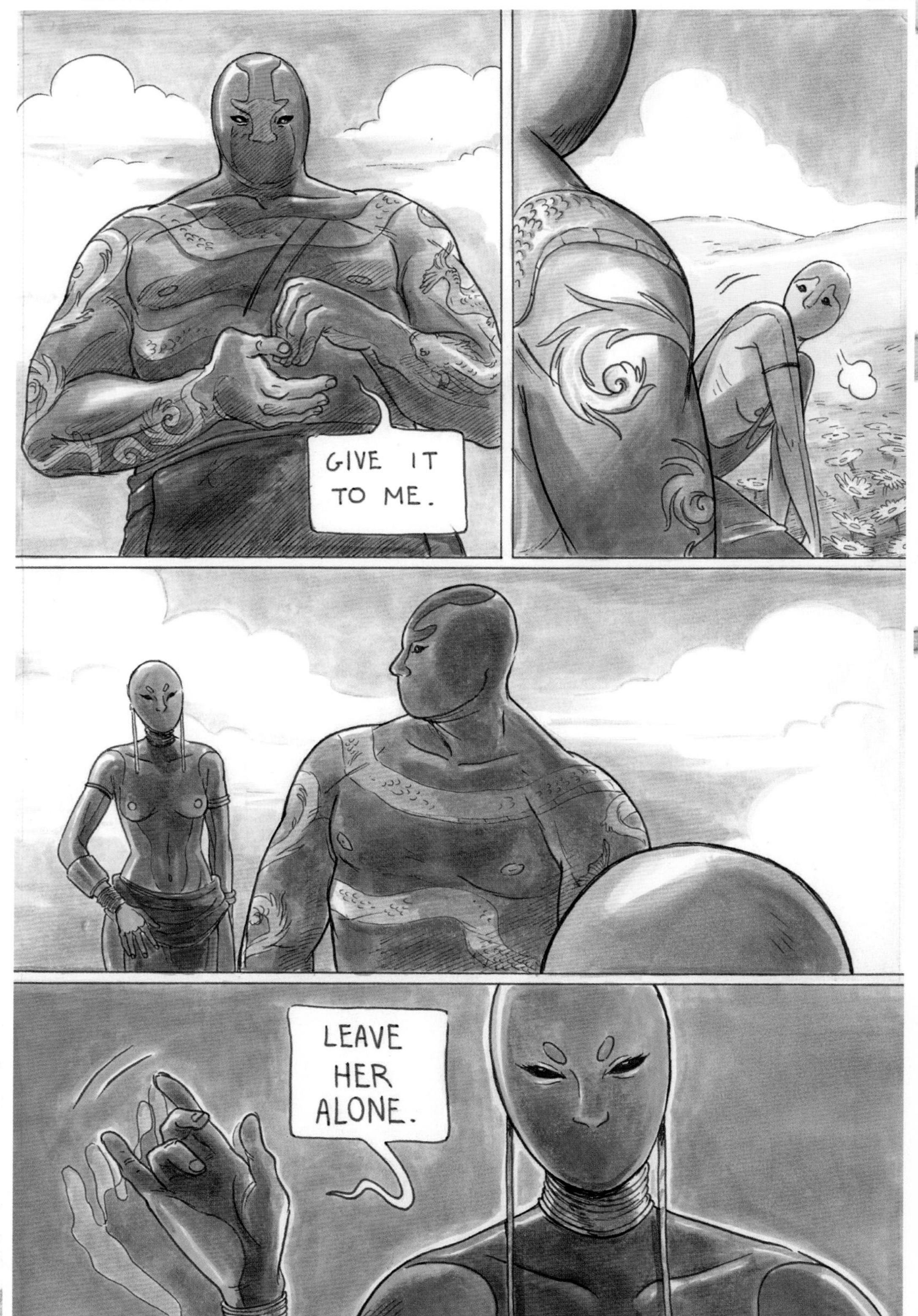
GIVE IT TO ME.
LEAVE HER ALONE.

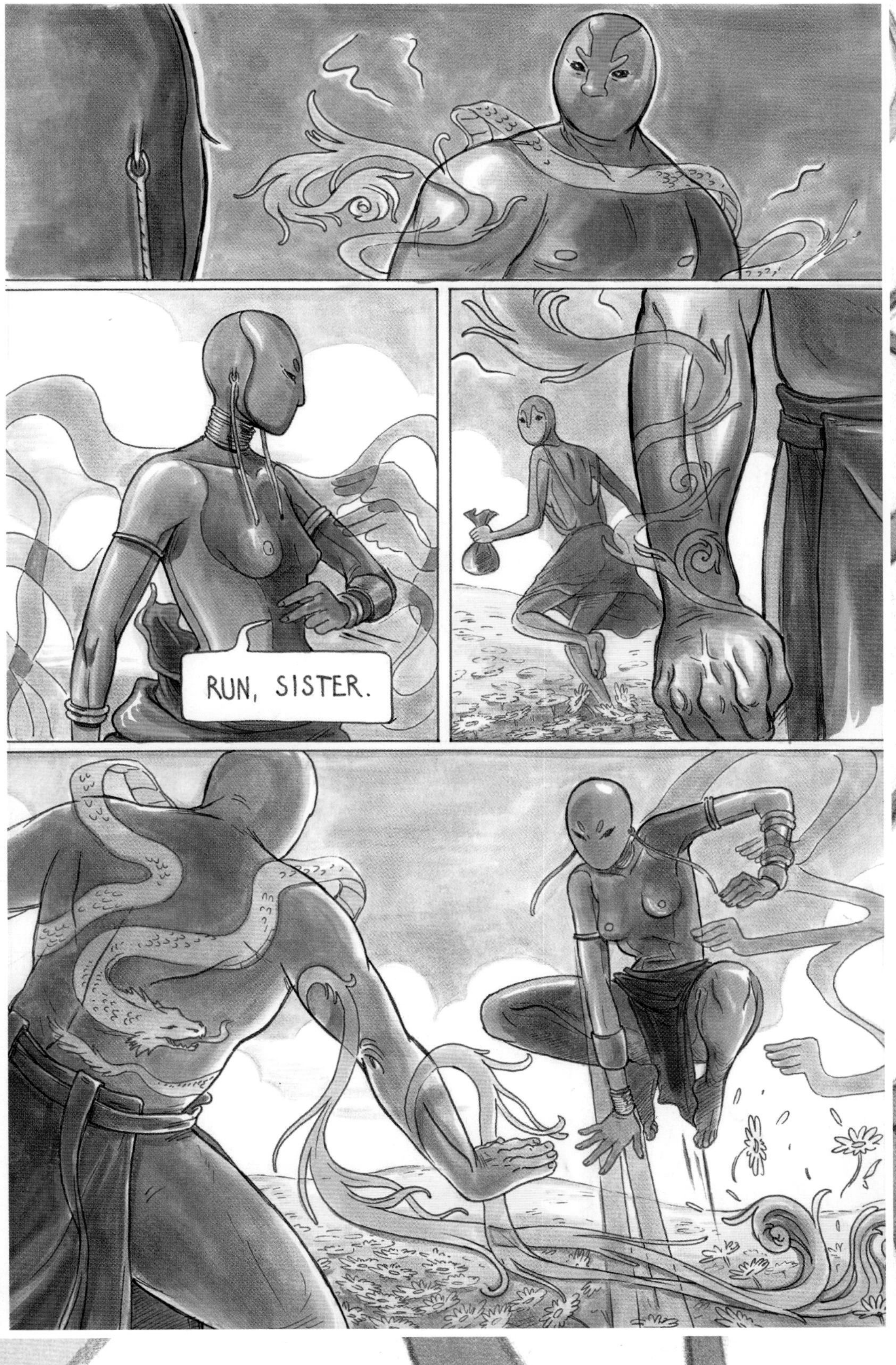
RUN, SISTER.

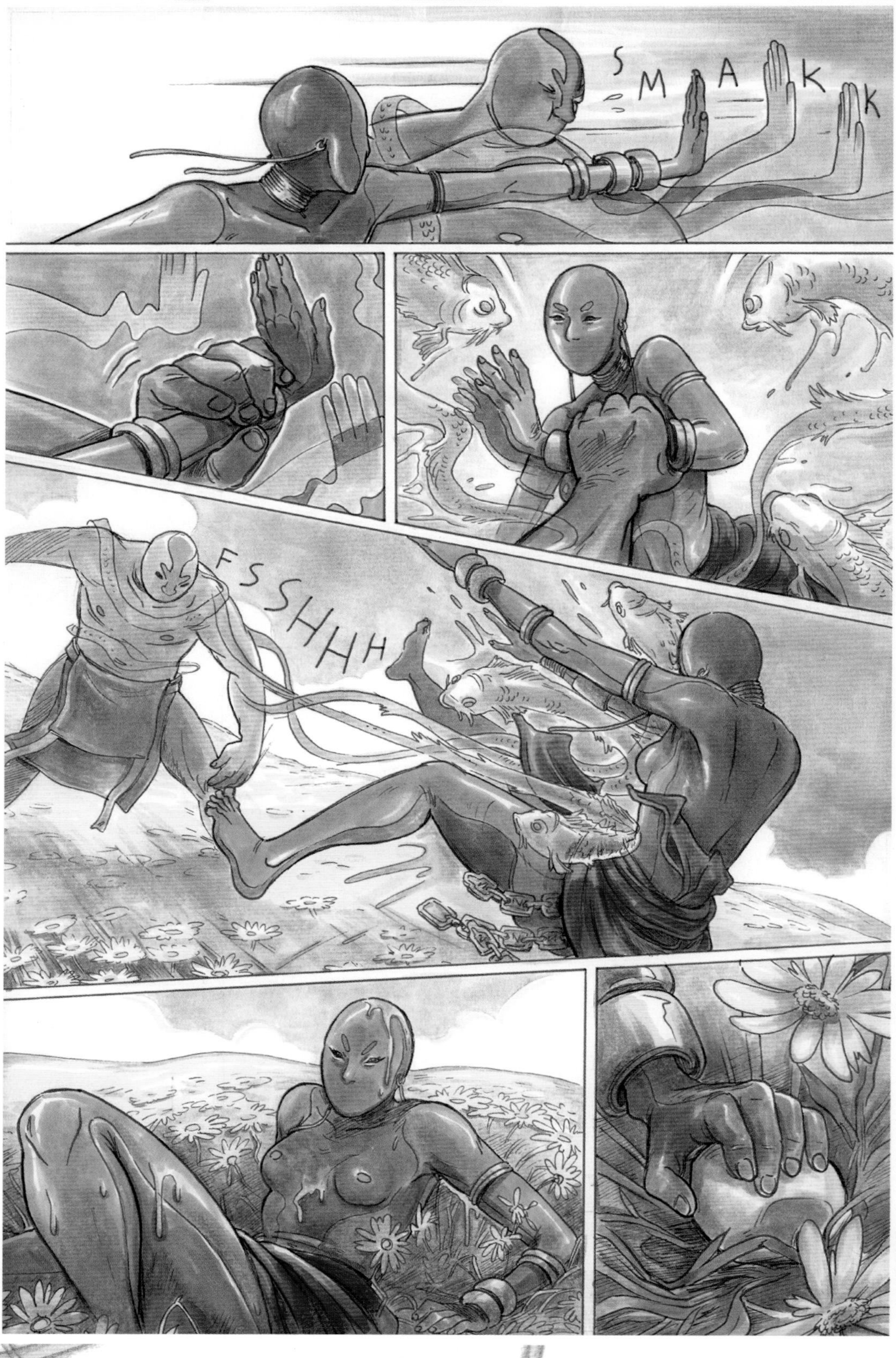
SMAKKK
FSSHHH

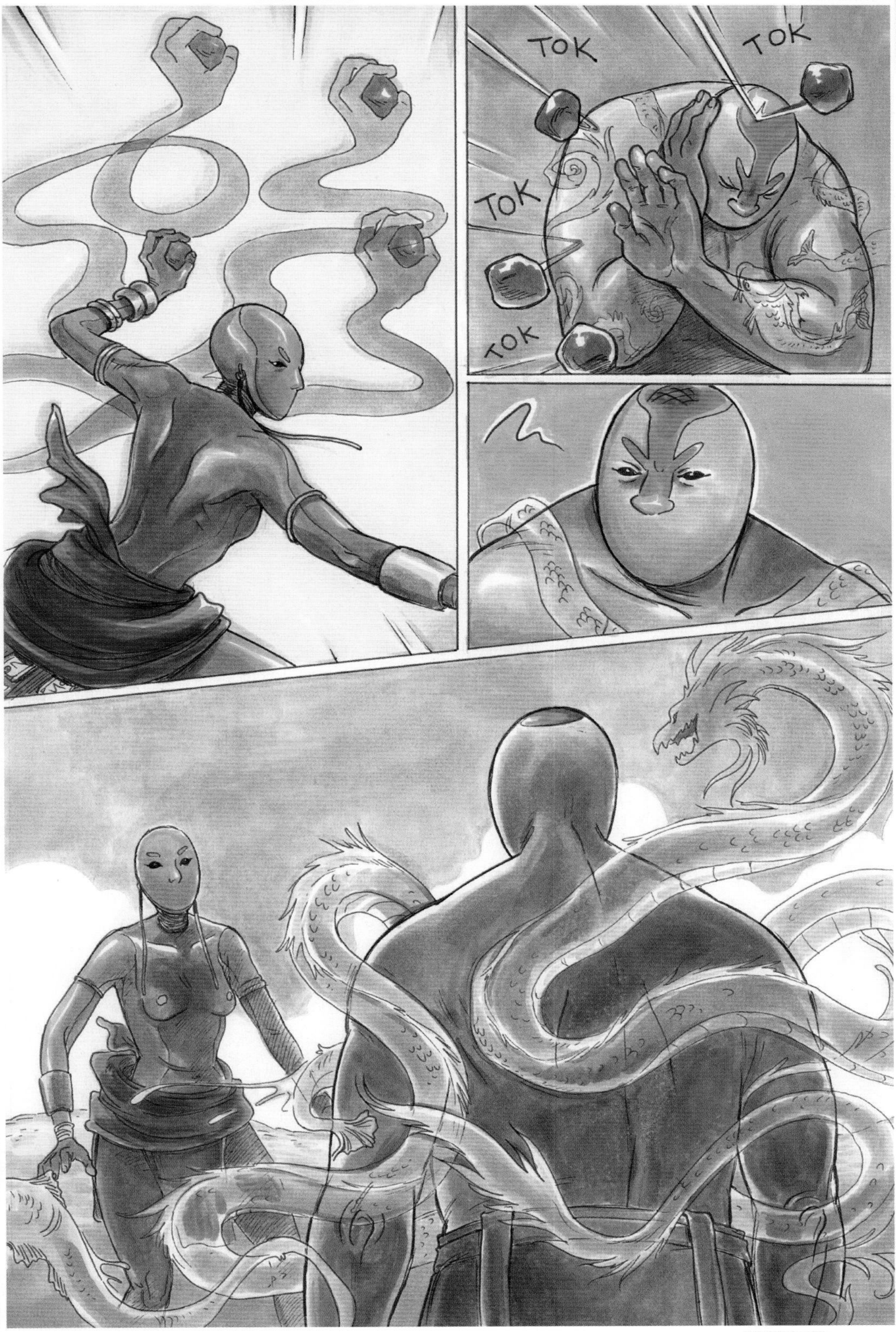
TOK
TOK
TOK
TOK

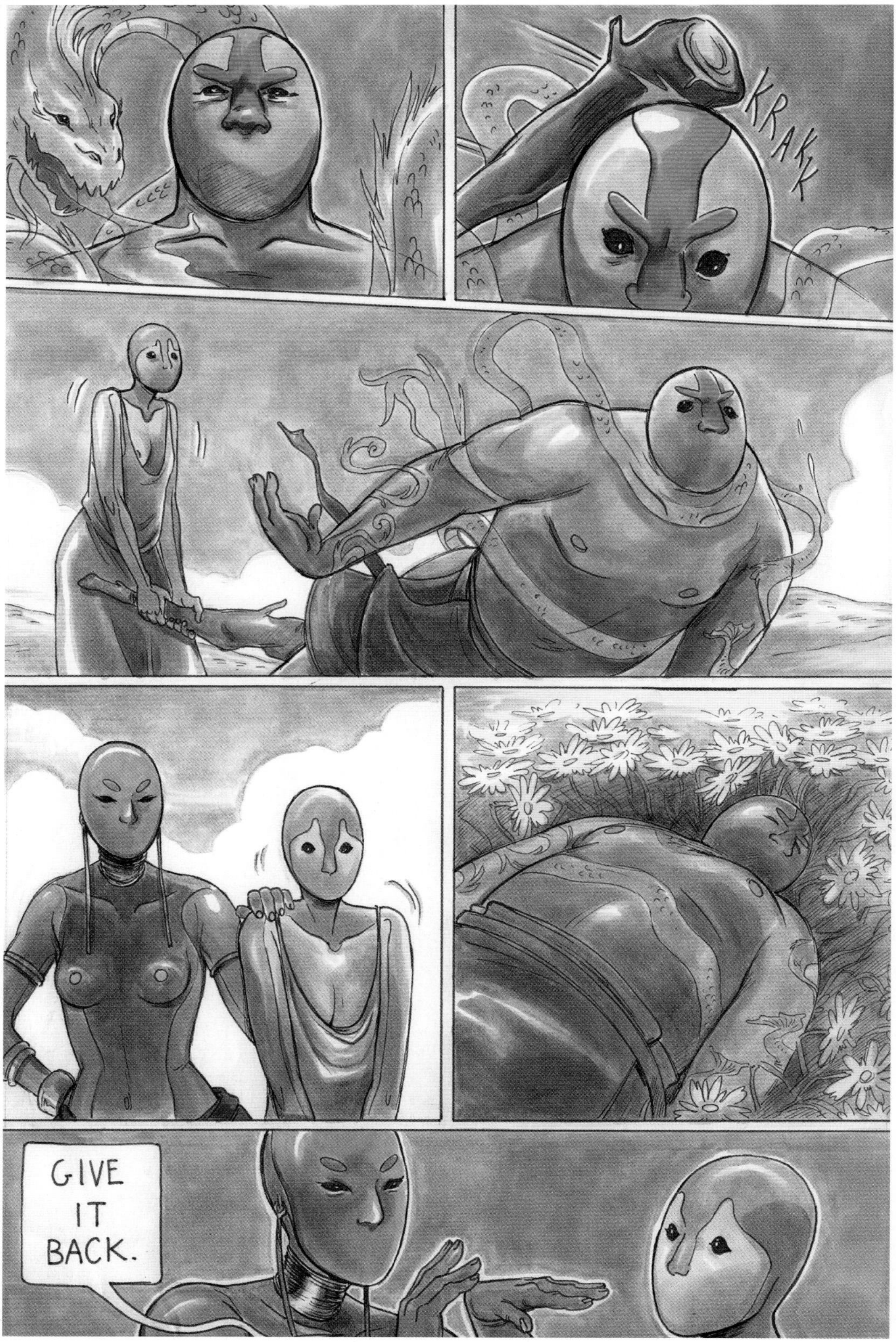
KRAKK
GIVE IT BACK.

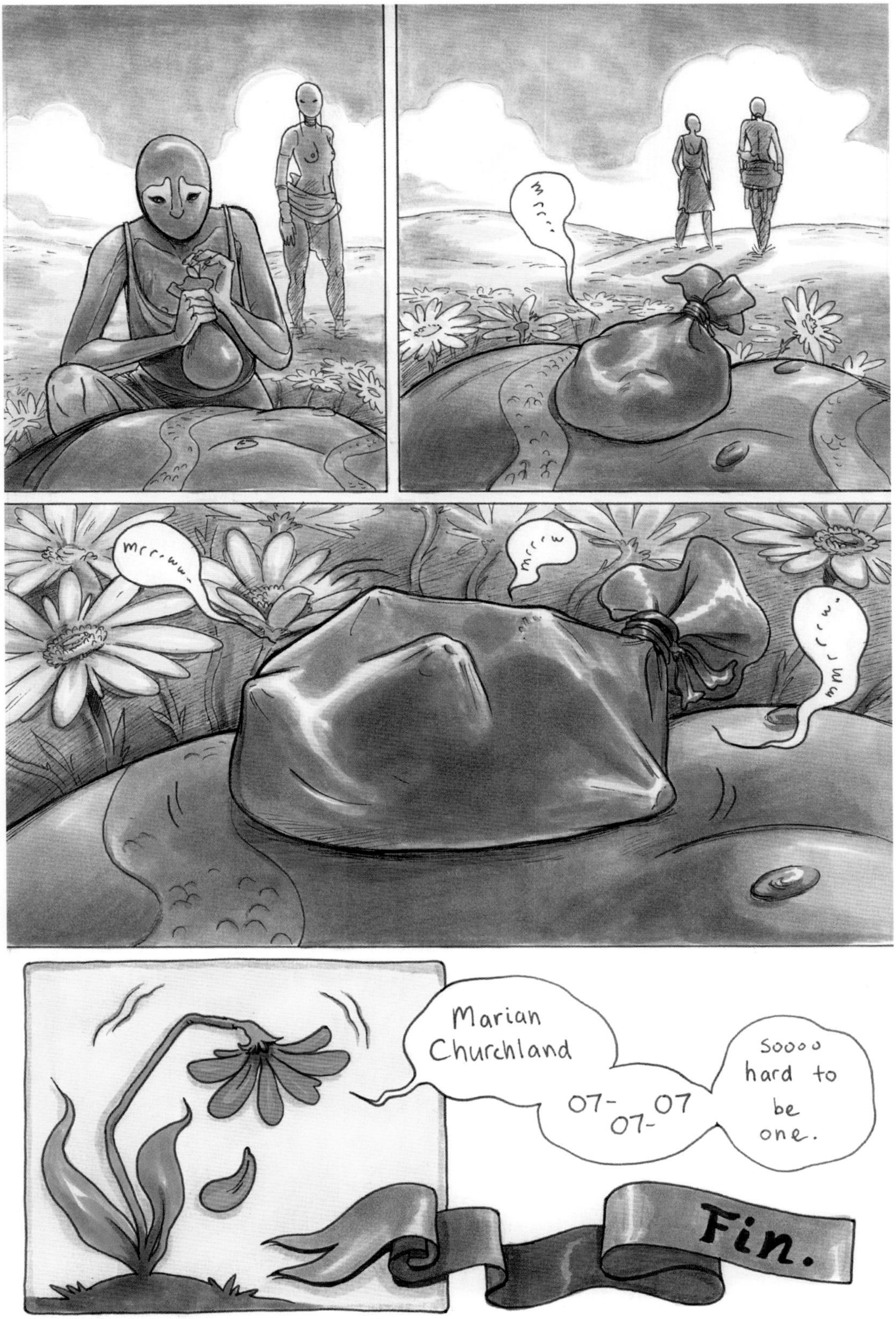
Marian Churchland
07-07-07
Soooo hard to be one.
Fin.

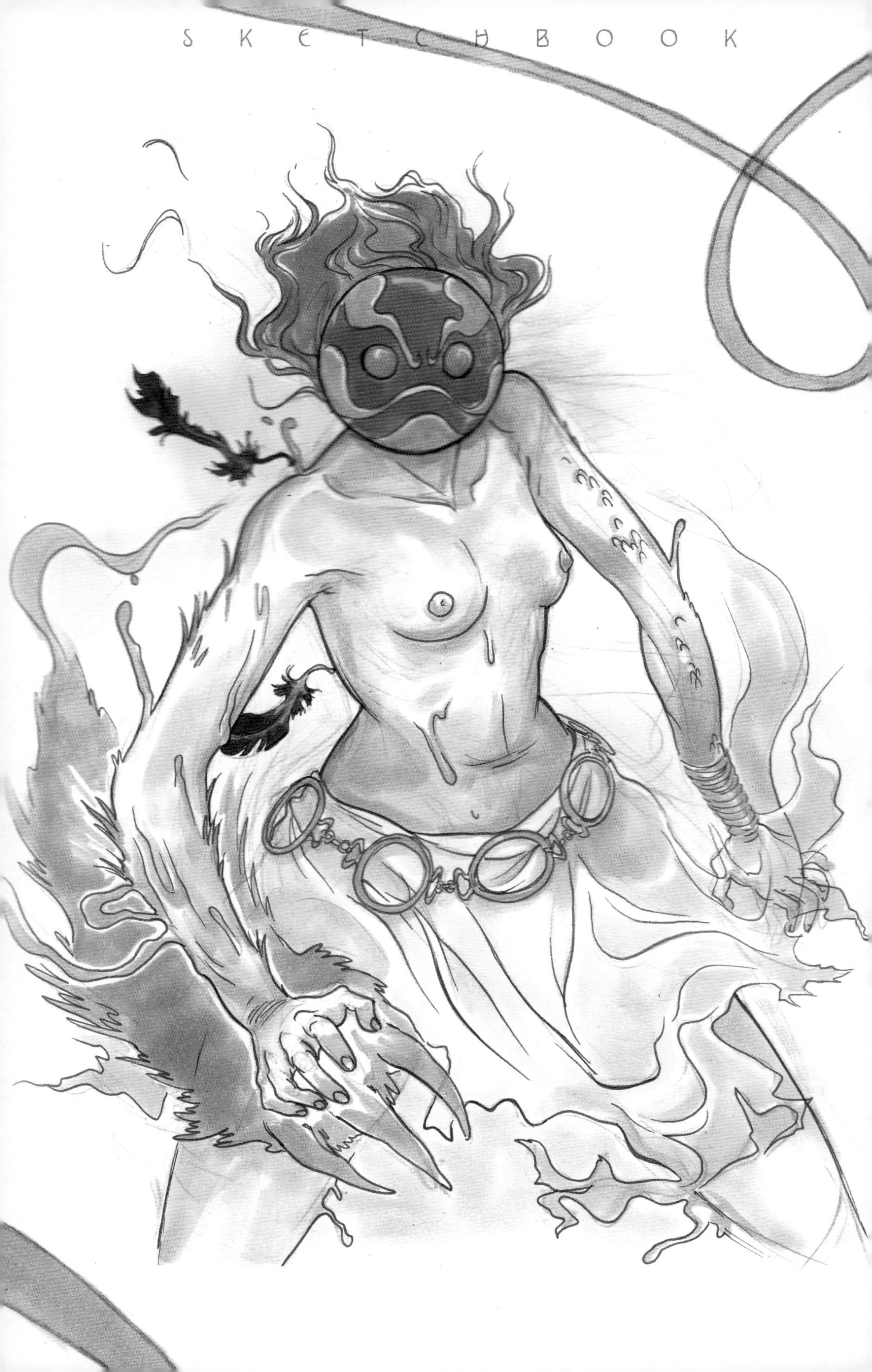

MARIAN CHURCHLAND

Marian can draw hot looking chicks and yummy looking food. What a dream! Write to Marian via DeviantArt or LiveJournal and demand she draws another issue soon!

Rich!

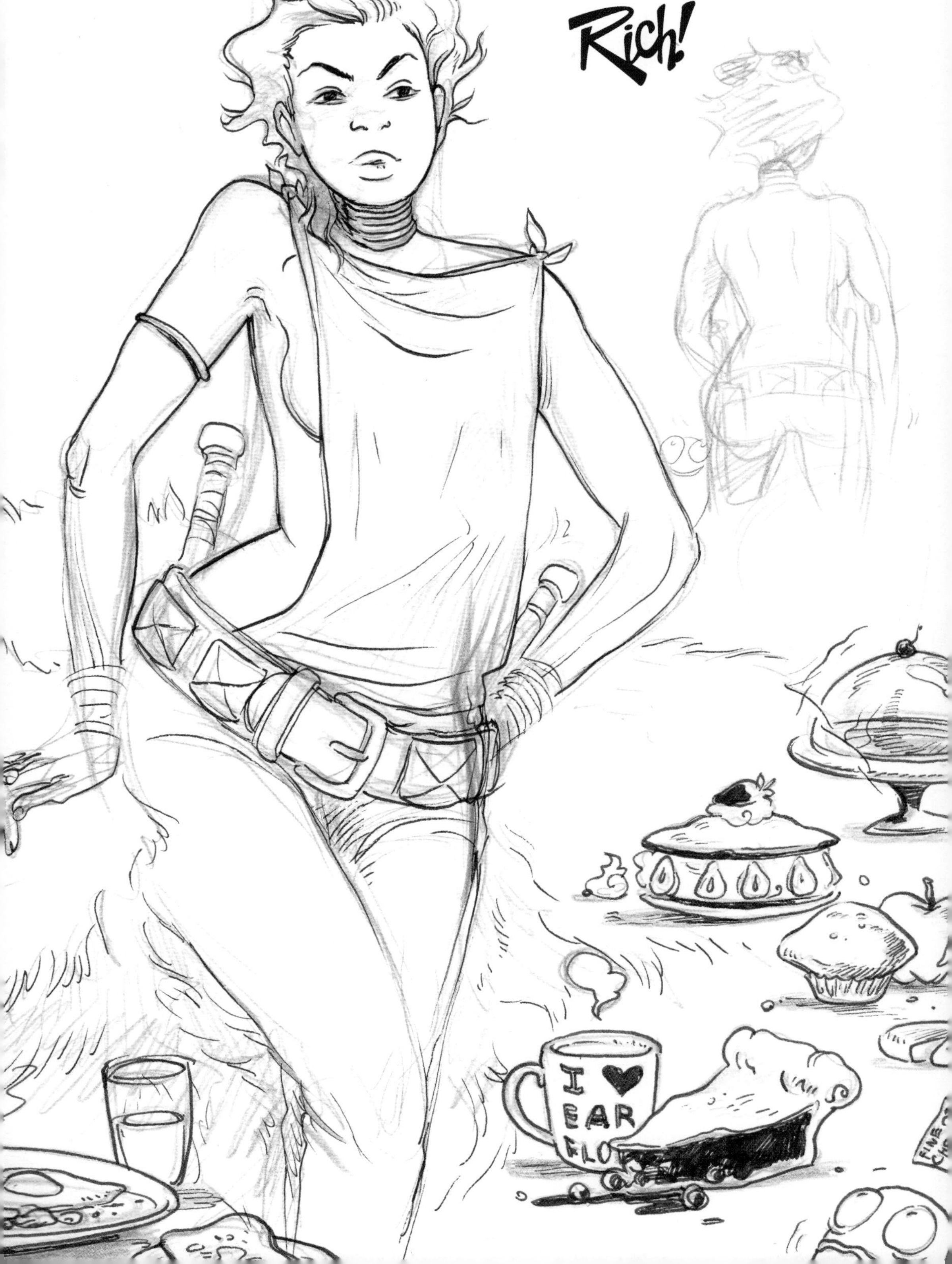

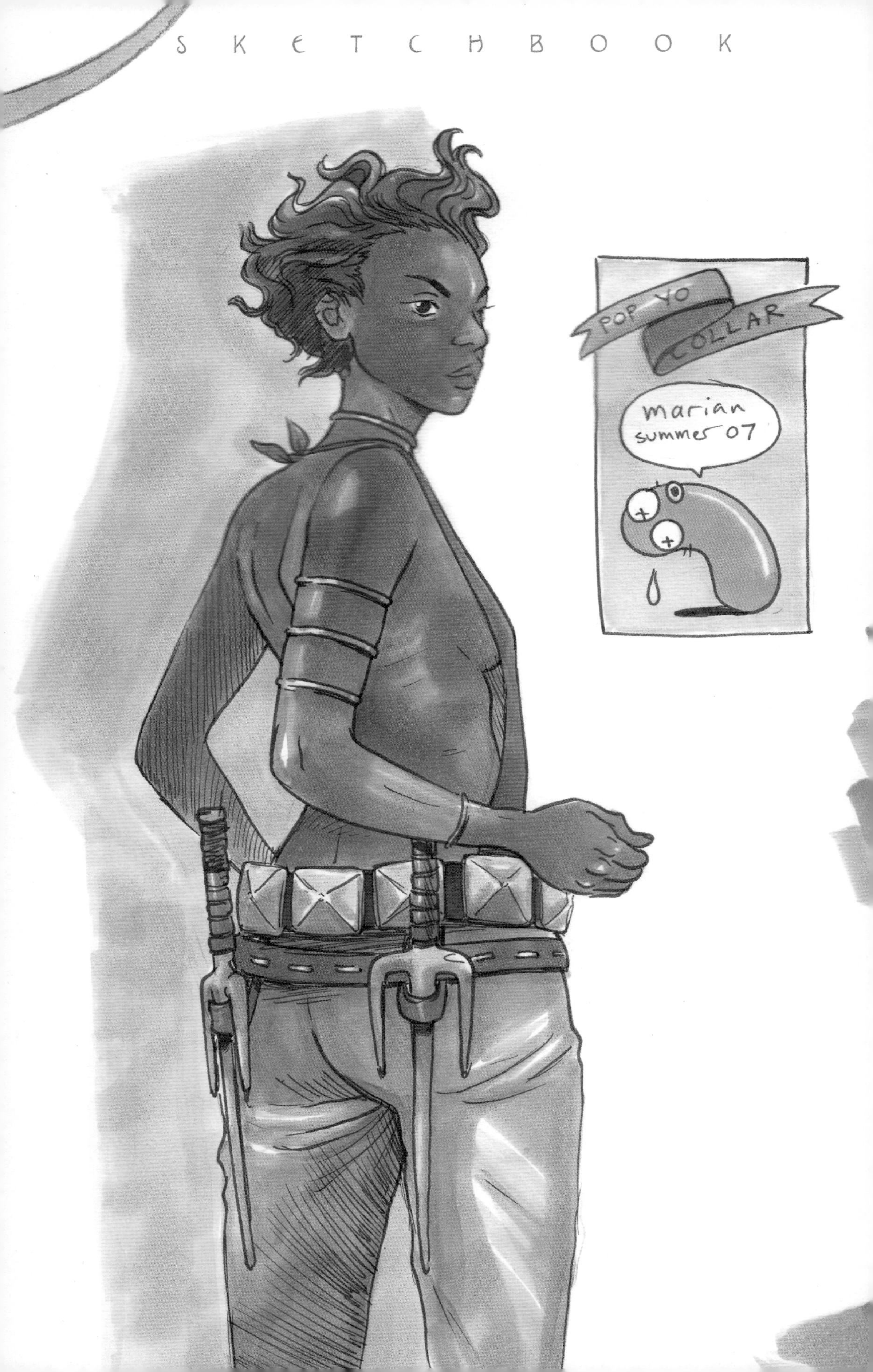
POP YO COLLAR
marian
summer 07

MARIAN CHURCHLAND

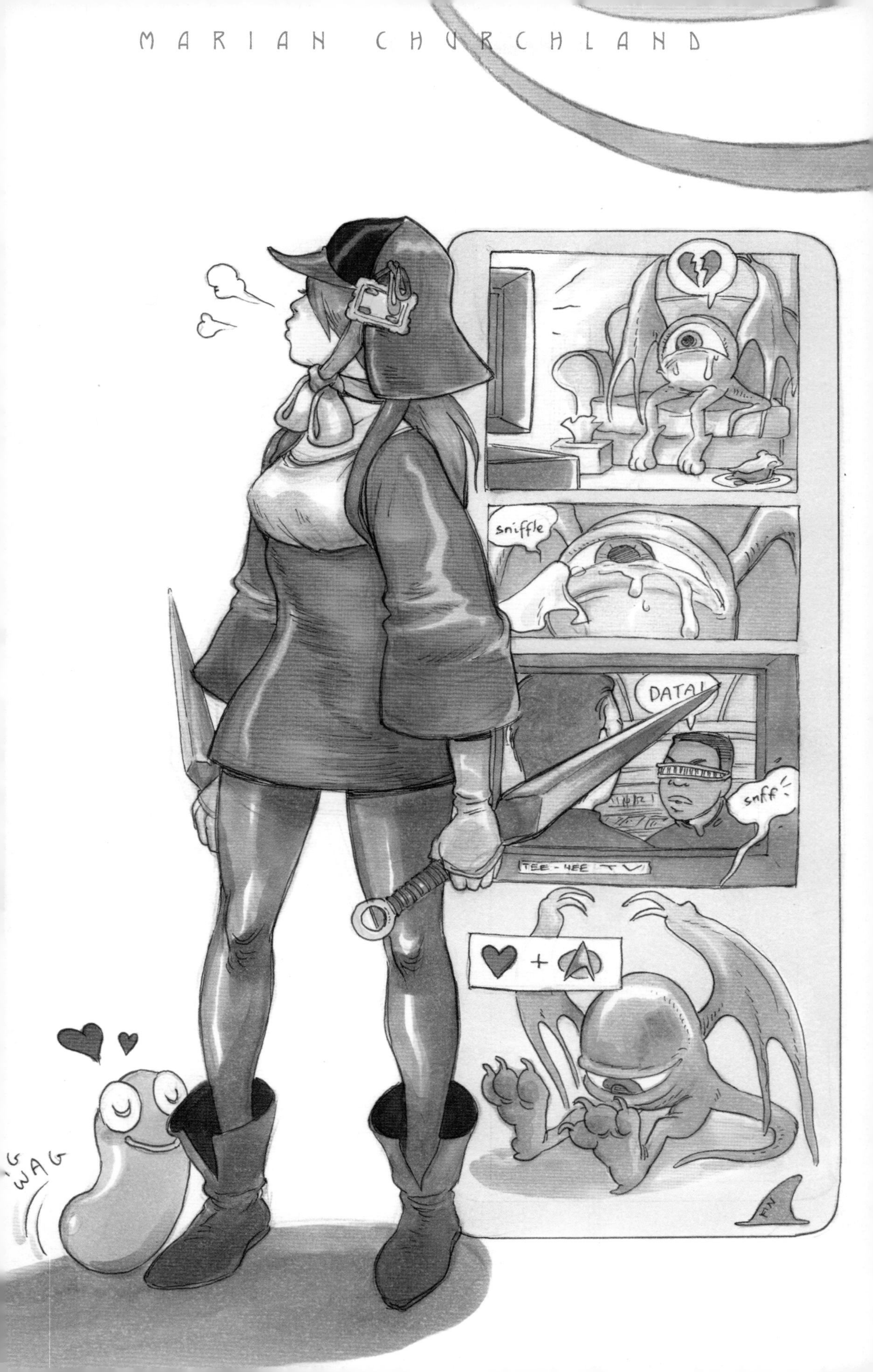
sniffle
DATA!
snff
TEE-VEE TV
WAG
FIN

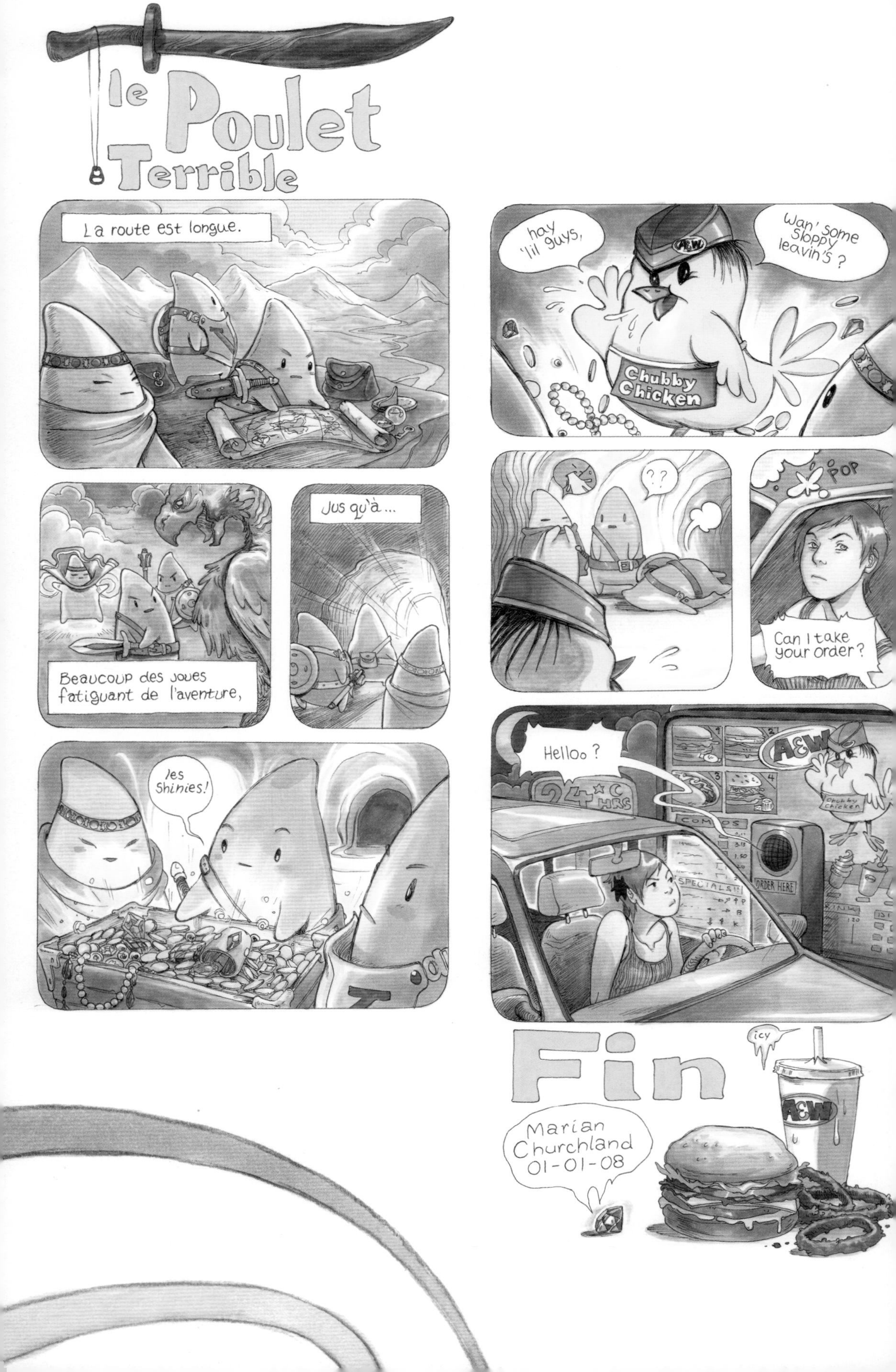
le Poulet Terrible
La route est longue.
Beaucoup des joues fatiguant de l'aventure,
Jus qu'à...
les Shinies!
hay 'lil guys,
Wan' some Sloppy leavin's ?
Chubby Chicken
??
POP
Can I take your order?
Helloo ?
24 HRS
A&W
ORDER HERE
SPECIALS
Fin
icy
Marian Churchland 01-01-08

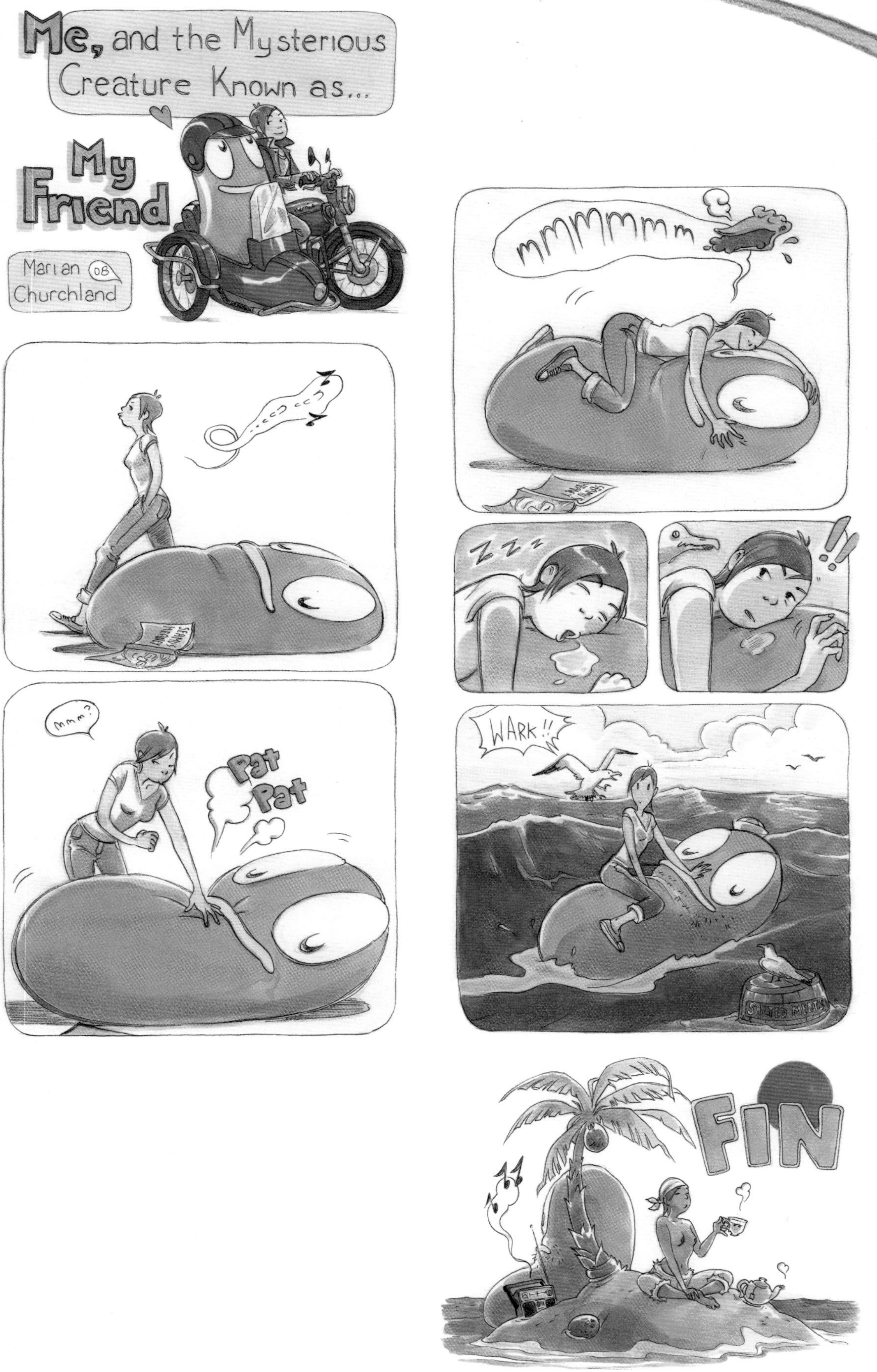

Me, and the Mysterious Creature Known as...
My Friend
Marian 08 Churchland
mmm?
Pat Pat
mMMmmm
Z z z
!!
WARK!!
SALTED MEATS
FIN

AFTERWORD
BRANDON GRAHAM

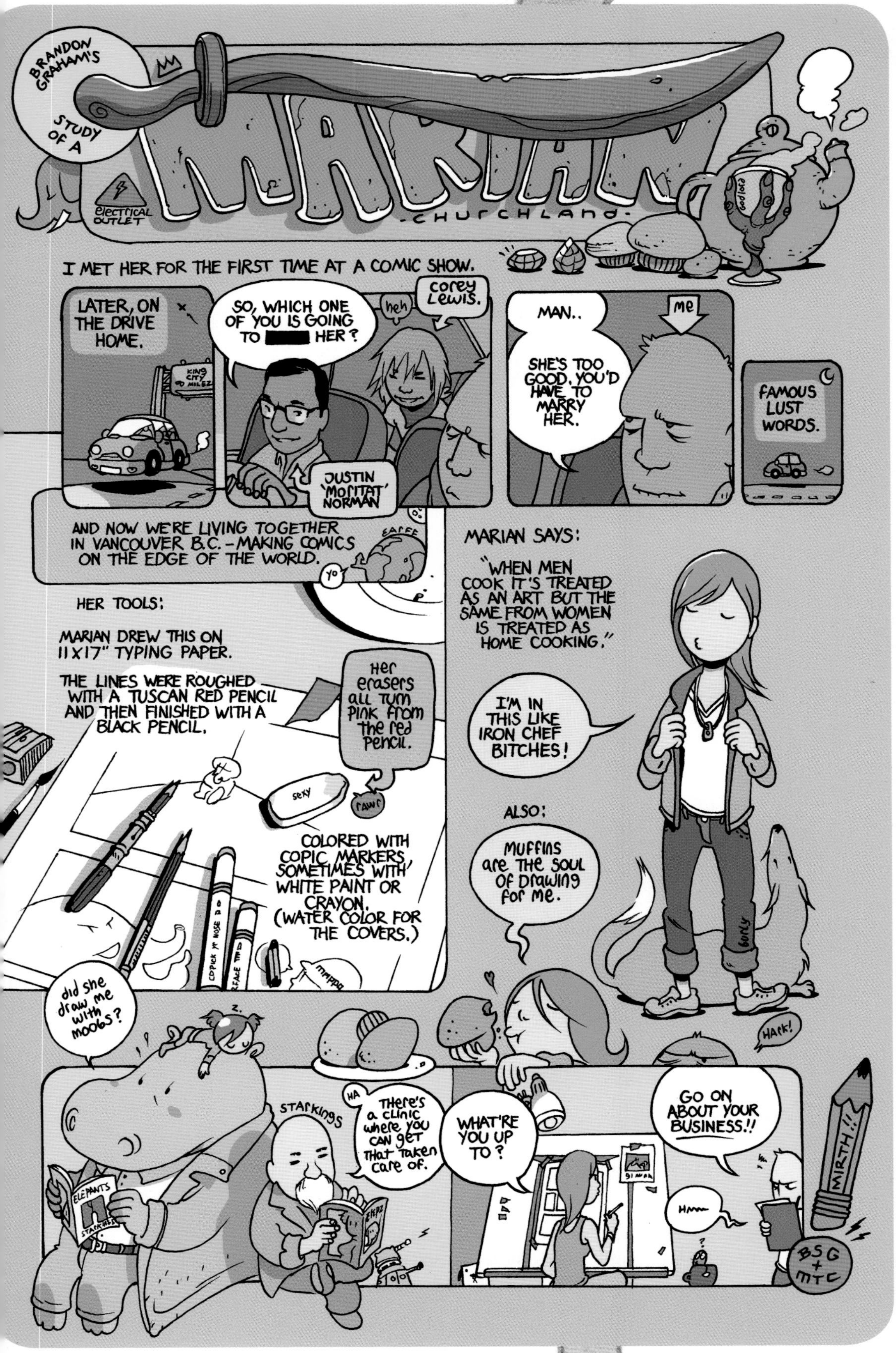

BRANDON GRAHAM'S STUDY OF A
MARIAN
-CHURCHLAND-
ELECTRICAL OUTLET
Godzora
I MET HER FOR THE FIRST TIME AT A COMIC SHOW.
LATER, ON THE DRIVE HOME.
KING CITY TO MILEZ
SO, WHICH ONE OF YOU IS GOING TO [redacted] HER?
heh
corey Lewis.
JUSTIN 'MORITAT' NORMAN
MAN..
me
SHE'S TOO GOOD, YOU'D HAVE TO MARRY HER.
FAMOUS LUST WORDS.
AND NOW WE'RE LIVING TOGETHER IN VANCOUVER B.C. - MAKING COMICS ON THE EDGE OF THE WORLD.
EARTH
yo
HER TOOLS:
MARIAN DREW THIS ON 11X17" TYPING PAPER.
THE LINES WERE ROUGHED WITH A TUSCAN RED PENCIL AND THEN FINISHED WITH A BLACK PENCIL.
Her erasers all turn pink from the red pencil.
sexy
rawr
COLORED WITH COPIC MARKERS, SOMETIMES WITH WHITE PAINT OR CRAYON. (WATER COLOR FOR THE COVERS.)
MARIAN SAYS:
"WHEN MEN COOK IT'S TREATED AS AN ART BUT THE SAME FROM WOMEN IS TREATED AS HOME COOKING."
I'M IN THIS LIKE IRON CHEF BITCHES!
ALSO:
MUFFINS ARE THE SOUL OF DRAWING FOR ME.
did she draw me with moobs?
HARK!
STARKINGS
HA
There's a clinic where you can get that taken care of.
ELEPANTS
WHAT'RE YOU UP TO?
GO ON ABOUT YOUR BUSINESS!!
Hmm
MIRTH!!
BSG + MTC

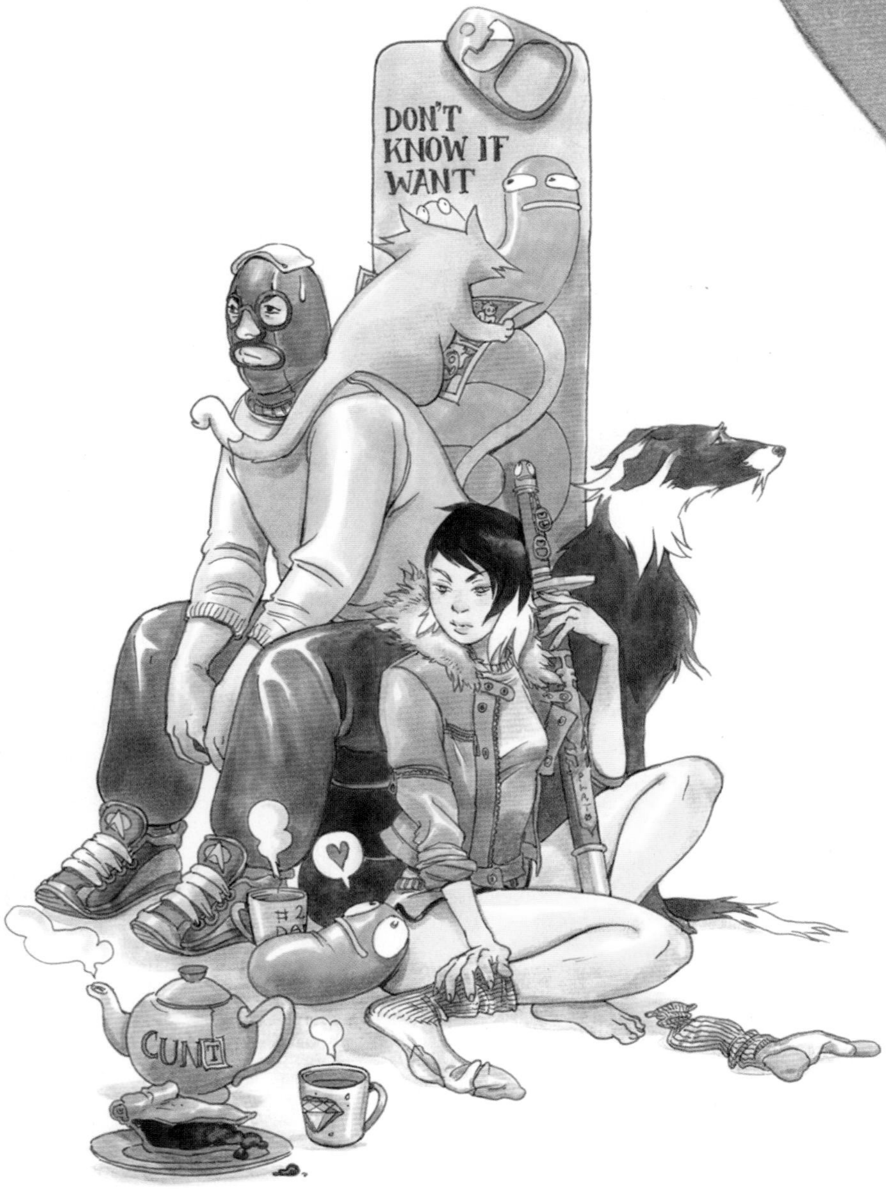
DON'T KNOW IF WANT
CUNT

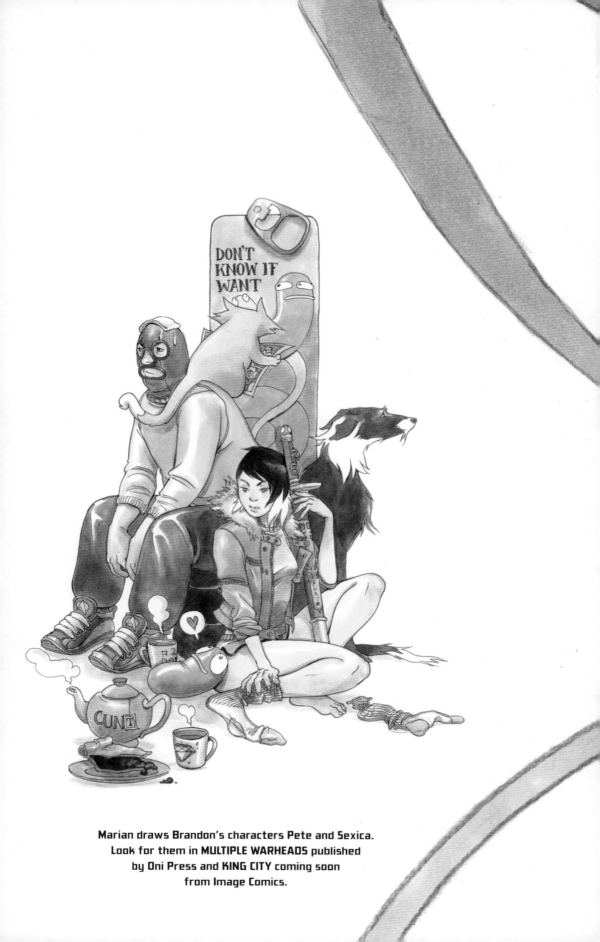

Marian draws Brandon's characters Pete and Sexica. Look for them in MULTIPLE WARHEADS published by Oni Press and KING CITY coming soon from Image Comics.

The Artist at work.

Visit Marian online at
incertus.livejournal.com &
nernie.deviantart.com

ALSO AVAILABLE

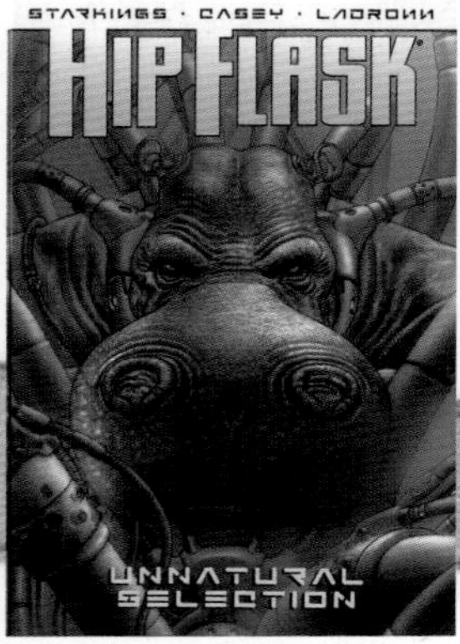
STARKINGS · CASEY · LADRONN
HIP FLASK
UNNATURAL SELECTION

HIP FLASK: UNNATURAL SELECTION

2218: The birth of Hieronymous Flask and the Elephantmen, and their eventual liberation from the torturous world of MAPPO.

ISBN 0-97405-670-7
DIAMOND #STAR19898

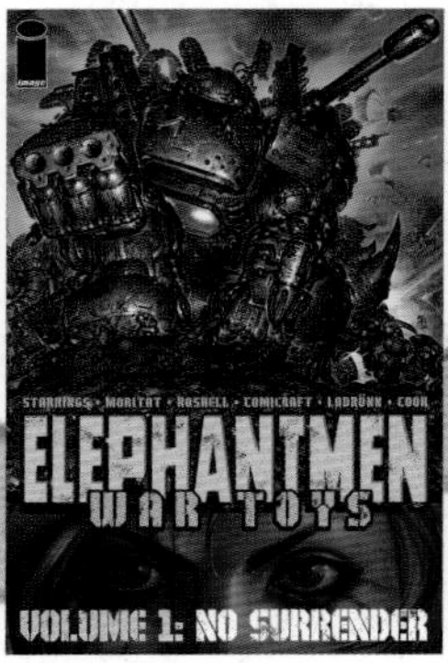
ELEPHANTMEN
WAR TOYS
VOLUME 1: NO SURRENDER

ELEPHANTMEN: WAR TOYS

2239: Europe has been devastated by a lethal virus. A war begins between Africa and China for the remnants. Enter: MAPPO's footsoldiers, the Elephantmen.

ISBN 1-58240-980-3
DIAMOND #MAY08 2184

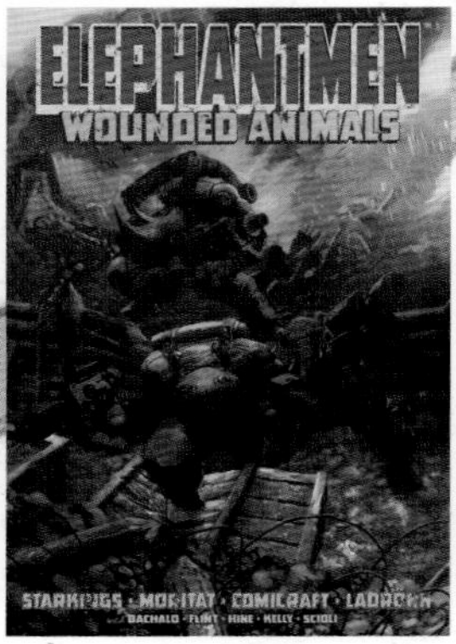
ELEPHANTMEN
WOUNDED ANIMALS

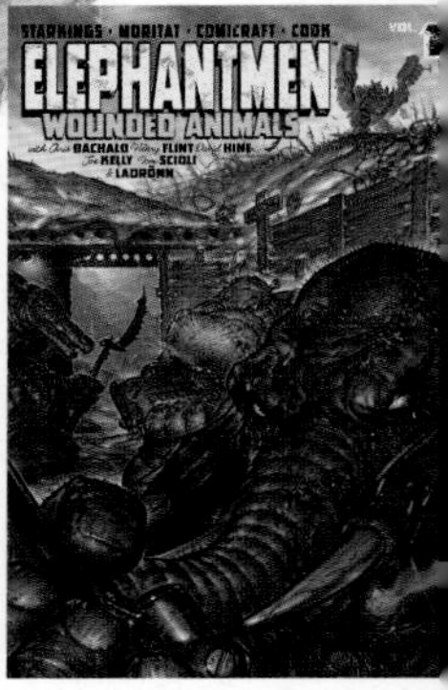
STARKINGS · MORITAT · COMICRAFT · COOK
ELEPHANTMEN
WOUNDED ANIMALS

ELEPHANTMEN: WOUNDED ANIMALS

2259: Freed and rehabilitated, Nikken's creations struggle for survival and acceptance in the world of man. Collects ELEPHANTMEN #1-7 featuring art by Ladrönn, Moritat, Henry Flint, Tom Scioli, Dave Hine and Chris Bachalo.

HARDCOVER:
ISBN 1-58240-691-X
DIAMOND #JAN07 1927

SOFTCOVER:
ISBN 1-58240-934-X
DIAMOND #FEB08 2135

THE ORIGIN · THE WAR · THE SURVIVORS